SPECIAL MESSAGE TO READERS

This book is published under the auspices of

THE ULVERSCROFT FOUNDATION

(registered charity No. 264873 UK)

Established in 1972 to provide funds for research, diagnosis and treatment of eye diseases. Examples of contributions made are: —

A Children's Assessment Unit at Moorfield's Hospital, London.

•

Twin operating theatres at the Western Ophthalmic Hospital, London.

•

A Chair of Ophthalmology at the Royal Australian College of Ophthalmologists.

•

The Ulverscroft Children's Eye Unit at the Great Ormond Street Hospital For Sick Children, London.

You can help further the work of the Foundation by making a donation or leaving a legacy. Every contribution, no matter how small, is received with gratitude. Please write for details to:

THE ULVERSCROFT FOUNDATION,
The Green, Bradgate Road, Anstey,
Leicester LE7 7FU, England.
Telephone: (0116) 236 4325

In Australia write to:
THE ULVERSCROFT FOUNDATION,
c/o The Royal Australian and New Zealand
College of Ophthalmologists,
94-98 Chalmers Street, Surry Hills,
N.S.W. 2010, Australia

KU-665-962

Stuart Harrison grew up in England and always wanted to be a novelist. He finally decided to have a go after forty or so other careers failed to work out. He now writes full time and currently lives in Auckland, New Zealand. His website address is: www.stuartharrison.com.

APHRODITE'S SMILE

When Robert French travels to the tranquil Greek island of Ithaca after his archaeologist father goes missing, he meets Alex, a young woman in search of her roots and the truth about her grandmother's exile from the island sixty years earlier. Gradually, it seems possible that there is a link between an ancient treasure that Robert's father spent many years searching for and the tragic events surrounding Alex's grandmother during the Second World War. Then, suddenly, Alex vanishes and Robert is embroiled in a desperate search — for the woman and for the solution that had evaded his father. To find the truth he must come to understand his own past . . .

Books by Stuart Harrison
Published by The House of Ulverscroft:

LOST SUMMER

STUART HARRISON

APHRODITE'S SMILE

Complete and Unabridged

CHARNWOOD
Leicester

First published in Great Britain in 2004 by
HarperCollins Publishers, London

First Charnwood Edition
published 2005
by arrangement with
HarperCollins Publishers, London

The moral right of the author has been asserted

This novel is a work of fiction.
The names, characters and incidents portrayed in it
are the work of the author's imagination.
Any resemblance to actual persons, living or dead,
or events is entirely coincidental.

Copyright © 2004 by Stuart Harrison
All rights reserved

British Library CIP Data

Harrison, Stuart, *1958 –*
Aphrodite's smile.—Large print ed.—
Charnwood library series
1. Ithaca Island (Greece)—Fiction
2. Suspense fiction 3. Large type books
I. Title
823.9'14 [F]

ISBN 1–84395–637–3

Published by
F. A. Thorpe (Publishing)
Anstey, Leicestershire

Set by Words & Graphics Ltd.
Anstey, Leicestershire
Printed and bound in Great Britain by
T. J. International Ltd., Padstow, Cornwall

This book is printed on acid-free paper

For Dale, who has to put up with me

STAFFORDSHIRE
LIBRARIES, ARTS
AND ARCHIVES

3 80l4 03885 6719	
ULVERSCROFT	0 7 FEB 2005
F	£18·99

Acknowledgements

Thanks as always to Susan Opie, my editor at HarperCollins, and to Stephanie and the team at William Morris.

Prologue

French was drunk, which wasn't in itself an extraordinary event. He wobbled slightly as he stood at the bar and, raising his hands in the air, surveyed the assembled crowd.

'My friends,' he began loudly, 'in gratitude for the welcome you have extended to me during the years that I have been privileged to live among you, I will make a gift to the people of Ithaca.' He paused for dramatic effect, and waited until he was sure that he had everybody's attention before he continued. 'This year the *Panaghia* will once again take her place at the head of the procession to Kathara.'

There were murmurs of surprise from those who had not heard the Professor, as he was known among the locals, make this same claim two nights earlier. Everybody on the island knew that the statue of the Holy Virgin had been stolen more than sixty years ago, and the Professor's claim was greeted with interest or scepticism, depending on the listener's point of view.

The bar was in a narrow street at the far southern end of the harbour around which the town of Vathy had been built, separated from the wharf by a row of run-down houses. Half a dozen zinc tables lined the footpath outside where old men played checkers and drank ouzo. Inside the air was thick with cigarette smoke.

French leaned against the bar to steady

himself and peered around at a blur of faces, wagging a finger at nobody in particular. 'I know there are those among you who will doubt me. I confess that for a time I myself thought that all of these years I have spent searching had been in vain.' A slight wave of nausea momentarily overtook him and French belched softly.

Some of those present crossed themselves or briefly touched the crucifixes they wore around their necks, silently praying that the Professor's claims weren't merely the result of drinking too much wine. Before she was stolen, the statue of the *Panaghia* had been at the centre of the festival. After the procession to the monastery, the people would approach her one by one and silently pray for her blessing for the coming year. Perhaps if she was returned, the Holy Mother might send more tourists to the island so that it could prosper as its neighbour Kephalonia had. All summer long the charter jets disgorged their cargoes of package holidaymakers across the strait, though distressingly few of them made the ferry trip to Ithaca.

Spiro, however, was not among the more optimistic of those present in Skiopes bar that night. He had come to drink beer and forget his terrible day. To begin with, the engine on his boat wouldn't start, and then, when he had managed to coax it into life and eventually put to sea, it was only to rip a hole in his main net after it became entangled with some piece of junk floating beneath the surface a mile offshore. In the end he had returned with barely enough in his catch to cover his costs and he was not in a

2

good mood. 'You talk too much,' he muttered sourly to French, lifting his eyes from his almost empty glass.

Annoyed at having his train of thought interrupted, French frowned briefly. He was in full flight now, his imagination fuelled by the realisation of a dream he had pursued for almost a quarter of a century. 'You will see, Spiro,' he replied. 'Even you will have reason to thank me, though of course gratitude is not what I seek, nor has it ever been.'

'And pigs will fly,' Spiro sneered. He was in the mood for an argument with somebody and this arrogant Englishman would do. He was sick and tired of hearing his crap anyway.

'You are an ignorant man,' French proclaimed. 'You should stick to fishing, about which you at least know a little.'

There were a few chuckles around the smoky room, since it was common knowledge that Spiro was possibly the worst fisherman on the island. Spiro glowered from beneath heavy brows. 'At least what I do is honest work, fit for a man. I do not waste my time with my nose stuck in books.' He held up his hands for emphasis. His fingers were short and thick with calluses.

The Professor was an educated man, however, engaged in scholarly work, and for such men life was different. So though one or two heads nodded in sage agreement, most did not. Besides, Spiro had few friends.

French dismissed Spiro's remarks with a wave of his hand. 'I would not expect you to understand, Spiro, but some men, like myself, are destined not for the toil of workman's labour as honourable as that may be, but rather we are driven to pursue knowledge through history, promoting understanding of ourselves through the understanding of our forebears. This work may look easy to you but it too has its difficulties, believe me.'

'Difficulties!' scoffed Spiro. 'What do you know of difficulties? Do you put to sea every day even when the wind is howling from the south? When the waves toss the boats of poor fishermen like children's toys and the cold freezes your fingers to the bone? Do you risk your life just to feed your family?'

Though it was an impressive speech, nobody in fact could remember Spiro risking anything worse than the possibility of a headache in the morning from drinking too much wine, and that alone would prevent him from putting to sea. French, however, barely heard him; he was addressing himself to a wider audience.

'Consider the years of painstaking research that does not always bear fruit. Do you think that Sylvia Benton and her colleagues from the great British School of Archaeology in Athens simply stepped out one morning and made their discoveries in Louizos cave by mere happenstance? A site that is considered by many of my esteemed colleagues today to be the rival of Olympia and Delphi. Perhaps the very first site of Panhellenic worship in all of Greece.'

Most people present had little idea of what precisely French was talking about, partly because he had a habit of slipping from Greek into his native English when he'd been drinking, though all of course knew of the cave at Polis Bay where a famous archaeologist from the thirties had discovered some pieces of ancient pottery. Nevertheless, to show their support a chorus of vocal approval rippled about the room.

But Spiro was not to be so easily beaten in an argument. 'At least nobody can say that Spiro Petalas lives off the money his wife earns,' he declared. 'How can a woman respect a husband who cannot put food on the table, eh? And if a woman cannot respect her man, how can he satisfy her? Soon she will look elsewhere to find a real man, a man who can take care of her.'

It was true that French had lived for years primarily off the money that Irene earned and it was common knowledge that she had left him last year, as Spiro had indelicately reminded them. But though this might once have bothered him, it no longer did. 'When the world learns of my discovery,' French said, 'there will be money. More than you can imagine. The tourists will come in their thousands and the whole island will prosper.'

'You have been too long in the sun I think, old man, or perhaps it is the wine,' Spiro scoffed. 'Why should tourists come here to see a statue of the *Panaghia*? To us she is important, of course. But not to anybody else.'

Spiro gloated in triumph when it seemed for a moment that he had the upper hand, because what he said was undoubtedly true. Unfortunately even if the Professor had found the missing statue, it was difficult to see how even she could work a miracle.

French, however, merely smiled secretively. 'Perhaps the *Panaghia* is not the only discovery I have made,' he said. 'Perhaps there is something else, something that all the world will want to know about.'

The room waited with anticipation for the Professor to continue. People leaned forward in their seats and an expectant hush fell over the room. Spiro Petalas was suddenly ignored as if he had become invisible.

French blinked. It occurred to him that he had been indiscreet and that in fact it would have been better to have kept his mouth shut for now. For a moment the room wavered and wobbled so that he felt disconcertingly as if he were trapped inside a large smoky jelly. His stomach lurched and he wished that he hadn't eaten quite so much of the seafood stew earlier. Food was one of his weaknesses and he'd long since given up trying to prevent his waistline expanding further. Sobered by a sense of unease that overtook him as he focused on the faces staring back at him, he searched for one in particular. Even though it wasn't there, he decided that he should leave.

'I refuse to bandy words with an ignoramus,' he announced loftily, dismissing Spiro and putting an end to their discussion, though the fisherman gave a sly grin of triumph.

'You are full of shit,' Spiro said.

Those looking on shifted awkwardly on their chairs, averting their eyes to the walls or the ground. Though it was regrettable that a fat pig like Spiro had been so impolite as to humiliate the Professor, there was truth in what he said. It seemed that French had unfortunately indulged his love of wine a little too enthusiastically again. The crowd looked on in silence as he set down his half full glass and managed the short walk to the door. One or two of them wished him good-night and advised him to get a good night's sleep.

At the door, French looked around one last time searching among the faces for one that held sinister intent, but he found only expressions of sympathy.

Reassured, he began the walk home.

★ ★ ★

It was a half hour walk from the bar to the house. The route took him away from the waterfront along narrow streets that zigzagged up the steep hillside, connected at intervals by sets of concrete steps. The climb was exhausting and French stopped often, his heart pounding deep in his chest as it struggled to supply his bulk with oxygenated blood. When he had caught his breath he pressed on. The night air was fragrant with the scent of jasmine and bougainvillaea, although French admitted that it was spoiled somewhat by the sour odour of his own sweat mingled with the reek of alcoholic fumes. His head was clearing a little now that he was out of the foggy atmosphere of the bar. Enough that he was already regretting the hangover he would have in the morning and being so careless with his talk. Careless talk cost

7

lives they had said in the war, though he had been too young himself to remember.

Half-way up a set of steps, a single lamp fixed to a wooden power pole cast a light that glistened on the waxy leaves of a large magnolia in full bloom with pure white flowers. The sky was lit with a myriad stars. They seemed almost close enough to touch, creating the illusion that upon reaching the top it would be possible to step off into space. From behind, French heard the sound of a stone skittering on concrete. When he looked back he saw only deep shadows close against a wall. His heart skipped a beat but nothing moved. After a while he hurried on.

From within patches of garden the sweet powerful smell of mint wafted on the night air. Another time it might have been pleasant, but by the time he reached the top of the steps, French felt quite ill. He paused until an attack of dizziness passed. Far below, the lights from the restaurants were mirrored in the harbour. As he admired their effect he glimpsed a movement and this time he swore that he heard the sound of footsteps. He experienced a prickling of unease. It was just his imagination, he told himself, though not very convincingly.

Moving on, he hurried along a street past terraces shadowed with grape vines supported by rusting iron trellis. The houses petered out and the road wound upwards through olive groves. As he turned a corner the lights from the harbour were lost from sight and the road was abruptly smothered in thick, heavy darkness. Breathing heavily, French paused to mop his

8

brow with a handkerchief. He was sweating profusely. Behind him the sound of footsteps dogged his progress, any pretence at stealth now abandoned. There was something chilling in their purpose. He felt the darkness close in around him like a shroud. Unfortunate analogy he thought grimly.

'Who's there?' he called out with false bravado. The footsteps stopped briefly, then resumed and quickly picked up pace.

A peculiar sense of calm descended over him. He would not spend his last moments consumed by fear. If he were going to die he would face his killer and look him in the eye. He wondered if it was the alcohol that fuelled his bravery, though he no longer felt drunk. Briefly, he wished he hadn't said so much at Skiopes. If he'd kept quiet he might finally have found a measure of success towards the end of his life. He might also have had the chance to put things right with Irene and Robert, and at this thought a wave of regret welled up inside him.

The footsteps were almost upon him. French drew himself up and prepared to face his fate, determined to cling to the remnants of his self-respect. And then from around the bend came the unexpected sound of an approaching engine. The road wasn't used much at night, but perhaps on this evening some greater force was at work. Or perhaps it was just luck.

The footsteps stopped. An indistinct figure was visible no more than twenty feet away. Something glinted in the light. A blade perhaps? Seizing his chance, French turned to run, though his bulk reduced his flight to more of a shambling stumble. He gasped for breath, his heart bursting. He could feel the spot in his back where the blade would enter and pierce his liver. The sound of the approaching vehicle grew louder, drowning out the footsteps behind him and then he was bathed in the headlights of a truck and a voice called out.

'Professor? Is that you? What are you doing? Slow down before you hurt yourself.'

It was Nikos. He ran a haulage business between the towns on the island and as he climbed down from the cab French almost wept with relief. He turned to face the figure pursuing him but the road was empty.

Suddenly a devastatingly sharp pain gripped his chest. His mouth opened and closed silently as his knees gave way and he felt himself sinking to the ground. He heard Nikos call his name, but it sounded as if his voice came from a long way off, and slowly the lights from the truck shrank to a pinprick.

His last conscious thought before darkness overcame him was that this must be the gods' idea of a grim joke.

PART ONE

1

The phone rang at six. I was already up so I took the call in the kitchen hoping that it hadn't woken Alicia. She had been working long hours lately, leaving at seven in the morning and sometimes not getting home until nine or ten at night. I thought her boss could manage without her for an hour or two.

I wondered who was calling so early. I lifted the receiver feeling the faint stirrings of disquiet, unexpected calls at odd times being harbingers of bad news. When I heard Irene's voice I experienced an odd reaction of both relief and dread combined.

'Robert, is that you?' Her accent conjured an image of the house where she and my father lived overlooking the town of Vathy. I could almost smell the dry earth and olive trees and, involuntarily, I glanced to the window. Outside, London was waking to a leaden May sky. The leaves on the trees in the square dripped steadily onto the pavement below.

'Irene, yes it's me.' I became aware that I was clenching the phone with a vice-like grip and I took a breath to relax myself. 'What's happened? Is something wrong?'

'It is your father. He had a heart attack.'

I closed my eyes, waiting for the inevitable.

'He is in the hospital in Argostoli. They

13

brought him on the ferry to Kephalonia this morning.'

The knowledge that my father wasn't dead gradually seeped into my brain. The attack was serious, but no longer immediately life-threatening. As she continued to explain what had happened, Irene's normally thickly accented pronunciation of English was exacerbated by emotion. She sounded distraught.

'Where are you?' I asked her. 'Are you all right?'

'Yes. Yes, I am fine. I am phoning from the hospital. Your father is sleeping. They have given him medicine.'

'You sound tired,' I told her, though what I meant was that she sounded shattered. Emotionally spent. I recalled her saying that she had been at the hospital most of the night.

'Yes, I am a little tired. But I will be all right.'

'You should get some rest. Why don't you go home? I don't suppose there's anything you can do there anyway.' She didn't reply, and in the silence that followed I thought we had been cut off or else she hadn't heard me. 'Irene, did you hear what I said? You should go home.'

'Yes, yes. I am sorry. I heard you. But I will stay here. They have put a bed in Johnny's room for me.'

She seemed hesitant and I wondered if she really was OK but she assured me that she was.

'It is just that I am tired, and I have been so worried about Johnny.'

She had always called him Johnny. I'd never

14

become entirely used to it because when I was a child and we still lived in Oxford, my mother had always called him John. Everybody had. He taught at the university then, and John seemed natural for a middle-aged academic who wore corduroy trousers and tweed jackets. But when he went to live on the island of Ithaca he seemed to shed that persona, and when I first saw him there he was born again as a tanned and bearded figure who wore shorts and short-sleeved, open-necked shirts for most of the year. He had developed a fondness for Greek food and wine and indulged heavily in both. Johnny suited him, and in some ways he was like somebody I had just met.

I continued to offer Irene long-distance advice as if she were the one who was ill. 'Make sure that you eat something,' I told her. 'Don't worry too much.'

There was a short silence and then she said, 'Robert, you understand that your father is very ill?'

I realised that I hadn't mentioned my father. I hadn't questioned anything that she had told me. 'But didn't the doctors say he's in no danger?'

'They say that he will recover if he rests. But he will need to take medicine and he will need to change the way that he lives.'

'He's a tough old bird. He'll be fine, Irene.'

'He is not so tough as you think, Robert. He is getting old.'

I detected a vague censure in her voice. It was several years since I had last seen him. I counted back in my head and surprised myself when I realised that it was actually closer to eight. He'd seemed robust enough then but a lot could happen in that length of time. I had to admit that I had picked up on the changes in him during our infrequent phone calls. There was a time when he'd always put on a cheerfully optimistic front. He'd talk about some dig that he was working on or about the museum he ran, and pretend not to notice my lack of interest. When he asked what I was doing I gave monosyllabic answers. After every call I would feel tense and physically drained. But for a couple of years now it had begun to seem that keeping up the pretence had become too much for him. His enthusiasm for his work had waned. Occasionally he'd even been drunk when he called and I'd been subjected to long self-pitying monologues about his life being a failure.

'How old is he now?' I asked Irene.

'Seventy-two.'

I was eleven when he left England, almost twenty-five years ago. He would have been about my age when I was born. Seventy-two didn't seem so old, I told myself.

'I thought perhaps you could come and see him,' Irene suggested.

I leaned my forehead against the wall. 'I'd like to. Things are busy at the moment. But I'll see what I can do.'

A heavy accusing silence reigned over the phone line. I felt a pressure building in my head. A hiss of static prompted the temptation to replace the receiver quietly as if we had been disconnected, a notion I dismissed instantly.

16

'He is your father, Robert,' Irene said gently.
'I know.'
'He needs you.'
My eyes stung and my chest felt tight, as though I was being constricted by an iron band. 'No, he doesn't,' I said. I coughed, a choking involuntary sardonic laugh. My father needing me. That was almost funny.

★   ★   ★

Alicia was there when I hung up the phone. 'What is it?' She put a hand on my arm, a gesture of concern. As I looked at her I experienced a sudden tidal flow of tenderness mixed with gratitude that she was there. I had never seen her look more beautiful. She was wearing a long nightdress and her hair was mussed from sleep, a crease in her otherwise flawless skin where she'd lain on the edge of the pillow. She was a little pale I thought, and there were faint smudges beneath her eyes.

'It was Irene.' I put my arms around her and hugged her tight. I was a head taller than her and she felt slight against me. There was something of the wide-eyed innocent about her even though she was almost thirty. The first time I saw her I thought she'd looked lost, which in fact she had been. Literally. She was studying a street map with a worried frown. That had been three years ago.

She laid her head against my chest. 'What did she want?'

I breathed in the scent of the shampoo she

17

used and her face cream mingled with the early morning sexiness of her skin. I'm an inch short of six feet, but holding Alicia always made me feel taller somehow. It was the way she sank into me. Surrendered. Her body moulded against mine. 'My father had a heart attack. He's in hospital.'

She drew back a little so that she could look at me. 'Will he be all right?'

'Apparently.'

Alicia had never met him, or Irene, but she had spoken to both of them on the phone. I'd explained early on in our relationship that I didn't get on with my dad. She knew the history. 'I'm sorry.' She rested her head against me again. She didn't offer advice, she didn't question me and she didn't try to comfort me except by her presence and I loved her for that.

'Families,' I said wryly. I smiled and kissed her. 'Who'd have them?'

As I turned away I glimpsed Alicia's quick anxious frown and I realised my mistake. She wanted children and I was fairly sure that she was afraid that I didn't. When she'd moved in with me we'd agreed that if we were still together and felt the same way about each other in a year's time then we'd get married and start a family. The year had come and gone, but when we talked about it I always found a reason to delay things. It wasn't that I didn't love her. I just thought it was a big step.

I went back and kissed her again. She looked surprised. 'What was that for?'

'Because I love you.'

She studied me intently. 'Do you? Really?'
'Really.'

She kissed me back. 'God. I love you too. I really do.'

At the weekend, I decided. At the weekend I'd ask her to marry me.

★ ★ ★

I spoke to Irene on the phone twice over the next forty-eight hours. My father's condition continued to improve and the doctors were ever more confident that he would make a full recovery providing he made the necessary changes to his lifestyle. Every time I called, Irene asked me when I was going out there. I told her as soon as I could. I decided that since he was out of danger I should wait until he'd regained his strength, besides, there were things that needed my attention at work. She didn't completely buy it, but she didn't push the issue. She kept telling me that she would take care of him when he was allowed home. She'd make sure he kept to the doctor's regime. I thought it was a little strange the way she kept assuring me, almost as if I doubted her, but I put it down to tiredness.

In fact it wasn't a good time for me to be leaving London. I had started my company when I was still in my mid-twenties, having come out of university with a BA and not much idea of what I wanted to do with my life. All I knew for sure was that I wanted to spend it in the present rather than in the past like my dad. After a few years of intermittent travelling, and having tried

19

banking and marketing, I decided that I didn't really mind what I did so long as I didn't have to work for anybody else. I raised some money and bought a run-down flat in North London which I fixed up and sold on for a profit. Since the work had been easy enough and the rewards surprisingly good, I did it again, so next I could afford to do up two places at once. Then I bought a big old house in Chingford that had been let as bedsits and tiny flats with shared bathrooms. With a daunting amount of debt, I set about converting the place into three apartments, each occupying a single floor. I sold two for what it had cost me to buy and renovate the entire building. The third one was pure profit, and London prices were about to take off.

By the time I was thirty I was worth several million on paper, but a year later I was not only broke but badly in debt. I'd invested heavily in an office tower but the main contractor had cut corners on a previous project and one of his recent buildings had been declared unfit. A whole morass of corrupt dealings with suppliers and officials had been exposed by one of the national newspapers, and when the contractor filed for bankruptcy nobody would come within a mile of the half-completed building I part-owned.

In the five years since then I had clawed my company back to profitability. I was more cautious about where I invested and for the most part I followed a strategy of developing a broader range of smaller properties. In another year or two I could begin to relax a little.

My company offices were within walking distance of my house. The day after Irene first called with the news about my father I arrived at work early. Tony Allen was the only one there. I had a small team who all had a stake in the business, and Tony had been with me the longest. He was ambitious and hard-working and was usually at his desk around seven. I'd given up telling him he didn't need to burn himself out a long time ago.

That morning he didn't know that I was there. His office door was open and, as I went to the coffee machine, I could hear him talking on the phone. He mentioned the name of a warehouse property that we had been trying to buy in Fulham. We already had plans to turn the building into the kind of trendy offices favoured by advertising agencies and the like who didn't mind paying high rents. It was a big project and I had taken a lot of convincing, but Tony had been chipping away for a long time. He thought I was too conservative and, though I reminded him that I'd almost gone under once, he told me that was in the past and I shouldn't let it hold the company back. In the end I'd relented enough to agree to the deal, but a couple of weeks ago Tony had told me the seller had suddenly upped his price by a third and he didn't think we were going to be able to reach agreement. The last I'd heard the deal was dead in the water. I wondered if something had happened to resurrect it. The way Tony was talking it sounded that way.

Back in my own office I forgot about the

Fulham project. I couldn't stop thinking about my dad. Part of me wanted to fly out to Ithaca but another part looked for excuses not to. I was thinking about Alicia too and my decision to ask her to marry me. I loved her, but I wondered if this was the right time to be making that kind of decision. Half an hour later Tony passed my office and when he saw me he looked surprised, even startled. He started to come in, but my phone rang and as I reached for it he pointed to his watch and mouthed that he'd see me later.

It was some time in the afternoon when we crossed paths again. As we chatted I recalled the phone conversation I'd overheard that morning and I was about to ask him if things had changed when he said that he'd heard again from the company that owned the warehouse.

'Might as well forget that one for now. They're not going to sell,' he said.

I said that it was a pity and he joked that I was probably secretly relieved. I smiled but didn't say anything. After he left I remembered his expression when he'd seen me that morning and I thought about the call. I went to my office and sat down. After a while I called a friend of mine and asked him to do me a favour.

That night at home Alicia came and sat beside me on the couch. 'What are you thinking about?'

'Nothing.'

'Liar.' She play punched me. 'Is it your dad? Did you speak to Irene today?'

'Yes. She said he's improving. I can speak to him tomorrow probably.'

'That's good. Do you think you'll go out there?'

'I don't think I can. Not right now.'

'OK.' She yawned. 'I'm tired. I'm going to go to bed. Are you coming?'

'You work too hard,' I told her.

'Tell Mitchell that.' She pulled a sour face.

I knew she hated Mitchell. He was the worst kind of boss. The kind who is so insecure about himself that he resents anybody who might be a threat. Alicia could do his job in her sleep and he knew it and so he made her life a misery. It was a shame because she was talented and she gave herself heart and soul to her career, but now she hated it.

When I went to bed an hour later the lights were off in our room. I cleaned my teeth and tried to put Tony out of my mind. Alicia had left her birth control pills on the vanity top. I thought about the doubts I'd had earlier and it occurred to me that if we got married she could stop taking her pills and she could tell Mitchell to shove his job.

When I got into bed, Alicia wasn't asleep. She turned and snuggled up to me and I realised that she was naked, which always meant one thing.

'I thought you were tired,' I said.

She kissed me and her hand slithered over my belly and took hold of me. 'Not that tired.'

★ ★ ★

In the morning I was at work early. I went to Tony's office and closed the door. He saw

23

something was up, and his grin lost some of its lustre.

'You remember that Fulham deal?' I said. 'David Jones talked to the company yesterday. Apparently they're developing the site themselves. They've got a new partner.'

Tony didn't say anything. We both knew who the new partner was. I waited for him to deny it, but he didn't. I had thought of Tony as a friend. But not any more.

'You're fired,' I told him calmly. 'Get out of here and don't ever set foot in this building again.'

He stared at me, surprised I think by my coldness. But then he stood up and began to gather a few things together. 'It's business, Robert. Nothing personal. You don't want the high risk projects. I'm only trying to do something for myself. Maybe I could've done it differently, I'll admit that.'

He didn't seem to be too concerned. He was losing his job and I knew he must have leveraged everything he owned to make himself a partner in the deal he'd done with the owners of the site. He stood to make a lot of money if things worked out. He would have quit his job with me eventually anyway, but he wanted the security of a salary for as long as possible.

When he had packed up his things he looked around the office. 'I'll send somebody around for the rest of this stuff.' He looked as if he were wondering whether to offer to shake hands.

'You should know that after I spoke to David I had him make an offer on the building,' I said.

24

'Twice the original price.'

Tony's face fell. 'You can't be serious. It isn't worth that much.'

'You're right, it isn't. But the way prices are going, in a couple of years I'll be able to sell it on. Until then, I'll just sit on it and pay the interest.'

He smiled. 'You wouldn't do that. You still stand to lose a lot of money.'

He was right about losing money, but I had found that all lessons in life come at a cost. In business I wouldn't make the mistake of trusting anybody the way I had trusted Tony again. When I didn't say anything he realised that I was serious. He looked ashen.

'Your shareholding in this company of course reverts to me for the price you paid,' I reminded him. 'There's a loyalty clause if you remember.'

Since he hadn't actually paid anything for his shares, in effect he had to gift them back. It was all legal and above board. He probably hadn't even read the small print when I had made the transfer. At the time he hadn't been planning to try to cheat me. 'You can't do that,' he said desperately. 'I'll contest it. You won't fucking well get away with it.'

'That's your right,' I said calmly. 'But I'd consult a good lawyer if I were you. Now get out.'

He wavered, indecision raging in his expression. I thought for a moment he would try to plead with me, invoke our friendship and the years we'd worked to build the company together. But there was no friendship any more. As far as I was concerned he didn't exist.

2

My father sounded tired when I spoke to him at the end of the week. But underneath his fatigue I detected a spark of his old resilience.

'The gods haven't finished with me yet, Robert,' he said when I asked him how he was feeling. 'They work in mysterious ways. In the face of peril they struck me down. A peculiar method of saving my wretched life, but effective nevertheless.'

I had no idea what he was talking about but I assumed that he was referring to his heart attack being a wake-up call. 'The doctors told Irene you were lucky,' I said. 'You have to listen to their advice.'

'Yes, yes. Don't eat this, don't drink that. I know all about it. A life of medicines and abstinence awaits me.'

Despite the curtailments he faced he sounded cheerful enough. I thought he wasn't taking it seriously, which annoyed me because it was Irene who would have to take care of him. I told him how worried she had been and that he should think of her instead of himself.

'Of course,' he said, sounding suddenly regretful. 'Poor Irene. I've put her through a lot. But I'll make it up to her now. I've always loved her you know. She's a remarkable woman.'

He was rambling, I thought. I wondered if it was the effect of his medication.

'She tells me that you've been phoning,' he said. 'That's very good of you.'

'I was concerned about her,' I said pointedly.

'Yes, yes, of course,' he murmured, the hurt evident in his voice.

I regretted being cruel, but my father had always brought out the worst in me. I tried to make amends by telling him that I was glad that he sounded better. We spoke for another minute or two and then, preparing to hang up, I said, 'I should let you rest.'

'Irene mentioned that you might come out some time soon,' he said quickly.

The hopeful note in his tone made me uncomfortable. 'When I can get away,' I said.

'It would be wonderful to see you. It's been quite a long time hasn't it?'

'Maybe in a few weeks,' I said. 'I'll let you know. In the meantime just remember to do what the doctors tell you.'

'Yes, of course. You know, Robert, it's funny but it's true what they say you know. While I've been lying here I've had a lot of time to think. I know I've made a lot of mistakes in my life. Things I regret. I've always wanted to try to explain.'

'You can do it when you're stronger,' I cut in, but he wasn't listening.

'I thought I was doing the right thing when I left England. I never meant to leave it so long before I wrote to you. I suppose I thought it was for the best . . . '

'It was a long time ago,' I said. I had heard this before, but it hadn't made any difference then

27

and it wouldn't now. What was done couldn't be undone. 'We can talk when I come over.'

'I understand what you must have felt,' he went on, as if he hadn't heard me. 'I didn't at the time of course, but in retrospect . . . '

'No!' In the startled silence that followed I took a deep breath to calm myself. 'You don't know how I felt,' I said quietly.

'No, of course.' He sounded suddenly exhausted. 'Perhaps you're right. This isn't the time.'

'You should rest,' I said. 'Let me speak to Irene.'

He said goodbye and handed me over. She must have been right beside him. I could hear the concern in her voice as she told him to lie back and rest, and when she came on the phone she spoke quietly.

'You must try not to upset him.'

'I'm sorry. Look, maybe it's better if I don't call for a few days.'

★ ★ ★

I wasn't about to let the wounds of the past intrude on the present. I'd planned that Alicia and I would go away for the weekend and so I'd booked a cottage in the Cotswolds. She loved the country and I'd reserved a table at a restaurant that I knew she liked. I'd bought her a ring. I was going to do the whole corny thing of proposing and then I'd open the little box and put it down in front of her.

The night before we left, she got up from her

28

chair and kissed the top of my head. 'Sleepy?'

I'd been brooding, my thoughts occupied with Tony and my father. I knew from her tone that Alicia wasn't thinking about sleep. Suddenly I wanted to make love to her. I wanted to feel close to her. A kind of reassurance.

I turned out the lights and followed her upstairs. When I went into our bedroom I glimpsed her reflection in the bathroom mirror. She was completely naked which was a sight that never failed to arouse me. Alicia took care of herself. She ran and worked out at the gym and it showed. As I began to turn away I saw her pop a birth control pill into her hand and then she dropped it into the sink and I heard the rush of water as she turned on the tap.

For a second I couldn't move. I was shocked. Then I went back downstairs before she came out of the bathroom. I wondered how long she'd been throwing her pills away. When I thought about it, our sexual relationship had been fairly active recently even though Alicia had been working so hard. I couldn't believe that she was trying to get pregnant. I thought I knew her, but I suddenly felt as if I didn't know her at all.

When I went back upstairs again she was in bed and when I slipped in beside her she cuddled up to me, but I caught her hand as she slid it across my chest.

'It's been a difficult week,' I said.

She hesitated in surprise but then she kissed me. 'Go to sleep. You'll feel better in the morning.'

I turned my back on her and lay in the

darkness with my eyes wide open. Alicia snuggled against me, her arm draped across my hip. She shifted position and I felt the soft warmth of her breasts against my back as her fingers trailed against the top of my thigh as if by accident. I didn't respond. I breathed slowly and evenly so that she would think I was asleep, and eventually she fell asleep herself. After a while she turned over and I raised myself on one elbow to watch her. Her lips were slightly parted, her hair had fallen over her cheek.

In the morning we drove down to the cottage, and later we went to the restaurant I had booked for dinner. I didn't give her the ring I'd bought or ask her to marry me. Earlier I'd pretended to fall as I was climbing over a fence, and when we went to bed I used the excuse of a pulled muscle to avoid having sex. I couldn't hide the fact that something was wrong however, I couldn't bring myself to look her in the eye any more.

When we were packing to leave on Sunday afternoon she saw the ring when the box fell out of my bag. When she picked it up she looked at me questioningly then opened it. She stared at it for what seemed like a long time and then she gave it back to me and sat on the edge of the bed.

'Did you buy that for me?' she asked quietly. I didn't answer. 'The other night at home you saw me didn't you? You saw me flush my pill down the sink. I thought you had. I caught a glimpse of something moving in the mirror. Why didn't you say something?'

'I'm not sure. I needed to think about it I suppose.'

She nodded to herself and looked at her feet before she met my eye again. 'And now that you've thought about it?'

'Why did you do it?'

She smiled sadly. 'I shouldn't have, I know. But every time we talked about it you kept putting it off.'

'So you decided to make the decision by yourself.'

'It was wrong. But I thought . . . no I think . . . that you'll never agree to have children. I think you're afraid to. You think your children might hate you the way you hate your father.'

'Christ.' I shook my head at her amateur psychology. 'That's bullshit. The truth couldn't be more different. I want kids. It's true I don't want to fuck things up for them, but that's why I've put it off. I just wanted to be sure.' I gestured angrily toward the ring. 'And I was sure. Why else do you think I got you that?'

Alicia looked at me. Her eyes were shining. 'Nothing's changed then,' she said in a quiet voice. 'I love you. I always have. You must love me if you bought that.'

But I didn't know any more. She was wrong to think nothing had changed and she knew it.

★ ★ ★

The following morning in London Alicia told me that she was going to stay with a friend for a while.

31

'I think it would be for the best.' She wrote me a number and left it by the phone. 'I'm sorry for what I did. But it doesn't mean that I don't love you.'

That night when I came home to an empty house I wanted to phone her, but I told myself I needed time to think about it all, to decide how I felt. I missed her. I felt as if I was rattling around in my big house that suddenly felt empty. But as the days passed it began to get easier.

A week later Irene phoned to say that she was taking my father home from hospital. I was surprised. He'd barely been in there for two weeks.

'The doctors have advised against it,' she said, 'but he will not listen.'

I had the feeling there was something she wasn't telling me. I sensed her indecision. When I asked her what was wrong she said it was nothing, but she asked me again when I was going over.

'A few weeks,' I said. 'I promise.'

After I'd hung up I picked up the number Alicia had left me. I stared at it for a long time, and then I crumpled it up and threw it in the bin.

3

The plane landed just after midday Greek time, swooping down over the Ionian Sea past hills scorched brown by the sun. It hit the runway with a series of bone-jarring bumps and shudders before finally coming to a halt beside two Second World War vintage fighters parked at the side of the apron.

The young woman sitting next to me breathed an audible sigh of relief, and, catching my eye, smiled self-consciously.

'I don't really like flying,' she confided, only now releasing her white-knuckled grip on the armrest between us. Her friend in the window seat was looking outside, anxiously searching for something that resembled the pictures she'd seen of Kephalonia in holiday brochures.

'It looks hot,' was all she could manage by way of uncertain pronouncement, no doubt unimpressed by the concrete and glass terminal and the featureless hills beyond.

'The beaches are nice around Lixouri,' I assured them.

'Is that where you're staying too?' the one beside me asked.

'I'm going to Ithaca,' I reminded her.

'Oh, yes. You told me that earlier didn't you? Is that near Lixouri?'

'It's another island. You have to catch a ferry.'

She looked disappointed. 'That's a shame. We

could have met up. Had a drink or something.'

She held my eye, emboldened by duty-free vodka. She was quite pretty, in her late-twenties with short hair and elfin features. In fact she reminded me a little bit of Alicia and for a moment the thought of her caused me a sharp pang of loss. It had been a month since she left. I had seen her once in a restaurant with a man I didn't recognise, but I'd hurried on before she noticed me. She had called me at home a few days afterwards, the coincidence making me think she must have seen me after all. I wasn't at home when she called, but when I came in and turned on the answering machine and heard a hesitant silence I knew it was her. I waited to see if she would speak, my pulse racing.

'It's me,' she said finally, and then there was another long pause before she hung up. I checked to see if she'd called back but there were no other messages and I hadn't heard from her again.

The seat-belt sign over my head went out and I put thoughts of Alicia out of my mind as all around me people got up and began to haul luggage down from the overhead lockers. When we emerged from the plane it was to a sudden and unfamiliar heat. Even in June, England had been chilly and grey. As we crossed the Tarmac to the terminal beneath a cloudless sky I could already feel the prickle of perspiration through my shirt.

I said goodbye to the girls I'd sat next to and after I'd collected my bag went outside to find a taxi to take me to Efimia. Already a throng of people had emerged dazed into the sun, clutching their luggage. They mingled with the crowds heading home who had just been disgorged from a line of buses. A few sat on a low wall exposed to the sun, their brown or sometimes livid red bodies bared for a final time.

The airport is on the western side of the island, but Ithaca lies in the other direction, reached by ferries that ply back and forth across the strait from ports on the eastern coast. The road led over the mountains, climbing high above fertile valleys past olive groves and vineyards where the taxi driver kept offering to stop so that I could buy some of the local wine. When I repeatedly declined he eventually gave up and for the rest of the journey contented himself with chain-smoking.

At Efimia I found that I had to wait an hour for a ferry to take me to Ithaca so to fill the time I ordered coffee at a nearby *kefenio*. The town had been built on the slopes of low hills surrounding a pretty bay that formed a harbour. A few yachts were tied up against the wharf where some children were fishing and a group of Greek men smoked cigarettes and chatted. Beneath the hot sun I could feel life slowing down, changing gear. When the ferry arrived I went to pay my bill, remembering too late that I hadn't changed any English currency into euros. The owner shrugged, waving away my pound coins.

'Next time. Next time.'

I thanked him, making a mental note to be

sure I remembered to come back here on my way home.

There were perhaps twenty or so passengers besides myself making the trip across the strait. Once out of the bay, Ithaca revealed itself as a hazy series of rocky humps resembling some sleeping sea monster. The colours of the landscape brought back memories of childhood visits. The sun flashed like silver on the impossibly blue sea. Kephalonia retreated, its coastal hills bare and brown while Ithaca's coast in comparison seemed lush with dark green growth. I sat on the top deck wondering what I would find when I arrived.

Since my father had left the hospital he'd been making a steady recovery. According to Irene he was resting and eating properly and drinking only half a glass of wine a day with dinner. When I spoke to her she sounded strained, but I put that down to worry and the stress of coping with my father. My father had regained some of his old bluff manner on the phone. I kept saying that I would come out some time soon, but I had never been precise about dates. I had told him I thought it would be better if I waited until he was stronger and, though he was disappointed, he tried not to let on. My vague plans had changed abruptly two days earlier. Irene had called me at five in the morning. I was only half awake, but as soon as I heard her voice I knew something was wrong.

'Irene? What is it?' I said, glancing at the clock by my bed and sitting up.

'It is your father, Robert.' I gripped the phone

tightly, fearing that she was about to tell me he'd had another heart attack, but instead she said, 'He has vanished.'

'Vanished? What do you mean?'

'Yesterday he left the house early in the morning. Before I was awake. Since then, nobody has seen him.'

I swung my legs over the side of the bed. I wondered how anybody could disappear in a place the size of Ithaca. 'Do you mean he's left the island?' The first thing that occurred to me was that he might have gone to Kephalonia to catch a plane and was on his way to England. I even glanced toward the door as if at any moment I might hear the doorbell downstairs.

'I do not think so,' Irene said. 'Nobody remembers him buying a ticket for the ferry, and the police found his car at the marina.'

'The police?'

'When he did not come home I phoned them. I thought something might have happened to him.'

I was fully awake by then and I tried to think logically. 'Hang on, you said his car was at the marina. What about his boat?'

'The *Swallow* is still there.'

'But if his car is there surely he must be around somewhere.'

'The police have asked everybody. Nobody has seen him.' She paused and when she spoke again her voice caught in her throat. 'They are searching around the harbour.'

I understood then that she was afraid he'd had another heart attack and I understood how worried she was. I tried to reassure her. I said that I was sure he would turn up but I was already thinking about how quickly I could get out there. By the time we hung up I'd promised I would get a flight as soon as I could. As it turned out, the next available seat on a scheduled flight to Kephalonia wasn't for forty-eight hours. Even after I'd booked my ticket I expected him to show up before I left, but the last time I'd called Irene from London there still hadn't been any news. By then my father had been missing for three days.

As the ferry approached the small port of Piso Aetos on Ithaca's western coast I searched for Irene on the wharf. Nothing much had changed since I was last there. There was just a dock and a couple of low-roofed buildings at the bottom of a steep hill. A handful of people stood waiting and among them I spotted Irene. Despite the years that had passed since we'd last met, I had no trouble recognising her. She wore a simple sleeveless jade-green dress that clung to her figure in the afternoon breeze, reminding me that she was twenty years younger than my father. As a boy I used to spend a week or two with them every summer during the school holidays. When I was fifteen, Irene would have been in her thirties. I used to wonder what she saw in my father, who by then was steadily thickening around the waist. She had made an effort to be especially nice to me and, with youthful confusion, I misinterpreted her kindness and indulged in fevered guilt-ridden sexual fantasies. A father cuckolded by his own son. It

38

couldn't have been more fitting on a Greek island.

Once the ferry had docked, Irene scanned the disembarking passengers anxiously. I waved and when she saw me she raised a hand in return but there was something hesitant and forlorn in her greeting. When I met her we hugged briefly and then she took both of my hands in her own.

'Robert, it is good to see you again.'

'And you Irene. Is there any news?' She took off her sunglasses revealing eyes that were reddened and puffy and I knew. Instantly I regretted not having come earlier. I was shocked. Somehow I hadn't believed it could happen. When I found my voice I said, 'He's dead isn't he?'

She managed to nod. 'I am so sorry.'

I looked past her to the hills beyond. I wasn't sure exactly what I felt but I knew that it wasn't the grief that a son should feel on hearing such news. I wasn't sure which was the greater tragedy; his death or my reaction to it.

* * *

The road that led from the port wound back and forth up a steep hill in a series of switchbacks. It was flanked on one side by an almost vertical plunge. From the top we looked down on the causeway that joined the southern and northern halves of the island. Beyond lay Molos Bay and in the distance were small hazy islands, faint smudges against the blue of the sea and sky. Mount Nirito rose almost vertically from the shore of the bay, its slopes surprisingly green from the wild oak that grew profusely all over the island, while on the other side a narrow gap between two headlands marked the entrance to Vathy harbour.

Instead of going to the house, we drove north. From the coast road I glimpsed the terracotta roofs of the occasional hamlet among the olive groves below. I remembered driving along this road with my father years before. I saw a curve of brilliant white beach where I was sure we had once gone for a swim.

When we reached the village of Stavros, Irene parked beneath the shade of a pine tree in the square.

'I grew up here,' she said. 'When I was a child I came to this church with my family.' Two towers flanked the entrance to the church opposite, and behind them was an impressive blue, domed roof. 'If you do not mind waiting I would like to go inside. You can wait for me in the *kefenio* across the street. I will not be long.'

'Of course,' I said. 'Take your time.'

When she had gone I lingered in the quiet drowsy heat of the square, but after several minutes curiosity got the better of me and I followed her. I had never seen inside a Greek Orthodox church before. Compared to the sombre austerity of the chapel I remembered from boarding school, the contrast could hardly have been greater. Instead of cold stone walls and rows of unwelcoming pews, the style was almost gaudy. The walls and the inside of the dome were painted a pale eggshell blue and a strip of what had once been bright red carpet led up the central aisle. Massive glass chandeliers hung from the ceiling and elaborate painted icons looked down on the rows of seats. Several huge throne-like carved chairs stood on a dais where I imagined the priests sat during services.

Irene genuflected before an icon of the Virgin Mary and then lit a candle that she took from a brass holder. She sat on a chair with her head bowed, her lips moving in silent prayer. As I watched her I wanted to feel something, but quite what I didn't know. I wondered if my father had become religious though I couldn't imagine him in a place like this somehow. If there was an after-life, if some essence of him was present here, I wondered what I would say to him. No answer was forthcoming and in the end, feeling that I was intruding on Irene's grief I slipped outside again to wait for her.

When she emerged, she offered a wan smile and led the way to a *kefenio* where we sat on a shady terrace. Stavros was built on top of a hill where several routes converged. From where we sat we looked down on Polis Bay where a yacht drifted at anchor, gleaming white against the deep blue of the sea. Irene and the owner of the *kefenio* knew each other and when he brought us menus he greeted her as an old friend.

'*Yassou* Irene,' he said warmly and kissed her cheek.

They spoke rapidly in Greek and though I didn't understand what they were saying I heard my father's name mentioned.

'*Kalos-orissate*,' the man said before reverting

41

to English. 'Welcome to Ithaca, Mr French. I am sorry for your father. I know him a long time. He is a good man.'

I thanked him, and when he'd left with our order Irene said, 'Johnny was very popular on Ithaca. He will be missed.'

We hadn't talked about what had happened yet, but now I said, 'I assume it was another heart attack.'

She hesitated. 'It is not yet certain. There will have to be an examination.' She gestured helplessly. 'I do not know the right word in English.'

'You mean an autopsy?'

'Yes. That is it. An autopsy. Your father was found in the harbour, Robert. At the marina where he kept the *Swallow*. The police think he may have drowned. They are bringing somebody from Kephalonia.'

I was surprised, not so much about where he was found but at the circumstances. After my parents were divorced, I eventually spent part of the school summer holidays each year on Ithaca. It was an arrangement I went along with grudgingly because I wasn't given a choice, but the one part of it I'd always looked forward to was spending time on my father's boat. For a while at least I was able to put aside the resentment I felt towards him. I could picture him vividly as he dived off the side into the cool, clear sea. His body was brown and powerful and though he was beginning to run to fat, he swam like a seal. 'I can't imagine him drowning,' I said to Irene.

'They think he may have fallen from the boat after he had another heart attack.'

I could see how it might have happened. Perhaps as he climbed aboard he was hit with a sudden crushing pain and he stumbled backwards into the water. But I had read somewhere that drowning victims quickly float to the surface buoyed by gases in the body. He had been missing for three days. 'Why did it take so long for anybody to find him?'

'Apparently his clothes were caught up with the propeller.'

I imagined my dad struggling to free himself, eyes wide, his mouth opening in a silent cry, only a stream of bubbles escaping. Horror plucked at my insides and I banished the vision with a hasty gulp of wine.

Belatedly I realised that tears were sliding unchecked down Irene's cheeks and I reached out for her hand. 'I'm sorry,' I told her. They had been together ever since my father had come to Ithaca, almost twenty-five years earlier. Whatever my own feelings towards him, I knew Irene had always loved him.

'It is my fault,' she said heavily.

'It isn't anybody's fault.' I was surprised that she was blaming herself. 'It was an accident.'

Irene shook her head. 'He was supposed to be resting. I should not have let him leave the house.'

'But didn't you say he left before you were awake?'

'Yes,' she admitted.

'Then there was nothing you could do. You

couldn't watch him every minute of the day. Besides,' I added, voicing a feeling that had been forming since I had arrived, 'if anyone should feel guilty it's me. I should have come earlier.'

'You should not feel badly. You have a busy life in London. Your father knew that.'

Both of us knew that wasn't the reason I'd delayed my trip, but I was grateful for the gesture. 'Then nobody's to blame. You always stood by him, Irene. He was bloody lucky to have you.'

I thought back to the times I'd spoken to him on the phone over the last couple of years as he'd begun to sound increasingly defeated, and especially the last six months, when he was often half drunk. I was subjected to long self-pitying monologues during which he bemoaned a wasted life. I thought Irene must have had to put up with a hell of a lot and I felt a twinge of guilt that I hadn't offered her any support. Before Dad's heart attack I hadn't even spoken to her for months. I couldn't remember exactly when the last time had been. It was clear now just how much strain she had been under. She was pale, her eyes were dull and she looked a little thin.

'You do not understand, Robert,' she insisted sadly. 'Your father was not so lucky as you think. There is something I must tell you. Before his heart attack, Johnny and I had not been living together.'

I gaped at her in confusion. 'I don't understand.'

'Last year, I left Johnny. You see, I am not such a good person after all.'

44

'You left him? But I've always thought of the two of you as being so happy together.' Even as I spoke I realised that I hadn't actually seen them for a long time. A lot can change in eight years. I thought about Alicia. Things could change in the blink of an eye, which is about how long it took for me to see her flush her pill down the sink.

'I should have told you when it happened,' Irene said. 'But of course I did not because I was afraid of what you would think of me. I have always been a little bit frightened that you would see me as the wicked stepmother. Like in the fairy-tales.'

'I never thought about you that way.'

'Is that true, Robert? I always wondered. After all you did not know me when you first came here. And you were so angry even though you were not much more than a little boy. How old were you?'

'Thirteen. But if I was angry it wasn't because of you.'

'No. Of course I realised that it was your father who made you feel that way. It was very sad. But I thought perhaps you would not like me because you would think I had taken him away from you and so some of your anger was for me too.'

'Maybe I wanted to feel that way to begin with. I hadn't heard anything from him in two years and then suddenly he writes to announce he's getting married again. I suppose part of me wanted to lay the blame on you. But you weren't anything like I imagined. I've always liked you Irene. If I'd known about you and Dad I would

45

have phoned to make sure you were OK.'

She smiled sadly, but was grateful I think for the assurance.

'He never mentioned it you know,' I said.

'Yes, he told me.'

'When did it happen?'

'In September, but things had been difficult for a long time. Your father had become depressed. He always hoped that one day he would achieve something important with his work. It was his dream. But with every year that went by I think he believed in his dream a little less. Do you remember the digs he used to work on every summer?'

'Yes, of course.' I recalled the trenches and excavated hollows where he would happily spend his days on his knees in the dirt carefully revealing some long-buried crumbling wall.

'There is a temple that Homer mentions in The *Odyssey*. It has been lost since ancient times. It was dedicated to the goddess Aphrodite.'

He had often talked about this temple where the fabled hero Odysseus had worshipped. In archaeological terms it was the equivalent of the Holy Grail. 'He thought if he could find it, it would make him famous,' I said bitterly.

'It was not fame he wanted, Robert. He simply wanted to feel that his work meant something. But in the end after so many years when he did not find the temple he began to give up hope. He thought that he was a failure. He began to drink too much. At first I was not so worried because I thought it would pass. Often at the end of each

46

summer he used to say that he would not make another excavation, then always after a few months he would change his mind. But last year for the first time since he came to Ithaca Johnny did not dig. Instead he was spending all of his time in the taverna.'

She broke off for a moment, her gaze drifting away from me across the bay. When she turned back to me she said, 'Have you ever been in love, Robert?'

'I suppose I have,' I answered, surprised by the sudden change in direction.

'It is a strange thing, don't you think? When we love somebody we forgive them their weaknesses and their failings because we know we are not perfect ourselves. We can manage to overcome all kinds of troubles. Do they not say that to be with another person we must always compromise, and we must expect that there will be difficult times as well as good? And yet we need to know that the person we love cares for us equally. Without that the sacrifice is too great. It is all give, with no reward for our efforts.'

I had some idea of what Irene was talking about. I had loved Alicia, though once I knew that she was trying to get pregnant I no longer believed that she loved me. How could she if she had made such a unilateral decision? I couldn't help wondering if her intent hadn't been to make sure that I would marry her. The instant I saw her that night in the bathroom I felt betrayed and afterwards I knew I could never trust her.

In Irene's case it wasn't a betrayal that had driven her away, but my father's repeated

47

insistence that she should leave him. She told me that he began telling her that he was too old for her. When she tried to talk him out of his depression he said she ought to be with a younger man. I thought of his drunken phone calls and I could imagine how it must have been.

'At first I told him that he was being foolish,' she said, 'but it was difficult. It is hard for me to explain. I loved Johnny, ever since we met I felt this way. But he changed and for so long I heard these same things. I did not feel that he loved me any more. How could he when he was always telling me to leave him? I did not know what to do.'

She broke off, her voice choked with emotion. 'You don't have to do this,' I said. 'I understand what you're saying.'

She shook her head. 'No. There is more that I must tell you. There was a man, an old friend. I needed somebody to talk to and he was there to listen.'

I understood then why she felt guilty to the point of blaming herself for my father's death. I listened quietly while she explained that when she realised that her friendship with this man was becoming something more than that, she decided that she couldn't continue to live with my father.

'I needed to be alone for a little while,' she said, 'so I rented a small house in the town and last September I moved in there. Of course I still saw Johnny, but it was difficult.'

'He knew about the other man?'

'Yes. He tried to pretend that he was happy for

me, but I knew that it was not true. I felt very bad because I knew that I had hurt him.'

'He hurt himself,' I pointed out. 'By the sound of it he practically drove you out.'

'Perhaps. But only because he wanted me to be happy. He explained this when I went to him after his heart attack. He was different then. More like the old Johnny. I told him that when he came out of hospital I wanted to go home to take care of him.'

'What about the other man?' I wondered. 'How did he feel about that?'

'He understood. You see when I was afraid that your father would die I realised how much I loved him.'

'Then you did everything you could, Irene. You went home and you took care of him. You can't blame yourself for what happened.'

I could see that my reassurances weren't enough. There was something desperate in her eyes, some turmoil of uncertainty and I guessed at once that there was something else that she hadn't told me.

'What is it?' I asked. 'Why are you punishing yourself like this?'

'Because I could have stopped Johnny that morning,' she said finally. 'If I had taken him seriously, perhaps he would not have gone to the marina without telling me.'

'I don't understand. If you had taken what seriously?'

'When he told me that somebody had tried to kill him,' she answered.

I stared at her dumbfounded, not certain at

first that she was serious, though it was clear that she was. 'Kill him? Why the hell would anyone want to kill somebody like my father?'

For a moment she hesitated and then she shook her head. 'I do not know.'

I remembered something he had said to me when I'd spoken to him on the phone when he was in hospital. He was talking about the gods saving his wretched life, as he put it, with their mysterious ways. 'In the face of peril they struck me down.'

4

After Irene's startling revelation we drove back to Vathy from Stavros. Along the way she explained that my father had been in the hospital for two weeks before he told her that somebody had tried to kill him. Irene had moved to a nearby hotel. Every morning she would spend a few hours with him and then return again in the evening after he had rested for the afternoon, then together they would talk or watch television or perhaps read. He was no longer bitter, she told me. He would hold her hand and often told her that he had been a fool to drive her away. While I listened I couldn't escape the suspicion that my father's reformation was remarkably convenient, perhaps explained by his close brush with mortality.

'But he was not quite the same,' Irene said. 'There was something on his mind. What is the English word for this? I felt he was thinking about something else, even when he was talking to me about coming home. I could sense that part of him was not with me.'

'You mean he was preoccupied?'

'Yes. That is it,' she agreed. 'When I asked him about it he denied that it was true, but he could not deceive me. When you have lived with somebody for a very long time there are things that you understand without the need for words. There was a time when Johnny would never keep anything from me. We had no secrets from one another. It is difficult, I think, for a relationship to be strong when one person hides things from the other.'

'You felt he was deliberately hiding something?'

'Yes. I think he did not trust me to tell me what it was. He was worried I think. But also excited.'

'Excited?'

Irene frowned as she drove. 'I do not know how else to put it. He was not unhappy or depressed any more. Sometimes when we talked of the way things were before, how he had talked so much of failure, I had the feeling that there was something he wanted to tell me, but then he would draw back and it would be gone. And then one morning when I went to visit him I found him out of his bed demanding that the nurse bring him his clothes. He was very upset.'

'About what?'

'I do not know. He insisted that I take him home.'

'You mean upset as in angry?'

She thought about that. 'Not angry. Perhaps a little with the nurse because she refused to fetch his clothes, though it was not her fault, she was only doing her job. It was more that he was in a hurry. I do not know how to explain it. As if he was anxious about something. When he saw me he was very pleased. He pleaded with me to make them bring his clothes. At first I did not know what to do. I told him I would have to speak to the doctors.'

'What did they say?'

'That he was not well enough to leave.'

'But he wouldn't listen?'

'No. And when they saw how upset Johnny was they became alarmed. They checked his medication because at first they wondered if the nurse had given him the wrong drugs. I felt sorry for her. She had not given him anything except what was written on his chart. She thought she was going to get into trouble but she told the doctors the same thing she had told me, that Johnny had seemed quite all right when she had brought him some juice and the newspaper after he had woken up. He had been sitting up in bed and talking to her, though of course he was complaining about being in hospital because he did not like being stuck in bed all day and he said the food was terrible, but Johnny always complained of these things, so it was nothing new. But when she went back later he had changed. He was very agitated and that was when he said that he was leaving.'

Irene told me that after the doctors had checked him over they had taken her aside and warned her that though my father wasn't ready to go home it was dangerous for him to be in such an excitable state. She had to try to calm him down or else they concluded it might actually be better if they agreed to his demand, though there were forms she would have to sign absolving them of culpability.

'It was then that Johnny told me that somebody had tried to kill him,' Irene continued. 'He said that it was dangerous for him to stay in hospital and that was why he needed to go home.'

'Maybe he was talking about the hospital food,' I joked, though she didn't see the humour.

'No. He was talking about the night of his heart attack.' She explained how a truck driver going home late at night had seen my father collapse on a road high above the town. 'If Nikos had not seen him, Johnny would have died. But your father told me that he was being chased when he collapsed.'

'Chased by whom?' I tried to imagine him running under any circumstances. Even when I had last seen him he had been quite overweight.

'He would not say at the time. Later he said that he did not know who it was.'

'But whoever it was wanted to kill him? Why?'

She shook her head. 'I thought that it might be his medicine. The doctors had told me that there might be side-effects. He might have confusions.'

'You mean delusions?'

'Yes, that is the word. But when Johnny saw that I didn't believe him he would not say any more. I think it hurt him. But later I thought about it again. I signed the forms and took him home and that night I wondered why he would say such a thing if it was not true.'

'Are you serious?' I said. 'He was ill, and like you said he was probably on some pretty potent medicine. You don't really think there was anything to it.'

'But there is the way he behaved at the

hospital. And afterwards at home. As if there was always something on his mind. He was worried, I am sure.'

'Did you ask him why?'

'Of course. But he told me that I was right, that it was the medicine that had made him think strange things. He laughed it off.'

'Then surely that's your explanation.'

'But I felt that he was keeping something from me. If I had listened to him at the hospital he might have told me what it was, but because I did not believe him he would not confide in me again. After I took him home he behaved in strange ways sometimes. Every night he would lock the doors and windows, even though there is very little crime on Ithaca. It is not like the cities or what you see on television. He would often wake up at night thinking that he had heard something outside.'

'You never saw or heard anything?'

'No, of course not. And there were other things. He would shut himself in his study, even though he was not supposed to work. He wouldn't tell me what he was doing. And he wouldn't let me ask anybody to come to the house. He refused to see anybody.'

To me my father's behaviour, while smacking of mild paranoia, sounded consistent with the possible side-effects of the drugs he was on, or else he was simply suffering withdrawal symptoms because he wasn't drinking. I felt that guilt had distorted Irene's view.

'It can't have been true,' I reasoned. 'I mean, what possible reason could anyone have for wanting to kill him? He was simply a harmless old man.'

She met my eye, uncertainty written into every troubled line in her face. For a moment I thought there was something else she wanted to tell me, but then resignedly she said, 'I suppose you are right.'

★ ★ ★

The house where my father and Irene had lived for more than twenty years sat on a hillside high above the main town of Vathy. Stone retaining walls formed terraces where olive trees grew. It was a common feature of the island, evidence of cultivation going back thousands of years. Often these walls had fallen into disrepair because the landowners lived abroad, but here they were well maintained, reminding me that Irene ran a successful company.

She had bought a small olive-pressing plant from a family member a few years after she met my father. She must have understood early on that they would struggle to live on the money my father made as an archaeologist and curator of the small museum he had started to house his finds. At first she had pressed the crops of local smallholders, mainly for their own use, charging them a percentage for the process. Later she had begun bottling her own brand and, as European regulations loomed, she had invested in more sophisticated plant and gradually had turned the business into a full-scale commercial operation. Her oil was exported all over the world, albeit in

56

relatively small quantities.

The whitewashed plaster façade and terracotta tiled roof of the house were typical of Ithaca. It had been built over two levels with shutters on the windows and wrought-iron balconies outside the upper-floor rooms. A large terrace over-looked the town and the sheltered harbour far below. To the north, Mount Nirito rose dramatically to a darkening sky, splashed by late golden sunlight.

When we arrived, Irene showed me to my room. It was the same one that I had used during my reluctant visits there as a child. After she had reminded me where everything was, she told me that I should feel at home and she gave me the keys to my father's Jeep.

'I am afraid that the last few days have been tiring,' she said. 'If you do not mind I will go to bed early. But perhaps you would like to go into the town.'

I was sure that I wouldn't be able to sleep, so I took the keys and thanked her. 'I might do that.'

She smiled wearily and kissed my cheek. 'Then I will say goodnight, Robert. *Kalinichta.*'

'Good-night.'

★ ★ ★

It was dark by the time I drove into Vathy. The town was built around a picturesque harbour. The entire place had been destroyed during the devastating earthquake that had hit the Ionian Islands and part of the Greek mainland during the early fifties, but Vathy had been rebuilt in

57

traditional style. Unlike neighbouring Kephalonia, there were no strips of tacky bars and nightclubs or huge tourist hotels. The twisting, narrow streets were full of small shops selling fresh vegetables or books and magazines, groceries or clothes, and on every corner there was a *kefenio* or taverna where the tables spilled out onto the pavements. Closer to the waterfront there were a few souvenir shops catering to the tourist trade and all of them had racks of paperback translations of Homer's *Odyssey* and *Iliad* on display.

Outside the towns, the beaches were not sandy like those on Kephalonia, but rather were made of smooth stones bleached by the sun. As a consequence, the island didn't attract the package-deal hordes that descended on its neighbour. Instead, many of those who came to Ithaca were Italians or mainland Greeks. Some stayed in small apartment complexes or rented rooms in private homes, others had their own properties that remained shut up during the winter months. The island was also popular with the many boats that cruised the area during the summer, their owners attracted by its unspoilt beauty and its history.

As I drove along the waterfront I could see that almost every available berth was taken and a few yachts lay at anchor further out in the harbour. In the main square the restaurants and bars were busy. I found somewhere to park and searched for a free table outside but they were all taken. I was about to look for somewhere quieter in the backstreets when I saw a girl sitting alone.

58

At first I thought she was a local. She had dark blonde hair, the olive complexion of the Mediterranean races and there was something distinctly Greek about the angular slant of her features. But when I noticed the book she was reading I saw that it had an English title and I approached her and gestured to the unoccupied chairs.

'Excuse me, do you mind if I share your table?'

She looked up in surprise and then glanced around at the busy tables as if noticing them for the first time. Her eyes were hidden behind dark glasses even though the sun had gone down an hour before. I wondered how she could see to read. 'No, I don't mind,' she said quietly and then returned to her book.

The way she spoke immediately conjured images of private schools and a well-to-do family. She appeared to be in her mid-twenties or so and I wondered if perhaps she was from one of the visiting yachts. The book she was reading was by a well-known and fairly literary author.

The air was warm and the smells of grilled food and the sea mixed pleasingly. The slap and suck of water against the wharf was soothing. A waiter arrived and delivered the beer I'd ordered. I drank while I watched the life of the town go on around me. Whole families were out to eat dinner or simply stroll along the waterfront. Groups of people stopped to talk while their children ran around shouting and playing games.

I thought about my father lying somewhere

nearby, his body cold and lifeless, and it hit me that I would never hear his voice again. There would be no more phone calls and conversations that never went anywhere but saw us endlessly skating around each other on thin ice. He was always wary of cracking through the surface of normalcy while I silently resented the pretence. I always felt agitated during those calls. Part of me wanted to air my grievances with confrontation, another part to punish him with silence the way I had been doing for years. I always ended up doing the latter. It struck me that I'd never have to worry about it again, but also that everything I'd wanted to say would have to remain unspoken.

My thoughts turned to my father's claim that somebody had tried to kill him. I didn't believe any of it. It sounded as though he had been doing a pretty good job of it himself anyway. The thing that had really killed him was selfishness. It was what had brought him to Ithaca in the first place and had ultimately led him to clog his arteries and pickle his liver. Years ago he'd fled Oxford after a professional scandal that had ruined his reputation and destroyed my parents' marriage, which had been far from perfect in the first place. My father had taken refuge here on this pretty but insignificant island, and for the next quarter of a century had buried himself in the past. I'd always thought he had taken the easy option.

I could still remember the last time I saw him in England. I was eleven years old and I had been in a fight at school with a boy who'd said my dad was a cheat. I went home with a blackened eye and when I told him what had happened, instead of being proud of me for sticking up for him, my father couldn't look at me. He went to his study and shut himself away while my mother put an ice pack to my face. When I told her what the boy I'd fought with had said she was tight-mouthed and furious. That night I heard her voice raised in shrill anger and accusation and in the morning my father had left. Within a fortnight I'd been sent away to boarding school with the flimsiest of explanations about where he had gone and when he was coming back.

Until then, our house had been divided. Though I'd always known that my parents were not particularly happy together, they never actually argued much. But they weren't affectionate towards one another either. My mother exuded a more or less permanent air of dissatisfaction and disapproval of which I somehow understood my father was the root cause, though I never knew why. He seemed to accept his lot and tried hard to keep the peace, but his nature seemed coloured with the resignation of defeat. They were out of balance with one another and I was caught in the middle.

During the summer breaks, when my dad went off on one of his digs I would go with him. We'd camp out or stay in a small country pub, and for the time we were away he didn't seem to have any worries bearing down on him. For my part I was happy to escape my mother's attention to tidiness and cleanliness, qualities my dad didn't consider important. During those summer digs everything was different. It was like shrugging off clothes that were a size too small, and I sensed that he felt the same way. Out of that shared feeling a deeper bond grew between us, though in a sense it was a secret. After the summer was over and we went home again there was an unspoken agreement that we didn't talk about the time we'd spent away. We simply resumed our structured way of life.

Boarding school was even more regimented and excessively orderly. I didn't fit in. Our family didn't have money and everybody seemed to know about my father and what had happened at Oxford. At first I defended him, but later, when I realised that the things the other children said were true, I simply ignored their taunts. All the time I expected to hear from him any day and I couldn't understand why I didn't. My mother finally told me he was living on a Greek island. I compared a mental picture of blue seas and sunshine with the cold grey stone walls of the school and the wet wind that came off the river. I was still certain that he would come back for me as soon as he could, or at least write and tell me when that would be. But every week my disappointment grew like a cancer. He never came or sent word.

My reflections were abruptly disturbed when a child bumped into the table as he chased a ball. '*Signomi*,' he said, grinning apologetically.

As he ran off to continue his game I glanced at the girl opposite me. She didn't appear to have noticed what had happened. Though she still held her book open, I was sure she hadn't read a page since I'd sat down. She seemed completely absorbed in her thoughts. Perhaps lost was a better term. She exuded a kind of melancholy aura. I wondered what gave me that impression and decided that it was her stillness and the fact that she took no notice of what went on around her. The dark glasses she wore made her seem removed from the world, but imprisoned rather than unobserved.

I finished my beer but couldn't attract the attention of a waiter so I got up to go inside to fetch another. When I returned, the girl had gone. I saw her crossing the square among the crowd, but somehow apart from them. As she retreated into the darkness she looked small and vulnerable.

When I had finished my beer I decided to go for a walk. I hoped that the exercise would tire me out so that I'd be able to sleep later. Away from the centre of town there were fewer bars and restaurants and the streams of people thinned to a trickle. Small fishing boats replaced the yachts and launches at the wharf and across the road tiny cottages looked over the water. I walked almost to the very end of the wharf beyond the last of the iron lamps that cast a string of pools of yellow light in a crescent along the waterfront. There, only the moon that had risen above the hills softened the darkness. It was very quiet, the water like oil close to the shore, turning to silver grey further out. Cicadas chirped from the trees on the hillside. I paused to take it all in.

About thirty feet away somebody else was gazing across the harbour. Whoever it was didn't seem to be aware of me and I had the feeling I was intruding on a moment of quiet reflection. I was about to turn away when I recognised the girl whose table I had shared. Her melancholy air struck me again. Without warning she seemed to waver, then, as if in a dream, she vanished into the darkness and I heard a splash as she hit the water below.

It felt afterwards as if I had been rooted to the spot in surprise for a long time, but it couldn't have been more than a moment before I ran to where I had last seen her. The wharf was perhaps seven or eight feet above the water. I couldn't tell how deep it was because it was black as pitch, but I saw a streak of movement below and heard a gasp. Without thinking, I leapt in. Immediately I sank. I couldn't see a thing. The water was cool but not cold. When I didn't touch the bottom, a flutter of panic rose in my throat and I kicked for the surface. A second later I took a breath of warm air. I spun around looking for the girl. She was half-floating face-down only a few feet away from me and with a stroke I caught hold of her and turned her pale face to the air. Her eyelids fluttered and she coughed. Grasping her underneath her shoulders I struck out for shore. My feet touched the ground within seconds and I hauled her onto the rocks.

She had been in the water for no more than half a minute. As I laid her dead weight down I pushed her over onto her side and almost immediately she began to cough up sea-water.

64

She gasped for breath and was gripped by a bout of retching. I did what I could for her until she finally collapsed from the effort with a low moan of either despair or pain. When I was sure that she was breathing normally I asked if she was all right.

She turned her head weakly and peered at me with a mixture of surprise and mild shock. She could only nod feebly. I got up and, helping her as much as I could, encouraged her to stand. 'You're cold,' I said, feeling her skin. Her hair was plastered to her scalp and she looked even paler now that I had her out of the water. She did not resist as I led her back to the wharf and then she began to shiver. Her features were oddly expressionless and, though I tried to get her to rub her arms, she seemed incapable of doing anything.

'Wait here,' I said, guiding her to the kerb by the road so she could sit down. When I let go of her she reached out for me.

'Where are you going?'

'To get help.'

She stared at me slackly and then something in her brain seemed to kick-start into life again. 'I'll be all right. Just give me a few minutes. Please.'

I hesitated, persuaded by the appeal in her voice. She seemed to have snapped out of her trance-like state, but I was still worried that she was shivering so much even though the night air wasn't cold. I looked back toward the nearest cottages. 'All right. Just wait for a moment.'

I remembered seeing some washing hung out

to dry on a small terrace, and when I found it I took down what looked like a bedspread and left some sodden euros under a stone. When I got back, the girl hadn't moved. She sat hunched over and shivering and when I put the bedspread around her shoulders she looked at me gratefully and clasped it tightly around her.

'Thank you.'

For a couple of minutes we sat in silence. I studied her as best I could in the darkness. Wrapped up in the huge, threadbare bedspread and without the glasses she'd worn earlier, her hair plastered to her skull, she looked even more vulnerable than she had before. Gradually she stopped shivering.

'What happened?' I asked. She didn't look at me.

'I don't know. I was thinking. I sort of forgot where I was. The next thing I knew I was in the water and then you were dragging me out.'

When I thought about what I'd actually seen I couldn't say that she had jumped. It seemed rather that she had deliberately fallen, though for the time being I didn't say so. Instead I decided to try to get her somewhere warm and dry. 'Is there somewhere I can take you?' I asked. 'Do you have family here, or friends?'

She shook her head.

'You mean you're here alone?'

'Yes. I'm renting a room. It isn't far.'

'You need to get out of those wet things. Can you walk there?'

After a moment she nodded and got to her feet. I put my arm around her shoulders and she stiffened slightly but then leaned against me and allowed me to lead her away. The top of her head barely reached my shoulder. We didn't speak at all except when she gave me directions. I was trying to think about what to do when we arrived wherever we were going. I knew if she really was alone I couldn't leave her. For all I knew she'd turn around and go straight back to where I had found her.

It took nearly thirty minutes to reach the house where she was staying, though as she'd told me it wasn't actually far. It was on a narrow street on the hillside, a largish place surrounded by a low wall with a sign outside advertising rooms for rent. There were lights on inside, but when I headed for the front door the girl gestured towards a low building that had probably once been a garage.

'That's my room.'

At the door she dug in her wet clothes and produced a key. Inside I found a light. The room was simply furnished but clean and tidy and there was a small bathroom attached. From the few things I saw hanging in a cupboard and the single bed, I gathered that she really was alone.

'I'll just get changed,' she said, and then noticed for the first time that I was wet through as well. She also recognised me. 'I saw you earlier tonight didn't I? You sat at my table.'

'Yes.' Her eyes were a startlingly pale shade of green. She caught me staring and looked momentarily self-conscious, though I imagined she must have been used to it.

'Did you follow me?' she asked.

'No.'

She appeared to consider whether or not to believe me, then she went into the bathroom and came back with a towel. 'I haven't anything to give you to wear I'm afraid.'

'This is fine,' I said and took the towel.

'I won't be long.'

She went back into the bathroom and closed the door, then I heard her turn the shower on. While she was gone I looked around her room, and spotted a bottle of pills that were on the bedside table. I picked it up to read the label, which was in Greek. It appeared to be some kind of over-the-counter pharmacy medicine, and the bottle was about three-quarters full. I was about to put it back again when the bathroom door opened. I hadn't noticed that the shower had been turned off.

'They're to help me sleep,' the girl said when she saw me with the pills.

'Did you take any tonight?'

'A few. They didn't help. I didn't want to take any more so I went out.'

'Did you drink anything?'

She nodded. 'That probably wasn't a good idea was it?'

'Probably not.'

She sat down on the edge of the bed. She looked better for the shower. She'd towel-dried her hair and her skin had a fresh glow. 'It's funny. I feel as if I could sleep for a week now.' She looked at her hands on her lap, then back at me. 'I don't even know your name.'

'It's Robert.'

'Robert. Thank you.'

'I don't know yours either.'

'Sorry. It's Alex.' She looked away and thought for a few moments. 'What happened earlier, it was an accident. I feel stupid now. I think it must have been the pills and the alcohol. I felt really strange. But I'll be OK now. I promise.'

I wasn't sure whether I believed her. I didn't think the sadness I'd sensed earlier could be explained by the sleeping pills she'd taken. 'Look, if there's something you'd like to talk about . . . '

She shook her head. 'I'm so tired. Honestly. I'll be fine.'

There was a chair in the corner. My clothes were wet and uncomfortable but it was warm in the room and tendrils of steam were rising off me. I sat down. 'I'll just wait here for a while to make sure you're all right.'

For a moment I thought she'd protest, but then she smiled resignedly and I thought she was actually glad in a way. She got into bed and lay down so that she was facing me. For a while her eyes remained open.

'Thank you,' she murmured again. Her eyes flickered shut. I waited until she was breathing evenly, then I got up and turned out the light. Eventually my eyes adjusted to the darkness so that I could see her small, huddled form lying in bed. She slept deeply with her knees drawn up to her chest, curling herself into a tight ball.

She barely stirred for the next few hours. It seemed a little peculiar to watch over her the way I did, but I felt a kind of responsibility, as if she'd entrusted me with her well-being. She looked so defenceless in her narrow bed. Almost like a child. I stayed there until early in the morning and then, certain that she was safe and unlikely to wake for some time, I looked around for something to write her a note. I found a pen and wrote my name and Irene's address, and that I would come back later.

After I left, I took the bedspread back to the cottage where I'd borrowed it from, though I left the money. I smiled to myself, wondering what they'd make of it. By the time I got back to the Jeep, the first faint streaks of light were visible in the sky over the hills.

5

It was mid-morning when I woke. The events of the previous night came back to me in a rush, but in that groggy state between sleep and full consciousness I wondered whether I had dreamt it all. I recalled turning towards the figure muffled by shadow at the end of the wharf as she appeared to fall slowly forward into space and be swallowed by the darkness, then the splash of water. I thought of how Alex had watched me later as she had lain in bed, her eyelids flickering as she succumbed to sleep.

I got out of bed. My clothes were on a chair where I'd left them, still wet from the night before. The shutters over the window were closed and the air was stiflingly hot. I threw them open, squinting at the harsh light. Outside, the sun was beating down on the roof of the house from a still and cloudless sky. I could see the back of a dark-coloured sedan parked by the Jeep and the sound of voices reached me from somewhere in the house.

After I'd showered and dressed I went downstairs and found Irene and a man wearing the uniform of the local police sitting at the table on the terrace. They were speaking quietly in Greek, their heads close together. When they saw me, Irene drew back quickly, some indecipherable expression flashing in her eyes. It was gone in a moment, and smiling she rose to introduce us.

'*Kalimera*, Robert. Did you sleep well? This is Captain Theonas from the police department. Miros this is Johnny's son.'

The policeman rose to shake my hand. He was middle-aged, tall and thin with a deeply tanned face. '*Kalimera*, Mr French. May I extend my sympathies for your loss?'

'Thank you.'

'Sit down,' Irene told me. 'I will fetch you some coffee.'

'Are you here about my father, Captain?' I asked after Irene had gone inside.

'Yes. I have the results of the autopsy carried out by the examiner from Kephalonia.'

Beyond the terrace the deep blue sea glittered with slivers of light. The cicadas were going at full force, a startlingly loud cacophony of sound. I was aware that Theonas was watching me with professional reserve.

'I am sorry to have to discuss these things. I understand that this must be a painful situation for you,' he said sympathetically.

'I suppose I'm not used to the idea that he's dead yet.'

'Of course. You are aware, I believe, of the circumstances surrounding the discovery of your father's body?'

'Irene told me that he was found in the harbour.'

'That is correct. As I was explaining to her, the examination shows that your father drowned. It appears that he had been in the water since early on the morning he vanished.'

72

Just then Irene returned with coffee. Theonas glanced at her and I saw a sudden quickening change in his expression. It was gone before I could interpret it, but it made an impression on me, like a vivid painting glimpsed through a crack in a doorway before it closed.

'How can you tell he drowned?' I asked him.

'By the presence of water in his lungs.'

'Did he have another heart attack?'

'This the examiner cannot determine for certain. There is evidence of thrombosis. This is the narrowing of the arteries supplying blood to the heart. However, this is to be expected given your father's history. Perhaps he simply lost his footing and fell . . . his clothes became tangled in the propeller and he was unable to free himself . . . '

It seemed straightforward enough, and I glanced at Irene wondering if the autopsy results had allayed her misgivings. She guessed what I was thinking.

'Miros is aware that your father claimed somebody had tried to kill him,' she said. I was surprised that she had gone as far as reporting it to the police.

'After Irene came to me I made some discreet enquiries,' Theonas said. 'On the night your father was taken to hospital he had been drinking heavily in a bar on the waterfront. There were many witnesses. Everybody that I spoke to said that he was in good spirits. In fact he had been making a speech.'

'A speech?'

'This was not unusual where your father was

73

concerned. On this occasion he claimed that he had discovered the missing *Panaghia*.'

Seeing my incomprehension, Irene explained. 'Your father was referring to a statue that has been lost since the German occupation ended during the war. The *Panaghia* was a statue of the Holy Virgin that was kept in the monastery at Kathara. The monastery was looted by the Germans.'

I knew what she was talking about then. When I was young there had been a man who worked for my dad whose name I couldn't remember. They would have been about the same age. The three of us used to go out on the *Swallow* and my dad would talk about finding some statue that was meant to be on a sunken wreck from the war. We'd drop anchor at some spot or other and the two of them would take turns diving. I had a vivid recollection of watching them strap on their scuba gear, and their tanned bodies glistening when they came out of the water. When I asked if this was the statue she meant, Irene said that it was.

'The ship was called the *Antounnetta*. Johnny used to spend part of each summer trying to find her. He wanted to return the *Panaghia* to the people of Ithaca, as a way of thanking them for making him welcome on the island.'

'The statue is worthless in monetary terms,' Theonas said. 'However, to the people of the island it has great significance as a religious symbol. The night he was in the bar, your father became involved in a mild argument with a fisherman called Spiro Petalas. It seems that

Spiro was sceptical of your father's claim that he had at last discovered the *Panaghia*. It is possible that this incident might explain your father's belief that somebody wished him harm. Perhaps he was confused . . . '

'You mean he was talking about this fisherman?'

'Perhaps.'

'Could there be any truth to it?'

'I do not think so. Many people have told me that Spiro remained in the bar for several hours after your father left that night. And though he is certainly a moody fellow, I do not think Spiro is a violent man. In fact violent crime is almost unheard of on the island. On the rare occasion when it occurs, it is usually committed by a visitor. We had an incident recently in fact. I am afraid that it is an unpleasant irony that though we need tourists to survive, sometimes the people who come here are not entirely desirable.' Theonas shrugged before he went on. 'Your father was alone when he left the bar that night. It is a steep walk to the Perahori road from the harbour. There are many steps. For a man in his condition . . . ' He paused tactfully and I assumed he meant for a man as drunk as my father was. 'I spoke also to the driver of the truck who took him to the doctor. He saw him collapse with his own eyes and he swears there was nobody else on the road.'

'Then you think he imagined it?'

'In the absence of any evidence to the contrary it is likely. I can think of no reason why anyone should have wished to harm him.'

Irene was frowning, deep in thought. She realised we were both watching her. 'I suppose that you are right,' she agreed, though she didn't sound entirely convinced. She got up and began clearing the table. As she picked up a cup she disturbed Theonas's folder and a photograph fell out from between the typewritten sheets. It was a shot of my father's pale bloated corpse on the autopsy table, the flesh grey and wax-like. Irene blanched.

Theonas picked it up quickly, looking stricken as he murmured an apology. '*Signomi*, Irene.'

His hand strayed to her arm in an instinctively intimate reaction and suddenly I understood the look I'd seen pass across his face earlier. But Irene hadn't noticed. Instead she picked up one of the typewritten sheets and, frowning, said something in Greek to Theonas.

'I am sorry, Robert,' she said, remembering me. 'I was asking Miros about something that is written here. It says the examiner found a wound on Johnny's head.' She touched the back of her skull above the neck to demonstrate.

'What kind of wound?'

'Some bruising,' Theonas explained. 'A small cut. It is conceivable that your father struck his head when he fell into the water. In fact that would explain how he drowned . . . if for a short time he lost consciousness . . . '

Irene stared at the sheet of paper, her brow deeply lined. 'What is it?' I asked her.

She shook her head in frustration. 'I do not know. This. Everything. Perhaps Johnny had a heart attack. Perhaps he fell. Perhaps he struck his head. Nothing is for certain.'

'This wound, couldn't the examiner be more specific about what caused it?' I asked Theonas, hoping he could add something to quell Irene's anxieties.

'The examiner found wooden splinters. Perhaps he hit his head on the wharf. It is impossible to say for sure. By the time he was found, your father had been in the water for several days. If there was any blood it had washed away.'

Irene gave him back the notes, though she still appeared to have her doubts. There was nothing more Theonas could tell us and, when he rose to leave shortly afterwards, Irene went with him to his car. I watched them from the terrace. They spoke quietly together in Greek. I couldn't understand what they were saying and they were careful to maintain a degree of distance between each other, but they couldn't disguise what I had already seen. When she came back Irene avoided my eye.

I helped her clear the table and followed her into the kitchen. 'Can I ask you something?' I said. 'Did my father know Theonas was the man you were seeing?'

She looked momentarily surprised but didn't attempt to deny it. 'Yes. I sometimes wondered if that was why your father was so secretive.'

I didn't understand what she meant. 'Did he know you told Theonas that he thought somebody tried to kill him?'

'No. I think that is why he tried to pretend he did not mean it. He did not want me to say anything.'

'Because of your relationship with Theonas?'

She hesitated. 'Yes,' she answered, though I had the feeling that wasn't what she'd meant at all. Before I could ask her any more she turned away leaving me puzzling as to why else my father wouldn't have wanted her to say anything to Theonas.

★ ★ ★

Later, Irene told me that she had to go to her office. They were very busy, she said apologetically. 'But there is something we must discuss. I must arrange your father's funeral. Unless you would like to bury him in England?'

The idea hadn't even occurred to me. 'Did he make any requests in his will?'

'Your father was not a religious man. I do not think he ever gave it any thought.'

'You were his wife,' I said. 'It's for you to decide. But if you want my opinion, I think he should stay here.'

'Then I will speak to the priest today. You will stay for the funeral?'

'Of course.'

She suggested I might like to go for a drive and fetched a map to show me some places where I could stop for a swim, suggesting we would have dinner together later. I hadn't told Irene about Alex, but after I left I drove to the house where she was staying. There was nobody about, so I went to her room and knocked and when there was no answer I peered through the window. The bed was made and her backpack

78

was still there and though Alex wasn't anywhere to be seen, everything looked quite normal.

I found a note she had left for me by the door. It was brief, thanking me again and assuring me that she was all right. She said there was something she had to do, but she would be back later in the day. As a postscript she had written that I needn't worry about her, and had added a smiley face and some exclamation marks in an effort to be convincing. It worked. Had she been planning on doing something rash I was sure she couldn't have written anything so jaunty. I thought what had happened the night before was probably as she had said, a mixture of pills and alcohol that had caused a temporary loss of perspective.

I was disappointed that she wasn't there, but since she hadn't said anything about where she was going I decided to spend a few hours at a beach somewhere. When I got back to the Jeep I consulted the map Irene had given me. Other than the village of Perahori and the main town of Vathy, the remainder of the southern half of the island was uninhabited and largely inaccessible except by sea, so I decided to drive north to the more populated part of Ithaca.

When I reached the village of Stavros where Irene and I had stopped the day before, I drove down to the beach at Polis Bay, descending a perilously steep and rutted track to park in the shade of a small olive grove. There were a few local fishing boats tied up at the small wharf and a couple of buildings housed a shop of some kind and a bar. A plaque fixed to a large olive tree inscribed in both English and Greek described the history of an archaeological site on the far side of the bay that had been excavated during the thirties. I remembered my father telling me about it. Louizos cave, as it was known, had become famous as the place where, among other things, a fragment of a clay mask bearing the inscription of Odysseus had been found, proving that Homer's hero had been worshipped as a god since before Homer himself had lived. The cave, however, had been buried during the devastating earthquake of 1953.

The beach was deserted. I sat in the shade afforded by a ruined stone hut and for a while I tried to read a book I'd brought with me, though I couldn't concentrate and eventually I put it aside. Out in the bay several large yachts rode at anchor, brilliant white against the deep blue of the sea. I went down to the shore and swam out towards them. The water was clear and cool and almost completely flat. I swam hard, powering myself out into the bay with long, even strokes, the salt water sluicing off the dead cells, shedding old skin. I didn't stop until my muscles ached and my chest was heaving, by which time I was almost alongside one of the yachts.

It was deserted, perhaps forty-five or fifty feet long. I wondered where it came from and who owned it. The idea of sailing the islands, stopping where I wanted, moving on without any particular destination or schedule seemed appealing. I trod water for a while engaged in this idle fantasy before I swam back again and came ashore dripping onto the pebbles where I lay down to dry and fell into a light sleep.

When I woke it was early in the afternoon. I'd had too much sun and I felt thick-headed. I was bathed in an uncomfortable sheen of sweat. I staggered groggily to the sea to cool off and lay with my head immersed looking up at the sky through the water. The images of a dream I'd had filtered back to me. My father had been standing by his boat when a shadowy figure approached from behind with his arm raised. He brought it down and my father collapsed. I knew it was only the workings of my unconscious mind fuelled by Irene's suspicions. My father was seventy-two when he died. He had a bad heart and a history of drinking. Maybe his wild claims had all been a ploy to gain Irene's sympathy. In fact I thought that made sense. Maybe he'd been trying to win her back from Theonas.

Once I had towelled off I decided to drive up to Stavros and find somewhere I could buy a beer and sit in the shade. At a junction just back from the beach I checked carefully for traffic, wary of the erratic driving habits of the locals. Fifty yards away a figure was squatting beside a scooter stopped at the side of the road. I almost drove on but then she stood up and I realised that it was Alex.

She looked around when she heard the Jeep approaching, but she didn't realise who it was until I stopped.

'Hello again,' I said.

She smiled uncertainly. 'Hello.'

'How are you feeling today?'

'Fine. I slept late.'

'I went to the place where you're staying earlier. I got your note.'

She gestured to the scooter. 'I wanted to get out and take a look around so I hired this. I couldn't face being in my room all day.'

I looked at the scooter. 'Is there a problem?'

In a gestured of frustration she pushed a damp strand of dark blonde hair back from her forehead. 'Yes, actually. It won't go.'

In the light of day she looked a lot better than when I had last seen her. The dark smudges beneath her eyes had already begun to fade. I was struck again by the colour of her eyes. Now that they weren't reddened and puffy, the full effect of them was even more pronounced. Their unusual paleness somehow added to her vulnerability. It was as if I could look right inside her. She was, I thought, quite beautiful. But the overriding emotion I felt was one of protectiveness as I had when I had sat watching her sleep. Tearing my gaze away I bent down to have a look at the engine, checking that the lead and plug were secure, then opening the fuel tank.

'I filled it before I left Vathy,' she commented drolly. I smiled and gave up pretending that I knew what I was doing.

'The best thing would be to leave it here. I'll give you a lift back to the place where you hired it and they can come and pick it up.'

'I suppose you're right.' She sounded disappointed and glanced toward the hills across the bay.

'Is that where you were going?'

'Yes. There's a village I wanted to see.' She pointed to a towering hill where the hazy outline of a few buildings was visible perched precariously on the steep upper slopes. 'But it doesn't matter. I can go another time.'

'I could drive you there if you like,' I offered.

'I didn't mean to suggest . . . '

'Suggest what?'

'I mean you've done enough for me already,' she said awkwardly. 'Look, about last night. I feel terrible about it. I mean I feel like an idiot.'

'You shouldn't,' I said. 'I'm just glad that I was there.'

'I haven't even thanked you have I?'

'Yes you have. Last night.'

'Did I? I don't remember much to be honest. Anyway I really appreciate what you did. I don't know what came over me. I'd had a few drinks. Actually more than a few. I don't think they mixed well with those pills I took.' She shook her head in disbelief at her own actions. 'I just felt this black mood sink over me. I couldn't shake it off.'

'At least you seem better today.'

'I am. Much better.' She looked at me intently, almost beseechingly. 'I didn't really mean to kill myself you know. I mean I don't know what I was doing. But it wasn't that.'

'Like you said, it was probably the pills. If I were you I'd get rid of them.'

She smiled gratefully. 'I already did.'

I looked back towards the village on the distant hillside. I wanted to ask what had brought her to Ithaca and why she had been drinking alone and taking pills to help her sleep, but I thought if she wanted to tell me she would. 'So, how about that lift? I'll take you up there if you like.'

She hesitated. 'I don't think there's much to see,' she warned.

'That's OK, I haven't got anything else to do. Besides there are probably great views from up there.'

I still sensed a residue of uncertainty in her, but then she suddenly smiled, whatever doubts she had melting away. 'Well, if you're sure, that would be great. Thanks.'

It turned out the village was called Exoghi and the road that led to it ascended in a series of tight switchback curves. At times the drop to Polis Bay far below was perilously close to the wheels, and the Jeep's engine, stuck in first and second gear the entire way up, howled in protest. Now and then I glanced at Alex and though she smiled when our eyes met, most of the time she was preoccupied with her thoughts. Despite everything she'd said earlier I could sense that her assurances were a thin veneer to mask whatever was troubling her. As we got closer to the village however, she began to take a keen interest in it, craning her neck for a better view as we glimpsed the tower of a church among some cypress trees.

When we arrived it turned out there was a small parking area beside the church where I pulled over. I'd been right about the views. We could see for miles. To the east was a broad fertile valley where olive and fruit trees grew and beyond the coast, the blue-grey shapes of scattered islands were visible in the far distance. To the west across the strait the towering coastline of Kephalonia seemed close enough to touch.

It was very quiet and there was a curious stillness about the place that heightened its distinct feeling of isolation. 'It looks deserted,' I commented.

'I think a lot of the houses are owned by people who come here for the summer,' Alex said. 'I read somewhere that only two families live here all year round.'

She studied the village intently as if comparing it to some mental image she had, perhaps from a guidebook. She wanted to look around, so we left the Jeep and went on foot. We walked past houses that overlooked the roofs of the ones below. Most were small, simply-built stone affairs with shuttered windows that had probably stood there for generations, but one or two had been built in recent times. One we saw even had a pool. Alleyways and sets of steps connected the streets, which was really a single road that ran back and forth through the village. Behind stone walls there were overgrown gardens and from one the familiar smell of wild mint and thyme sweetened the musty stench of something long dead. Weeds pushed through the cracks between the uneven paving slabs. The only sign of life we saw was a cat that regarded us suspiciously, frozen in surprise on a wall, as startled by us as we were by it.

Beyond the houses we came to a sign that indicated the way to a monastery at the summit of the hill. Alex frowned and looked back the way we'd come.

'What's wrong?'

'To be honest I'm looking for something,' she admitted. 'A house. Or what's left of one anyway. That's why I wanted to come here. My grandmother was born in this village.'

I recalled that when I first saw Alex I'd mistaken her for a local, which made sense now. As we began to retrace our steps she told me a little about herself. She had grown up in Hertfordshire where she had attended a private girls' school. Her mother was a doctor and her father a barrister working in London. It was her maternal grandmother who came from Ithaca, though she had lived much of her life in England until she had died the previous year.

'It wasn't until then that I realised how little I knew about her,' Alex said. 'I knew she was Greek of course, but I didn't know where she was from exactly. It's funny how you think you know somebody, and then suddenly you find that you really don't at all. And then it's too late.' She shrugged philosophically. 'And now here I am.'

We had reached an alleyway that we'd missed earlier. It ran between two houses, but it was overgrown with wild oak. Beneath our feet what had once been a paved path had succumbed to nature.

'Let's try this way,' Alex suggested.

We emerged into a stand of gnarled and

86

long-neglected olive trees beyond which stood the ruins of a cottage. The roof had gone and the walls had partly collapsed. It stood in an overgrown clearing. Sunlight splashed on the ruins, but instead of cheering them it somehow emphasised the emptiness of the windows, the shadowed spaces inside. There was an odd atmosphere about the place. I had the feeling that nobody had been there for a long time, but also that it still resonated with the lives of those who had once lived there. It was the sort of place that gives credence to the idea of the existence of ghosts.

'Is this it do you think?' I asked Alex.

'I think so.'

She seemed absorbed with whatever private thoughts the place evoked in her and, sensing that she wanted to be alone, I wandered around to the back where I found what had once been a terrace. A rusted pole protruded from the ground at an angle — what remained of a trellis to support a grapevine. On the hillside, olive trees grew in ranks, the stone retaining walls badly in need of repair, the terraces themselves heavily overgrown and neglected.

Inside the ruin itself there was nothing to see except some faded graffiti painted on a wall. Overall there was an air of desolation about the place. A sort of heavy silence in the air.

A sound from behind startled me, but when I turned it was only Alex. I smiled self-consciously, my heart thumping. 'I didn't hear you.'

'Sorry. There's a strange feeling here isn't there?'

'Yes,' I admitted, glad that I wasn't alone in my perception. 'You said this is where your grandmother was born?'

'My mother too actually, though she was only a baby when Nana took her to England.' Alex hesitated and I had the distinct impression that she wasn't sure if she wanted to share this with me. Then she said, 'Have you ever felt that you don't really know who you are?'

It was an odd question, but in a way I thought perhaps I knew what she meant. 'When I was young I was sent to boarding school,' I told her. 'I never felt as if I belonged. I didn't know what I was doing there.'

'Yes, that's it isn't it? When everything we're used to changes and suddenly we're not sure where we fit in?'

'Something like that.'

'When I was growing up I never questioned anything. I think it's incredible really when I look back on it, but my brother and sister didn't either. I suppose my parents are quite well off. I went to a good school. There was pony club, a house in the country, all that sort of thing. The only thing that was out of place was my Nana. She lived in this little flat in North London where my mother grew up. She was quite happy there. She didn't want to move because her friends and everyone she knew were all there. All these Greek families. But the funny thing is I never heard her speak anything but English. Even though she had this terrible almost unintelligible accent. You'd think I might have wondered why.'

'Maybe not. I think kids accept something if it's always been that way.'

'I suppose that's it. It must be why I was never really curious about my grandfather. Nobody ever talked about him. I grew up knowing that he died a long time ago, but that was all. There were no photographs of him anywhere. Even my mother never mentioned him.'

Alex looked around the inside of the ruined cottage. Her gaze settled on the faded graffiti. It was written in Greek so I had no idea what it meant. She dug in her pocket and found a pen and a notebook. 'I want to know what it means,' she said, copying it down as best she could.

We went back outside and before we left Alex stopped to take another look at the ruin. Sunlight fell in shafts through the branches of the olive trees, splashing in pools on the dry earth below. My gaze wandered beyond the clearing to the tangled undergrowth where it was gloomy and shadowed. I glimpsed a movement that at first I took to be an animal or a bird, but when I looked more closely I was surprised to find that I was wrong.

'We've got company.' I nodded towards the old man who stood almost hidden back among the trees. He stared at us silently and though I couldn't make out his features clearly I had a strong impression of dark eyes filled with malevolence. I could feel it pouring out of him, a black stain that soaked into the earth.

'*Kalimera*,' Alex called out. '*Oreos keros.*'

89

The old man made no response. 'Maybe we should leave,' I suggested. 'I don't think he likes visitors.'

We began to make our way back along the path. At the edge of the trees I looked back and he was still there, staring after us. I was slightly relieved when we emerged back onto the street. As we made our way to the Jeep I half expected to see him following us, so when a figure appeared from an alleyway some way in front I wasn't surprised that it was him.

'What do you think he wants?' Alex asked.

He stood by the side of the road watching as we approached.

'He's probably harmless. I expect he's not used to seeing strangers around. Maybe he's not quite all there.'

His face was as wrinkled and brown as a walnut. He had to be seventy or eighty years old. The clothes he wore were rough and patched, encrusted with ancient dirt. But it was the intensity of his gaze that was unnerving. As we passed, I nodded to him but I don't think he even noticed. His baleful glare was fastened exclusively on Alex. He muttered something under his breath. I couldn't make out the words, but it sounded harsh and unfriendly.

'Did you catch that?' I asked.

'My Greek isn't very good.' She looked shaken.

He watched us until we reached the Jeep. He was the only living soul we had encountered in the entire village and, as we drove back down the hill, I was glad to put the place behind me.

When we reached Polis Bay I suggested we stop for a drink. We sat at a table outside the bar on the beach and ordered beers and some bread and salad. Some fishermen were working on a boat tied up to the wharf, and two young children were playing in the water. It was all very normal and reassuring.

'That old man, he was looking at me wasn't he?' Alex asked. I admitted that it had appeared that way. She searched through her bag until she found what looked like a diary. From inside the back cover she took out some photographs and handed one to me. It was of an old woman with iron-grey hair.

'My grandmother. It was taken just before she became ill.'

Despite the difference in their ages the resemblance was clear, especially since they both shared the same strikingly pale green eyes. She handed me another picture, this one much older and taken in black-and-white. The image wasn't as clear, but the resemblance was even more obvious.

'That was taken when she was a year or two older than I am now. I wonder if that old man mistook me for Nana.'

I supposed it was possible. 'You think he might have known her?'

'Perhaps. She left here after the Second World War. I never knew that until she was moved to a hospice for the last few months before she died. She started telling me stories about the village where she grew up. I'd never heard any of it before. She talked about her parents and about

91

her brother who I never even knew existed. It was incredible. She was dying and I suddenly realised I didn't know anything about her.'

'Is that why you came to Ithaca?'

Alex hesitated. 'Partly.' I had the feeling she was trying to decide how much to reveal of herself. 'I wanted to know more about her life. And about my grandfather.'

'Was he from here as well?'

She shook her head. 'You remember I said earlier that nobody ever talked about him? The first time I heard him mentioned was when Nana was dying. I went to see her one evening. They were giving her a lot of morphine. I think she was a bit confused. She seemed to think she was back here again and she talked about this man that she fell in love with. His name was Stefan.'

'Stefan? That's German isn't it?'

She nodded. 'I didn't find out any more until after she died. When I asked my mother she told me that her father was a German soldier. That's why nobody ever talked about him. When Nana left Ithaca she was pregnant. Her family name was Zannas. They had lived here for generations, but after the war, the family disowned her and forced her to leave. They said she was a traitor.'

I began to understand what Alex had meant when she had talked earlier about not knowing who she was, and why she'd wondered if the old man in the village had recognised her. 'Do you know what happened to your grandfather?'

'No. That's partly why I'm here. My mother told me that she went through a phase once of wanting to find out everything she could about

92

him. Even if he was dead, she thought he must have family. She wondered if she had half-brothers and sisters somewhere. She was an only child, so I suppose it was important to her. For a long time Nana wouldn't tell her, but in the end she gave in. I think she was afraid that if she didn't my mother would find out some other way, which would have been worse.'

'Because he was an enemy soldier?'

'Not just that. There was more to it. Have you noticed how many churches there are here?'

I said that I had. 'The Orthodox Church is still a big part of life for many Greeks. Especially in places like Ithaca.'

'Nana went to one in North London all her life. Her flat was full of those little icons of the saints. You see them all over the place here. When she grew up, her life was dominated by her family and by the church. In those days it was unthinkable for a girl to get pregnant before she was married. She told my mother that she was raped. I don't think she actually used that term, but it's what she meant.'

'But didn't you say she told you she was in love with this soldier?'

'Yes. I think she might have told my mother she was raped to put her off looking for his family.'

'That's a hell of a thing to say if it wasn't true isn't it?'

'Yes, but it worked. Maybe she did it because he was already married. Anyway, after that my mother didn't want to know any more.'

'But you do?'

'Yes. I think back then the war was still recent enough that Nana thought she was doing the best thing. I don't know why. Perhaps to protect his family. But it is a long time ago now. I want to know the truth. There's so much I don't know. When I discovered all this I also found that I had a whole set of relatives in London. Nana's estranged brother and his family. They own a restaurant in Camden. My mother told me that when she was little Nana was ill once and hadn't been able to work so she went to ask her brother for help. My mother never even knew about them before then. A man came to the door and Nana spoke to him in Greek. He looked at them both for a long time and he didn't say anything. But my mother said she never forgot his eyes. How full of hate they were. In the end he slammed the door on them. Nana never mentioned him again.'

'Nice guy.'

Alex made a face. 'He's still alive actually. And he's still horrible. His name is Kostas. I think after that Nana decided it would be better for my mother not to know about her Greek side. She brought her up as English, and my mother brought us up the same way. I suppose we all have different ways of dealing with these things. My mother's was to bury it all. When I knew that I had relatives I hadn't even heard of I wanted to meet them, though my mother tried to persuade me not to.'

'I gather it didn't work out.'

'No. They still own the restaurant and so, of course, I went there. That's where I met Dimitri.'

'Dimitri?' I thought she was referring to some relative or other.

'He was working there. He's from Ithaca. He's the other reason I'm here.' She paused and looked out across the bay for a few moments. After a while she turned back to me and smiled ruefully. 'Anyway, things haven't worked out in that department either. But since I'm here, I want to try to find out more about my family.'

I was curious about Dimitri, but I didn't want to ask any more questions. I assumed that he was the cause of her unhappiness. It was clear when she mentioned his name that the wounds were still raw, but it was getting late by then, and Alex reminded me that she had to get back to the place where she had rented her scooter so, after I'd paid the bill, we left.

During the drive back to Vathy she was quiet, though she asked me a little about myself. I told her my father lived on the island and that I had come to see him, and she was interested when I said that he was an archaeologist. I didn't tell her that he had died because I didn't want to introduce a maudlin note. Instead we talked a little about Homer, whose work she had read when she was at school. She knew the story of the *Odyssey* much better than I did. She was surprised when I told her that my father had spent the past twenty-five years or so looking for Aphrodite's Temple.

'I didn't know Odysseus really lived,' she said. 'I always thought he was a mythological figure. Our teacher taught us the *Odyssey* was a metaphor for life. She said Odysseus's travels and struggles to return home were a search for the truth about what was really important. Family, home and so on.'

'Maybe Homer blended fact and fiction,' I said. 'But some experts believe Odysseus really existed.'

When we arrived back in Vathy I drove her to the rental shop tucked away in a narrow street behind the main square and I waited outside while she went in to talk to the owner. I could see her through the window. I gathered the owner's English wasn't that good and she was having difficulty getting him to understand where she had left the scooter. He kept scratching his head and shrugging. Eventually she drew him a map and he smiled and nodded vigorously.

When she came back outside she said, 'You needn't wait. He's going to give me another one.'

There was a moment of awkwardness as I realised this was my cue to leave, but I knew I wanted to see her again even if my reasons were less clear. 'How long will you be staying on Ithaca?' I asked.

'I'm not sure.'

'Maybe we can meet for a drink or something,' I suggested.

'To be honest . . . ' she broke off and whatever she had been about to say seemed forgotten. 'I'd like that. But . . . '

'I understand,' I assured her, guessing what she was about to say.

I couldn't have put into words exactly what passed between us. Some recognition perhaps that we were both in our own ways adrift. I think then my overriding emotion was one of protectiveness towards her, and possibly she felt safe with me. But there was more to it than that, even though it was tempered with uncertainty and caution on both sides. We were both caught unawares by the moment.

When I drove off I looked back in the rear-view mirror and she was still standing outside the scooter shop watching me. I waved and she raised a hand in return.

6

By the time I reached the house Irene was home. She told me that she had spoken to the priest at her church and that the funeral would be in two days' time. Later we were having a drink on the terrace, watching the sun go down over the hills of Kephalonia across the strait when a white Mercedes raised a cloud of dust as it drove towards the house. When it pulled over the driver opened the passenger door for another man who looked up to the terrace and raised a hand in greeting.

'*Kalimera*, Irene.'

He was tall and thin with a fringe of white hair around his otherwise bald head. He regarded me with interest before his features creased into a friendly smile. 'You have the look of your father about you. *Kalos-ton* Ithaca, Robert. Though I wish that I could welcome you under more happy circumstances.'

Irene stood to meet him as he climbed the steps. She held out her hands and when he grasped them in his own she turned to me. 'Robert, I would like you to meet Alkimos Kounidis. Alkimos and your father were great friends.'

Kounidis kissed Irene on both cheeks then extended his hand to me. 'May I offer you my sympathies? Your father spoke of you often, Robert. I hope you do not mind if I call you that? I feel as if I know you already.'

'Of course.'

We shook hands and then he turned back to Irene. 'And you Irene? *Iste kala?*'

'*Ime entaxi,*' she answered. I'm OK.

Kounidis joined us and Irene made him a glass of sweetened iced coffee, and one for his driver who remained by the car, sitting in the shade smoking a cigarette. Kounidis and Irene spoke about the funeral arrangements and then Kounidis began reminiscing about my father and the time they had spent together over the years. He told a story about a time they had gone to a nearby island after diving on a reef off the coast and had spent the evening eating and drinking in a taverna there.

'Your father climbed up onto the table to sing us all a song, Robert. Even though many of us begged him to spare us. He would not listen and he sang a traditional ballad in its entirety but when he came to the most moving part at the very end, he lost his footing and crashed to the floor.' Kounidis shook his head and chuckled. 'There was much applause, though I do not think it was in appreciation of Johnny's talent as a singer.'

I had difficulty reconciling this gregarious image of my father with the one I carried of him. 'It sounds as if you knew a side of him that I didn't, Mr Kounidis,' I commented.

'I came to know him quite well I think. He spoke of you often, though of course I am aware that your relationship was not always close,' he added tactfully.

'That's one way of putting it I suppose.'

'Unfortunately this sometimes happens between fathers and their sons I think. Your father liked to remember happier times. He talked of when you were very young. I believe that you used to go with him on his archaeological digs in England.'

'That was a long time ago.'

'Time changes many things. Your father regretted that living here meant that he did not know you better. Even though he loved Ithaca.'

I snorted derisively. 'If he told you that, I'm afraid he misled you. The reason we didn't know each other had nothing to do with the fact that he chose to live here. It was because after he left England he conveniently forgot that he had a child. I didn't hear from him for almost two years. That's a long time for a boy, Mr Kounidis.'

'Robert, please,' Irene interrupted.

I held up my hands in mock surrender. 'I know I don't sound like the grieving son, but the truth is that my father had a talent for glossing over certain things.'

'What happened to your father before he left England affected him very badly,' Irene said. 'It took him a long time to get over it.'

I knew the scandal had ruined his career but I had heard this excuse before and I always had the same answer. 'It didn't stop him marrying you while he was busy getting over it.'

'Forgive me,' Kounidis interjected hastily, 'I should not have brought the subject up.'

Irene looked at me with a mixture of hurt and reproach, and I wished I hadn't said anything. It was pointless going over this same old stony ground now that my father was dead and I knew it. I had never blamed Irene for any of it, though it had sounded as if I had, if only a little.

'I'm sorry, Irene,' I said. 'You too, Mr Kounidis. Please accept my apologies.'

He made a gesture as if to dismiss any further thought of it and I tried to divert the topic of conversation. 'How did you come to know my father, are you also an archaeologist?'

'Please, call me Alkimos. And to answer your question, I am afraid that unlike your father I was never a scholar. I am retired now of course, but for many years I was a simple businessman.'

'Alkimos is being modest,' Irene said, seizing on the change of direction. 'He owned a very successful shipping company in Patras on the mainland.'

'I had an interest in a few ships. It is not such a big thing.'

I doubted that. I hadn't seen too many people on Ithaca who drove around in large, nearly-new chauffeur-driven Mercedes. 'Then you're not from Ithaca originally?'

'As a matter of fact I was born here, but I left when I was a very young man, after the war.'

I was surprised. According to my quick calculation that meant Kounidis had to be at least in his late seventies, though he didn't look it.

'I went to sea,' he went on, 'and over the years I saved a little money. Eventually I managed to raise enough to buy an interest in a small freighter. I was fortunate to have a little success.

101

Did you know that Ithaca has a great seafaring tradition, Robert? Some of the great Greek shipping families came from here. The Stathatos brothers and the Charalambis family to mention two. My own accomplishments were much more modest of course.'

'You moved back here after you retired?'

'Yes. I have had a house on Ithaca for many years. Like Odysseus I always longed to return home. You are familiar with Homer?'

'A little.'

'Alkimos helped your father with his work,' Irene said.

'I made small contributions towards the cost of some of his excavations over the years, no more. I was honoured to help. Unfortunately in Greece there is never enough money for such important archaeological work.'

'Without Alkimos's help, your father's museum would never have been able to remain open,' Irene said.

'Irene exaggerates of course,' Kounidis demurred. 'I had great respect for your father, Robert. He was an educated and intelligent man, as well as being a good friend. If I was able to assist in some small way then I regard it as a privilege. You know of course about Aphrodite's Temple? Your father always hoped that one day he would discover its whereabouts.'

'Yes.'

'Did you know that a man named George Dracoulis claimed to have first discovered it in the thirties?'

I was surprised. 'I thought it had been lost since ancient times.'

'And so it was. In fact scholars have always disputed its existence. But Dracoulis wrote a letter to his sister in which he claimed to have found the temple. Unfortunately this could never be proven because Dracoulis died during the war, and by the time the letter came to light the earthquake of 1953 had buried the site he had unearthed. At least that was the theory of some. Including your father.'

'Though I gather from what Irene has told me that in recent years even he had given up any hope of finding it.'

'This is true, of course. It was a great shame to see him become so despondent. Though he knew in the end that Dracoulis was proved right.'

'Oh?'

'Yes. Some of the artefacts that Dracoulis recovered from the site were discovered in a private collection last year in Switzerland. It was proof that everything he wrote in the letter to his sister was true. At least Johnny knew that the temple really existed. I am sure that someday it will be found.'

I wondered if that might have added to my father's despair. To know that the temple was actually somewhere on the island, but that even after twenty-odd years he hadn't found it and probably never would.

'I recall that your father mentioned that you are in business?' Kounidis said, changing the subject.

'Property development, yes.'

103

'Your father also said that you are quite successful.'

'Prices have been going up,' I said. 'It doesn't take a genius in those conditions.'

'But it does take work, and commitment, I think. You have those qualities in common with your father at least. Will you be staying on Ithaca long?'

'I'm afraid not. I'll be leaving after the funeral.'

'Then I hope you get to see some of our wonderful scenery before you return. As I'm sure you know, there are some beautiful beaches where it is pleasant to swim. And unlike our neighbour, Kephalonia, most of them remain unspoilt by crowds of holiday-makers.'

That much we agreed on, and I told him that I had been to Polis Bay that day.

'Ah. You know about the cave there? It is very famous.'

'Yes, I read about it.'

'Did you also know that there is a sunken city in the bay? It was called Jerusalem. It is believed to be the remains of a town that sank during an earthquake centuries ago. There are some amphorae on display in your father's museum that were recovered from the sea-bed. Have you visited there yet?'

'Not on this trip,' I admitted.

'You should. There are some remarkable finds from an excavation he made at Platrithias several years ago. It was his last excavation in fact.'

Kounidis seemed to be knowledgeable about Ithaca's past and I wondered if he knew as much about the island's more recent history. It occurred to me that he might know something about Alex's grandmother and I mentioned that I had gone to Exoghi that afternoon.

'Ah yes, the views from there are excellent. Did you go inside the church? There are some wonderful examples of religious icons.'

'I'm afraid not. Actually I gave a lift to a girl I met whose scooter had broken down. She wanted to see the house where her grandmother was born.'

'A local girl?' Irene asked.

'Actually no, she's from London, but her grandmother came from Ithaca.'

'What was her name?' Irene asked. 'Perhaps I know her family.'

'Zannas, I think she said.'

'Julia Zannas?' Irene and Kounidis exchanged quick glances.

'Do you know the name?'

'Yes,' Kounidis said. 'I am afraid that many people on Ithaca know the name of Julia Zannas. Though perhaps not so much the young. You say this girl that you met is her granddaughter?'

'Yes. Her grandmother died last year. She wants to find out more about the Greek side of her family. From what she told me it was a bit of a taboo subject when she was growing up.'

'I can imagine that it might be so. If you see her again, Robert, you should advise her to be careful who she speaks to. For some people the past is never forgotten.'

I was reminded of the old man we had seen in the village. I told them what had happened and about Alex's resemblance to her grandmother.

'As you see, Robert, it might be better for your friend not to go back there.'

'She told me that her grandmother was involved with a German soldier. But surely nobody would hold that against Alex. Especially after all this time.'

'Do not be so sure. For some people the name Julia Zannas brings back unpleasant memories. Many of them blame her for the deaths of members of their families during the war.'

'Why? What did she do?'

'It is a long story,' Kounidis said, 'and an old one, as you say.'

I gathered that he was reluctant to repeat it, and when he changed the subject I didn't press the matter. He and Irene became involved in a discussion about her business and were soon talking about the company that handled her distribution, and how best she could address a problem she was having. They spoke in English out of deference to me, and it was interesting to note that Kounidis seemed well connected. He offered to speak to various officials both on Ithaca and elsewhere on Irene's behalf.

Eventually he rose to leave and again he shook my hand. He invited me to visit him at his house near the town of Kioni before I left.

'If you have the time, of course. My housekeeper is an excellent cook. I think I can promise you a good lunch,' he said.

I thanked him and said I'd do my best.

'Irene will give you my phone number.'

Irene walked with him to his car and when she

106

returned I remarked that Kounidis seemed an interesting man.

'And a very good friend, yes. I did not exaggerate before when I told you that he helped your father a great deal.'

'It sounds as if he can help you too.'

'Alkimos knows many people and he is very well respected.'

'Because of his business days?'

'Yes, but also because as a young man he was involved with the Resistance during the war. He was captured by the Germans. That is why he did not wish to talk about what happened. Although your father asked him about it many times.'

'My father? Why was he interested?'

'Do you remember we spoke of the *Panaghia*? Alkimos tried to help your father find the German ship that sank during the war.'

'The *Antounnetta*?'

'Yes. In fact the story of what happened involves your friend's grandmother, Julia Zannas.'

The coincidence surprised me. I had a sudden sense of events in time colliding gently, nudging one another like great shifting plates in some impenetrable machinery.

* * *

That night after we had eaten dinner Irene excused herself, saying that she had some work to do.

'Why don't you go into the town? It would be good for you to be among people,' she suggested.

107

I decided that she was right, but as I negotiated the dark twisting bends of the Perahori road I found myself thinking about Alex. I drove past the house where she was staying, but I could see from the road that there were no lights in her room so I continued on into town. I had no particular idea about where I was going so I parked the Jeep near the square and strolled among the cafés and restaurants looking for a spare table. There weren't any, so I explored some of the side-streets away from the waterfront that I knew wouldn't be so busy. I found a small taverna with a scattering of tables outside. The place was filled with men, mostly locals, drinking and smoking cigarettes. The air was blue with smoke, so I sat outside and when somebody eventually appeared to take my order, I asked for a beer.

For a while I watched the flow of people, a few making last-minute purchases before the shops closed for the night. Across the street there was a travel agent and next door to it a shop selling magazines and books. The owner was dragging a rack of magazines inside, the covers of which featured pictures of naked women. It always surprised me that in a country with such a strong religious tradition, soft porn was openly displayed on every street corner alongside icons of the Virgin Mary and the myriad saints that are revered in Greece.

Further along the street a group of young men wearing the ubiquitous Greek uniform of tight jeans and T-shirts chatted among themselves and smoked cigarettes, openly staring at any woman who walked past. It was another paradox of daily life there that had any of them witnessed a stranger ogling their own sister or girlfriend the way they did other women the consequences would undoubtedly have been violent.

A girl emerged from the travel agent across the road and called something in Greek to whoever was inside. The men on the corner whistled and called out to her as she passed, and she stopped to exchange a few words with them. A few moments later the lights were extinguished in the travel office and a man in his early-thirties appeared. As he locked up, one of the men on the corner shouted something to him and the others quickly joined in. I gathered they were trying to persuade him to join them, but he simply shook his head and replied good-naturedly and after a while they gave up. As he turned away, a young woman appeared in front of him and when he saw her he stopped dead. It took me a moment to realise that it was Alex.

At first I thought she must be asking about travel arrangements but, as I was about to call out to her, I heard her voice rise in anger. The man glanced around nervously as if he were afraid they would be overheard and at that moment I saw a sign over the door which I hadn't noticed before. *Classic Tours. Prop. Dimitri Ramanda.*

The man who I assumed was Dimitri had the uncomfortable look of somebody who would rather he were somewhere else. He seemed to be trying to explain something, but Alex cut him off with an impatient gesture. She fired a question at him and fixed him with a withering look while she waited for his answer. He appeared to be caught in an agony of indecision, but eventually he shook his head. There was a moment of charged tension between them and then abruptly Alex turned and strode away. He called her name but she didn't look back. Suddenly he ran after her and grabbed her arm, but she whirled around and shook him off furiously. For an instant she glared at him as if daring him to speak and then she turned again and moments later vanished around the corner, leaving him alone while onlookers stared curiously.

The entire scene hadn't taken more than a minute or two. Dimitri eventually turned and walked away in the opposite direction. When he had gone I left some money on the table and went after Alex. I had visions of her crossing the street without looking and being run down by a car, but when I emerged onto the square she was nowhere to be seen. Uncertain where to look for her I walked quickly to the wharf and looked first one way then the other. When I still couldn't see her I broke into a trot as mild concern began to turn into slightly panicked worry. On a hunch, I began to run towards the far end of the waterfront where I had found her the night before, but before I had gone even a quarter of the distance I passed a set of steps that led down to the water. She was sitting on the bottom step with her back to me, though when she heard me she turned around, the flash of anger that lit across her features turning quickly to surprise.

'Oh. It's you. I thought . . . ' She broke off and

made a gesture as if it didn't matter.

'I was having a drink across the road from the travel shop a few minutes ago,' I said.

Comprehension dawned in her eyes. 'You saw then.'

'Yes. That was Dimitri I take it?'

She nodded grimly. 'I suppose you thought that I was going to jump into the harbour again.'

'Are you?'

She shook her head. 'No.'

'I'm glad to hear it.'

She picked up on something in my tone and her brow furrowed. 'Are you?'

'Yes, I am.' I gestured to the step. 'Do you mind if I join you?' I sat beside her. There were tears in her eyes, which she brushed away with the back of her hand.

'I'm all right.' She turned her gaze across the harbour. 'I went to tell him that I was leaving,' she said eventually. 'I suppose I thought it might make him change his mind. About us I mean.'

'I gather it didn't?'

'No.'

'How long have you known each other?'

'A little over a year. He came back here three months ago to start his business. That was why he was in England. To make contacts. The idea was that I would come over and we would live together. I was going to resign from my job before I left. I didn't actually.' She thought about that and then turned to me. 'I suppose that means I must have known all along something like this would happen doesn't it?'

I guessed it was a rhetorical question, so I

didn't offer an opinion.

'I had the feeling things had changed before I left London. As soon as I saw him I knew that I was right. We had a fight and I found the room where I'm staying. The rest you know.'

'I'm sorry,' I said.

She picked up a stone and threw it into the water and we watched the ripples spread outwards. 'I just wish he'd told me before I left.'

'If it's any consolation, he didn't look very happy back there.'

'No, that's the funny part about it. I don't think he is. He told me that part of him wants me to stay. He's just not certain. At least he's trying to be honest.'

'So what will you do?'

She shrugged. 'I don't know. Perhaps I should go home.'

An idea occurred to me and as it did I knew I didn't want Alex to leave yet. 'What about your grandmother? Do you still want to find out about her?'

'I hadn't thought that far ahead. I do, but I'm not sure this is the right time.'

'Maybe it is. It might take your mind off things. And I might be able to help.'

'Oh?'

'I found out today we've got something in common. I didn't tell you this before, but when I told you I came here to visit my father, what I didn't say was that I was too late. He died before I arrived. I just found out yesterday.'

'Oh God,' Alex said, looking stricken. 'I'm sorry.'

'Don't be. He had a heart attack not so long ago, so it wasn't a complete surprise. And to be honest we were never close anyway. The thing is, I was talking to an old friend of his earlier and I mentioned that I'd been to Exoghi.' I told her about my conversation with Irene and Kounidis and how they had recognised her grandmother's name. 'Irene has lived here all her life. I think she can probably tell you at least some of what you want to know.'

'Really? Do you think she would mind?'

'I'll check first. Actually I'm interested myself anyway.' I explained about my father's search for the *Antounnetta*. 'So we're connected in a way. Albeit tenuously. Your grandmother is mixed up in the story behind the *Antounnetta* somehow.'

'In what way?' Alex asked.

I told her that I didn't know.

She thought for a moment and then gave a small shake of her head. 'It's strange isn't it? The way we met, and now this?'

'Karma,' I said jokingly, though not entirely. 'Look, what are you doing tomorrow?'

'I hadn't thought.'

'Do you like boats?'

'I don't know much about them.'

'My dad owned one. I'm sure Irene wouldn't mind if I borrowed it. We could take her for a sail along the coast and then afterwards you can come to dinner at the house and meet Irene.'

'I'm not sure,' Alex said uncertainly. 'I mean it sounds wonderful, I just don't know if I'm good company at the moment.'

'What else are you going to do? Maybe it

113

would be good for you.'

She thought about it for a few moments. I could see her struggling with conflicting impulses, but in the end she gave in. 'OK, I'd like that. Thanks.'

'Good.'

I arranged to pick her up in the morning but when I offered to walk her back to her room she said that she would prefer some time to think, so shortly afterwards I left her. As I walked away I looked back. She was hugging her knees gazing out across the harbour. I paused, struck by the feelings that she aroused in me. I felt some kind of connection between us. Maybe it was the island, the sense of time there. It was almost tangible, stretching back centuries into prehistory, to ancient civilisations and then leaping forward to more recent events. The Second World War. My father. Her grandmother. Love and passion, tragedy and death. The island was steeped in it. I felt as if we were bit players in a cast of characters endlessly trapped within the same human frailties.

Much later when I was back at the house I thought of Alicia. For the first time since she'd left I didn't experience a pang of loss. Neither did I feel resentment or bitterness towards her. I hoped things worked out for her, as I was sure they would. And then, unbidden, the thought flashed in my mind that perhaps they might for me too.

7

When Irene came down in the morning I was already dressed. She found me with a cup of coffee on the terrace where I'd watched the sun rise. As it gained height, the harbour changed colour from the deep reflected green of the pines growing on the surrounding hills to the endless blue of the sky.

'Good morning,' Irene said as she joined me. 'Did you sleep well?'

'Very. And you?'

'Quite well, yes,' she answered, though from the shadows beneath her eyes I thought that perhaps this was not entirely true.

'Do you have any plans for today?' she asked. 'I am afraid I must go to Kephalonia this morning. Alkimos telephoned last night to say that he has arranged for me to meet a man who can help me with some business problems that I am having at the moment. I thought you might like to come with me. Perhaps there is something you would like to see in Argostoli, and after my meeting we could have lunch somewhere together?'

'I appreciate the offer but actually I wanted to ask a favour.'

'Oh?'

'You remember the English girl I met who I told you about?'

'The granddaughter of Julia Zannas?'

'Alex, yes. I ran into her again last night. I wondered if you'd mind if I took her out on the *Swallow*?'

'Of course I would not mind,' Irene said. 'I will pack you some lunch to take with you. You can have a picnic. Do you know where you will go?'

'Not far. Somewhere along the coast I expect.'

I followed her to the kitchen, protesting that there was no need for her to go to any trouble, but she insisted, and so, while she produced cheese and salad and some cold meat, I helped pack it all into a cooler.

'There's something else I wanted to ask you,' I said. 'Alex would like to know more about her family. Especially her grandmother. I gathered from what you said yesterday that you know what happened to her during the war?'

Irene stopped what she was doing. 'I know a little of what happened. But it is only the things I heard as a child. I was not even born then.'

'Would you tell Alex about it?'

'It was a long time ago,' Irene said reluctantly. 'Sometimes it is better that these things are forgotten, I think.'

'It was her grandmother. She wants to know. Is what happened really so bad?'

'Perhaps it would not seem so to you. But it is different for people who have lived here all their lives. People were killed. Sons and brothers and fathers. You must remember that Ithaca is a small island, Robert.'

'Then wouldn't it be better if Alex hears about it from you?' I reasoned. 'Mr Kounidis said I should warn her about asking too many questions, but I don't think that's going to stop her.'

Irene sighed. 'I suppose that is true. Bring her here this evening then. I will tell her what I can.'

I thanked her and as we finished packing the food I said, 'Do you know somebody called Dimitri Ramanda? He runs a travel agency in town.'

'Yes of course. Do you know him?'

'No, but Alex does.'

'Ah, I see. They are friends?'

'In a way. They met in England. What's he like?'

'He is a very nice young man I think.'

I'd asked because I was curious, but I almost wished that I hadn't. I was aware of the speculative way in which Irene glanced at me when she thought I wouldn't notice, and I could almost hear the whirring of cogs in her head.

★ ★ ★

It was around ten by the time I drove into town to pick Alex up. She heard the Jeep pull up and came outside to meet me.

'Good morning.' I took the bag she'd brought with her containing a towel and a change of clothes and put it in the back. 'How are you feeling?'

'Better,' she said with a determined smile. 'I've decided to enjoy today and forget about everything else.'

'Good for you.' I gestured towards the harbour

117

where the sunlight skipped across the waves. The sky was clear, but there was a light breeze. 'It'll be perfect out there today. And I talked to Irene this morning. You're invited to dinner tonight and she's agreed to tell you what she knows about your grandmother.'

'That's great. You're sure she doesn't mind?'

I decided not to tell her that I'd had to overcome Irene's initial reluctance. I wondered if Alex was aware that she might discover things about her grandmother that she wouldn't necessarily like, though now didn't seem the time to prick her bubble. She'd obviously made a mental effort to look forward to the day and I didn't want to spoil things for her.

It was only a short drive to the marina, along a narrow road that wound along the side of the harbour for about a mile or so from the edge of town. A concrete wharf with half a dozen pontoons provided berths for perhaps fifteen or twenty boats, and a couple of buildings by the road housed an office and repair shed. Several boats had been hauled out for maintenance in the shade of a stand of tall gum trees. When we arrived, the place seemed deserted and, other than the ever-present sound of cicadas among the trees, was quiet and still.

I recognised the *Swallow* though it was a long time since I'd last seen her. She was a forty-two foot motor ketch which my father had bought soon after he arrived on Ithaca. Her hull was painted dark blue above the waterline, while her cabin-housing and decks were a mixture of teak and varnished timber. She was a classic boat, built for cruising and ease of handling.

'She was a virtual wreck when my dad bought her,' I told Alex when we reached her. 'He did a lot of the restoration himself.'

It was only then that it struck me that this was where my father's body had been found. The water was clear and deep, but shadowed by the pontoon and the boat itself so I could understand how it had been possible for him to remain unseen for so long. It was less clear how he'd managed to end up in the water at the stern however, which is where I assumed he must have fallen in if his clothing had tangled with the propeller. The boat was moored lengthways against the pontoon so that climbing aboard was best done about midway along her length, which meant it couldn't have happened then. Either he was already on board or else he'd been on the pontoon. If he'd been on board I couldn't see anything that he could have hit his head on before he hit the water, so he must have been on the pontoon, but when I crouched down near the back of the boat to look for any sign of blood there was nothing there. It was puzzling. The wood was dry and solid.

'Is something wrong?' Alex asked, watching me with a puzzled expression.

'Sorry. I was thinking about my dad. This is where they found him.'

She looked down at the water in consternation as if she might see him still floating there.

'He had a heart attack five weeks ago,' I explained. 'After he'd been home for about three weeks he disappeared one morning. He was supposed to be resting, but he left the house early, before Irene was awake. They found his car here later. It was three days before somebody spotted his body trapped under the boat. That was a couple of days ago, the same day I arrived. The police think he must have fallen in after he had another heart attack.'

'That's terrible. I'm so sorry. It must have been awful for you.'

'It's been harder on Irene.' I got up and looked around, still trying to see how it must have happened. 'The thing is, the autopsy report was inconclusive. The cause of death was drowning, that much the police know for certain, but there was a wound at the back of his head they're not sure about. The theory is that it happened when he fell, but there's no sign of blood here and the wood is dry. Look how far it is to the water.'

Alex leaned over, but she didn't understand what I meant.

'That's about a foot. The police captain I spoke to said if there was any blood it would have been washed away, but there's virtually no tide here, and the water's like glass. No waves.'

'But if it had been windy . . . ?'

'Possibly,' I said, though I wasn't convinced. The weather was generally fairly stable. I could see that Alex didn't understand what I was getting at. 'The day I arrived, Irene told me something a bit strange. Apparently my dad thought somebody had tried to kill him.'

I could see that Alex didn't quite know whether I was serious or not. 'Are you saying he was murdered?'

I shook my head. 'No, I'm sure it was an accident. You have to know what he was like. He'd been drinking pretty heavily for quite a while. Either he imagined it or it was a play for sympathy.'

'Sympathy?'

'He and Irene had problems. Last year she left him. There was another man involved. Actually, he's the local police captain. Maybe after his heart attack, Dad decided it was a way to get her back.'

'So he said that somebody had tried to kill him?'

I shrugged. Out loud it did seem like a bizarre idea, but not as bizarre as the notion that there might be any truth to his claim. If he'd really believed it, then why had he later denied saying it? And as Theonas had pointed out, what possible reason could anybody have for wanting to harm somebody like my father? I explained the whole sequence of events to Alex, including Theonas's suggestion that my father's claim might have been prompted by the argument he'd had that night with a fisherman in the bar where he was drinking.

Despite my rationalising however, I couldn't entirely dispel a lingering doubt. Theonas had been quick to explain away the wound to my father's head, but now his explanation struck me as ill-conceived, even glib. I also had to wonder what my father had been doing at the marina in the first place. I didn't think he could have been planning to take the *Swallow* out alone. But what bothered me mostly was that Irene hadn't seemed convinced. I also had the vague feeling there was something she wasn't telling me. I wondered again about her comment that Theonas may have been the reason for my dad's secrecy. In the end though, there was nothing substantial in any of it.

'Come on,' I said to Alex, 'help me get these things on board.' I picked up the cooler and a bag and slung them over the rail onto the deck.

★ ★ ★

It had been a long time since I'd been on board the *Swallow* and it took a few minutes to re-familiarise myself with everything. She was in perfect condition. The brass gleamed, the varnished wood shone with a deep lustre and when I started the engine it ran smoothly with a rhythmic thump.

I went forward and slipped the bowline and asked Alex to release the stern, then I put the *Swallow* in gear, idled her out of the berth and we headed for the mouth of the harbour. I found a set of charts below and among them was one which showed the eastern coast of the island. There were plenty of small coves to choose from, but I picked one out that was only a few miles south and appeared to be only accessible by sea. Once we left Molos Bay beyond the harbour I handed the wheel over to Alex.

'Just aim for that headland,' I told her, pointing to a landmark about a mile ahead of us. While she concentrated on holding our course, I went on deck to raise the sails. There wasn't

122

much wind, but it was steady from the south-east so it was taking us in the right direction. When I was done I went back into the wheelhouse and turned off the engine. All at once the vibration under our feet ceased and the only sounds were the hull slipping through the sea and the breeze in the sails.

'It'll take us a while this way,' I said to Alex, 'but it's pretty relaxing.'

She grinned but kept her eyes on the point she was aiming for. 'It's fantastic. Where did you learn about boats?'

'It was the one thing I used to like about coming here when I was young. Dad used to spend part of every summer looking for the wreck of the *Antounnetta*. Apparently there's supposed to be a statue on board which the Germans looted from a monastery.'

At the reminder of the war and its connotations for her family Alex frowned. 'Before I came here I read some books about the German occupation of Greece. Some pretty awful things happened. I was thinking about that old man we saw in Exoghi yesterday. He was probably old enough to remember it all. And what you said just now about the Germans looting a monastery? It made me realise that one of them might have been my grandfather.'

'I suppose that's true,' I agreed, though I guessed she was thinking of things far worse than looting. 'Would that bother you?'

'Do you think it should?'

'It depends. Have you considered the possibility that if you're determined to find out about your grandmother you might not like everything you learn?'

'I hadn't before I came here to be honest. But the way that old man looked at me made me think about it. Why? Do you know something?'

'No. But the man I told you about, Mr Kounidis, he did say I should warn you to be careful who you speak to. And Irene has made a couple of remarks about certain things being better left in the past. I was going to tell you later.'

Alex thought for a moment, and then she said, 'But I don't think it's right to bury our heads in the sand just because we might not like what we see, do you? I want to know what Nana was like when she was young. I want to know what happened to her. But I want the truth, not just some palatable version of it. We can't understand anything unless we're prepared to be honest about the past, can we?'

'I just wanted to warn you.'

'Because you're worried that if I find out something unpleasant I won't be able to deal with it?'

'No.'

'I couldn't blame you if you did think that. But I'm not really some pathetic female who goes jumping off wharves in the middle of the night every time something goes wrong in my life.'

'I didn't think you were.'

She studied me for a moment to see if I was telling the truth. 'Tell me about you,' she said suddenly. 'You know my darkest secrets and I don't know anything about you.'

'What do you want to know?'

'What do you want to tell me? Where do you live?'

'London. In Kensington. I'm thirty-six and I own a small property development company. What else? I like Italian food, going to the cinema, reading books, and I force myself to run for three or four miles several times a week.'

'Are you married?'

'No.' I hesitated. 'There was somebody who meant a lot to me. It was quite recently actually. But we're not together any more.'

'I'm sorry.'

It might have been an uncomfortable moment, but in fact it wasn't, perhaps because failed relationships gave us something else in common. Alex looked towards the island half a mile off our starboard side. 'I'm glad that I came,' she remarked. 'It's beautiful. You said you used to come to Ithaca when you were young?'

'Reluctantly. My dad moved here after he and my mother split up. I used to spend a couple of weeks here during the summer holidays.'

'You didn't get on with your father did you? Did you always feel that way?'

'Not when I was very young. Most summers I used to go with him on whatever dig he was working on. He'd be unearthing some Roman villa in deepest Sussex and I'd be off roaming the fields and woods with a catapult looking for squirrels.'

'A typical boy. Why do boys always want to kill things?'

'It's in our nature.'

'Were you ever interested in archaeology?'

'Not really. I suppose if Dad had dug up some old helmets or swords it might have been different, but mostly it seemed to be bits of mosaic.' I remembered how in the evenings we'd all sit around the camp-fire eating sausages and fried potatoes and I'd half listen while my dad and his colleagues talked about what they'd found that day. I'd pretend to be interested because I didn't want to hurt his feelings. 'I think he was always worried that I thought his work was dull.'

'Did you?'

'His work maybe, but not him.' It was around those summer camp-fires that he'd first told me he liked boats and the sea. As a child he'd grown up on the Norfolk coast where his father had owned a wooden sail-boat. My dad would sail to coves along the coast where he'd spend the day gathering shellfish or looking for fossils in the rocks.

The more I talked to Alex the easier I found it and I ended up explaining the whole sorry story of how we had become estranged.

'One summer he was excavating a Saxon settlement,' I said. 'He had a particular theory about burial practices during the era he was interested in then. If he could have proved that he was right he would have set conventional thinking on its head and some of the finds he made that year seemed to validate his theory. He wrote a paper and had it published. The trouble was it turned out he'd manipulated some of the

126

evidence. I'm sure it was an accident. He probably just got some of his calculations wrong or something, but by the time he realised it the paper was already attracting attention in archaeological circles. In the end he had to admit to his peers publicly that his findings were wrong. The professional fall-out ruined him.'

'It doesn't sound so terrible,' Alex commented. 'Not enough to ruin somebody.'

'At Oxford a person's reputation is everything. It's far more important than money. The competitiveness is ruthless. There were rumours of cheating. Dad was forced to resign in the end.'

'It must have been terrible for him.'

'It was. I was only a kid, but I can guess what it would have been like. The whole petty social machinery of the place came into play. Suddenly people my mother thought were her friends were ringing her up cancelling invitations to afternoon tea parties on some pretext or other. Women she'd known for years ignored her on the street. It was vicious really. And it was especially hard for her because she'd grown up there. Her own father was a respected academic.'

'How old were you when all this happened?'

'Eleven.'

I told her how I was sent to a boarding school and that the fees were paid for by my grandfather. 'It was his old school. The kind of place where children are taught to be small adults instead of kids. Or at least some outdated upper-class notion of what small adults should be. My mother was completely dominated by her father. He was entrenched in the snobbish

127

hierarchical system at Oxford. I think my dad always felt he couldn't compete, that he'd never be good enough in the eyes of his father-in-law. He was probably right. I expect that had a lot to do with everything that happened. Anyway, the next time I heard from him was almost two years later.'

'And he'd been here all that time? Why didn't you hear from him?'

'Funny you should ask,' I said cynically. 'Anyway, I had a letter to say that he was getting married.'

'Which you must have resented.'

'I did, but it was the implication that he'd been merrily getting on with his life that hurt. I didn't resent Irene. Not once I met her anyway. What got to me was that during those two years my life was a fucking misery. I spent the first six months believing he'd come and get me out of there, but gradually I realised that wasn't going to happen. I felt . . . ' I paused, struggling to describe what it had been like. ' . . . I suppose abandoned. Even betrayed. And when I finally heard from him and he talked about this terrific sunny island where he was living and that he'd met some woman he was going to marry . . . '

'It made it worse.'

'Yes. I never forgot.'

'But didn't he ever explain why?'

'He tried. But what explanation could there be? He said he thought he was doing the right thing because he thought I was ashamed of him. He told me that for a long time he couldn't face thinking about England. The whole experience had been humiliating I think. It wasn't just his career and his reputation, it was his marriage too. His failure to live up to my mother's or her father's expectations of him. Or maybe in her father's case it was the reverse. But people have to deal with things all the time. He had a child. Me. He had responsibilities. In the end he ran away. He took the easy option and he salved his conscience by convincing himself that he was doing the right thing.'

Alex was quiet. I knew I sounded bitter, but even after all the years that had passed the hurt was still there. It had become a part of me. As much as any other facet of my make-up.

'Anyway,' I said finally, 'none of it matters any more.'

'Why not?' Alex asked.

I was surprised at her question because I thought the answer was obvious. 'Because he's dead.'

She smiled uncertainly. 'Oh, I see.'

⋆   ⋆   ⋆

Not long afterwards we approached the cove I'd picked out as our destination, so I went out on deck to lower the sails and we motored the rest of the way. As we rounded the headland we saw a strip of white pebbled beach fringing an aqua bay. The water was still and clear, protected from the breeze by the headland and steep rocky cliffs, which made access from the landward side all but impossible.

'It's lovely,' Alex said with delighted surprise.

129

I dropped the anchor in ten yards of water and lowered the dinghy over the side, then Alex passed down the cooler and we rowed to shore. While I hauled the dinghy onto the beach she laid out a rug near the shade of a tree. As I turned around she had her back to me. I watched her unzip her skirt and let it fall to the ground revealing a bright red bikini cut high on her hips. When I went over to join her she was rubbing sun lotion into her legs, and as I sat down she handed me the bottle.

'Can you put some on my back?'

She rolled over onto her stomach and I squeezed a blob of cream between her shoulder blades and spread it across her smoothly tanned skin, briefly envying her Mediterranean blood. When I was finished, I spread a towel beside her and lay down with a book.

'Thanks,' she murmured, her eyes closed.

The sun was fierce. Within ten minutes rivulets of sweat were running down my face. I glanced at Alex. She hadn't moved and I thought she was asleep. Out in the cove the *Swallow* drifted serenely at anchor. With her twin masts against a cloudless sky and the deep blue of the bay behind she looked like something from a holiday brochure. I got up and walked down to the water's edge. It was cool and refreshing after the baking heat of the sun. I began to swim out into the cove and when I'd gone a hundred yards I turned to look back towards the beach. Alex was sitting up, hugging her knees and watching me. Then she walked down to the water and with smooth, even strokes swam out to meet me.

'It's gorgeous,' she said. Her hair was plastered to her scalp, emphasising the planes of her features and the startling green of her eyes. She pointed to some rocks on one side of the cove. 'I'll race you.'

Without waiting for an answer she promptly kicked out and within seconds she had a five-yard advantage. I went after her but, though I swam hard, she kept inching away from me and by the time we were almost half-way there she had doubled her lead. I dug deep, putting everything I had into the race, but when we reached the rocks she was still ahead and I was gulping air like a beached fish. Alex climbed out and looked on with an amused expression as I hauled myself out and collapsed.

'Where did you learn to swim like that?' I managed to ask eventually.

She grinned smugly. 'I was school champ in the hundred-yard dash.'

'Christ,' I moaned, but at least I felt less of a failure.

I closed my eyes, letting the sun warm me while my heart rate returned to something like normal. When I opened them again Alex was watching me with a distant, vaguely puzzled expression. She smiled self-consciously then unexpectedly reached out and touched my cheek. Her fingers lingered and impulsively I started to reach for her but, before I could, she turned and slipped back into the water. I sat up and watched her swim back towards the beach.

For the rest of the afternoon that moment seemed to sit between us like some invisible barrier. I kept thinking about the questioning, almost perplexed look in her eyes, as if she couldn't understand what she was feeling.

Later, when we were sailing back towards Vathy, I went below and fetched a couple of cold beers. When I took one up for Alex she thanked me and then said in a rush, 'I'm sorry about what happened earlier. I don't want to give you the wrong impression.'

'You haven't.' She glanced at me quickly and I realised that I'd sounded dismissive. 'We're both a bit off-kilter. Let's forget it.' I touched my beer to hers. 'Cheers.'

'Cheers,' she responded tentatively.

It was late afternoon when we tied up at the marina again. Alex wanted to have a shower and freshen up before dinner, so I said that I'd drop her off and come back for her later. Before we left I took the chart I'd been using back down below and put it with the others. The one on top of the table covered the area to the south-east of the island, towards the mainland coast, and I noticed that it was covered with clusters of tiny crosses annotated with numbers. The markings puzzled me until I realised that the numbers were dates. Above the chart table a shelf held a number of leather-bound journals. I pulled one down at random and flicked through the pages. It was a record of my father's search for the wreck of the *Antounnetta*, written in the neat hand possessed by people who have lived much of their lives before the proliferation of computer keyboards.

I turned to the front page, which was dated

April 17, five years earlier. The final entry had been made at the end of October the same year, and during the intervening summer months my father had made notes for each day which he'd spent searching for the wreck, recording every location and dive and what had been found, or more accurately what had not been found. I looked through several more of the journals. They were arranged on the shelf in consecutive years and each of them followed the same pattern. The entries were sometimes weeks apart and at other times only days, and I soon figured out that the dates corresponded to the clusters of crosses on the chart. Over time a clear pattern had emerged. During twenty-odd years of searching, my father had covered a broad swathe of open sea to the east, beginning a mile or so off the coast of Ithaca. Looking at the vast expanse of water as a whole it was painfully evident that his task had been almost impossible. Towards the mainland coast there was a single large cross without any annotations beside it. I wondered what it meant.

In all of the journals my father frequently mentioned the old man who had crewed for him. Normally he was referred to by just the letter G, but I remembered then that his name was Gregory. During the last few years, my father had been unable to dive himself, and Gregory it seemed could only manage one a day, but when I took down the last journal covering the previous summer I saw that my father had hired a foreign student to help. It meant that rather than search for odd days at a time, they had concentrated their efforts over several blocks lasting a week or so. Nevertheless the final entry made in September revealed that as usual nothing had been found. I put the last journal back with the others in the order they belonged.

The chart with its visual record of years of dogged fruitless searching graphically seemed to sum my father up. He had spent years looking for the wreck of a World War Two ship because it contained a worthless statue which he wanted to return to the people of Ithaca. At the same time he'd searched for a lost temple, a discovery that would have restored his reputation and made his name around the world. And yet he had never displayed the same kind of doggedness and determination where I was concerned. His efforts were for the attention of others. It seemed to me that I had never had my fair share of the man, that he had kept the best of himself for his work, for the past, for the people of Ithaca and even for Irene. For anything in fact but me.

Fuck him, I thought angrily and I turned and went back on deck.

8

Irene had roasted a leg of lamb, which she served with side-dishes of butter beans cooked in a tomato sauce and boiled greens dressed with oil and lemon. We ate on the terrace with the lights of Vathy below us. Alex was wearing a simple white dress which contrasted with her tan and the mesmerising colour of her eyes. I kept thinking about the incident between us that afternoon, the sudden look of confusion which I saw in her expression. Now and then our eyes met across the table and I felt my pulse quicken.

The conversation over dinner tripped from one subject to another without mention of Alex's grandmother or the war. Irene asked Alex about her job as a teacher at a private school for expatriate Europeans in London, and in turn she told us stories about her own family and what it had been like growing up on Ithaca. The food was excellent and between us we drank several bottles of wine.

After our main course Irene brought out dessert. 'It is called *galactoboureko*,' she announced.

It was very good. Some kind of custard in a filo pastry case topped with sweet honey. Later over coffee which we drank with glasses of peach brandy, Irene finally broached the subject of Alex's grandmother.

'What do you know about why she left the

island, Alex?' she asked.

'Not very much actually. I know that she was involved with a German soldier during the war, and that when she left she was pregnant with my mother but that's about it.'

'Your grandmother never spoke about it?'

'Not until she became ill. I know it sounds strange but it was something that was never discussed when I was growing up. I always thought my grandfather had died when he was young, but I can never remember anybody saying so directly. He was simply never mentioned.'

'And your mother? Did your grandmother never speak to her about what happened?'

'Only once. My mother wanted to know about her father. Until then Nana had never talked about the war, but I suppose she decided my mother was entitled to know the truth. She told her that during the war she was raped. Obviously my mother didn't pursue it after that.'

'I see. And yet you wish to?'

'I'm not sure Nana told my mother the full truth,' Alex said. 'When she was dying she talked about the German soldier who she had known. She said that she fell in love with him. The way she talked it was as if she still felt the same way even after all this time. I don't see how that could be if he had raped her.'

Irene sighed. 'I do not think that I can answer that question. Perhaps only your grandmother knew the truth. But certainly it is not what I have always understood.'

Alex glanced at me and then said to Irene, 'No

matter what the truth is I want to know.'

Irene saw then that nothing would dissuade her, and finally she agreed to tell what she knew.

★ ★ ★

The Germans arrived in Greece in 1941, after the Italians who came before them. On Ithaca there was a small garrison based in Vathy. It was not an important posting, perhaps twenty soldiers commanded by a young officer called *Hauptmann* Stefan Hassel. He would have been in his late-twenties. Not much more than a boy. The men he commanded were mostly very young, or too old to be of much use on the front line.

Relations between the German soldiers and the islanders were friendly. At least as much as circumstances would allow. There were few of the restrictions which existed on Kephalonia or Corfu. The people had enough to eat and the restrictions on their movements were not too rigorously enforced. There were no instances of men being beaten or women raped, nor any of the other atrocities that were common during the occupation in other parts of Greece. This was due partly to the fact that on Ithaca the Resistance was not very active, at least to begin with, and so the potential for friction was lessened. Mainly the Resistance provided food and other supplies to groups on Kephalonia.

The relationship between the islanders and the German soldiers remained, however, one of conqueror and the conquered. Though on the surface, the atmosphere was generally good, the true nature of the situation sat ever present in people's minds. Nevertheless it is true that things were much better on Ithaca than in other places. The Germans were a long way from home and they were lonely. The posting they had been assigned was not arduous. Under such circumstances people began, if not to forget their differences, at least to put them aside. The soldiers wished to be seen as friends and not the enemy. It was not their fault that they had been sent there. Gradually they sought acceptance from the islanders. Rules were relaxed and in return for the co-operation of the people the soldiers tried to make life seem as normal as possible. For a while it seemed as if the war didn't exist on Ithaca.

It was soon clear to everyone that the young German *Hauptmann* in charge of the garrison was in love with Julia Zannas. He had first seen her in the marketplace in Vathy where every week she went with her father to sell the produce which they grew on the patch of land they owned in a village in the north of the island. Julia was a beautiful girl. Her long hair was thick, the colour of honey shot through with sunlight. Her eyes were wide, a startling shade of green, like the silvery underside of the leaves of the olive trees which grew on the hillside above the village. When *Hauptmann* Hassel passed by the makeshift stall she and her father had set up in the square by the waterfront, he paused to examine the vegetables laid out in shallow boxes. As he picked up the ripe tomatoes his eyes were on Julia. He spoke to her but she did not understand. Once or twice when he wasn't looking, she gazed at him with interest, this tall, fair-haired foreigner with his pale blue eyes. After that he came every week and he always bought a box of whatever she had to sell.

After a month, Hassel arrived in the village of Exoghi, driven in the open-top armoured car he used to patrol the island. People came out of their houses, curious to see what the commander of the German garrison was doing in their village. It transpired that he was considering posting two men outside Exoghi on the cliff high above Polis Bay. From there they would be able to monitor the comings and goings of boats in the channel between Ithaca and Kephalonia a few miles distant. The villagers wondered what Hassel expected his men would see, since the only boats were those which belonged to the fishermen and, though they occasionally carried supplies to the Resistance on Kephalonia, they did so only at night. The supplies were carried overland along trails known only to the islanders themselves, over the hills and mountains through the thick holm oak and stands of cypress to isolated coves where the boats waited.

The young *Hauptmann* made a great show out of touring the village. He stopped at the house of the Zannas family to request a drink, and in exchange he offered Julia's father a cigarette from a packet in his tunic pocket. He stayed for half an hour asking questions about the Zannas's land, showing great interest in the affairs of the family. If he saw Julia through the window as she worked in the garden he did not show it. When he stood to leave he put his packet of cigarettes on the table insisting that Julia's father should keep them.

After that, Hassel visited Exoghi often, though he never did post any men on the cliff. Every time he came he would call on the Zannas family and would sit with Julia's father outside beneath the grapevine. He would be offered a cup of wine and the two men would talk, though since Hassel knew only a few words of Greek and Julia's father knew no German at all their conversation was limited. Eventually they began teaching each other the rudiments of their respective languages. In time Hassel began to pick up a smattering of Greek, though Julia's father was less proficient at learning German and soon gave up the attempt altogether.

All the time as Hassel sat outside on the small terrace his eyes wandered ceaselessly back and forth among the olive trees on the hillside. Outwardly he was polite and well mannered. He always arrived looking as though he had brushed down his uniform and wiped the dust from his boots. He never came without bringing some gift of food or wine or a bolt of cloth he had managed to find somewhere, and these he would present to Julia's mother with great courteousness, though he was careful not to give so much that his gifts might arouse feelings of jealousy or suspicion among the other villagers.

He was attentive as Julia's father taught him new words and phrases, though it was clear that at least part of his mind was elsewhere. Only

140

when he spied Julia did his demeanour change. His eyes would shine with a fervent light, following her every movement with a yearning hunger.

The Zannas family were aware of the true reason for Hassel's frequent visits. Julia's father was angry, and since he couldn't make his anger known to Hassel himself he made sure that his family understood his feelings. Julia was his only daughter. He knew with the mix of a father's pain and pride that she was extraordinary. She attracted the interest of young men from all over the island and one day she would marry one of them, and though the dowry she would take with her would not be large, he was determined that she would be married well. In addition to being his daughter, she carried his hopes for an improvement in the circumstances of the family.

Nevertheless, the German *Hauptmann* had to be handled carefully. He must not be encouraged and yet care had to be taken to ensure that he did not feel that his attentions were spurned. The gifts he brought were useful. But more than this, Julia's father had to consider the people of the island who were aware that they were lucky to have Hassel as the commander of the occupying force. Nothing must be done to jeopardise the fine balance of their relationship with the German soldiers.

Julia was constantly reminded of her part in all of this. She must be pleasant to Hassel when he came to the market. She must speak to him politely, but she must not do or say anything that could be misconstrued. She must greet him if she saw him when he came to visit the house, but she must never linger. Above all, should she by chance encounter Hassel when she was on the hill above the village tending the goats or else on the road as she walked to Stavros to fetch something for her mother, she must never be alone with him for longer than it takes to exchange pleasantries. Julia listened to all of this and she did as she was told. She knew that people were gossiping about the *Hauptmann*'s visits to the house but, so long as she did as her father instructed, they could find no fault with her.

Every week when she went to church she knelt before the icon of the Holy Virgin and prayed for her help and guidance, and every evening before bed she would also pray. She would think of the young *Hauptmann*'s attempts to speak her language when he came to the market. She smiled at his broken Greek and thought his eyes were like no blue that she had seen before. She imagined they were like the sky viewed through a layer of ice on a clear day, but when he smiled they were full of tenderness and sometimes she could see in them that he was lonely. He was separate from the men under his command. Too young, she thought, for the responsibility he bore. She saw the way he looked at her and after a while she didn't mind. She found herself thinking about him. His teeth were white, his face had become tanned and his hair bleached by the sun. He was unlike anybody she had ever known.

One morning Julia was collecting shellfish

from the rocks along the edge of the bay when she heard the sound of a vehicle and knew it was Hassel's. Shading her eyes with her hand she saw it turn the corner at the bottom of the long hill which led to the village and she guessed that he had been to her house. She had been out all morning, however. She experienced a tug of disappointment that she had missed him. As his car drove along the track above the beach she had a sudden impulse to wave her arms to attract his attention. She could see him behind the wheel. He wasn't wearing his uniform cap and his hair was startlingly fair in the glare of the sun.

As she watched, the car slowed and then stopped. Hassel got out and clambered down to the beach where he sat on a rock and smoked a cigarette while he looked out across the water. It was almost midday and the sun was directly overhead. The white pebbles on the beach were almost painful to look at, the water flashed and glittered. The bay was deserted. A single boat was pulled up beyond the water's edge, a net spread out beside it to dry. The distance was too great for Julia to see Hassel's expression, but she formed the impression that he was thinking of her. He looked so alone as he sat there. She wondered who he talked to at night.

She wanted to go to him and talk to him, to sit with him for a time. She wondered what it would feel like to be alone with him, and from there her thoughts wandered and she began to imagine what it would be like to put her hand against his face and feel his skin. She imagined it would not be as coarse as her father's. She pictured his smile and before she knew it she was imagining placing her mouth on his. All at once she rose, shocked at her own thoughts, colour rising into her cheeks, her heart pounding. She hurried towards the path which led back up the hill. What would her parents say if they knew she had entertained such shocking ideas? She began to pray to the Holy Virgin, asking for her forgiveness. A little way up the path she paused to look back. *Hauptmann* Hassel was on his feet, staring up at her. Their eyes met for several seconds and then Julia turned and fled.

A few weeks later men came to the house one evening. Julia and her brother were sent to bed, but she heard their voices late into the night. Once one which she recognised as her father's cried out in a mixture of pain and anger. The following evening after they had eaten supper and she had helped her mother clear away, Julia's father told her to sit down at the table. When he spoke he could not meet her eyes.

'Tomorrow, when the German *Hauptmann* comes here, I want you to take him for a walk.'

'A walk?' she echoed, not comprehending his meaning. 'Where to?'

'It does not matter. Show him the view from higher up the hill,' her father said. He sounded angry, though she did not know why. She understood that her father meant for her to be alone with the *Hauptmann*. She had never been alone with any man before, except her father and the priest. She glanced at her mother for help but she was busy in the kitchen, her eyes

144

determinedly downcast.

Her father looked her directly in the eye at last. 'You know he likes you, my angel? You must encourage him. Let him think that you return his feelings. When he comes here, take him for walks, spend time with him.' Her father gripped her hand, his expression almost fierce. She didn't understand it. His eyes flashed anger but also he seemed to be in pain. 'You are my daughter and you are Greek. Never let him touch you. Never let him lay a hand on you. Do you understand?'

'Yes, yes, of course,' she answered, bewildered that he should even ask. 'But why am I to do this?'

'Because it is important, my angel. If it were not I would not ask this of you. Just remember that you are my daughter,' he added again sternly.

She did not know what he meant. Of course she was his daughter. How could she forget?

The *Hauptmann* did not come for two days. She was working in the garden when she heard his car coming up the hill and then her father appeared. He seemed anxious. For the past few days he had barely spoken to her, and at night he often went out and came home very late. Julia sometimes caught her mother looking at her strangely too. She would murmur endearments and stroke her hair as Julia sat at the table.

As usual her father and the *Hauptmann* sat outside beneath the grapevine and Julia's mother brought them wine. Hassel gave her a gift of a piece of ham, bowing stiffly from the waist. Then he sat down and offered Julia's father a cigarette.

They talked a little, but her father seemed ill at ease. When he had smoked his cigarette he got to his feet and, apologising, told the *Hauptmann* that he had just remembered something he must do. Hassel began to get up too but her father insisted he stay and finish his wine. At the same time he looked towards the trees on the hill where Julia was hiding and, taking her cue, she started walking down towards the house.

Hassel didn't even see her father leave. He stared at her the way a starving man might look on a meal another is eating, the agony of the unattainable in his eyes. Beneath the intensity of his gaze Julia felt heat rise into her cheeks. She was conscious of every move she made. Her stomach clenched and her heart began to beat faster. When she was close, Hassel realised that her father had gone and he rose.

'*Kalimera, Kyria* Zannas.' He stood and bowed slightly.

She smiled at the way he spoke. '*Kalimera, Hauptmann.*'

For a moment he didn't know what to say. 'I was passing, so I brought your mother some ham,' he managed in the end. His Greek was heavily accented, but understandable, though he stumbled on some of the words.

'You are very generous. She will be grateful.'

Unused to being alone with her he sought for a way to communicate. 'Have you been working this morning?'

'Yes.'

'It is hot.' He looked toward the sky.

'My father said that I can take you for a walk,' she said.

He looked around as if he expected her father to be standing somewhere close by, his surprise evident. 'Your father said that?'

'If you wish to.' Julia pointed up the hillside. 'I could show you a place where you can see the whole bay.'

He said something then in German that she did not understand, but she didn't need to. His smile told her everything she needed to know.

After that day *Hauptmann* Hassel came more often. Things followed the same routine. He would arrive and present Julia's mother with some small gift, then he would sit with her father and they would have a glass of wine and a cigarette until her father found some excuse to leave. Then Julia would appear and she would take him for a walk. Sometimes they went through the olive trees towards the monastery at Pernerakia high up at the top of the hill, other times they followed the path that led along the cliffs above the bay. They would find somewhere to sit and talk. He did most of the talking, often lapsing into his own language and, though she understood little of it, she was happy enough to listen. His voice was tender. He looked at her sometimes in a way that made her heart beat faster and her throat tighten so that she couldn't speak. Sometimes when they were walking his arm would brush against hers and the muscles in her belly would convulse. She kept her expression impassive however and averted her eyes until she could breathe normally again.

Each time after these walks when they returned to the house her mother and father would smile and stand outside to wave the *Hauptmann* off, though afterwards her father's mood would change. His face would darken and he would ask her what had happened. She assured him that Hassel had not touched her in any way and, though he seemed relieved, she could see the agony that still burned in his eyes.

A few weeks passed. One evening after she had gone to bed she heard men's voices. Her father's was among them. They talked for a long time and in the morning her father spoke to her. His manner was strange. There was an odd light in his eyes, as if he had a fever. He said that Hassel would come the next day as he always did. She was to take him for a walk as usual only this time she was to make sure they went along the path above the cliffs. On the way back, she was to lead him through the olive grove above the village, along the path which passed between the two slabs of rock where it was always shady, even in the middle of the day.

The next afternoon when Hassel arrived he gave Julia's mother a gift of a can of olive oil. Outside he smoked a cigarette with her father and drank a glass of wine and, if he noticed anything different about the way her father was acting, he didn't show it. When her father got up to leave Julia emerged from the trees where she had been watching. The *Hauptmann* met her half-way, his eyes fastened on hers as he approached. She felt the familiar tug in her breast as they walked side by side, close together

148

but never touching.

They did not speak much that day. They went to a place on the headland high above the bay where they sat in the grass and looked out over the sea towards the brown hills of Kephalonia. Behind them the village was lost from sight. The sound of goat bells reached them from the hillside. Hassel lay back in the grass and looked at the sky. He said something and when she turned to him he smiled. He looked so young, his tanned face smooth, his eyes clear and strong. He spoke again and though Julia didn't comprehend his words she thought she understood the emotion behind them. She knew he was wishing that there was no war, that they were not separated by the fact that he was a German soldier and she a Greek. But she knew also that if this were not so, he would never have come to the island and they would never have met. She wondered about his home, his family.

Something stirred inside her and she shifted her position so that she sat close to him. She reached out and smoothed his hair. He rose to one elbow, surprise registering in his expression, but she made him lie down again, though this time with his head resting in her lap. She wanted to lean down and kiss his mouth. Sadness filled her because she thought of the men's voices she had heard in the house, and she thought of the way her father had been acting and how he had looked that morning. She knew why he had made her bring the *Hauptmann* here and why he had insisted she return along the path between the two big rocks.

A bird rose from the hillside behind them, its wings whirring as it took to the air. Hassel watched it, and for a second his brow furrowed but then he relaxed again. He closed his eyes and the hand that had shielded them from the sun lay in the grass. Julia wanted to hold it within her own hand, to press it against her cheek. She wondered how his skin would feel, what he would smell like. Sometimes when she was alone in the dark of her room she thought of him and her breasts ached and she could not sleep unless she walked barefoot for a while in the cool night air.

She knew at once she could not do what her father had asked of her. It was not a decision made out of reason, but one from her heart. She looked down on Hassel's face and she was filled with feelings which burst inside her, feelings which took hold of her with such force she could hardly breathe. There was little time. She did not think of the consequences. She roused him and when he opened his eyes he looked startled and uncomprehending. She told him urgently that they must leave. He didn't understand her and suddenly she was overwhelmed with fear for him. She held his face in her hands and leaned close to him and she told him again that he must go, that men were coming to kill him, and she gestured toward the hill where even now they must be approaching. And then somehow she saw that he understood her. Her fear for him communicated itself and in so doing she revealed her love for him.

He rose hurriedly to his feet and unfastened

the pistol at his side, then he pulled her up and started back the way they had come. His face was different now. She saw a shadow of tension in the lines around his eyes, but he was determined too.

They heard a sound above them, perhaps a rock which had been dislodged by a goat, but then again it could be the men who were meant to come for him. She stopped and when he turned to question her, she pulled him away, leading him by another path. He resisted, then looked back the way they had come and he understood and went with her, putting his trust in her. They ran, and when she slipped he stopped her from falling and for an instant he held her against him. She looked into his eyes and he into hers. When they arrived at the village, he pushed her towards the armoured patrol car. She hesitated, knowing suddenly that if she went with him she was taking an irrevocable step. A hundred thoughts flashed in her mind, a thousand images. Her home, her family, everything she knew. Her entire life seemed intensified and concentrated into this one moment, this one decision. As if everything she had experienced until then had meant to lead here. All at once a sense of calm descended over her.

She looked at the *Hauptmann* and he understood. He got in the car and she climbed into the seat beside him.

★   ★   ★

Irene had stopped speaking. The images her story had created fled and dissolved into the night. The lamp still glowed on the table, casting us in light and shadow. With surprise I saw that several hours had passed. Alex wore a look of intense concentration.

'What happened?' she asked.

'I think it is better that you hear the rest from somebody who was there. He can tell you far more than I can,' Irene said. She turned to me. 'You must take Alex to speak to Alkimos Kounidis.'

'He's the man I mentioned to you. A friend of my father's,' I explained. 'During the war he was a member of the Resistance.'

'He knew your grandmother, Alex,' Irene added. 'Tomorrow he will be at the funeral.' She turned to me. 'I am sure he will agree to talk to Alex if you ask him then.'

She rose and cleared away our glasses, announcing that she was tired. I said that I would run Alex back to where she was staying. We drove in silence down the dark road, both of us still affected by the story we'd heard. When we stopped, Alex turned to thank me. She looked beautiful. I recalled again the way she had looked at me that afternoon in the cove, and how she had reached out to touch my cheek. Without thinking about it I leant across and kissed her on the mouth. When I pulled away she stared at me in confusion. Then she got out and went to the door where she turned and looked back.

'Good-night,' she said quietly.

9

On the day of my father's funeral I went to his study, a room I'd avoided since my arrival on the island. The walls were lined with books and his desk was strewn untidily with papers and various archaeological magazines. At one end of the room a collection of fragmented clay vessels was laid out on a trestle table like pieces from a jigsaw puzzle. One pot had been completed, save for a missing hole in the side. From the card beside it made out in my father's hand I read that it was a Corinthian *aryballoi*. The outside was decorated with intricate black-figured designs.

I sat at the desk. The papers were a mixture of household accounts and invoices relating to the small museum he ran. A half-finished article written in longhand described a dig he'd worked on, but when I looked at the date I saw that it had been written eighteen months ago. The text was heavily edited. Much of it had been crossed out and rewritten in an effort, it seemed, to make what was essentially dry academic reporting appear even mildly interesting. It was an attempt that appeared largely to have failed, which I gathered was the conclusion my father had also arrived at.

In one of the drawers I found a slim paperback, its cover faded and dog-eared. It was called *The Dracoulis Enigma*. I recognised the name of the man Alkimos Kounidis had mentioned, so I took it out to flick through the pages. Underneath was what I at first thought was a piece of rusted jewellery of some sort, but when I took a closer look I recognised the shape for what it actually was; a Maltese Cross. The four arrowhead-shaped points tapering towards the centre were unmistakable. It was the design used by the Germans during the First and Second World Wars for the medal known as the Iron Cross. I had seen it a hundred times in films and on book covers. I wondered where my dad had found it and why he had kept it.

The paperback fleshed out the story that Kounidis had already told me. It had been written in the late-fifties after a letter sent by the curator of the museum in Argostoli to his sister in Athens came to light. The curator's name was Dracoulis. He was an archaeologist and in the letter, written in 1940, he claimed that during the summer of 1938 he had discovered the location of Aphrodite's Temple at an unnamed location on Ithaca. During his excavation he had removed a number of artefacts but he had never made his discovery public due to the imminent outbreak of war. Dracoulis had died in 1943 without ever revealing to anybody what he had found. In fact until the letter he wrote to his sister surfaced he was remembered only as a mild-mannered and unremarkable curator. The letter changed all of that. Suddenly his name became famous and his claims the subject of intense debate. At the time the book had been written, neither the temple nor the artefacts he

154

mentioned had ever been found.

The author of the book, somebody called Donald St James who had a string of letters after his name, debated the authenticity of the letter. Though some experts believed it could be genuine, arguing that the excavation of the temple might well have been buried during the devastating earthquake of the early-fifties, many did not agree. They focused on the missing artefacts. It was well documented that during the latter stages of the war the German commander on Kephalonia, an SS officer called Manfred Bergen, had systematically looted the antiquities kept in the museum in Argostoli and had them flown to Berlin. Many of these had subsequently been recovered, as had some documents referring to the event made by the ever-meticulous Germans.

Donald St James asserted that if the artefacts Dracoulis wrote about had actually existed some trace of them would have been found, since Bergen surely must have included them with the shipments he'd flown to his masters in Berlin. Since this was not the case, St James concluded that the letter was false, a hoax perpetrated by persons unknown, though he gave no compelling reason why anyone would bother to do such a thing. Towards the end of the book there was a photograph of Manfred Bergen. It was a grainy black-and-white shot showing a very thin, unsmiling man wearing the uniform of the SS. There was a short piece about the sinking of the *Antounnetta* which occurred after it had left Ithaca. Bergen himself had survived that event

155

but had died before the remaining survivors were picked up by another German ship near the mainland coast. Unluckily for them however, the rescue ship itself was attacked only hours later and all of the men from the *Antounnetta* were killed.

I was about to put the book back where I'd found it when some pieces of folded paper fell out onto the desk from between the cover and the back page. They were both press clippings from a Greek newspaper. The text was indecipherable to me but one of them had several accompanying photographs. In each of them groups of people were pictured standing beside what appeared to be a museum display. The photograph had not been posed, but rather seemed to catch them informally, champagne glasses in hand, at some function or other. Another picture was of the display itself, a collection of figurines and various drinking vessels and the like in a glass case.

There was one photograph which caught my attention over the others. In it the unmistakable figure of my father was clearly visible. He appeared to be talking to another man while slightly behind him and to his right another less distinct figure looked on. My dad was holding a glass, smiling broadly. I stared at his image for some time, thinking about the man I had known as a child before he left England. The man with whom I had spent my summers, while my mother preferred to stay at home in Oxford. Throughout my life I had never been able to reconcile that person with the one who had left me at the age of eleven. And there was another side to him of course — the side which Irene had loved for so long, the side which his friend Alkimos Kounidis had spoken of, testament to the affection in which he was held. A side I had never known.

I didn't hear Irene come to the door so it gave me quite a start when I looked up to find her there. I gestured to the things on the desk, feeling slightly embarrassed that I'd been caught going through them.

'I was curious,' I said.

She smiled and looked around the room. 'He spent a great deal of his time in here.'

'I found this,' I said, showing her the clippings.

'Ah, yes. These pictures were taken in April. It is at the opening of the Dracoulis exhibit in Argostoli after the artefacts were returned from Switzerland.'

I showed her the book I'd been reading. 'In here it says there was no record of the artefacts leaving the island.'

'It is assumed that they were sold after the war. Many antiquities stolen by the Germans fell into private hands. When the man who had bought these died and his collection was discovered, the Greek government claimed them back.'

Irene saw the other clipping on the desk and picked it up. As she read it she appeared puzzled and then some darker, more troubling reaction flashed in her eyes.

'What is it?' I asked.

'It is an article about a man who was found

dead on the island recently. It was terrible. He was murdered. Stabbed.'

I remembered that when Irene had talked of my dad's behaviour after he came home, the way he'd insisted on locking the house at night, she'd said crime was almost unheard of on Ithaca. Theonas had said the same thing, though he'd referred to a recent unusual incident and I assumed this was what he'd meant.

'Who was he?' I asked.

'He was not identified. Nobody knew him.'

'Then he wasn't from the island?'

'No. He did not appear to be Greek.'

'Presumably the police didn't find whoever stabbed him?'

'No.'

I wondered what had interested my father enough about this for him to keep a clipping of the story. Suddenly his claim that somebody had tried to kill him seemed less fanciful. 'When did this happen?'

Irene read the date. 'In May,' she said, 'about three weeks ago.'

Around the time my dad left hospital. Irene's brow was deeply furrowed.

'What's wrong?'

'Nothing. It is nothing,' she said. 'I must get ready.'

I didn't believe her. When she'd gone I returned the clipping to the drawer and made a mental note to ask Theonas about the dead man the next time I saw him.

★ ★ ★

The funeral was held that afternoon at a small church in Vathy on the hill above the western side of the harbour. I was surprised by the number of people who arrived to pay their respects. They filed into the churchyard in small groups and pairs and bowed their heads as the priest recited the service.

'Na *zisete na ton thimaste*,' Kounidis said solemnly as he paused by Irene. She thanked him and kissed his cheek, then Kounidis went to the closed casket and kissed it before he paused in front of me.

'May you live to remember him,' he said, offering the traditional funeral-saying in English.

On the way to the church, I had called in at the place where Alex was staying and asked if she would like to come and meet Kounidis. She'd been uncertain about attending the funeral at first, given that she hadn't ever met my father, but I persuaded her that I'd like her to come and in the end she agreed. When Kounidis saw her his eyes widened, registering a brief shock as if he'd received a low-voltage jolt from some unexpected source. It was gone in a moment and he moved on.

As the casket was lowered into the ground I tried to summon some kind of emotion, but all I could manage was a kind of confused regret. I met Alex's eye and she offered a sympathetic smile.

At the end of the service the mourners began to drift towards the gate, pausing to offer words of condolence to Irene, who looked pale and tired. Miros Theonas stood at a respectful distance watching the proceedings, his gaze riveted on her. I wondered whether they would resume their relationship. Theonas had the look of a patient man. He would bide his time until a suitable period had passed, but he would not give up. I couldn't help harbouring a vague resentment towards him for being there, though I told myself it was unjustified.

I told Alex that I had spoken to Irene earlier and she was going to talk to Kounidis to see if he would agree to tell her the remainder of the story about her grandmother. We hung back, waiting until the last of the mourners had gone before joining Irene to take her back to the house where food and drinks had been laid on in the Greek custom. I introduced Alex to Alkimos Kounidis.

'It is remarkable,' he said as he shook her hand and gazed at her face with a vestige of the shock I had seen before, only now it was overlaid with wonder. 'When I first saw you it was as if sixty years had not happened. For an instant I truly believed that you were your grandmother. The resemblance is quite astonishing. I had almost forgotten how beautiful she was.'

'Thank you,' Alex said, blushing a little.

'I was very sorry when Robert told me that she had recently died.'

'Did you know my grandmother well, Mr Kounidis?'

'No, I cannot say that I did. I was a few years older than Julia, and we came from different villages, though of course I knew who she was. Everybody knew Julia Zannas. She was the most beautiful girl on all of Ithaca. I spoke to her a few times in the market at Vathy but only when her father was present. In those days a girl of Julia's age was never allowed to be alone with a man who was not from her family.'

'Has Irene explained that Alex wants to find out more about what happened to her grandmother during the war?' I asked. 'She said that you knew the story better than most.'

'Yes, this is true,' Kounidis agreed.

'Irene told us how my grandmother met *Hauptmann* Hassel,' Alex said, 'but I would like to hear the rest of what happened.'

Kounidis considered this. 'In that case I would like to invite you both to come and stay at my house for the weekend. Have you been to Kioni?'

'Years ago,' I said, and Alex shook her head.

'It is a very pleasant town. The harbour is popular for visiting boats, and my house is nearby. I would be honoured if you would be my guests. Come for lunch tomorrow and bring your swimming costumes with you. There is a small private cove below the house.'

I glanced at Alex and she nodded her assent. 'Thank you, Mr Kounidis. That would be lovely.'

'Excellent. I shall look forward to your company. Unfortunately I cannot join you now.' He turned to Irene and murmured something quietly to her.

'Thank you, for coming, Alkimos,' she said.

'Until tomorrow then.' As an afterthought he turned back to us as he left. 'When you come tomorrow stop in Frikes. There is a plaque on a rock there that you should read.'

When he'd gone, we returned to the house.

161

Irene was kept busy with the twenty or thirty people who had returned. Some of them approached me to shake my hand, often taking the opportunity to relate some anecdote or other concerning my father. It was clear that those who had known him had also held a genuine affection for him. The tales they told portrayed him as Kounidis had two days earlier — a fun-loving, gregarious man who though he may have enjoyed a drink had been well liked and respected.

Miros Theonas joined us briefly, and when I introduced him to Alex he regarded her with interest. 'I trust that you are enjoying your stay on Ithaca?'

'Yes, thank you. It's a lovely island.'

The two of them got talking and so I excused myself and went out onto the terrace where I had just seen Irene. She was standing alone gazing down to the harbour, and when she saw me she turned and smiled.

'Would you rather be alone?' I asked.

'No. I was just thinking about your father. I will miss him.' When I didn't say anything she looked towards Theonas and Alex who were standing close to the door. 'She is a lovely girl, Robert.'

'Yes, I suppose she is.'

'May I say something?'

'Of course.'

'I could not help but notice the way you looked at her last night. Is there anybody waiting for you at home in England?'

'No, but it isn't like that,' I said. Then I

thought of the night before, how I'd kissed her. 'Besides, I don't think she's ready to think about anything like that.'

'Ah, you mean because of the young man she was seeing, Dimitri?' I must have looked surprised that she knew, because she smiled knowingly. 'Ithaca is a small island. But she is not seeing him any more?'

'No.'

'I am sorry. It is none of my business. But sometimes I wish . . .'

'Wish what?'

'I only mean that I would like to see you happy. Your father used to feel the same way. Despite what happened between Johnny and I in recent years, we were very happy together before. I think he used to worry about you.'

'About me?' I said doubtfully.

'He was afraid that because of your own childhood you would not have children of your own. Perhaps he thought that if you did you might understand him a little better.'

'I don't know why he'd think that. But if I ever do have children, I know I'll make sure I'm always around for them.'

Irene smiled sadly. 'When your father was alive I always tried not to interfere between you. When you were younger I was afraid that if I did you would resent me.'

She was probably right. Part of the reason I'd always liked her was her neutrality.

'I sometimes wonder if I did the right thing. Perhaps if I had tried harder you would not have always been so angry with him.'

163

'Christ, Irene. What did he expect? He buggered off and left me when I was just a child.'

'I know.' She sighed heavily. 'And he always regretted it. There is only one thing that I can tell you about him, Robert. He loved you. He said it many times. You should try not to be angry with him any more. But not for him. He is gone now. Do this for yourself.'

Some people came out onto the terrace then, and Irene left me to go and speak to them. I went to join Theonas and Alex who were still talking, but I was preoccupied and I didn't join in their conversation much. Eventually Theonas saw that Irene was alone in the kitchen and he excused himself, but before he left I remembered the news clippings I'd found in my dad's study and I asked him about the murdered man.

'Ah, yes. The tourist.'

'Then you have identified him?'

'I am afraid not. But the taxi driver who took him from the ferry to the monastery at Kathara said that he spoke with a foreign accent.'

Alex looked perplexed by our conversation so I explained what we were talking about.

'But please do not be alarmed,' Theonas assured her. 'Ithaca is very safe. There has not been such a crime here in living memory. Once a man killed his neighbour in a dispute over some land, but nothing like this. Unfortunately even here we occasionally get unwelcome visitors. I think whoever did this terrible thing has long since left.'

'Then you don't believe the murderer was local?' I said.

'It is unlikely. The motive appears to have been robbery, since we found no wallet or personal belongings on the body. Also we know that on the day that this man visited the monastery, the only other vehicle to take the road to Kathara was a tourist bus. The passengers were from the inter-island ferry. Many of them were young people travelling among the islands. They come from all around the world. They stay a night here and there in cheap rooms or they sleep on the beach. Some are students and they are welcome. But there is also a bad element. They sell drugs and steal the belongings of others. We managed to trace some of the people on the bus, but most we could not. There is no way of knowing who they were.' Theonas shrugged resignedly. 'I am afraid it is likely that this crime will never be solved.'

'But if it was a robbery committed by some backpacker, why was my father interested?' I wondered.

'This I do not know,' Theonas answered. 'And now if you will excuse me . . . '

When he had left us I went outside with Alex. I was still bothered by the murdered tourist. I was also thinking about my conversation with Irene. 'I think I need to get away from here,' I said. 'Do you feel like having a drink somewhere?'

'All right. But do you mind if we don't go into Vathy?'

I wondered why until I realised that it was probably because she didn't want to run into Dimitri. I said that Irene had recommended a place, and we took the Jeep and drove up to the village of Perahori, which was nestled in a fold of the hill a couple of miles away. We went to a small taverna where the owner had built a concrete pad on stilts on the hillside across the road to serve as a terrace. Sitting in the shade of a grapevine it felt as if we were hovering in space. Far below us the harbour glittered in the afternoon sun and to the north, Mount Nirito towered over the landscape.

The wife of the owner brought drinks and snacks. 'If you want something more, you shout, yes?' She smiled and then retreated again.

'Look at that view,' Alex observed. 'Sometimes I find it hard to think of going back to London.'

'I wonder what would happen if you lived here though,' I mused. 'Would it all become so familiar that you wouldn't notice it any more? Would food like this stop tasting so good?' I gestured to the bread and the salad swimming in olive oil.

'I don't know,' she admitted reflectively.

'You would have found out if your boyfriend hadn't let you down.'

'Yes, I suppose I would.'

I could smell the scent of her perfume and once again I remembered what it had been like to kiss her — the stiffened, surprised response, and then just for a moment or two the soft yielding of her mouth.

'Can I ask you something?' I said. 'How do you feel about Dimitri now?'

'Now?'

'After last night.'

She thought for a moment and then said, 'I'm not sure what I feel.'

'But you feel something? Between us?'

'Yes.' She frowned, struggling to rationalise it. 'I thought at first it was because of the night you pulled me from the harbour. I think I wanted that to explain what I was feeling. I kept asking myself how it could be anything else. I was in love with Dimitri.'

'Was?'

She made a helpless, frustrated gesture. 'I don't know anything for certain any more. I never thought of myself as the kind to fall in and out of love.' She broke off, realising the implication of what she'd said. 'What about you anyway? You said there had been somebody in England recently.'

'There was. But it didn't work out between us.'

'Would it be nosy of me to ask why?'

I tried to think of a way to explain. 'Alicia, that was her name, did something that made me feel as if I couldn't trust her any longer. After that . . .'

'I'm sorry. And then you came here to find your father had died. Perhaps we're both a bit vulnerable at the moment.'

'I'm not sure it matters why things happen, does it?' I countered. 'Only that they do.'

'Perhaps,' she agreed.

For a time we sat quietly. It was a comfortable, easy silence. Eventually Alex began to talk about her grandmother. She said that she had been thinking about what Irene had told us, and about the decision Julia had made at the end.

'Do you think she was right to go with him?' she asked.

'I'm not sure. I think we need to hear what happened afterwards.'

'But if there was nothing else. If that was the end?'

'It couldn't be,' I insisted. 'There are always consequences. I don't see how you can judge an action without knowing what they are.'

'But put yourself in her place,' Alex insisted. 'She couldn't have known what the consequences might be. None of us ever can.'

'No, but we can make a judgement based on experience.'

'Then what would your judgement have been?'

I could see that she wasn't going to let it go, so I tried to explain how I saw it. 'It's basically a case of divided loyalties. Which is the greater? Her loyalty to her family and people? Or to her feelings towards the man in charge of an invading force?'

'You make him sound brutal. But that wasn't how Irene depicted him.'

'It's a fact that the Germans were invaders, however you sugar it.'

'All right,' she conceded. 'So what's your answer?'

'I think she was in an impossible position, and her own people should never have put her there without her agreement.'

'Then you agree with what she did?'

I wanted to say that I did, because I knew it was what Alex felt, but I couldn't. The best I

168

could manage was a compromise. 'I think we need to know the rest of the story. I'll tell you when we've heard what Kounidis has to say.'

She smiled, acknowledging that I was avoiding the issue, but for the moment she was willing to let me off the hook.

★　★　★

After I had dropped Alex back at her room later that evening and returned to the house, the guests had all gone. Irene, drained from an exhausting day said that she was going to bed. Left alone I tried to read for a while, but I couldn't concentrate. I was thinking about Alex. When I'd walked her to her door we'd kept a distance between us. I hadn't even kissed her on the cheek.

In the end I gave up on my book and went to my father's study. I stared at the picture of him in the newspaper article. I couldn't reconcile myself to the knowledge that he was dead and buried. In the end, too restless to sleep, I decided to drive into town and have a nightcap. The streets were busy, and as I drove around the square I knew I didn't want to sit alone nursing a beer so I drove on until I found myself heading out of town along the dark stretch of road that led to the marina.

It was quiet when I arrived. I parked the Jeep and made my way past the buildings to the water's edge. I wasn't sure what I was doing there. An enormous full moon hung over the harbour, its pale light casting deep wedges of shadow among the boats. I listened to the comforting slap of water against their hulls and the creak of ropes straining against cleats. It wasn't until I'd almost reached the *Swallow* that I saw a light in one of the windows. It grew dim and then bright again and, after a while, I decided that it must be somebody moving around with a torch.

As quietly as I could I climbed aboard at the stern. The wheelhouse was directly in front of me, the cabin-housing further forward where a short flight of steps led to the cabin door. From that angle I couldn't see the light any more. As I felt my way forward something slid beneath my hand and before I could catch it, it clattered to the deck. I froze, certain that whoever was on board must have heard.

Seconds dragged by into one minute, and then two, and when still nothing happened I began to breathe again and my heart slowly ceased its heavy thumping. I started cautiously forward again to the cabin door. It was open a crack. I pushed it wider to reveal complete darkness within. There was no sound, no movement, and I wondered if I'd been mistaken about the light. Perhaps it had come from somewhere on the harbour and I'd been fooled when it reflected through the window. I stepped inside and in that instant the door was suddenly slammed into my face. As I staggered backwards, a figure charged towards me and the impact of a shoulder drove me down against the steps. Something hard slammed into my spine and I gasped in pain, but even as my attacker leapt over me somehow I had the presence to grab for a leg. A man's voice cursed in a low breath, then with a violent kick he jerked himself free and clattered up the steps.

I scrabbled to my knees and went after him, but he'd anticipated me. Too late I saw a shape leap from the dark and a pair of powerful arms locked around my waist and propelled me towards the side of the boat. Realising that I was about to be driven over the side I flung my hand out and my fingers closed around a winch handle. I hung on tight, bringing us both up short with a wrench which I felt all the way up into my shoulder. My attacker grunted in surprise and, seizing the momentary advantage, I brought my knee up hard. I felt it connect and heard a muffled exclamation, but as I was released I lost my footing and thumped my head against the rail. For a few brief moments I was too stunned to move.

It was long enough. The man leapt to the wharf and by the time I was on my feet I was twenty feet behind. I hit the ground as the other man reached the cover of the shadows between the buildings. I followed blindly into the pitch darkness and before I'd gone more than a few steps I knew I'd made a mistake. I glimpsed a movement near my feet and, though instinctively I leapt to one side, something hard whacked into my shins and swept my legs from beneath me. As I fell I rolled to avoid a vicious kick aimed at my head and then, curling into a foetal position, I wrapped my arms around my skull for protection and waited for a rain of blows.

Seconds passed but nothing happened. Warily

I struggled to my knees as somewhere close by a car started. It accelerated hard, the engine note changing with the gears, and by the time I reached the road it was a hundred yards away, the headlights illuminating the trees before it vanished around a bend. Gradually the sound of the engine faded.

When I reached the *Swallow* again I lowered myself into a chair by the chart table. My shins were bleeding and the right one, which had taken the force of the blow, was already turning a nice shade of green. By the light of a battery-operated lantern I searched the galley and found a bottle of Scotch and a glass in a cupboard. I poured a stiff measure and looked around. The cabin was a mess. Cupboards had been opened and the contents taken out, though nothing was broken and, in fact, on closer examination everything had been arranged tidily. A considerate sort of thief I thought wryly. I noticed that the radio remained in its place, as did a CD player and the electronic navigation aids, which struck me as odd. I wondered why the thief hadn't taken them first, since they were the most visible items of any value.

The charts I'd used the day before lay where I'd left them on the table and next to them was one of the journals I'd been looking at. I saw the gap on the shelf where it came from and suddenly I was certain that I'd put it back there. It was open at the final page, dated September the year before. A typical entry describing a fruitless, and it appeared final, dive to search for the wreck of the *Antounnetta*.

When I went back on deck the air was soft and warm, absolutely still. By the light of the moon the hills around the harbour were silhouetted against the sky. The landscape was unfamiliar, the water black as oil. I tried to convince myself that I had disturbed some opportune thief but I felt uneasy, adrift in an alien environment.

PART TWO

10

I was up early in the morning. I hadn't slept much with everything that had been spinning around in my head. When Irene came down I was sitting on the terrace applying some ointment I'd found in her cupboard. When she saw my shins she was horrified. Overnight they had turned the colour of an aubergine.

'Robert, what happened? Did you have an accident?'

'Not exactly.' I told her about my late-night trip to the marina and about the intruder I'd disturbed on the *Swallow*.

'He did this to you? Do you need to see a doctor?'

'Actually I think it looks worse than it is. Nothing's broken.' I straightened up and winced from a sharp pain in my ribs.

'Are you sure?' Irene questioned doubtfully.

'I'm OK. I took a bit of a knock when I fell down.'

'I will phone Miros at once. We must report what happened. Did you see the man who did this?'

'It was too dark.' I hobbled after her as she went to the phone.

'You may not believe it, Robert, but there was a time when such things would never happen on Ithaca. That somebody should do this on the day of your father's funeral, it

177

would have been unthinkable once.'

'If it's any consolation I don't think anything was taken.'

'I cannot imagine what this person hoped to find. There is nothing worth stealing on the boat. Certainly nothing that is worth this.' She dialled a number and as I limped towards the kitchen for some juice I heard her speaking urgently on the phone. When I returned she told me that Theonas had asked that I go to the police station to make a report.

I was still thinking about what she'd said before. 'So Dad never kept anything valuable on the boat?'

'No. Can you get down the stairs?'

'I think I can manage.'

'Of course there is the radio and some other equipment.'

'That hadn't been touched. You're sure there was nothing else? Something somebody might have known about? Money maybe?'

'I am certain. Perhaps a few euros. Why do you ask?'

I described what I'd found. The cupboards all open and the contents taken out, but in an orderly, methodical fashion rather than simply rifled through. 'Whoever it was had been there for a while before I arrived. If it was just some opportunist thief, why didn't he grab the most obvious things first? Like the radio?'

Something flickered in Irene's expression. It came and went in a split second but my question had sparked some thought in her. 'I do not know.' She turned away from me and went towards the door. 'We should go now, Robert. Miros is expecting us.'

I went after her but when we reached the car I said, 'You know something, don't you?'

'What do you mean?' She tried to appear as if she really didn't know what I was talking about.

'I mean that don't you think it's time you told me what's going on?'

She regarded me blankly, but I held her look. 'I do not understand,' she said.

'Ever since I arrived I've had the sense that there's something you haven't told me. When you blamed yourself for Dad's death, at first I thought it was guilt because you'd left him for Theonas. But it's more than that isn't it? The other day when you saw the newspaper clipping about the murdered tourist, that meant something to you. And now this.'

She resisted a moment longer but then she sighed heavily. 'Yes, you are right. I kept something from you. But I did so because I loved your father, and because I have tried to believe that I was wrong.'

'Wrong about what?'

'Come and sit down, and I will tell you.' She sat on the steps and I went over and joined her.

'First, tell me this, Irene, do you believe Dad's death was an accident?'

'I do not know what I believe.'

'When he said that somebody tried to kill him, you think he was serious don't you? It wasn't his medication or some ploy to get you back.'

She looked surprised at my second suggestion. 'Of course not. Your father knew that I still loved

179

him. But yes, now I think he was serious. I tried not to believe it. But I cannot pretend any longer.'

'Why?'

'Because of something that happened a year ago. It was before I left Johnny. Things were bad between us, but I had not yet reached the point where I could not take any more.' She smiled, but it was a crooked, ironic smile. 'It is strange how fate works. It was because of what happened that I went to see Miros Theonas. He was sympathetic. I told him more than I had intended and he listened . . . I never imagined what would happen. We had known each other for many years, but only as friends.'

I begrudged Theonas his relationship with Irene. It seemed to me that he had taken advantage of the situation in a way which was unethical in the circumstances. Perhaps he'd long harboured romantic feelings toward her and suddenly he had found his opportunity.

'What was it that you went to see him about?'

'A man approached your father. He was a Frenchman I think. He was visiting the islands. A wealthy collector of antiquities. He asked Johnny to sell him some of the pieces in the museum.'

'But Dad didn't own them did he?'

'No. They are owned by the Greek government. It is illegal to transport antiquities out of the country. In the past so much of this country's history has been stolen by foreigners and placed in museums in other countries.'

'Like the Elgin Marbles?' I said. 'I've read that

180

the Greek government is campaigning to get the frieze back from the British Museum.'

'Yes. Johnny was approached many times over the years. Of course he always refused such offers.'

'But not this time, is that what you're saying?'

'No, of course he did refuse. But not at first. To begin with he asked me why he should not sell some of his collection. Though it did not legally belong to him, he had discovered everything in the museum himself. He said that at least he would have something to show for all of the years he had spent digging in the stony ground of Ithaca. Of course he did not really mean it. He was drunk.'

'But you must have wondered,' I said, guessing at the truth. 'That's why you went to Theonas.'

'Perhaps,' she admitted.

'So what happened?'

'Nothing. By the time I spoke to Miros, the French collector had left. But Johnny mentioned the subject once or twice afterwards. It was always when he had been drinking of course. I did not take him seriously, but one day I read an article in a magazine about something that had happened in Athens. A man had become involved with a gang who were planning to smuggle some antiquities out of the country. He was the curator of a museum. He let them into the building at night but something went wrong with the plan and he was killed. I showed it to Johnny.'

'To warn him?'

'Yes.'

'And now you think he may not have listened. Is that it?'

'It is possible,' she confessed, though it was clear she didn't want to believe it. 'After Johnny told me he thought somebody had tried to kill him I was worried about the way he was behaving. I remembered this French collector and I asked him if he had become involved in something illegal. He denied it. But I was never sure.'

'And now?'

'When you found the newspaper cutting about the murdered tourist and I saw the date I remembered it was the same day that Johnny came home from the hospital.'

'You think there's a connection?' It made sense. If he was somehow involved with the murdered man it explained why he kept the clipping and why he'd suddenly insisted on leaving hospital. It also explained why he hadn't told Irene the truth.

'Perhaps.'

'And you think the person I disturbed on the boat last night could have been involved too?'

'It is only a possibility,' she insisted.

'But if he wasn't simply an opportunist thief, it makes sense, doesn't it? He was looking for something specific,' I reasoned.

Irene didn't answer. Instead she looked sadly out across the harbour, and I knew this was exactly what she thought, or perhaps feared, might be true.

Far below us the water was changing from dark green to blue as the sun rose higher above the hills. The sails of a yacht flashed white as it slid out to sea looking like a pretty toy. On the Perahori road a truck laden with rocks for repairing the walls in the terraced olive groves chugged steadily upwards. Everything appeared normal and yet the tranquillity was deceptive. I understood why Irene hadn't said anything until now. It wasn't simply that what she suspected my dad of doing was illegal, but rather that she hadn't wanted to face the possibility that the man she had loved for so long had in the end betrayed the people of the island he had made his home. Including her.

The question was, if all this were true, what had my father planned to sell that somebody had thought was worth killing for?

★   ★   ★

On the way into town we discussed what we would say to Theonas. Now that Irene's suspicions were out in the open she was reluctant to accept that she may have been right.

'I still cannot believe Johnny would do this,' she said, though she sounded as if she was trying to convince herself more than me.

'Let's see what Theonas has to say.'

The police station in Vathy was a squat, single-storey building shielded from the road by a high wall, the entrance guarded by wrought-iron gates that, judging from the overgrown weeds, were permanently open. Inside, Irene spoke to a bored-looking policeman who fetched Theonas. He greeted Irene warmly and took us

183

to his office at the rear of the building.

I went over what had happened on the boat and then reminded him of the French collector that Irene had spoken to him about the previous year. He glanced at her and I knew immediately that he had guessed all along why she was concerned about my father's death.

'You believe that your father was involved in illegal smuggling, Mr French?' he said.

'From what Irene says it fits.'

'And the attack on you last night, this is connected to your father's activities?'

'Nothing was taken. I think whoever was on the boat was looking for something.'

'And what do you think that might be?'

I detected a faint note of polite scepticism in Theonas's questions though I wasn't sure why. 'I have no idea,' I said. 'But on the way here something did occur to me. You're aware that my dad spent part of every summer looking for the wreck of the *Antounnetta*?'

'Yes, of course.'

'He recorded it all in a set of journals, one for each year. I was looking at them when I was on the boat the other day. Last night I found one open on the chart table, but I know I put them all back on the shelf.'

Theonas looked puzzled, and so did Irene for that matter. 'I think whoever attacked me was reading it,' I explained. 'It was open to the last entry he made, dated last year. He wrote that he hadn't found anything. But that doesn't fit with what he said in the bar the

184

night of his heart attack.'

'Johnny said that he had found the *Panaghia*,' Irene said. 'Is that what you mean?'

'Yes. And if he had found the *Panaghia* that means he must have found the *Antounnetta*.'

'Your father had been drinking heavily that night, Mr French. It was not the first time that he had talked of returning the *Panaghia*. Many times over the years he claimed that he was close to finding the wreck. And if it was true, why did he not write it in his journal?' Theonas reasoned.

'Maybe he did. What if there's another journal? The most recent one on the boat is for last year.'

'And you are suggesting that the person you disturbed was looking for this journal?'

'He was looking for something. I know the *Panaghia* isn't valuable, but the Germans had a history of looting valuables and works of art during the war. Isn't that how the artefacts which Dracoulis found ended up in Switzerland? So it's reasonable enough to assume there might have been something else on the *Antounnetta* other than a religious statue.'

Theonas regarded me impassively while he considered this, then he said, 'There is no evidence to support this theory, Mr French. It is pure conjecture.'

I appealed to Irene. 'Did he mention the *Antounnetta* to you after you first saw him in hospital?'

She thought hard but then shook her head. 'No. I am certain of it.'

'All right. It's conjecture, but what about the

185

tourist who was killed?' I said to Theonas. 'Why did Dad keep the news clipping I found?'

'Murder is almost unheard of on Ithaca. Perhaps your father was simply interested in the case because of this.'

'And maybe Dad knew who he was. Didn't you say yourself the taxi driver said he spoke with a foreign accent? He might have been a collector like the Frenchman who was here last year.'

'Again, Mr French, this is mere speculation.'

It dawned on me that no matter what I said Theonas would never be convinced. 'You don't want to take this seriously do you?'

'On the contrary, I can assure you that I take the matter very seriously,' he countered stiffly.

'What Miros says is true, Robert. There is no evidence for any of this,' Irene said.

'There's no smoking gun if that's what you mean. But there's at least enough to investigate. I suppose it wouldn't look good though would it? The captain of the police having an affair with the wife of a murdered antiquities smuggler.'

I had gone too far. Irene was stunned into silence while Theonas regarded me with a cold stare. 'There is no evidence whatsoever to indicate that your father's death was anything other than an accident,' he said. 'Nor that he was intending to smuggle anything. In fact I have never believed that he was capable of such a thing, as I told Irene when she came to me last year.'

I saw from her expression that what he said was true. Theonas rose from behind his desk. 'Of

186

course I do not deny that my relationship with Irene placed me in a difficult position with regard to your father. However, I always regarded him with the greatest respect. It is for this reason more than any other that I find it difficult to accept your theory.' He fixed me with a withering look. 'I am not so ready as you are, it would seem, to accuse a man who is unable to defend himself.'

'What the hell does that mean?'

'It is no secret that you did not get on with your father. Your theory relies on the assumption that he was engaged in illegal activities. Perhaps you wish to see wrongdoing where in fact there was none.'

'Are you serious?' I said. 'You think I'm making it all up because I have a grudge against my father?'

Theonas said nothing, which was answer enough.

'What about Irene?' I said, turning towards her. 'You've always suspected something like this.'

Irene regarded us both uncertainly, unwilling to commit. It occurred to me that Irene's suspicions had always been at war with her desire to continue to believe in my father.

Theonas rose and opened the door to signal that the meeting was over. I got to my feet angrily, but Irene hesitated and asked me to go ahead. I went outside to wait and when she emerged a few minutes later she wore a troubled expression.

'You should not have accused Miros,' she said.

187

'He is a good man.'

'Good men make mistakes like everybody else,' I pointed out.

'Yes,' she agreed, and regarded me in a way that seemed to imply that I should take note of my own words.

*   *   *

When we arrived back at the house I told Irene that I was going to go with Alex to visit Alkimos Kounidis. I thought that if my father's death had anything to do with the *Antounnetta* then Kounidis would be a good person to talk to anyway, and there was obviously no point expecting Theonas to do anything further.

Irene drew me a map to show me how to find his house and when I picked Alex up I explained everything that had happened.

'What will you do?' she asked when I had finished.

'Talk to Kounidis. Find out if he knows whether the *Antounnetta* could have been carrying something that somebody was prepared to kill for. After that I'm not sure. Try to find the missing journal I suppose.'

'Then you don't think the man who attacked you found it?'

'No. I would've noticed if he was carrying anything and I know he searched the boat pretty thoroughly. But just to make sure I want to take another look.'

I drove to the marina and pulled up near the *Swallow*. Nothing had been disturbed since the night before. Together we went over the entire boat from one end to the other, but after a couple of hours I was convinced the journal wasn't there.

After we left, we drove north to Stavros and from there took the road to the eastern coast across a broad valley where the land was fertile and more cultivated than in other parts of the island. We passed vegetable patches and fruit orchards with lemons and oranges ripening on the trees. A sign pointed to Platrithias and in the distance a church tower crowned a low hill. I remembered going there as a boy, to a site my father had excavated where graves and the ruins of buildings dating from the Mycenaean period had been discovered. It was one of the possible locations for Aphrodite's Temple, though nothing had ever been found.

When we reached Frikes I pulled over. It was a fishing village built around a small harbour. A cluster of restaurants and tavernas huddled close to the waterfront sharing space with a few shops selling gifts for the tourists. The bay was flanked by hills and on the southern side, just beyond the village perhaps sixty or seventy feet above the road, stood a ruined fort made of stone. At the foot of the cliff directly beneath it was the plaque Kounidis had told us about.

FROM THIS ROCK ON 13/9/1944 GUERRILLAS OF *ELAS-ELAN* ATTACKED WITH SELF-SACRIFICE AGAINST THE NAZI VESSEL *ANTOUNNETTA*, THUS WRITING ANOTHER PAGE OF GLORY

DURING THE STRUGGLE OF OUR NATIONAL RESISTANCE AGAINST FASCISM.

NEVER FORGET: EVERY STEP OF OUR LAND IS A HEROIC MONUMENT. EVERY FATHOM OF SEA, THOUSANDS OF DROPS OF BLOOD!!!

The rock above the plaque was scarred with pockmarks and indentations, the visible effects of bullets perhaps. It was difficult to imagine the harbour as the scene of a battle. Frikes was picture-perfect, a pretty village nestled in the embrace of green hills. The tables and awnings of the tavernas clustered invitingly along the wharf beside deep clear water where a few brilliant white yachts were moored next to gaily-painted fishing boats. A line of ancient olive trees provided welcome shade. And yet sixty-odd years earlier the tranquillity must have suddenly erupted with the flash of gunfire and the blossoming heat of explosions, the air heavy with cordite and the screams of the dying.

Beyond Frikes, the road to Kioni where Kounidis lived wound past a series of tiny, picturesque coves fringed with white pebble beaches. Eventually it climbed a steep hill and the views broadened to wide, open vistas of the sea and the islands in the distance. Close to the shore the water was aquamarine and crystal clear, the seabed clearly visible even from a great height, but further out the blues deepened to navy, flecked with splashes of white where the surface was whipped by the breeze.

190

Below us was the town of Kioni; its small deep harbour hemmed in by hillsides so steep that no roads connected the houses which clung to them, only a series of steps and narrow walkways. The buildings were painted in muted yellows, pinks and blues. The occasional one painted simply white reflected an almost painful glare from the bright sun. Vivid purple bougainvillaea erupted from the edges of walls and terraces competing with splashes of scarlet geraniums like flecks of paint from a carelessly wielded brush.

Following Irene's map I took the road which traversed the ridge above the town before it dropped away to run parallel to the cliff. Several imposing properties, screened from view by belts of trees, had been built where they commanded unobstructed views over the sea. The house where Kounidis lived was hidden behind a dark row of cypresses. Wrought-iron gates and a high wall protected the entrance. When I announced our arrival into an intercom set in the wall, the gates swung smoothly open and, as I drove towards the house, the cypresses gave way to a manicured emerald lawn, a rarity on Ithaca. I could only guess at the cost of bringing in the water by tanker to maintain it.

The house itself was large and square, built over three floors, painted white with a terracotta roof and dark-green window shutters. It was striking as much because of the simplicity of its design as because of its proportions. We were met at the door by the man who had driven Kounidis's car.

'This way please,' he said in heavily accented English and led us across a hallway tiled in a pattern of fired reds and earth browns, past open doors that offered glimpses of tastefully and expensively furnished rooms. At the back of the house, folding doors opened onto a wide shaded terrace and steps led down to a lawn that ended at the edge of the cliff. For a moment we were transfixed by the view. Sea and sky merged in hazy blues on the horizon, one bleeding into the other.

'It is beautiful is it not?' a voice said, and we turned to find Alkimos Kounidis rising from a seat where he had been reading a book. '*Kalimera*, Alex.' He shook her hand, holding on to it for a moment as he gazed at her, wearing the same slight, almost bemused smile he had the day before. 'Forgive me. Every time I see you I think of your grandmother.' He gestured towards some chairs. 'Please, sit down. Would you like something to drink? You must be thirsty after your drive. The sun here is very hot this time of year.'

As he spoke, a middle-aged woman dressed in black appeared carrying a jug of iced juice and some glasses, which she set down on the table.

Kounidis murmured something to her then introduced us. 'This is Eleni, my housekeeper. She takes excellent care of me.'

The woman smiled and shook our hands.

'You had no trouble finding the house, I hope,' Kounidis said as Eleni left us.

'No. Irene gave me a map,' I said.

'You certainly live in a lovely house, Mr Kounidis,' Alex said.

'Thank you, Alex. Later I will show you around if you would like. But please, you are both my guests. Call me Alkimos.'

Alex smiled, obviously charmed by Kounidis. He turned to me and his manner became grave. He told me that Irene had already phoned and so he knew of the recent events.

'I must say that I find it impossible to believe that your father was involved with anything illegal.'

'He never said anything to you?' I asked.

'For the past year I did not see him very often,' Kounidis said regretfully. 'He did not wish to see his old friends. As you know he became increasingly depressed. Of course I tried to offer support, many people did, but it was difficult. After Irene left him, he became worse.'

'You mean he was drinking more.'

'That is part of it, yes.'

'Do you have any idea what he was doing before his heart attack?' I asked. 'Could he have been looking for the *Antounnetta*?'

'As I said, I am afraid I had not seen your father for some time. In other years he did not begin looking for the wreck until May or June, when the weather is warm. Before that he would be at the museum. It was closed for the winter, but usually he would be there cataloguing the finds from his digs the previous summer. But he had not worked on an excavation for two years. From what I heard, Johnny spent most of his days in the bars in Vathy.'

193

'Supposing that for some reason he started looking for the wreck early this year. And this time he found it. What do you think could have been on it?'

Kounidis shook his head. 'That I am afraid I do not know.'

Just then Eleni returned and she and Kounidis spoke briefly. She smiled and left us again.

'I have asked Eleni to bring us some lunch. You have not eaten yet?' We said that we hadn't. 'Good. Then we will eat and later I will tell you what you wish to know about your grandmother, Alex. But first, perhaps you would like to see some of the house.'

'Thank you, yes,' Alex said. 'It is beautiful.'

Kounidis inclined his head in acknowledgement. 'Of course it is much too big for one old man.'

'Don't you have any family, Alkimos?'

'Unfortunately no,' he said with a note of regret. 'I have many relatives on the island, of course, but no immediate family of my own. Come, let me show you both something.'

He led the way along the terrace to the southern corner of the house where he pointed through the trees to some cottages further down the hillside reached by a dusty unpaved track. Beyond them the land sloped toward the sea, dotted with olive trees and some rough cultivated land. At the bottom was a rocky cove where several wooden boats had been hauled up out of the water and fishing nets had been draped over the rocks to dry.

'I was born in one of those cottages,' Kounidis

told us. 'I grew up helping my father to fish and grow vegetables to feed our family. A long way from there, to all of this, eh?' He chuckled and gestured to his surroundings. 'And yet not so far. I bought this land many years ago so that in my retirement I could be reminded of where I came from.'

'How long have you lived here?' I asked.

'I built this house thirty years ago to use as a summer home, but I did not move back to Ithaca permanently until I retired.'

As we went back along the terrace I looked through a window and saw a room full of children's toys.

'For when the children of my relatives come to visit,' Kounidis explained. 'I was married once, a long time ago, but we never had children of our own. When I was a young man I worked very hard. Long hours every day. I was consumed with my business. There was no time for anything else.'

For a moment he seemed lost in some inner reflection, and then he smiled and led us into the house. Our tour took half an hour, but I trailed behind for most of it while Kounidis and Alex went ahead. I got the impression that he liked her. She asked questions about the furnishings and the paintings on the walls, and he seemed happy to answer her. Now and then he would touch her elbow as they paused to admire something, or as he guided her through a door. His manner was courtly, old-fashioned even, and he constantly made subtle flattering remarks to Alex at which she laughed modestly though I could tell she was pleased.

When we returned to the terrace we ate lunch at a table on the northern side of the house. Cold white wine made from local grapes was served in chilled earthenware jugs, along with fresh warm bread and bowls of salads made from fat juicy olives, chopped tomatoes, cucumber, onion and feta cheese sprinkled with thyme. Later Eleni brought out a lamb pie and a plate of grilled octopus. As we ate, Kounidis talked about the writings of Homer about which he appeared to be quite knowledgeable. He was interesting to listen to, even for me. He knew great sections of both the *Iliad* and the *Odyssey* by heart, and even recited parts to us in classical Greek. Though I didn't understand a word of it I couldn't deny that there was a certain lyrical beauty to the sound of the passages, spoken in the language in which they had originally been written.

After lunch he apologised self-deprecatingly for having bored us, which we protested wasn't true. 'This evening,' he said, looking at Alex, 'I will tell you what I can about your grandmother. But for now I must rest.'

He told us that there was a path down to a small private beach if we felt like a swim.

'Please treat my home as your own,' he said. 'Eleni has made up rooms for you both. She will show you where they are.'

After he'd gone Eleni appeared to clear the table and when she returned she showed us upstairs. Our rooms were next door to one another on the top floor of the house at the back.

Like Alex's, mine had two large windows which, when the shutters were opened, revealed a view across the sea. I thanked Eleni, who murmured some quiet acknowledgement in Greek and, when she had gone, I went to knock on Alex's door.

'Do you feel like that swim?' I asked.

'Give me five minutes. I'll meet you downstairs.'

I went to my room to change and fetch a towel and was waiting on the terrace when Alex came down. The path Kounidis had mentioned was steep, with steps carved into the rock leading down to the cove below. The water was deep and cool, fringed by a strip of pale stony beach. We swam out to the entrance and explored the rocks before returning to the beach to dry off in the sun.

'What do you make of Alkimos?' Alex asked, hugging her knees, her wet hair dripping rivulets of water. I tried not to watch their progress across her thighs.

'He seems a bit lonely I suppose.'

'Yes, that's what I thought. He's very sweet. I think it's a shame that he lives here all alone. Except for Eleni, of course. And the man who let us in. Do you think that's her husband?'

'Perhaps. He drives for Kounidis.'

'That room with all the children's toys is a bit sad isn't it? I wonder what happened to his wife?'

'I get the impression he devoted too much time to his work. Maybe there wasn't enough left over for a wife.'

She lay down and closed her eyes. I watched

her breathe, the rise and fall of her breasts, the hollow of her stomach.

Late in the afternoon we went back to the house to rest for a while. I lay down on my bed to read, but there was too much going on in my mind. Thoughts of my father and of Alex kept insinuating themselves. In the end the heat made me drowsy and I fell into a light sleep.

When I woke, twilight was approaching, the sky darkening. I took a shower and changed, then knocked on Alex's door. When she opened it she had a towel wrapped around her and her hair was wet.

'I'll meet you downstairs,' she said.

I left her to get ready and went down to the terrace. Though there were faint sounds of activity from somewhere in the house there was nobody around, so I went back inside to the library where I spent half an hour browsing the shelves. Many of the volumes were in French and other European languages, including English. I recognised some of the English and American authors; Greene, Hemingway and Conrad, but most of the books were volumes on psychology, archaeology and history, both modern and ancient. Some were old texts, but the majority were pristine. First editions.

Near the library I found a room we'd passed earlier on our tour with Kounidis. The door had been closed then and he hadn't remarked on it. This time I tried the handle out of curiosity, but it was locked. From its position I guessed that it faced out onto the northern end of the terrace, but when I went outside the windows to the room were shuttered.

I was admiring the view over the sea as the light faded, when Kounidis appeared.

'Good evening, Robert,' he said. 'Did you have a pleasant afternoon?'

'Very. Thank you.' I told him that we had been for a swim. 'Alex is quite taken with your house. With everything actually.' I smiled, gently teasing Kounidis, who smiled in return.

'I have always appreciated beauty, Robert.' He gestured towards the chairs where we had sat that afternoon. 'Please.'

For a little while we were content to sit quietly. The light was almost gone, the otherworldly purple and pink fading to darkness. The breeze had dropped and the temperature was pleasantly warm. Eleni appeared carrying a tray with some glasses, a bottle of ouzo and a jug of cold water. She set them down and returned moments later with a variety of *opektika* dishes. *Dolmades* and *saganaki*, bread and an aubergine dip. Footsteps approached from within the house and Alex joined us. She looked quite stunning, dressed in a simple dark-blue skirt and top. She paused in the doorway self-consciously as we stared at her.

'Forgive us, Alex,' Kounidis said. 'We are, I believe, both of us made quite speechless by such beauty. Please, sit down.' He drew out a chair for her.

'Thank you.'

'Do you like ouzo?' Kounidis asked us both.

'I have to admit it's a taste I haven't fully

'acquired yet,' I said, and Alex admitted that she hadn't tried it.

'Then you must try this. It is a very good brand.' Kounidis poured some out for both of us and raised his glass. '*Stin-iyassas*.'

The ouzo did taste a little better than others I had tried, but I still found the strong flavour of aniseed disconcerting. We chatted for a while. Kounidis asked Alex about her family and her life in London. He seemed quite taken with her, even mildly flirtatious in an old-fashioned and courteous way. He refilled our glasses. I could feel the alcohol going to my head and there was a distinct shine to Alex's eyes. Eventually Kounidis asked Alex about her grandmother.

'Did she ever marry in England?'

'No. There was only ever her and my mother.'

'Your grandmother had a brother who also went to live in England.'

'Kostas, yes. His family run a restaurant in North London. But Nana and Kostas never saw each other. I didn't even know about the rest of the family until after she died.'

'Yes, I am afraid that I am not surprised,' Kounidis said.

Eleni appeared to tell us that dinner was ready. We ate on the terrace again. Eleni had prepared chicken cooked with herbs, potatoes and white wine. Kounidis directed the conversation as he had at lunch. He steered away from the subject of Alex's grandmother, instead relating stories from his childhood when his time had been taken up with fishing and working on the family land. He portrayed a life of work with virtually no luxuries, but he made it seem like a happy, simpler time in many ways. The land, the sea, the sun, the smell of pine and wild sage and days spent fishing when the nets would be hauled into the boat full.

As I listened I couldn't help wondering how accurate his depiction was, given that in the end he had been lured away to the mainland, driven by what must have been a powerful urge to succeed. At some stage a lamp was lit, attracting insects which flickered around the flame until Eleni returned with a candle. The smoke it emitted had a curious, powerful aroma which acted as a repellent. The glow from the lamp enveloped us in a cocoon of yellow light beyond which the darkness closed in. As the stars appeared, I felt a strange sensation which was probably heightened by the amount of wine and ouzo I'd consumed. Being high up and so close to the cliff edge created the illusion that we were no longer earth-bound but were instead drifting through space.

When the remains of dinner had been cleared away, Kounidis began to tell us the rest of the story of what had happened during the war.

'But before I take up where Irene left off, I must tell you about other events on Kephalonia, because they are important if you are to understand what happened here,' he said.

The way he pronounced English words and his slightly convoluted phrasing lent an almost poetic quality to his narrative, somehow making the words themselves unobtrusive, facilitating the conjuring of images. The lamp had been

201

turned down until it was barely a dim glow which cast Kounidis in dark silhouette. Beyond the terrace, figures seemed to be moving in the darkness, the past coming to life . . .

11

The guerrillas on Kephalonia were led by a communist named Metkas. They regularly harassed the Germans by sabotaging equipment and reporting intelligence to the Allies. But as the war in Europe turned and the Allies began to advance on all fronts, Metkas began openly to attack the German occupiers. In response, an SS officer named *Standartenführer* Manfred Bergen was placed in charge of the garrisons on Kephalonia and the surrounding islands, and he quickly decreed that any attack against German forces would be met with swift reprisals against the civilian population.

Metkas was aware of this decree as he sat with a group of men around a wooden table in a cottage outside the small town of Vaisemata. The room was dimly lit by only a few candles which had burned low, dripping pools of solidifying wax onto the rough pine boards of the table. The flames flickered in a thin, cold breeze which came through a gap in the door, the light reflected in the eyes of the half-dozen men. They were all unshaven and dark, several days of beard growth on their faces. Their features were half hidden in dense shadows, their expressions grimly impassive as they listened to Metkas speak. He jabbed at a map, pointing to a village on Mount Enos. The Germans had built a transmitting station nearby, a strategically important site which was guarded by a permanent garrison of soldiers.

'The attack will take place here,' Metkas said. 'From above.' His voice was rough-edged, his thick fingers ingrained with what appeared to be dirt but was in fact the stain of ink. Before the war he had been a teacher. He had also been a believer in Communism and a hater of Fascism. When the Italians had invaded Greece he had been teaching in a school in Lefkada. He had seen at once that his time had come. Far from being a disaster for his country, the war, he had believed, would prove in the end to be the force that would shake his countrymen from their lethargy. Metkas immediately joined a Resistance group, the National Liberation Front, whose aim was first to eject the invaders from their country, but also and even more importantly to position themselves for the aftermath when a communist government would be installed in Athens.

The first operation Metkas had taken part in was an attack on Italian troops stationed in Lefkada. The surprised soldiers had been quickly overwhelmed. The officer in charge of them had surrendered after several of his men had been killed and the rest surrounded. It was Metkas who had taken the officer's automatic pistol before leading him outside to a wall in the courtyard where he had shot the man once in the forehead. Metkas could still remember his expression of horrified disbelief. After that, it had only been a matter of time before he was sent to Kephalonia to organise resistance there before the monarchist factors gained the upper hand.

Now Metkas looked around the table at the men he had fought alongside these past few years. They had lived on the move, in the pine forests of the hills and mountains, evading first the Italians and then the Germans, descending to the ports on the coast to gather intelligence and sabotage supplies and sometimes to attack German soldiers. Of the five others present he knew he could count on two who were, like him, dedicated communists. Three others who sat together on one side of the table were right-wing monarchist sympathisers.

One of them, Aris Gratsos, met his eye. Metkas and Aris had known each other the longest. They had fought alongside one another, each watching the other's back. Aris, like the other men, led his own small group. He was older than Metkas, perhaps by ten years, in his fifties, a heavy-set, determined man with a scar on his forehead where a piece of grenade shrapnel had almost killed him. It was Metkas who had pulled the groups together, persuading each leader that they must work in concert, and it was Aris who had seen the logic of this argument and had persuaded the other monarchists to join with them. One day, Metkas knew he would have to kill Aris. There was a degree of regret inherent in this knowledge, but personal feelings were of no consequence if Greece was to become a true communist country after the war. Inevitably there would be a power struggle in the vacuum the Germans would leave in their wake and men like Aris must be eliminated before they became a threat. It was simply a matter of choosing the right time.

For now, Metkas turned his attention back to the map. First they had to defeat the Germans.

'While Kimon and his men attack the transmitter station the rest of us will launch an attack here, in Sami,' Metkas went on. 'Once the Germans realise the transmitter is under fire they will send men from Sami to help. Then Aris and I will attack what is left of the garrison while the rest of you fire on the ships in the harbour.'

He paused and looked around to gauge the reaction of the others. It was a bold plan. Kimon would draw the Germans away from protecting the port, leaving the gunboat and the two supply vessels, which Allied intelligence had informed them were *en route* there, under-defended. The supply ships, loaded with vital weapons and ammunition needed by the forces on the mainland, would anchor in Sami overnight.

Nobody spoke. They were all aware that there would be severe consequences for an attack such as this. The SS officer, Bergen, had a reputation for being merciless, and every man present at the table knew that regardless of the outcome of the plan Metkas was proposing, the civilian population on the island would pay a heavy toll. Eventually Metkas asked them each in turn whether they would commit their men and support the operation. One by one they nodded their assent. An hour later they slipped away, one after the other into the darkness.

★ ★ ★

The attack took place three nights later. As planned Kimon's group opened fire on the transmitter station with grenades and small arms fire. Flashes of light could be seen high on the summit of the mountain, and the distant crack of shots was heard on the coast. The Germans were pinned down under heavy fire, but Kimon held his men back to give the Germans time to summon help, and, from their position above the road outside Sami, Aris and Metkas watched as a convoy of trucks carrying troops sped along the road out of the town.

'We wait an hour,' Metkas said. Aris looked him in the eye as if he were about to say something, but in the end he merely nodded before melting away into the darkness to rejoin his men. Metkas pondered that look, wondering what it had signified, but he quickly forgot about it as the time drew near to launch the assault.

The Germans had made their headquarters in the town hall on the waterfront. The building was normally well defended, but only a handful of soldiers had been left behind after the others had driven away. Metkas and Aris led their men in the attack from opposite directions. Resistance was fierce but brief. As soon as the first shots were fired the other groups brought mortars into position near the wharf and opened fire.

A flare rocketed skyward and exploded, lighting the darkened ships in the harbour. Metkas and his men were bathed in the light as they advanced to the town hall, rushing from building to building. Metkas fired a quick burst from his British submachine-gun at two German soldiers who ran from a door. The soldiers crumpled and fell and Metkas paused to reload. All around him was the sharp crack of rifle shots and short bursts fired from machine guns, the crump of mortars and the following roar of explosions. Pressing himself against a wall, he scanned the scene ahead and returned fire at a pocket of German soldiers shooting from a first-floor window, then he crouched and ran forward. A bullet hit the wall close to his head and he ducked. The shot had seemed to come from behind, but when he turned he couldn't see any Germans. He ran on. As he passed between two buildings he glimpsed a ball of orange flame erupt from one of the ships in the harbour, thickening with black smoke as it billowed skywards. Another explosion followed and then he was past the gap, running inside a door firing ahead of him.

During the attack one of the supply ships was sunk, but the other managed to escape out of range, aided by the gunship *Antounnetta*, which pounded the mortar positions with deadly shellfire from her fore and aft guns. Heavy machine-gun fire raked the wharf and soon Metkas gave the order to retreat. As his men scattered through the town toward the safety of the hills he regretted that the mission had only been a partial success. They had underestimated the response from the *Antounnetta* and the speed with which the surviving supply ship had managed to steam out of range. The cost of the operation had been high, at least a dozen men killed and as many injured. His own group was the last to leave. As they ran through the narrow streets away from the waterfront the sound of explosions and the occasional burst of machine-gun fire continued from the harbour. Metkas slowed to a walk. His men were all ahead of him. He needed time to be alone. A few minutes to collect his thoughts.

It was as he passed along a narrow lane between rough cottages at the very edge of the town that he realised that somebody was following him. His immediate reaction was that it must be German soldiers, but even as he hid in the protective shadows cast by a terrace wall he knew that pursuing soldiers would not be so cautious. Whoever was there was moving stealthily. Metkas left his machine gun slung over his shoulder and took out his pistol. The moon was bright in a clear sky and the lane was shrouded in luminous grey light, flanked by deep shadows. A sound, like a footfall, and then a figure appeared moving from shadow to shadow. Metkas relaxed, breathing out loudly.

'Shit, you had me worried there,' he said.

Aris stopped and Metkas stepped into the open. They were only a few yards apart. It was the expression Aris wore that gave him away, mingling surprise and guilt. Even as his grizzled features hardened again into lines of resolve, Metkas recalled the curious way Aris had looked at him before the attack. He remembered also the shot that had almost hit him which he thought had come from behind. Aris pointed his pistol and Metkas knew he'd waited too long. He had fallen prey to his personal feelings for this man who was about to kill him.

Aris hesitated. 'I am sorry,' he said. Then he squeezed the trigger.

There should have been a shot, but instead there was nothing. They both realised what had happened. The gun had jammed. Even as Aris frantically tried to free the mechanism, Metkas raised his own pistol. The single shot echoed between the houses and Aris staggered backwards. Metkas strode forward to finish the job. He remembered the Italian officer's expression when he'd shot him. Aris didn't look surprised. Through his pain his expression was one of resignation. Metkas fired once into his temple, the barrel almost touching his skin.

★ ★ ★

The German convoy arrived in the village at dawn the day after the attack. It was led by an armoured patrol car and followed by a truck full of soldiers. SS *Standartenführer* Bergen, aged thirty-two, climbed down from the patrol car and lit a cigarette as the soldiers jumped out and formed orderly lines. They jogged into the village, rifles clasped at the ready and began going from house to house, systematically rounding up the inhabitants. Old men and women with children stumbled into the street.

Bergen eyed them dispassionately. These people eked out a thin existence from the land in this squalid, inhospitable place at the top of the mountain. A few goats and cows, some chickens. Olive groves which had been there for thousands of years. Their houses were made of stone, simple rough structures haphazardly arranged. The air smelt of animal dung.

As the villagers were herded past Bergen most of them averted their eyes, but a few looked at him with a mixture of apprehension and curiosity. They didn't know who he was, but he struck them as a fearful figure, immaculate in his black uniform with its death's-head insignia. His eyes were pale, almost colourless, his skin also pale and smooth. His hair thin and light yellow. He looked like a ghost compared to them. Their own skin was weathered and dark. In their rough clothes they looked shapeless, shambling. Mothers held tightly to small children.

When all the people from the village had been assembled, the soldiers lit torches soaked in gasoline and set fire to the buildings. Every one of the village's eighty inhabitants was forced to watch while their homes were destroyed, including the church. Shots rang out in the thin, cold air as the animals were slaughtered, bellowing in protest. Their carcasses were dragged to the buildings and they too were burned. A low wailing sound of despair came from the villagers who knew that in the winter they would starve.

After half an hour a thick grey pall of smoke hung over the hillside and the smell of roasted meat filled the air.

So intent had they been on witnessing the destruction of their homes that the villagers had not noticed the machine guns which had been put in place behind them. Gradually as they did, they fell silent. They moved closer together, perhaps for comfort, perhaps instinctively seeking protection. Mothers shielded their children. The quiet was eerie. Tension snapped in the air. The *Hauptsturmführer* commanding the soldiers glanced toward his senior officer, but Bergen did not acknowledge his look. He had given his orders earlier and saw no reason to repeat himself. Finally the command was given and the machine guns barked savagely.

The sound of bullets could clearly be heard thudding into flesh amid screams and cries of terror and pain. Bodies twisted and fell, sometimes jerking on the ground where they lay, a pile of tangled limbs. The carnage was brief, the ensuing quiet emphasised by the single shots that followed as the *Hauptsturmführer* walked among the dying with his pistol drawn.

It had taken less than an hour. The soldiers packed up their guns and climbed back onto the trucks, and the small convoy headed down the mountain road towards Sami, where fifty people had already been rounded up and were being held under guard on the waterfront.

As the sound of the engines faded, silence returned to the hillside. The smoke began to thin. Nothing moved.

★ ★ ★

Metkas stayed on Kephalonia after the attack on the ships at Sami. During the months that followed, the SS officer, Bergen, continued to take reprisals against the civilian population whenever the German forces were attacked. During these attacks, if one of the guerrillas was wounded and unable to walk, his friends, following Metkas's orders, would shoot him to prevent him falling into German hands. Despite this, and despite Metkas moving camp every second day, he was almost captured on two occasions after wounded fighters were taken before they could be shot.

Towards the end of the year, when it became clear that the Germans were losing the war, there were rumours that they would pull out of the islands. Metkas increased his harassment to hurry that day forward, but during an attack on a German convoy he and his men were ambushed. It was rumoured that he had been betrayed by the monarchists. Metkas was lucky to escape with his life. Most of his men were not. After that he could not stay on Kephalonia, and so one night he secretly took a boat and hid in the monastery at Kathara on neighbouring Ithaca. He quickly took control of the poorly-organised Resistance.

It was Metkas who devised the plan to lure *Hauptmann* Hassel to his death. He wanted to take the garrison at Vathy and he decided to use Julia Zannas to make sure that Hassel was separated from his men.

When Julia led Hassel away from the ambush, they returned to the armoured patrol car he had left in the village. Hassel had driven to Exoghi alone, as was his custom, leaving three of his men in Stavros where they relaxed, putting their weapons aside and unbuttoning their tunics while they sat in the shade outside a taverna. The owner of the restaurant brought them a jug of cooled wine. It was a hot day. The soldiers drank and talked. They were very young. They smoked cigarettes, made jokes and invited the owner to join them giving him cigarettes. Now and then he rose to refill the wine jug.

In the kitchen, three men with guns sat silently at the table waiting for the appointed time. Whenever the owner came inside the smile would vanish from his face. He would look nervously at the others and tell them that the soldiers suspected nothing.

The three men had risen from the table and were checking their weapons one final time when they heard a vehicle drive at speed into the square. They froze as orders were shouted in German, and then one of them crossed to the window and peered outside. The soldiers were scrambling to their feet, buttoning their tunics and grabbing their rifles, while below the terrace *Hauptmann* Hassel stood in his patrol car with a pistol in his hand.

The man at the window turned to the others. 'Something has gone wrong,' he hissed. The others crowded close in time to see the soldiers outside seize the owner of the taverna and drag him toward the patrol car.

The men looked at one another questioningly. Should they rush out and attack the Germans now? Perhaps they might still carry out their orders, even though they had lost the element of surprise. But the men were not soldiers, and Hassel was already looking suspiciously toward the very window where they were hidden. In a state of uncertainty they watched as the soldiers bundled the taverna owner into their vehicle, and then it was too late. Hassel barked an order and the vehicle accelerated out of the square. The last thing they saw was the face of Julia Zannas as she looked back, her expression full of sadness and regret.

The prearranged signal that Hassel had been killed was never received by the men waiting outside Vathy. Instead one small group waiting on the hillside above the road saw the patrol car speed past them towards the town, and they knew that Metkas's plan had failed. Alkimos Kounidis had been among one of the several groups waiting for the signal to attack the garrison, by chance the one led by Metkas himself. When they realised what had happened, the men dispersed. Kounidis went with Metkas and several other men. They travelled north, following the secret trails through the live oak and broom, and climbed unseen to the monastery at Kathara where Metkas had been hiding for several weeks. There they waited for news while Metkas fumed. At that point they still were not aware of what exactly had gone wrong, nor that the taverna owner had been seized and taken to Vathy.

It was dark when they heard the sound of shouting and the clatter of boots outside the gates. The Germans had left their vehicles on the road below and had climbed the last half mile on foot in darkness before surrounding the monastery. Some of the men managed to escape through the old passages which had been dug beneath the monastery walls centuries ago so that soldiers seeking refuge might escape the Turks, but Metkas and the young Alkimos Kounidis were not so lucky. Following a brief exchange of fire they were captured.

They were taken to Vathy and imprisoned in the basement of the old mansion on the waterfront which the Germans had commandeered as their headquarters when they had arrived on the island. Locked away in the darkness, Kounidis and Metkas heard the sound of vehicles, orders shouted and men running. Occasionally they heard the crack of rifle fire. They discovered later that a curfew had immediately been imposed. Meetings between groups of more than two people were banned, and patrols stopped everybody to question them. Houses were searched at gunpoint. The soldiers no longer shouldered their rifles. When they looked into the faces of the islanders they had drunk with, had laughed with and shared their food with, they saw only people who had planned to kill them. They felt betrayed, as if they, the German occupiers, were guests who had been treated vilely by their hosts. A strange irony.

Kounidis and Metkas were held for thirty-six hours before the bolts were drawn on the heavy wooden door and they were marched outside at gunpoint. When they emerged blinking into the morning light, Kounidis fully expected that they would be shot. Though Metkas seemed calm, even fatalistic, Kounidis could not stop himself from shaking. He was young. Only nineteen. He had taken no part in the discussions after Metkas had arrived and assumed command of the Resistance on the island, though he had listened as some of the men had argued politely that perhaps it was unnecessary to attack the garrison as it was clear that the Germans would soon leave as they were losing the war. Metkas, however, had been adamant that it was their duty to kill the fascist invaders.

The sky to the west in the direction of Kephalonia was smudged with dark brown and grey smoke. Kounidis and Metkas exchanged glances. The entire German garrison in Vathy had been assembled and a convoy of trucks filled with soldiers and supplies was waiting in the street outside the mansion gates.

Hauptmann Hassel stood beside his patrol car overseeing the final stages of the evacuation. His uniform was immaculate, his boots gleamed. He stood with his feet apart and his hands clasped behind his back, and Kounidis was struck by how much older he looked. As if he had aged years overnight. But it was his bearing that was most striking of all. He held himself stiffly and, when he looked upon his prisoners as they were led towards one of the trucks, his eyes were cold.

Kounidis and Metkas were bundled into a truck. Two soldiers brought another man towards them, his feet dragging in the dirt. Even when he was thrown into the truck Kounidis didn't recognise him at first. They tried to help him, but the man was only partly conscious. He had been beaten badly and one of his eyes had been smashed to a bloody pulp. His teeth were gone, both his knees smashed. With shock Kounidis saw that it was the taverna owner.

The convoy drove north along the coast road. It turned at the foot of the mountain to follow the perilous route towards the monastery.

When the trucks arrived, the soldiers jumped down and brought out the monks who were then lined up against a wall in the courtyard. While a few of the soldiers guarded them with machine guns, the others went inside the buildings and began to carry out anything which appeared to be of any value. They took everything. Pictures, dishes, candle holders, even the ceremonial vestments which were decorated with jewels, though in reality these were coloured glass. The very last thing they carried out was the statue of the *Panaghia*. By the time the Germans left, they had stripped the monastery bare.

The convoy reached Frikes late that afternoon. A German gunboat lay at anchor in the harbour. The villagers had been driven from their homes and Metkas and Kounidis were imprisoned with the dying taverna owner in a house on the waterfront. All night they could hear the sounds of small boats ferrying everything the Germans could take with them out to the *Antounnetta*. Anything that was to be left behind was destroyed. Now and then they heard the muffled thump of an explosion and the occasional crack of rifle shots. Houses and shops were looted and burned and the acrid smell of smoke lay heavy in the air.

A few hours before dawn the door to their

makeshift prison opened and two soldiers entered and stood stiffly at attention. Hassel entered followed by an officer wearing the black uniform of the SS. Metkas recognised him at once as Bergen.

Bergen appeared colourless, as if he had assiduously avoided the Greek sun. He glanced dismissively at Kounidis, who was sitting with the unconscious taverna owner, but when he looked at Metkas his lips stretched into a thin smile, though his pale eyes were frighteningly devoid of expression. He and Hassel conferred in German, and then without another glance at the prisoners the two officers left.

When they were alone again Kounidis asked what Metkas thought would happen to them. The older man replied that he expected they would be taken to Patras on the mainland. When Kounidis asked why, Metkas looked at him and then rested a heavy hand on his shoulder. He said that they must be brave, though even Metkas was unable to conceal his fear. Everybody knew what happened to people who ended up in the hands of the SS at Patras. What the taverna owner had suffered was nothing compared to the torture that the SS were capable of.

Several hours before the sun rose on the following day, soldiers came for them again. They were marched to the wharf and ordered into a small boat. As they were taken across the harbour towards the gunboat, Kounidis looked back at the cliffs, convinced that he was seeing his homeland for the last time. There were fires in the town and along the waterfront. The flames were reflected in the water, and from their light he could see smoke rising into the sky.

The last boat to leave was the one which carried Hassel. As he climbed down he did not look back at the lone figure of Julia Zannas who stood on the wharf. Though he had brought her to Frikes, now she was to be left behind. Though Metkas stared at her with hate and fury burning in his eyes, Alkimos Kounidis felt a stirring of pity for her. He did not understand what she had done, but he had never seen anyone who looked so utterly alone as she did at that moment.

The attack began as they were climbing aboard the *Antounnetta*. Kounidis learned later that men had come from Kephalonia when they heard that Metkas had been captured. They brought with them seasoned fighters and weapons. Their leaders planned to sink the gunboat before it could leave the harbour. They launched their attack from the cliff above the harbour, opening fire with mortars and machine guns.

Kounidis was thrown to the deck with the first explosion which came from a mortar hitting the forward gun, and that was followed almost immediately by a second, even bigger explosion. He felt the heat from the blast singe his hair and scorch his face.

The harbour was suddenly lit as bright as day with orange flame. Men screamed. Debris and bodies were thrown into the air, the water hissed as red-hot metal fell like rain. A machine gun opened up and bullets slammed into metal

220

plating, whining as they ricocheted. The deck shook with the heavy thud of explosions. From the cliff, the flash of muzzle fire was almost continuous, blinking on and off. Mortar shells exploded and fountains of water erupted like geysers. A soldier was suddenly thrown against the structure behind Kounidis, his uniform shredded and blood-soaked as he crumpled like a pile of discarded clothing.

The *Antounnetta*, though damaged, returned fire. There were fires burning toward the bow, but the stern gun was undamaged and amid the smoke and confusion an explosion tore into the cliff above the town. The deck began to hum as the engines were started. The taverna owner was gone, lost overboard during the first seconds of the attack, but Metkas and Kounidis crawled through an open doorway. A German naval officer appeared, his face blackened by smoke and one arm hanging uselessly by his side, the sleeve of his uniform soaked with blood. He looked surprised to see them, then said something in German and pointed a pistol at them before slumping down to lean against the bulkhead, his face strained with pain and shock. He rested his good arm on his knee and kept the pistol trained on them. With a gesture he conveyed that they should put their hands on their heads, and when they were slow to respond he pointed the gun directly at Metkas's face.

For the next hour or so they could only sit helplessly as the vessel limped from the harbour and the sound of firing gradually eased as the *Antounnetta* moved out of range.

They saw soldiers running past on the deck outside to fight the fires. Eventually, a sailor, almost black from smoke, shoved his head through the door and when he saw the three of them he spoke to the officer and returned a few minutes later with two more men. Metkas and Kounidis were taken down a ladder and shoved into a bare cabin, the door locked behind them.

For what seemed like hours they listened to the unsteady beat of the engines. The smell of smoke and oil grew steadily worse, and a murky haze slowly leaked into the cabin. At one point the engines stopped for quite a long time, but eventually they started again. Within minutes the ship rocked with the force of an explosion.

When the door opened it was clear that the boat was sinking. They could feel it wallowing as it took on water. They were dragged onto the deck coughing and choking from the smoke and fumes. Hassel and Bergen were waiting for them. The sky was black, the sea lurching. Several lifeboats were already in the water full of men and, as soon as Kounidis saw them, he knew there would be no place for him or Metkas. Bergen glanced at them and spoke to Hassel and then he turned and began to climb down to one of the boats. Hassel ordered the last of his soldiers to follow and, as they climbed over the rail, he took his pistol from the holster on his belt.

The lifeboats had all moved away, except for the last one. One of the sailors shouted something, no doubt afraid of being dragged down when the *Antounnetta* went under. Calmly

Hassel raised his arm and fired a single shot. Metkas jerked, his head snapped back, blood spraying from his wound. Even as he began to fall the gun was swinging towards Kounidis and, in that moment, he acted out of instinct. He leapt forward and wrapped his arms around Hassel's waist. He heard a shot, which missed him by so little he swore he felt the heat of the bullet, then they both fell to the deck as the ship began to sink at the bow. The deck tilted and as they slid towards the water Kounidis crashed into the bulkhead. The breath was driven from him as he went under, suddenly alone. When he surfaced, he was gasping for air. He began to swim as hard as he could to escape the sinking ship. He didn't look back until his arms felt like lead and he could hardly breathe. As he rose and fell on the swell, he searched in the darkness for the lifeboats but they were already gone, as was the *Antounnetta*. There was no sign of Hassel.

For many hours Kounidis floated with the tide, sometimes swimming, but mostly just trying to stay afloat. He had no idea where he was until it began to get light, then he could see land to the west and the current was carrying him closer. Eventually, exhausted and freezing, half dead, he was washed up on the southern tip of Kephalonia.

12

After Kounidis had finished speaking, Eleni materialised to turn up the lamp. I wondered whether she had been lingering nearby, waiting for her cue. Alex was gazing into the darkness. Kounidis had gone to great lengths to bring his story to life. The combination of ouzo and wine, the subtle tension of anticipation he'd built by deliberately avoiding the subject earlier in the day, and even the lighting and the setting all seemed to have been arranged to add drama to his account. But when I saw the way he was observing Alex, I wondered if there was another reason for his preparations. Perhaps he had endeavoured, rather than simply to repeat the facts of the events themselves, to recreate some echo of the emotions, some sense of what had happened so that Alex might have a glimpse at least of why feelings among the older islanders still ran so close to the surface after all this time.

Eventually Alex returned to us. She smiled self-consciously. 'Thank you,' she said to Kounidis. He bowed his head slightly in acknowledgement.

'Did you ever see Julia again?' I asked.

'No. She left the island soon afterwards and lived for a short time on Kephalonia. But it did not take long for people there to learn who she was.' He hesitated diplomatically. 'Many people lost sons and fathers during the war. Sometimes entire families. Often people made little distinction between those who collaborated, no matter what the circumstances. Julia was lucky to survive. Many in her situation elsewhere did not. The civil war that broke out once the Germans had gone probably helped her. In the confusion there were other targets.'

It was late and Kounidis looked drained. I imagined retelling the story must have taken its toll on him too. He had glossed over his own part in it, but there must have been many times when he had been afraid, when he had thought that his next breath would be his last. He had seen men killed, had witnessed first-hand the cruelty of Hassel's revenge on the people of Ithaca. Those things must have affected him. I even wondered if they had in some way contributed to his ambition, to the drive which had seen him in later years leave the island and eventually become the man he was now, and if the failure of his marriage could be traced to the psychological impact of his trauma. Perhaps he had buried himself in his work to escape his memories.

He bade us good-night, and after he had gone to bed, Eleni again appeared to clear up. She didn't speak to us and we took her efficiency as a hint that we too shouldn't linger. When we reached Alex's room I asked her if she was feeling all right and she nodded and managed a smile of sorts.

'Yes, I'll be fine.'
'Good-night then.'
'Good-night.'

I went to my own room and stood by the open window. Outside cicadas creaked, but otherwise the night was still. Moonlight had washed the sea silver-grey and the sky seemed alive with stars. I was thinking about the evening and about Alex. I was tempted to go and knock at her door but before I could make up my mind I heard a tap at my own door and when I opened it Alex stood outside.

'Can I come in?' she asked.

'Of course.'

We sat by the window. 'I couldn't sleep,' Alex said eventually. 'I was wondering if Nana ever regretted the decision she made.'

'What do you think?'

'I don't think she did.' My surprise must have been obvious. 'You think what she did was wrong don't you?' Alex asked.

'I understand it. But it's hard to separate the decision from the consequences.'

'But there would have been consequences either way. We don't know what would have happened if she had let those men kill Hassel. If Metkas and his men had wiped out the entire garrison, surely Bergen would have taken reprisals.'

'I suppose that's probably true,' I admitted.

'I think what she did was brave.'

'Whatever decision she made would have been courageous,' I conceded.

'She chose what was right. What they did was cynical,' Alex said. 'What could be worse than encouraging her to fall in love with Hassel, and that's more or less what they did, and then expecting her to take part in his murder?'

'I doubt that anyone expected her to fall in love.'

'How could they blindly think he would fall in love with her without knowing there was a risk she would feel the same way about him?'

I had to admit she had a point, but in the end it came down to a question of loyalties. 'I can't agree with her decision because I can't discount what happened afterwards,' I explained. 'And maybe Julia couldn't either. Maybe she wouldn't have made the same decision again if she had had the chance.'

'What do you mean?'

'She told your mother she was raped. Maybe it was true. Maybe Hassel thought she'd known about the plan all along but only changed her mind at the last moment. He must have been angry. He felt betrayed. Once he thought about it maybe he felt like that about Julia as well.'

Alex shook her head. 'They were in love. She still loved him when she died, after all those years. She couldn't have felt that way if he'd raped her.'

'Then why tell your mother that? To protect his family?'

'Possibly. Or maybe because she was ashamed of the way she felt. She went against everything that she had ever been taught about family and the church. You can't just wipe that kind of indoctrination away, can you? She saw what he did to the taverna owner. And later she must have heard that he killed Metkas and almost killed Mr Kounidis. *But she still loved him.*'

'How could she? How could she love a man like that?'

'Because that wasn't all he was. She fell in love with the man who came to her village every day for months just so that he could catch sight of her. The man she walked with on the hillside. They were both young. To her he wasn't just a soldier, he was a gentle, lonely young man who made her heart beat faster every time he looked at her. And up until the point where the guerrillas tried to kill him, he had done his best for the people of Ithaca. Afterwards she saw another side of him.'

'That's the part I don't understand,' I argued. 'Even after she knew what he was capable of, you believe she still loved him?'

'Haven't you ever done anything you're not proud of?'

I could have answered glibly that I'd never tortured anyone, but I understood what she was getting at. There had been a war on and under those circumstances the normal rules don't apply however much people might want to believe that they do.

'It's like asking a wife whose husband goes to prison for some violent crime, maybe even killing somebody in a heated argument, does she still love him?' Alex reasoned. 'She might say that she does because she knows that one violent act doesn't define entirely who he is.'

Alex took something from her pocket. It was the piece of folded paper on which she'd copied the graffiti from the ruin of her grandmother's house in Exoghi.

'I found out what it means,' she said. 'Nazi whore.' She crumpled it in her hand.

It was easy to see why Julia had been branded a traitor. Perhaps it was unfair given the circumstances, but then who could blame the people of Ithaca given the moral complexities of what had occurred? It was a case of cause and effect. I still couldn't understand how Julia could have continued to love Hassel after what he'd done, but whatever the rights and wrongs, at least Alex knew the truth.

She looked tired and a little forlorn. I reached across and took her hand. Her eyes met mine and faint lines creased her brow. 'I should go,' she said, though she made no move to leave.

'You don't have to.'

She shook her head as if to dislodge a persistent notion which had become stuck somewhere.

I leaned toward her and kissed her. She didn't respond at first, and then her hand touched my face. Abruptly she pulled away.

'I can't.'

'Why not?'

'Because . . . because I don't know you. We don't know each other. A few days ago when we met I believed that I was in love with Dimitri.'

'Do you still love him?'

She looked me in the eye and opened her mouth to respond, but then shook her head. 'You see why I can't do this? I can't answer that question because I don't know. It's too soon. It doesn't feel right.'

There was, I knew, an undeniable strand of

truth and common sense about what she said. We had only just met, and we were both emotionally exposed for different reasons. But that was also why we were sitting there together, why we felt the way we did.

'I can't help what I feel for you,' I said simply. 'Perhaps it is too soon, for both of us. Maybe it's not a good idea. But that doesn't change anything.'

I leaned toward her again and she didn't move away. Her eyes were riveted to me like an animal paralysed in the middle of the road at night. I kissed her. She didn't respond. I pulled back and she moved her head, an infinitesimal movement of denial.

I kissed her again, and a low sound escaped her. It was a moan of uncertainty but also of desire. I broke off and looked deep into her eyes. A tear ran down her cheek. I tasted its salty wetness then kissed her eyes. Something rose up inside me, an almost overpowering tenderness. I wanted to hold her and be held, to love and be loved.

We kissed again and this time she responded. Her mouth was soft, pliant. Our kiss became urgent. She held my face in her hands. I kissed her neck, her throat. My senses brimmed with her scent, her taste, the heat of our bodies. She raised my face and we looked at one another for a long moment and then I led her to the bed where we undressed and lay down. When we made love she closed her eyes and wrapped her arms tightly around me. She raised her hips and matched my rhythm with a slow rocking motion, and when she tensed and a shudder ran the length of her body, it was more like a shiver than a crescendo.

Afterwards we held one another until eventually first Alex, and then I fell asleep.

★ ★ ★

When I woke it was still dark. At first I was disoriented by the unfamiliar room, the open window through which a breath of air flowed to cool my skin. I realised that Alex was no longer in bed and sat up in alarm thinking that she had gone, or worse that it had all been a dream, but then I saw her standing in the shadows by the window. She was naked, her arms wrapped around her body, hugging herself.

'Do you hear it?' she asked quietly, seeing me stir.

'Hear what?' But then I did hear something. Music. The notes very faint, falling and rising on the breeze. I got up and went over to her. The music was clearer by the window. 'It sounds as if it's coming from the terrace.'

'It's beautiful. So sad.'

'What is it?' I vaguely recognised the sound of some unfamiliar stringed instrument. The music it produced had a haunting, mournful quality.

'A bouzouki I think.'

It was difficult to follow the cadence of the piece as it was so faint, which perhaps added to its romantic mystery. And then as we strained to hear, it faded and was gone. We waited for a little while longer but when it didn't start again I put my arms around Alex. I felt a shadow of resistance, or perhaps uncertainty, and then she responded and turned towards me, lifting her face. We kissed and then we went back to bed.

13

Alex was still sleeping when I got up in the morning. She was lying on her side, one arm thrown around the pillow, the early light like warm honey on her naked back. I watched her, overwhelmed with unfamiliar feelings. Not least among them was an uncertainty which alarmed me. What happened now I wondered? Did we live happily ever after? I thought briefly of Alicia. I had believed that I loved her once, but that had all fallen apart. Alex had said herself that until a few days ago she'd been in love with Dimitri. I couldn't help wondering if love was such a powerful emotion that any relationship based on it was doomed to failure. Hadn't somebody once said love is blind? Did that mean it raised expectations which were so high they couldn't be met? Did it mean the very faults which precluded lasting happiness became invisible?

My doubtful philosophising didn't make any difference however. As I watched Alex sleep I was consumed with feelings for her. There was already nothing I could do. I wanted to be with her. I wanted to go to sleep with her every night and wake to find her beside me in the mornings.

Though I was tempted to wake her, I resisted the impulse and instead slipped quietly out of the room and went down to the cove for a swim. The water was fresh and cool. I swam hard out into the middle of the cove and then back to shore again and when I emerged, breathing heavily and dripping onto the stones, I felt renewed. After I'd towelled off and put a T-shirt on I walked back up to the house. When I got there I was surprised to see that Kounidis was already up. He was sitting on the terrace drinking coffee.

'Ah Robert, you have been for a swim I see. I hope it was pleasant?' He gestured to a chair. 'Please, sit down. Eleni will come in a moment and fetch you coffee. Did you sleep well?'

'Very, thank you.' I wondered if it was merely the light or was there a certain knowing flicker in his eyes?

'I have always been an early riser myself. It is the best time of the day. When it is still, and one can think,' he said. 'I have been considering what you told me yesterday about your father. It concerns me greatly. This man who attacked you, you did not get even a glimpse of him?'

'It was dark. He was tall and strong, that's about all I can say.'

'He did not say anything?'

'No.'

'When I saw you go down to the beach earlier I telephoned Miros Theonas. He has been unable to find anybody who saw anything unusual at the time you were attacked.'

'That doesn't surprise me. Theonas doesn't believe there's anything suspicious about my father's death. Or he doesn't want to believe it.'

'Do you still think that the person you disturbed on the *Swallow* was searching for one of your father's journals?'

234

'I'm fairly certain he was looking for something. Do you think it's possible that there could be something of value on the *Antoun-netta*?'

'Anything is possible,' Kounidis said. 'And the Germans are known to have removed a great many of our national treasures before they were driven from Greece.'

I detected a doubtful note in Kounidis's tone however, and I asked him why.

'Your father spent many years trying to find the wreck of the *Antounnetta*.' He gestured towards the sea beyond the cliff. 'There are many miles of open sea where the ship might have gone down. I cannot help wondering how likely it is that after all this time he finally found her. But if you are right there is also the question of why this year he began his search early. He was certainly not aware that there might be anything of value on board.'

I couldn't answer either point.

'What will you do now?' Kounidis asked.

'Look for his journal,' I said. I couldn't think of much else that I could do.

'If there is any way in which I can help you, please let me know.'

I thanked him and just then Alex appeared. 'Good morning. I heard voices.'

We both stood up as she joined us. She looked radiant, and as she sat down again she caught my eye and smiled.

'I hope you slept well,' Kounidis said to her.

'Yes, thank you,' she answered, faint colour rising in her cheeks.

Just in time Eleni appeared carrying a tray with coffee and pastries.

★ ★ ★

We spent the morning with Kounidis. Later he had his driver take us all to Kioni where we had lunch at a restaurant by the harbour. The tiny town was pretty and busy with tourists from the many visiting boats in the harbour. After lunch Alex and I went for a walk, wandering the alleys and steps which wound among the houses perched on the hillside. At a look-out point near the top of a steep climb we paused to admire the view.

'You seem quiet,' I ventured. 'Everything all right?'

'Am I? I'm sorry.' She sighed suddenly and turned to face me. 'I keep wondering how this happened. You and me.'

'Are you sorry it has?'

'No. Of course not. I'm not sorry we met, and I'm not sorry about last night. It's the timing. It's everything.'

'You mean Dimitri?'

'I suppose partly, yes. I'm confused. I thought I loved Dimitri, but now I feel this for you. It's different. It's something special I know. I want the same as you do, to be with you, to get to know one another. I just need some time. Please try to understand.'

I told her that I did, and she seemed reassured, but when she turned away the smile I wore faded. After that, whenever she was quiet or thoughtful, I found myself wondering what was on her mind. She would stop to admire a house and I would sense that her thoughts had slipped elsewhere. I'd imagine she was thinking of Dimitri. Once, when we reached the wharf, she stopped suddenly and the blood drained from her face. When I asked her what was wrong she smiled weakly and said it was nothing, she had remembered something she had to do later, that was all. It was a hasty and transparent improvisation. When I looked back I saw a man among a group of people who I thought resembled Dimitri. I began to get the feeling he was with us all the time, like an invisible presence.

Later that afternoon when we said goodbye to Kounidis, he shook Alex's hand.

'I am very sorry if the things that you have learned while you were here have been upsetting,' he said.

'Please don't be,' she assured him. 'I'm very grateful to you for telling me what happened.'

When I shook his hand, Kounidis again urged me to let him know if there was any way at all in which he could help with regards to my father. After we'd left Alex said, 'Does that mean you're not planning to go back to England yet?'

'Not immediately. What about you?'

'I don't have to be back until September,' she pointed out. 'It's the perk of teaching at a private school.'

I wondered whether she was thinking about spending the entire summer there. Although there was nobody in London to question my absence, I had a business to run. I had to go back soon and I wanted Alex to go with me. The fact that I didn't ask and she didn't volunteer seemed to yawn like a chasm between us.

When we reached Frikes, Alex asked if we could stop and look at the plaque commemorating the attack on the *Antounnetta* again. As we walked back to the Jeep I noticed a car further back parked by the side of the road.

'What is it?' Alex asked when she noticed my interest.

'Probably nothing. It's just that car there. I'm sure it was behind us on the way from Kioni.'

I'd slowed to let it pass because I was taking in the views, but each time I had, the car had dropped back to remain the same distance behind. I could see someone sitting behind the wheel, though it was too far away to make out any detail.

When we left Frikes I watched in the mirror. It was a nondescript blue Fiat which had seen better days. It pulled out and followed, keeping about a hundred yards back. At Stavros, rather than follow the coast, I turned off to take the longer mountain road. Before long I saw the Fiat again. I exchanged glances with Alex and she swivelled in her seat.

'Who do you think it can be?'

'You don't recognise the car?'

She looked puzzled. 'Why should I?'

'I just thought it might be somebody you know.' I'd been turning the possibilities over in my mind and one that I'd come up with was Dimitri. I think she guessed what I was getting at

238

and afterwards she kept looking back with a worried expression.

As we climbed the mountain I alternately sped up and slowed down, but the Fiat always maintained its distance. The road was steep and twisty, sometimes partly blocked by rockfalls. The small village of Anoghi near the summit looked abandoned. There was a central square that was little more than the confluence of two roads beside which stood a small shop which also served as a *kefenio*. On the other side was a church. I pulled over and went back to the corner to wait for the Fiat to appear. I heard it approaching, the engine pitch changing as the driver changed down for the corner, and then I stepped out into the road.

The driver braked, though I couldn't see who it was because of the sun's glare on the windscreen. As I made to step around the front the engine suddenly revved and the car shot forward. Taken completely by surprise I jumped out of the way, spinning into a wall. By the time I'd run back to the Jeep it had vanished around the corner on the other side of the square.

'Are you all right?' Alex asked in alarm.

'I'm fine. Did you get a look at the driver?'

'A man I think. It was too fast.'

I shoved the Jeep into gear and followed. We passed several small lanes at speed and then we were clear of the houses and the road twisted in a series of hairpin bends for a couple of miles, before we came to a turning signposted to the monastery at Kathara. I pulled over. The road above was empty and from where we sat we could see all the way down to the coast. The Fiat had vanished.

'He must have turned off in the village somewhere,' I guessed. 'He's probably half-way back to Stavros by now.'

'Who was it do you think?'

I thought again of Dimitri, but I was less sure. I also thought about the man who'd attacked me, but out loud I only expressed bewilderment. 'I don't suppose you got the licence number?'

'Sorry.'

'Me neither.'

I thought about the car all the way back to Vathy. By then Alex was urging me to report the incident to the police, but I could imagine how Theonas would react.

'What am I going to tell him? A car followed us from Kioni, and then vanished. I don't think he's going to get excited about that.'

'It almost ran you down.'

I shook my head. 'If that was his intention, he had plenty of opportunity before then. He could have done it in Frikes.'

'What if it was the same man who attacked you?' Alex asked.

Even if it was, I still couldn't give Theonas any kind of description.

When we arrived in Vathy I drove Alex to the place where she was staying and walked her to the door.

'Thanks,' she said. 'For everything.'

'What happens now?' I wondered aloud as we faced each other awkwardly.

'I need some time to think. And to be honest

240

I'm quite tired. Can we meet in the morning?'

I smiled to hide my disappointment. 'Of course.'

She hesitated, then leaned forward to kiss my cheek quickly and turned to go inside.

★ ★ ★

When I arrived back at the house Irene wanted to know if Alex had found the answers to her questions. I told her about the weekend, and then almost casually she asked if I was going to be seeing Alex again. There was a slight knowing edge to her probing and though I parried with as much vagueness as I could manage, I guessed that she had been speaking with Kounidis. Either way, once I had managed to change the subject, she told me that she had spent most of her own weekend searching the house from one end to the other. There was no sign of the missing journal. The only other place that she could suggest was my dad's museum in Vathy. Though it had been closed since my father's death, Irene had a key so I decided to go right away.

The museum occupied a squat, single-level building next to a vacant overgrown lot on a narrow street away from the waterfront. A rusting iron fence enclosed a patch of brown earth which supported a few patches of dry grass and some dusty flowers. The door was painted green, but the paint, like the plaster on the building façade, was peeling and faded. Bars guarded the windows and a sign over the door mirrored the one at the front announcing in several languages that this was the archaeological museum. Compared with the official museum of Vathy located a few streets away the one my father ran looked distinctly shabby.

I turned the key in the lock and went inside. The entrance hall was flanked on one side by a counter where somebody sat during opening hours to run the place and behind that was a door leading to my dad's office. Two arched entrances led to the display halls on the left and right. The display cases were arranged in rows, each filled with the kind of figurines and drinking vessels I had become used to seeing as a child. In one room there were some large amphorae which would once have been used to transport olive oil. Neatly printed cards explained that they came from the sunken city in Polis Bay which Alkimos Kounidis had mentioned. Until proper regulations had been imposed it had not been uncommon for people to dive from visiting boats and plunder the seabed of its treasure. I read that ironically there were artefacts from Polis Bay in museums and private collections all over the world.

When I went back to the office I found the door unlocked. As soon as I stepped inside I knew somebody had searched it thoroughly. Nothing looked obviously out of place, but I could see the dust marks where things had been picked up and put back again, though not exactly in the same position. A desk diary had been moved, as had a stack of file boxes.

Even though I knew I was probably wasting my time, I went through every file drawer and cupboard, all the time with the feeling that I was repeating what somebody before me had already done. It would have been easy enough to visit during opening hours and wait until the attendant was engaged with another visitor and then slip into the office.

I sat down at my dad's desk. I'd wondered from the beginning why he had gone to the marina on the morning he had vanished. I doubted that he'd intended taking the boat out. He must have known he wasn't capable of that in his condition. So he must have had another reason to go there. Had it been to retrieve the missing journal? But he had never left the marina, and the journal wasn't on the boat.

Of course it was all conjecture, as Theonas had pointed out. There was no proof the journal even existed. When I left the museum I wasn't sure what I would do next, or even if I should do anything. If my father really had been involved in smuggling antiquities, then perhaps it was better that nobody should know. It was this conflict which I knew plagued Irene; the desire to maintain the status quo, thereby possibly allowing a murderer to go free, or digging up an unpalatable reality that would finally destroy my father's reputation for ever.

As I drove back to the house I pondered the idea that perhaps it was true that some things really are best left in the past.

14

I hadn't closed the shutters over the window the night before and when I woke the first signs of dawn were lightening the sky. It was quiet, the cicadas and birds hadn't yet stirred. A faint breeze disturbed the leaves on the olive trees and carried the scent of wild mint and pine from the hillside. I heard the sound of a car on the road below the house, the engine note dropping as the driver changed gear before it faded and was gone.

I dressed and went downstairs. Irene wasn't up yet so I made coffee and took it onto the terrace. The tops of the hills seemed on fire as the sun rose behind them, while far below the harbour remained deep green and utterly still. I'd slept badly. All night I'd dozed fitfully thinking mostly about Alex.

I left the house while it was still early and drove into town to the house where Alex was staying. When I went to her room the shutters were closed and there was no response to my knocking. I called her name quietly once or twice, but there was still no reply. I didn't want to wake the whole household up and I was contemplating what to do when I heard a sound behind me. I turned to find a woman watching me from the door of the house.

'*Kalimera*,' I said.

'*Kalimera*,' she murmured, regarding me suspiciously.

'The young woman who's renting your room. Do you know if she's here?' The woman looked at me uncomprehendingly. 'Alex. The English girl.'

'Ah, Alex. Yes.' She beamed and came towards me. 'Alex is sleep?' She pointed at the door and the closed shutters.

'I don't know.'

The woman shrugged and knocked. 'Alex?' When there was no reply she shrugged again. 'Come again,' she said, it being evident that if Alex was inside she was asleep.

I had no alternative but to leave. The woman went back to her house and closed the door while I lingered outside in the street. The town was beginning to come to life. A small fishing boat chugged across the harbour toward the entrance and several scooters buzzed back and forth along the waterfront, their riders hunched over bags of fresh bread they had fetched from the bakery.

I got in the Jeep and decided to go and have a cup of coffee somewhere and come back in half an hour. As I slowed for the intersection at the end of the street I glanced up the hill to check for traffic and as I did, Alex appeared at the bottom of a flight of steps. She appeared engrossed in her thoughts and when I called her name she looked startled.

I got out of the Jeep and went to meet her. 'I've just been looking for you. I think I woke your landlady.'

Alex shot a nervous glance back the way she'd come. I looked to see what was wrong, but there was nothing there. 'We were having a slight communication problem,' I added.

Belatedly I realised that she was wearing the same clothes she'd had on when I'd dropped her off the day before. I noticed other small details. Her hair had been hurriedly brushed and she wasn't wearing any make-up.

'Have you been for a walk?' I asked, wondering why she hadn't said anything as a kind of dread seeped into me.

'Yes,' she said, though she didn't meet my eye. 'I couldn't sleep last night either.'

She started to say something then looked down at her feet. Everything about this was wrong. A second or two passed in silence and then, when she looked at me again, she wore a pleading expression. All at once I guessed where she had been. It felt like a punch to the gut. For a few moments I couldn't react. I didn't want to believe that I was right, but her silence was damning.

The sun had risen and it was already warm. Sunlight splashed on the wall behind Alex. I couldn't look at her while I tried to steady my feelings. Instead I studied the mortar between the pitted whitish blocks. It was cracked and decaying. A small clump of wild flowers had somehow managed to gain a tenuous hold and clung there hopefully, a cheerful but seemingly doomed dash of cheerful colour in an otherwise hostile environment.

'Robert,' Alex said in quiet appeal. But her voice triggered something in me. I turned on her.

'You didn't stay there last night did you?'

Her eyes widened at the coldness in my tone. I stared at her, knowing the answer even before she finally shook her head with a small, barely perceptible movement. She reached out, but I recoiled from her touch. She flinched and allowed her hand to fall away.

'Please, can we go somewhere so that we can talk? I want to explain . . . '

I cut her off. 'I just want to know one thing. So that there's no misunderstanding. Just tell me if you spent the night with Dimitri.'

'Please. I know how you must feel but . . . '

'Just . . . answer . . . me . . . ' I said, cutting her off again.

She closed her eyes for a moment and took a breath. 'Yes. I was with Dimitri.'

Though I knew that would be her answer I wasn't prepared for how I felt. I hadn't really understood how much she had got under my skin. Even now she seemed small and vulnerable and I felt a rage of conflicting emotions. Part of me wanted to embrace her and comfort her as if she were the one who was being hurt, but at the same time I wanted to lash out at her.

'I'm sorry,' she said. 'Really I am. You have to let me explain.'

'Christ! Explain what?' I demanded savagely. 'You must have gone to him as soon as I dropped you off!' I gestured to her clothes. 'Did you even wait for me to get to the end of the street?'

'Robert . . . '

'Was that him in the car which followed us?' I said, suddenly remembering the Fiat. I shook my head, beginning to see it all. 'It was, wasn't it?'

'No. Listen to me. It's not the way you think . . . '

'Isn't it? How is it then? Tell me, I'd like to know. You went there after I left. Then what? You got chatting, time slipped away and before you knew what had happened it was late and you thought you may as well stay over rather than walk all the way back? Because it must be what? Five minutes away? Ten?'

She shrank back from my mounting anger. 'I had to see him. You have to understand . . . '

'Oh, I understand. Just tell me this. It may be a stupid question given that you spent the night there, but did you fuck him?'

She recoiled as if I'd slapped her. 'Don't do this,' she murmured.

'Come on, Alex. You wanted to explain. Well here's your chance. Did you fuck him? It's a simple question.' I thrust my face close to hers. 'I ASKED IF YOU FUCKED HIM!'

Her eyes glistened. She stepped away from me and fear flashed in her eyes.

'What is it?' I said, moving a step closer. 'You can't be afraid of me, Alex. I'm the one who pulled you out of the harbour, remember?' I aped a sudden flash of insight, slapping my hand against my forehead. 'Is that what it was all about? The other night? Was that my reward? Or maybe I didn't come up to scratch, is that it? Is he a better fuck?'

Abruptly she slapped me. Her hand moved in a blur of speed and the force of it snapped my head around and left my cheek stinging.

Neither of us moved. We stared at each other in silence. Tears were leaking down Alex's cheeks. She stepped past me and I watched her cross the street.

'One thing,' I called after her, 'you don't know how I feel.'

* * *

After I left Vathy I drove north along the coast road. I had no clear idea of where I was going.

Without planning to, I arrived at Piso Aetos where a ferry was waiting to depart for Kephalonia and on impulse I bought a ticket. I told myself that I should never have become involved with Alex. Snatches of images came and went. I imagined her in bed in a darkened room, the sheets twisted and fallen to one side, two naked bodies, both tanned, her ankles locked around Dimitri's back as they moved in passionate unison. My knuckles were bloodless as I gripped the rail with such ferocity that the tendons in my wrists stood out like wire beneath the skin.

When the ferry slowed as it approached the wharf in Efimia I joined the other passengers to go ashore and found a taxi to take me across the island to Argostoli. There, I found a café close to the marina where dazzling yachts and sleek expensive launches filled the berths. A few people were drinking their morning coffee and reading the papers. An American couple sat nearby loudly discussing their itinerary for the day. The husband was complaining.

'I think we should just take a goddamn cab. I don't wanna drive on these roads the way some of these people handle a car. They're crazy.'

'I guess it wouldn't cost much in dollars anyway,' his wife agreed. 'Do we need to get some more of the money they use here, what do they call it now?'

'Euros. Jesus, what is this do you think?' The man prodded his breakfast with a fork and looked around for a waiter.

I heard him complaining, but tuned out his irritatingly intrusive drawl. When the waiter came to my table I ordered vodka on the rocks and he looked momentarily surprised. 'A big one,' I added, miming with my hands.

He shrugged. 'OK.'

My drink came and I polished it off. I've never been big on drowning my sorrows in alcohol, but it was a day for making exceptions so I signalled the waiter to bring me another. While I drank it I wondered how soon I could get a flight back to London. I had no desire to stay another day in Greece, and even less to return to Ithaca. But I had left without my passport, and anyway the least I could do was say goodbye to Irene. I supposed another twenty-four hours wouldn't kill me, especially if I found a painless way to pass the time.

I ordered a third vodka. The alcohol on top of an empty stomach was making me light-headed and numb, both feelings that I welcomed. I noticed a woman at a table nearby looking at me. She was perhaps thirty, obviously Greek, with long thick reddish hair and pretty features. When I stared back at her she held my gaze frankly.

'Would you like to join me?' I asked.

'It is early for drinking I think.'

I shrugged, and she got up and came over to my table.

'You have come here on holiday?' she asked.

'No. Actually for a funeral.'

She looked at me askance, unsure if I were serious. 'Who was it that died?'

'A man. I didn't really know him.' I waved a hand vaguely.

She gestured to my drink. 'Is that why you are drinking?'

'No.'

'Then you always have vodka in the mornings like this?'

'Always,' I assured her.

Her English was thickly accented, but a lot better than my Greek. She was wearing a cotton print skirt and a tight-fitting top which revealed little but hinted at a lot. I glimpsed slim brown thighs, and she caught my eye, a smile playing around the corners of her mouth.

'Are you married?' she asked.

'No.'

'I think you are not telling me the truth. You have left your wife at the hotel.'

'Why do you think I'm married?'

'You are good-looking. All men who are good-looking and are not fat are married.' She laughed throatily. 'Actually even the fat ugly ones are married.'

I laughed with her and emptied my glass,

251

vaguely surprised that I had finished it so quickly. 'You sure you wouldn't like one of these?'

She cocked her head on one side. 'Maybe I will. Yes. All right.'

I signalled to the waiter and this time ordered two vodkas. He glanced at the woman with a slight frown, but she ignored him.

'What is your name?' she asked.

'Robert. What's yours?'

'What is your wife's name?'

'I told you I'm not married.'

She smiled as if we were playing a game. 'Then you are divorced.'

'Never been married.'

'You have a girlfriend?'

'No.'

She sat back in her chair and regarded me quizzically. 'You are gay?'

I looked deliberately at her cleavage. 'Not gay.'

She grinned and leaned towards me. Her breasts pressed against the table and almost spilled from her top. Our drinks arrived and we clicked glasses.

'Do you like what you see?' she asked me, watching where my eyes strayed. I didn't answer, and then she stood up and for a few moments I sat blinking at her. The sun was behind her and the glare hurt my eyes. I reached for my drink but somehow the glass had emptied itself.

'Why don't you pay some money for the drinks,' the woman said. I couldn't have sworn to it but she appeared to be frowning, and I detected a note of impatience in her tone where

252

moments before there had only been a kind, coquettish flirting. Nevertheless I put some money on the table and stood up. She took my arm and we began walking along the street.

'I don't know your name,' I mentioned.

She gripped my arm more tightly as I stumbled, and then she decided that wouldn't do and put her arm around my waist, guiding my own around hers where it rested just below the soft weight of her breast.

She looked impatient again then shook her head and smiled, not without a trace of sympathetic humour. 'You have had too much drink.'

'A little.'

'Come with me. It is not far. You can rest.'

I was led through narrow streets to a building with an exterior which I hazily observed was shabby and unattractive. The doors were open to a gloomy hallway, its tiled floor splintered with cracks into which the grime of many years had accumulated. The woman guided me to a third-floor apartment that was simply furnished but clean. In the living room a collection of icons of saints arranged on a table by the window swam in and out of focus.

'I will fetch you a drink,' the woman said, and pushed me towards a couch. She went to the fridge in the kitchen and took out a jug and when she returned she gave me a glass of red juice which I drank thirstily.

'Would you like more?' she asked.

'No thanks.'

'OK.' She opened a window and the sounds of

the street filtered up to us. It was hot in the apartment. The air was stifling. I was sweating and beginning to feel sick.

'Can I use your bathroom?' I asked.

'Of course.' She gestured to a doorway.

I passed a room containing a bed and a set of drawers, on top of which were more icons. In the bathroom I turned on the cold tap and the pipes rumbled behind the walls before a stream of warmish water emerged. I closed my eyes and splashed my face. When I straightened up I was suddenly overcome with a bout of dizziness. Reaching out, I steadied myself against the basin and peered at my reflection in the mirror. I looked pale. I needed to sleep it off. As I went back towards the living room a voice called me from the bedroom. I went to the doorway and found the woman sitting on the bed. I still didn't know her name. She patted the space beside her.

'Sit down.'

Groggily I obeyed. Casually she pulled her top over her head and, before I could say anything, unhooked her bra. 'You must pay,' she said, interpreting my amused surprise as delight I suppose.

I took out my wallet and gave her some notes, then a few more until she seemed happy. 'Look, I just need to rest,' I said. 'This has all been a misunderstanding.'

'I do not think so,' she said.

I started to tell her she was wrong, but I stopped myself because of course she was right, I had known all along that she was a prostitute. She pushed me onto my back and started

254

tugging at my clothes. Before I knew it she had undressed me, and then she was naked herself. As if in a dream I watched her cup her breasts. She smiled and arched her throat as she pushed her hands back through her hair, then she positioned herself over me. I registered the smoothness of her skin, the dark patch of coarse hair at the base of her belly. Behind her on the dresser the icons watched us with their saintly expressions. They seemed uniformly unhappy I thought, before the idea dissolved. For an instant I thought of Alex. I felt the silken brush of hair against my chest and then I reached out for the stranger above me.

★　★　★

Sunlight streamed through the window and splashed onto the bed. I opened my eyes and squinted. My body was bathed in a sheen of perspiration and my head pounded. My mouth was so dry my tongue felt as though it was a foot thick. I looked at my watch and saw that it was almost five in the afternoon.

The woman was gone, as was all the money in my wallet. I got up and made my way unsteadily to the kitchen where I drank several glasses of water. A search through the cupboards turned up some aspirin. When I was feeling marginally better I searched the apartment for money so that I could get a taxi, but I didn't find any.

I let myself out and on the way down the stairs I passed a middle-aged woman carrying a bag of groceries. She regarded me with frank, unsmiling disapproval.

'*Kalimera*,' I mumbled.

The woman made some response and continued past, waving her hand and firing a staccato burst of unintelligible Greek at me. When she reached the top of the stairs she glanced back, a thick-waisted matron dressed entirely in black even down to her thick stockings, her brow creased into a frown of censure.

When I stepped outside into the street I paused. A few people drifted past, and across the road the owner of a *kefenio* chatted to an old man while he served him coffee and they both lit cigarettes. I went to the end of the street and followed whatever route appeared to lead toward the port. Now and then I caught glimpses of the sea, and within ten minutes I found a road that led all the way to the wharf where I eventually found a taxi that would accept payment by credit card. At Efimia I faced an hour-long wait for a ferry which I spent in the taverna where I had drunk a cup of coffee on the morning I had arrived from England.

The owner didn't remember me, but I used my credit card to buy three beers to quench my thirst and when I left I asked him to charge an extra amount so I would have some cash. I gave him a generous tip. I hadn't eaten anything all day and the beers went straight to my head. I bought another on the ferry and when I went into the bathroom to relieve myself I was confronted with my own bleary-eyed reflection. I stared at myself in surprise, then raised my bottle in a toast.

It was dark by the time I reached Ithaca. I drove back towards the house but I decided to stop at a bar by the waterfront on the way. As I weaved my way unsteadily from the side-street where I had parked the Jeep I was overtaken by a wave of dizzying nausea. I paused to lean against a wooden power pole that also served as a street lamp. The weak light it emitted was reflected in the dark bonnet of a car parked by the opposite kerb. I blinked and looked away, then looked back again. There was somebody behind the wheel. I could see a pale face watching me. I thought the car looked familiar, and then I realised that it was a Fiat.

My stomach lurched. Forgetting about the car I staggered to the corner. The bar I'd intended to go to was a few yards away. I sat at a table outside and when a waiter came I ordered a beer, then changed my mind and asked for a glass of water. A dull ache had begun to take root behind my eyes.

A man arrived and sat at a table beside the harbour wall, and though he appeared outwardly to be just another tourist, when I glanced his way our looks collided. He was tall and fair-haired, about my own age. I couldn't tell if it was the man from the Fiat, but I was sure that it was. The waiter delivered a bottle of sweating beer to his table. After a moment he got up and came over to my table.

'Excuse me?'

He was dressed in dark-coloured trousers and

a blue open-neck shirt and spoke with a north European accent. Perhaps Dutch or German. 'Yes?'

'Mr French?'

I wasn't surprised that he knew my name, and when I didn't say anything he said, 'Forgive me. I thought that I recognised you. I knew your father very slightly. By the way, please accept my condolences, I was saddened to hear of his death.'

'Thank you,' I said automatically while my brain tried to keep up with the conversation.

'It was an accident I believe?'

'Apparently.'

He looked at me with an oddly hesitant expression as if he weren't sure what to say next. 'May I be frank?' he said suddenly. 'Do you know if your father knew a man called Schmidt? Eric Schmidt?'

'I have no idea,' I said. 'Actually I don't know much about him at all.' The harbour wavered before my eyes, the lights on the far side shimmering like a mirage.

'Are you all right?'

'I'm fine.'

'I would like to talk to you about your father, Mr French.'

I looked across the road to where the blue Fiat was still parked. 'Did you follow me here?'

'Of course not. I happened to see you. A coincidence.'

I gestured to the car. 'Is that yours? I've seen it before.'

He appeared unsure how to respond, and then

behind him, a hundred yards along the waterfront I saw a woman pause by the wharf as she walked from the direction of the square.

'Mr French?'

'What?' I turned my attention back to the man in front of me.

'Perhaps there is somewhere that we could go. Some coffee perhaps . . . '

I stared at him. 'Look, Mr . . . ? What did you say your name was?'

The woman was standing close to one of the lamps that lit the waterfront. I thought it was Alex. She was alone, staring out at the water with her hands thrust in her pockets. Without thinking I got up and started towards her.

'Mr French?'

I half turned. Through my alcohol-fogged brain I realised that the man I'd been speaking to was not simply some acquaintance of my dad's looking to pass the time of day, but I didn't care. 'Listen, whoever you are. I don't know anything about my father or what he was doing, OK?'

The woman had gone. I began to run after her. The man called my name but I didn't look back. My heart was thudding in my chest, sweat broke out on my brow. I stumbled and almost fell head-long, then found my footing and ran on. When I reached the corner I was out of breath and a dull ache ground at my temples. There was no sign of the woman. I went to the next corner, looking in the shops and bars along the way but I couldn't find her. A set of steps led up the hillside, vanishing into darkness, but they were deserted. And then I saw her turning a corner down a lane. I called out and ran after her and when I caught up I grabbed her arm.

'Alex!'

The woman turned, startled to find a drunken foreigner accosting her. It wasn't Alex. She didn't even look like her.

Suddenly all that jostling of my stomach contents got the better of me. I turned away and threw up. The woman made a sound of disgust and walked off while I vomited again. Even when I had nothing left inside me the sour taste of beer and vomit made me retch until my stomach cramped in spasms. Eventually I straightened up, sweating and weak and managed to make my way back to where I'd left the Jeep.

The man who'd approached me was gone and so was the Fiat. I dug in my pocket for my keys and when I found them, I got in the Jeep and stabbed at the ignition until finally I got it started. Then I jammed it into gear and drove off to look for Alex.

15

The house where Alex was staying was dark and quiet. I pulled over in the street outside. When I had seen her I'd reacted without thinking, but now I'd had a chance to think. I knew I couldn't just forget her. I couldn't let her vanish from my life the way Alicia had, though at the same time I didn't know if I could let her back in either. A thin line divides extremes of emotion. I didn't know if I loved her or hated her or whether I vacillated between the two. I just knew that I had to see her again.

I gave up trying to rationalise my actions and went to the door of her room and hammered with my fist. The windows were shuttered and there was no light inside. Eventually the noise I made brought someone from the house. A man appeared, his face slack with sleep and shadowed blue-black. When he saw me a flicker of annoyance furrowed his brow.

'I need to see the English girl, Alex,' I told him and was met with blank incomprehension. 'Alex,' I repeated loudly and pointed at the door behind me. The woman I'd talked to that morning, though it seemed much longer ago, appeared on the step behind him clutching a heavy robe around her thick body. When she saw me a quick exchange took place in Greek and then the man scowled at me and barked something unintelligible.

'No Alex,' the woman said. 'No here.'

There was only one other place I thought she might be. I went back to the Jeep and drove back towards town. I stopped at the first bar I came to and asked for a phone book. I had to ask a waiter to look up the name I wanted.

'Ramanda,' I told him. When he found it he wrote the address down in English then pointed in the direction of the street. It was somewhere on the hill near where I'd met Alex that morning so I guessed it was the right one.

Many of the narrow streets and alleys above the town had no signs to identify them and I soon lost my way. After twenty minutes or so of fruitlessly driving back and forth I found myself at the bottom of the steps where I'd met Alex that morning, so I left the Jeep and went on foot. Half-way up a lamp cast its dim light on the waxy leaves of a magnolia. White flowers dripped to the ground and formed a fragrant pool. The steps divided. An alley ran to the left, but I followed another flight of steps further up the hill. Garden walls hemmed in the narrowing stairway and the houses above blocked out the sky so that I had to feel my way in shadowed darkness. The scent of herbs sweetened the air. A man's laughter, low and intimate came from some dark window nearby and then the low murmur of voices.

At the top I emerged onto another narrow street. A light fixed to a telephone pole illuminated a rare sign which matched the address I'd been given and I began searching the houses for numbers. When I found the one I was looking for I stood in the thick shadow of a wall. Opposite me was a terrace which during the day would be shaded by a grapevine, and beneath it was the street door leading into the house. I could hear voices, but they were muffled. At first I couldn't see anybody, then the voices became clearer and the next moment Alex appeared at the edge of the terrace. She looked out towards the harbour. We were no more than a dozen steps apart. If she had glanced down she would have seen me.

As I watched her I wondered what I was doing there. I was sweaty and probably didn't smell very good and I was still more than a little drunk. I told myself I should leave. She had made her choice. Why else was she with Dimitri now? And yet I couldn't move. I remembered the woman who'd taken me to her apartment. Even as I'd tried somehow to get even, take some kind of petty revenge, I had thought of Alex.

Suddenly I heard a man's voice from the terrace.

'Look at this.' A moment later Dimitri appeared behind Alex and placed his hands on her shoulders. 'Don't you think that it is beautiful?'

'Yes, of course I do,' Alex replied quietly.

'Then how can you think of leaving?'

She didn't answer. The silence was fraught with subtle tension.

'I was an idiot,' Dimitri said at last. 'I do not know what came over me.'

Alex replied without looking at him, her tone sorrowful. 'You had plenty of time to think about it, Dim. It was what you decided you wanted.'

'People make mistakes, Alex.'

'Yes.'

He paused, as if wondering what precisely her agreement conveyed. 'I love you,' he said. 'You know that I love you.' He put his arms around her.

'Don't. Please.' She moved away from him, turning and slipping from his embrace and, as she did, both regret and frustration flashed in his face. At the same time Alex glanced down to where I was standing and she froze in shocked surprise. Hurriedly she turned back to Dimitri and took his arm.

'Let's go inside,' she said, her tone suddenly coaxing.

She started to lead him away but it was too late. Puzzled by the sudden change in her manner he glanced down to the street and at the same time I stepped from the shadows. Ignoring him I spoke directly to Alex.

'I want to talk to you.'

Before she could respond, Dimitri stepped past her to the rail and glared down at me angrily. 'Get the hell away from here! She doesn't want to see you.'

'You owe me that much,' I said, holding Alex's look.

'I told you she doesn't want you here!' Dimitri said. 'You should go back to England.'

'If that's true she can tell me herself,' I said, still looking at Alex. She wore a trapped expression as Dimitri turned to face her as well, waiting for her to say something.

264

When she finally spoke it was in a quiet voice. 'What do you want?'

The brief scene I'd just witnessed between Alex and Dimitri made me wonder if I had made a mistake. I thought back to what had happened that morning. Had I overreacted? Had I made the wrong assumption? 'I want to talk,' I repeated.

She glanced at Dimitri then said to me, 'Wait there.'

I thought for a second that Dimitri was going to leap down on me from where he stood. Then furiously he turned to follow her. A few moments later the street door opened and Alex came outside, but as I took a step towards her she shook her head in warning.

'No! Listen to me. I want you to leave me alone.'

Dimitri appeared behind her and, when he heard what she said, he put his arm protectively around her shoulders. 'You heard what she said. You should leave now.'

But to his surprise Alex shrugged him off. 'I mean both of you. I want both of you to leave me alone.'

He took a step towards her. 'Alex. You are upset. Come back inside. Everything will be all right. I promise.'

'He dumped you once already, Alex,' I warned. 'So what's changed suddenly? Let me guess, you told him you met somebody and miraculously he wanted you back, is that it?'

'Shut your mouth,' Dimitri said.

'It's the Greek male psyche,' I continued regardless.

265

He took a step towards me, but Alex held his arm. 'Dim, don't.'

'What it is,' I said goading him, 'is he didn't want you, but he couldn't stand the thought of you fucking anybody else.'

I sensed rather than saw a blur of movement as he lashed out. I took a step backwards but alcohol had dulled my reactions and the blow caught me on the side of my head. I staggered, but though drinking had made me slow it had also numbed my senses. I bunched a fist and swung a punch that glanced off his cheek with a satisfying thud. Pain and surprise registered on his face as blood sprang from a cut.

Alex yelled at us. 'Stop it! Both of you!'

By then Dimitri had recovered his balance and he stepped in and jabbed me hard below the sternum, forcing the air out of my lungs in a tortured gasp. My vision swam red. For a second I thought my heart had stopped and then I was on my knees coughing and struggling for breath. He came in again, but I pushed myself to my feet and propelled my head into his stomach like a battering ram, then, wrapping my arms around his waist, I drove him backwards into the wall. He grunted and then started aiming short hard jabs at my kidneys. I kept my head down and punched him repeatedly in the ribs. I was hardly aware of his blows. I heard Alex shouting at us to stop, but she may as well have yelled at the wind.

We stopped when Dimitri finally managed to push me away. I sucked air into my lungs. Long slivers of sharp pain raced up and down my back where he'd pummelled me. Dimitri held his side, wincing with each laboured breath. The fight couldn't have lasted much more than a minute, but already the adrenalin in my system was all used up and I felt completely drained. My mouth was swollen and when I touched my lip I felt blood, though I didn't know when he had hit me there.

It was only then that either of us noticed that Alex had vanished. The street was empty. We stared at one another.

'Go back to England,' Dimitri said wearily and then he turned and slammed the door in my face.

Across the street I saw an old man watching with curiosity from an open window. He murmured something quietly and with a shrug went back to his bed.

16

In the morning I felt as if I'd gone ten rounds in the ring. Every joint ached and my torso was a patchwork of bruising. As I examined myself in the bathroom mirror, I wondered how I'd managed to sustain such damage in what I was sure had been a very short space of time. I hadn't been in a physical fight since I was at school. It amazed me how punishing it could be.

When I eventually went downstairs, Irene's eyes widened in alarm. 'Robert, what happened?'

'It's nothing. I got up in the night and walked into something.'

She frowned and, though she obviously didn't believe my feeble story, she didn't make any other comment. I hadn't spoken to her since I'd been to the museum, and now she asked me if I had found the journal. When I said that I hadn't I thought she looked relieved.

'Perhaps it does not exist,' she suggested, wanting to believe it just as she wanted to believe that my dad had not betrayed the trust of the people of Ithaca.

I didn't tell her that I was sure somebody else had searched the museum. It was only then that I recalled the man who had approached me the night before. 'Do you know of anyone called Eric Schmidt?' I asked.

'I do not think so. Who is he?'

I shook my head. 'Nobody. It isn't important.'

Irene made coffee and while we drank it on the terrace I made the decision to go back to England. There didn't seem any point in staying any longer. My father was dead and buried, and whatever the truth about him, perhaps it was better for everyone that at least Irene's memories of him remained intact. When I told Irene, she asked if Alex was leaving too.

'I don't know. I don't think we'll be seeing each other again.'

She looked at my battered face but didn't comment. 'When will you leave?' she asked eventually.

'I'll go into town and see when I can get a flight.'

'I hope that you will come back one day, Robert.'

I told her that I hoped so too, though we both knew that it was unlikely.

I borrowed the Jeep later, and drove into Vathy. Fortunately Dimitri's wasn't the only travel agency in the town. I stood at the counter while the travel agent tapped at her computer keyboard.

'There is a flight this evening to London Gatwick,' she told me. 'It is a charter flight, but there are one or two seats available.'

I hesitated. I asked myself if this was really what I wanted. The woman regarded me questioningly. 'I'll take it,' I told her. I got out my credit card and handed it over, and within ten minutes she had printed a confirmation.

'Check-in is two hours before the flight, Mr French. Your ticket will be at the airline desk when you arrive. Enjoy your flight.'

'Thanks.'

I stepped outside into the heat of the morning and went to the ferry ticket office to check the timetable. There was an afternoon ferry to Sami at four o'clock which allowed me enough time to catch a taxi to the airport. I had half a day to fill. I wandered to the square and sat down at a *kefenio* where I ordered coffee. As I considered how to spend my remaining time on the island, I was plagued by the unsettling sense that I was making a mistake. A young woman in blue shorts and a white top climbed down to the wharf from a yacht. She had her back to me but in the glimpse of her long tanned legs and the toss of thick blonde hair I was reminded of Alex. When she turned to head towards the bakery I saw that in fact she barely resembled her at all.

When I finished my coffee I left some money on the table and started back to where I'd parked the Jeep. I decided to go back to the house and pack, and then spend a few hours at the beach. I paused outside a bookshop, wondering if I should get something to read to distract myself. The rack outside was filled with English and European novels, and next to it was another rack containing translations of the *Odyssey* and the *Iliad*. They brought my father to mind amid a jumble of confused emotions. I changed my mind about buying a book.

When I went back to the Jeep I found myself driving towards the house where Alex was staying. I parked at the end of the street behind an old Toyota. I rehearsed the things I might say to her in my mind, but none of them made much sense even to me. In my imaginings I started off appealing to her and ended up accusing her. I must have been there for nearly forty-five minutes when I heard a scooter start. Alex appeared at the gate a few moments later wearing a bright red shirt and blue shorts. For a second I thought she would come my way, but then she turned and rode off in the opposite direction. I stayed rooted to the spot in an agony of indecision for perhaps a minute and then I started the engine and went after her.

★　★　★

Alex took the road north out of town and as I followed, I spotted her now and then as she rounded a distant curve. By the time I reached the end of the long, straight causeway at Molos Bay, I was stuck behind a truck laden with rocks. The road had become too narrow and steep to get past and I had to wait until the driver finally waved me by at the top of the hill. By then Alex was out of sight. Twenty minutes later when I reached Stavros I pulled over in the square, wondering which of the several possible routes she had taken. Acting on a hunch, I followed the road down to Polis Bay, past the place where her scooter had broken down almost a week before. The beach was deserted, though there were a few cars parked in the shade of the olive trees near the bar, and a schooner rode serenely at anchor in the bay.

I pulled over. There was a scooter under the

trees, but I didn't know if it was the one I'd seen Alex riding. I asked a girl at the bar, and when she finally understood my question her face lit up.

'Ah, the bike, yes?'

'Yes. Do you know whose it is? Have you seen a girl here?'

'This bike is mine.'

I thanked her and went back to the Jeep. Across the bay I could see the village of Exoghi high on the hill and I was suddenly sure that was where Alex had gone. By then she was almost a half-hour ahead of me. I thought about waiting for her to come back as there was only the one road, but in the end I decided I didn't have the patience.

A few minutes later I was negotiating the steep road up the hill. I changed down into first gear, hauling the Jeep around hairpin bends, inches from a sheer drop to the rocks hundreds of feet below. I had gone about two thirds of the distance when I heard the sound of an approaching car and, even as I looked for a space to pull over, it appeared around a bend ahead of me. I saw right away that it was travelling too fast and instinctively I yanked on the wheel to avoid a collision. The other car swerved the opposite way and passed me in a cloud of dust. I had time only to register that it was small and dark before I realised that I was headed towards the edge of the cliff. Empty sky loomed beyond the bonnet. I stamped on the brake and felt the wheels begin to slide on the loose rock. For an instant I felt as if my insides had been sucked out of me. I knew that I was seconds away from plunging over the edge.

A series of images from my life flashed in my mind. It was like rapidly flicking through the photographs in an album. I saw my parents in Oxford before they were divorced and then the gates of the boarding school as I was driven through them for the first time; my father on the *Swallow*, dripping water as he shrugged off a scuba tank; Alicia frozen in time, and then Alex as she lay in bed sleeping while I looked on from the chair in the corner. I doubt if the entire sequence lasted even a second, but it was almost long enough to distract me from my own imminent demise. Then suddenly self-preservation kicked in and I jerked myself back to reality.

I remembered the old instruction that in a skid the thing to do is accelerate. It is a difficult thing to do when you are sliding towards oblivion. It goes against all natural instinct. But in desperation I put my foot on the accelerator and pulled hard on the steering wheel. The tyres bit the ground and the Jeep swerved and shot across the road. It bumped violently as it travelled up the hillside and then lost momentum. There was a brief fragment of time where it teetered on the brink, and then somehow the bonnet was pointing towards the road again and the Jeep crashed down with bone-shuddering impact and came to a stop.

The engine had stalled. Very faintly I could hear the sound of the other car receding, and then there was silence save for the ticking of hot metal and the thunder of my heartbeat. I rested my head against the steering wheel. My hands shook, slick with perspiration.

It was some time before I could start the engine and put the Jeep in gear again. I drove the rest of the way cautiously. When I reached the village I found Alex's scooter outside the church of Agia Marina where we had parked the week before. The keys were in the ignition, so I took them out and put them in my pocket. There was no sign of Alex. The village appeared to be as deserted as it had been the last time I was there, enveloped in an almost eerie silence. Even the normally ever-present cicadas were absent. The ground absorbed the heat of the sun and exhaled it back into the air, causing the buildings and trees to shimmer in waves.

I started up the road past shuttered houses. A goat bell clanked, its distinctive flat tone clear in the pristine air. A small flock of animals grazed in the shade of an olive grove higher on the hill. I found the overgrown path that led to the ruined cottage where Alex's grandmother had grown up and once again I stood in the gloomy shade of the gnarled and blackened trees. The cottage with its crumbling walls and empty windows looked no different but, when I walked around the back, I visualised the young German *Hauptmann* sitting at a table in the shade, and I could almost see a young girl emerge from the trees on the hillside.

As I had the last time I'd been there, I felt there was an atmosphere about the place. The stillness seemed to gather in the shadows. The past almost a physical presence. I sensed passions once more aroused, coiled and waiting.

There was no sign of Alex.

As I went back to the Jeep I imagined that she was watching me from some hidden vantage spot. Far below, a small boat drew a line of white across the blue of the bay as it left the beach. When I looked again ten minutes later, the yacht I'd seen earlier was heading for open water, her mainsail rising and fluttering in the breeze.

Eventually I wandered to the church and tried the door but it was locked. A pathway led through a graveyard of bristling crosses to a stone wall, and from there some steps carved out of the rock led up the hillside and vanished among the cypresses. As I started up them I heard a sound from the church, and when I looked back a priest emerged dressed in long black robes. We observed one another and, as I turned to go back, I called out.

'Hello. *Yassas*. Do you speak English?'

He had dark eyes and a long beard, and his expression was stern, somehow disapproving. 'Can I help you?' he asked in heavily accented English.

'I'm looking for somebody. A young woman. I wondered if you'd seen her.'

'I have seen nobody. Except you.'

'Where does that path go?' I gestured to the steps cut in the rock.

'Along the cliff.'

I wondered if Alex might have gone that way. I thanked the priest and retraced my steps.

'Be careful,' he called out. 'The path can be dangerous if you do not know your way.'

I thanked him for the warning. He remained outside the church watching me until I was out of sight. At the top of the steps the path passed between the cypresses where it was shadowed and cool. I walked beneath a kind of silken roof formed by dozens of spiders' webs spun between the trees, one after the other, their fat black owners waiting patiently for their next meal. As I passed underneath, they quivered in the breeze and I was afraid a spider would drop onto my head. I shuddered at the prospect and was relieved when the path emerged into the open again.

A little further on two giant slabs of rock, which some long ago tremor had split apart like a nut, flanked the path. A few straggly bushes had found a tenuous hold at the top and there were fissures and ledges masked by shadows. I wondered if this was the place which Irene had described where all those years ago Metkas's men had gathered to ambush Hassel. Further on, the oak and olives gave way to dry grass and scrub, the soil too thin to support much more. The priest had been right about it being dangerous. Occasionally the path became so steep that it was little more than a goat track and the slope ended abruptly in a fringe of the ubiquitous wild oak growing at the edge of the cliff.

I had walked perhaps half a mile. From somewhere higher up came the sound of a goat bell. The land ahead tapered to a grassy headland which jutted out toward the open sea and the hills of Kephalonia. The channel between the islands was flecked with the sails of cruising yachts. Something startlingly red caught my eye, fluttering in the breeze, a piece of cloth caught on a bush at the edge of the cliff. I went cautiously down and plucked it free. It was clean, ripped along one edge and in an instant of recall I pictured the red shirt Alex had been wearing.

Beyond the bushes a vertical drop ended on the rocks far below. Vertigo made my head spin. In the open space in front of me the sky and the sea merged. I sucked in my breath and staggered backwards.

★ ★ ★

The priest allowed me to use the phone in the house beside the church. He stayed with me while I waited for the police, his expression somehow accusing, until eventually I mumbled some excuse and went outside.

When Captain Theonas eventually arrived he brought two uniformed officers with him. I explained what had happened and led them along the cliff. While his men began to comb the area, Theonas asked me if I was certain that the scooter parked by the church was the one Alex had been riding.

'I think so. When I saw her, she was wearing a red shirt.' I gestured to the scrap of cloth in his hand.

'You say that you followed her here?'

'Yes. In a way.'

'But you did not see her actually arrive?'

'No. I got stuck behind a truck,' I told him. 'But I guessed she might have come to Exoghi. We came here last week.'

'Then she did not tell you that she was coming here?'

'No.'

I watched his men walking back and forth through the thin grass and I wondered what they expected to find. From the edge of the cliff it was impossible to look directly down to the rocks far below because of the contours of the cliff face, but the beach was visible and the road running alongside it. I realised that Alex might have stood there and watched me drive past the bay. An image flashed in my mind of the night I had seen her on the wharf as she slipped forward into the darkness, and a hollow dread opened up within me.

'Mr French,' Theonas said. 'Mr French?'

I came to. I felt light-headed, as if the blood had drained from my brain.

'Is something wrong? Is there something else you have thought of?'

'I think she might have jumped.'

'Jumped?' Theonas seemed taken aback by the idea.

'It's possible.' I could hardly believe it, but the more I thought about it the more sense it made. I took an involuntary step closer to the cliff edge, but Theonas grabbed my arm in alarm.

'It is dangerous.' Theonas scrutinised me, his eyes and thoughts hidden behind the blank lenses of his sunglasses. 'Are you all right, Mr French?'

'Yes. Yes I think so. A bit dazed.'

His men found nothing and eventually we returned to the church. It was mid-afternoon by then. I had a little over an hour to make the ferry to Kephalonia if I was to catch my plane, but I had already abandoned my earlier plans. Theonas ordered one of his men to stay with Alex's scooter while the other got in behind the wheel of the police car. 'Please follow us, Mr French,' he said to me.

We drove down the hill to the bay where the three of us made our way along the rocks at the bottom of the cliff. I dreaded what we would find. I half expected to come across her bloodied corpse at every step and I followed along with a kind of numb resignation. Eventually, however, it became clear that Alex wasn't there. We began to search the waterline. In places it was deep and shadowed. Occasionally Theonas consulted with the other officer and they examined the cliff above us. It was often vertical, but there were areas where trees and bushes grew among the rocks, creating hollows and shelves where it was conceivable that a person who fell from the top might come to rest. Even so, it was almost impossible that anyone could survive such a fall. I cupped my hands to my mouth and called her name.

'ALEX.'

I shouted again but there was no answer. Theonas removed his glasses and regarded me with what might have been a trace of sympathy. We kept searching all the way out to the headland. All the time the sea lapped at the rocks, the waves getting stronger the further out we went. I don't know how long we were there before I felt a hand on my shoulder.

'I am afraid it is no use,' Theonas said. 'In the morning I will arrange for a boat.'

I stared at him. My initial shock had begun to wear off, to be replaced by an awful, gnawing guilt. I told myself that I should have known. If Alex had killed herself, it was my fault.

'I am sorry,' Theonas said. 'Come. I will drive you back to Vathy.'

17

Theonas arrived at the house early the following morning. As he got out of his car I watched from the terrace where I'd spent the last couple of hours, having eventually abandoned any possibility of sleep. I might have dozed for an hour or two, but that was about it. Every time I closed my eyes I saw that piece of red cloth fluttering in the breeze, and then the dizzying view of the rocks far below the cliff. An image of the rocks rushed towards me, filling my mind's eye. I was falling, plunging through space. My world shrank from sea and sky to a single black rock which rapidly expanded, getting bigger and bigger until it took on gargantuan proportions. And then abruptly there was nothing. Blackness. I would open my eyes with a start, my body damp with sweat, my heart thudding in my chest.

Theonas looked up at me. There were dark circles beneath his eyes and I had the feeling that he too had not slept much, though something about his expression caused me a prickle of unease. The sympathy which I had detected in his manner the day before, now seemed absent.

'What is it?' I asked.

He didn't answer my question. Instead he gestured towards the waiting car. 'Please, Mr French.'

It seemed less of an invitation than an order.

As I went down, Irene appeared.

'I am coming too,' she informed Theonas who, though he nodded his assent, seemed reluctant.

We drove to Polis Bay, where a party made up of police officers and local volunteers was assembled ready to begin another search along both the top and bottom of the cliff. I saw men with ropes who would be lowered from the top to examine the shelves and hollows where Alex might have come to rest. Though I wanted to help, Theonas instructed me to wait on the road above the beach.

'It is better that you remain here.'

A young officer was left to linger not very discreetly nearby. When Irene threw Theonas a questioning look, he avoided her eye.

As a group of searchers made their way down from the road I saw Dimitri among them. When he saw me he stopped and stared angrily. I thought for a moment that he would come over, but Theonas stepped between us and, speaking quietly, took his arm and firmly led him away, though Dimitri kept looking back at me over his shoulder.

As the search continued throughout the morning I looked on with growing dread. I was certain that it was only a matter of time before Alex's body was found. I blamed myself for what had happened. I saw her actions on the night I'd pulled her from the harbour in a different light. I had put it down to the effects of alcohol and sleeping pills, but now I realised how emotionally unbalanced Alex was. I couldn't escape the thought that I had driven her to this.

It was evident long before the searchers gave up that any hope of finding her alive was futile. Several fishing boats had been enlisted to help, and they trawled back and forth across the bay. Each time one of them hauled in its net I held my breath, expecting a shout to ring out across the water, but each time nothing happened. I became increasingly perplexed.

When Theonas eventually returned, he told me what I already knew. 'We have found no trace of Alex. She is not here.'

'Then where is she? She can't have simply vanished.'

'It is possible that her body may have been carried out of the bay by the currents. I have arranged for a boat to search the coast.'

As the last group of searchers returned, one broke away from the others. It was Dimitri. Theonas spoke quickly to the young officer nearby who intercepted him and issued a curt instruction, placing one hand firmly against Dimitri's chest.

Dimitri thrust an accusing finger at me. 'Where is Alex, you bastard? What have you done with her? If you have hurt her, I swear that I will kill you!'

Theonas barked an order to the young officer who took Dimitri's arm and led him away, though he continued to shout accusations and threats over his shoulder.

'What is he talking about?' Irene asked. 'How can he think that Robert would do anything to hurt Alex?'

Theonas didn't answer her. Instead he said to

me, 'This morning my men spoke to the people in Exoghi to see if any of them saw Alex yesterday.'

'And?'

'There was a boy tending goats on the hillside. He saw a woman wearing a red shirt on the cliff, and there was a man with her. He thought that they were arguing.'

I was completely taken aback by this news.

'Did you see anybody else yesterday, Mr French?'

'Nobody. Except the priest.'

'Ah yes, the priest. You said that you went to his house to use the telephone?'

'Yes.'

'The priest said that he had seen you before that.'

'That's right. I asked him if he'd seen Alex. He warned me about the path being dangerous.'

'Then it was after speaking to the priest that you went along the cliff?'

'Yes.'

'You are certain of this? Perhaps you spoke to him as you were returning?'

'No. I told you, he warned me to watch my step.' Exasperated I said testily, 'I don't see what difference it makes anyway.' Theonas made a vague gesture, but then I saw what he was getting at. 'This man the boy saw. You think it was me, is that it?'

'Was it you, Mr French?'

I shook my head incredulously as it dawned on me that Theonas suspected that Alex had not jumped or fallen from the cliff, but that somebody had pushed her. The somebody in question being me.

★   ★   ★

I was taken into the police station through the rear entrance after our small procession came to a halt in a dirt yard at the back of the building. The single officer left in charge was sitting with his feet on the desk smoking a cigarette while he watched a soap opera on a television in the corner. He looked over his shoulder and spoke to one of the returning officers.

'*Yassou,*' he called out. '*Ti nea?*'

'*Tipote,*' the officer replied. Nothing. Then he made some other comment and jerked his head towards me.

The man glanced curiously at me and went back to his soap opera. Theonas frowned and angrily slapped the man's boots from the desk, barking something which made him sit up and hastily turn off the television.

I was taken to a small room containing a scratched table and a couple of chairs. 'Please,' Theonas gestured that I should take a seat.

Irene had insisted on coming with us, even though Theonas had tried to persuade her to allow him to drop her at the house, assuring her that he merely needed to ask me some questions. When she started to follow me into the room, Theonas stopped her, his tone uncomfortably apologetic. She was surprised and irritated and a brief conversation followed which to me was completely unintelligible.

285

Finally Irene conceded, though she wasn't happy about it.

'Apparently I am not allowed to stay. It is ridiculous of course.' She made a vague gesture of impatience. 'I am sure everything will be all right but I will telephone a lawyer in Kephalonia. He is English. Your father knew him.'

'A lawyer?' My sense of unreality had deepened during the drive to Vathy, but the idea that I might need a lawyer brought my situation into sharp focus.

'As a precaution, that is all,' Irene assured me, though I detected a shimmer of uncertainty in her manner.

When Irene had gone Theonas sat down. 'There are some questions I would like to ask you, Mr French. Do you mind answering them?' His manner had changed. He was relaxed, almost friendly. 'It will take some time for the lawyer Irene mentioned to arrive. Of course you would be within your rights to wait until he does.' He took out a packet of cigarettes and lit one, offering the pack to me though I waved it away. 'Perhaps by then we can clear this up.'

'That depends what 'this' is exactly doesn't it?' I said.

He shrugged. 'For now, I would like to understand more about your relationship with Alex. You met when exactly?'

'Last week.'

'Can you be more specific?'

'The day I arrived on the island. The day my father was found.'

'And how did you meet?'

286

'We shared a table at a café in the square,' I said. 'She didn't stay long.'

'Did you speak to her?'

'Not then. Later.'

'The same evening?'

'Yes. I went for a walk. When I got to the end of the wharf I saw her again.' I hesitated, uncertain how to describe what had happened next. It wouldn't be exactly true to say she had jumped, but neither was it accurate to say she had fallen. Instead I told him I had heard a splash. 'It was dark. One second she was there, then I glimpsed a movement and she was gone.'

'You are saying Alex attempted to kill herself on the night you met?' Theonas's tone mixed astonishment with a note of scepticism.

'I'm not sure what she intended.'

He let the question go for the moment. 'What did you do after you witnessed this?'

'I ran over to where I'd seen her. She was floating face-down. I jumped in and turned her over and got her to the shore.' I could see that Theonas didn't believe a word I was telling him.

'Go on, Mr French,' he said when I paused.

I explained how I'd borrowed a bedspread from a cottage to keep her warm before I took her back to where she was staying. 'Eventually I got her into bed and she fell asleep. I stayed with her until some time in the morning.'

'And then?'

'I left her. I thought she would probably sleep for most of the day. I wrote a note in case she woke up.'

Theonas lit another cigarette. 'Tell me, did you

call for a doctor at any time during all of this?'

'No.'

'I see. Did you perhaps inform anyone of what had happened? Perhaps the owner of the house where she was staying?'

'It was the middle of the night.'

'So you left her sleeping. You were not concerned that perhaps she might wake up?'

'Look, I know what you're suggesting,' I said irritably, 'but she didn't seem to be suicidal. She told me she'd taken some sleeping pills and then had a few drinks on top of them. I didn't really think she knew what she was doing when she jumped or fell or whatever she did. She didn't strike me as the sort of person who would seriously try to kill herself.'

'I see. And after you left her that night, when did you next see her?'

'The following day. I went to where she was staying, but she wasn't there. She'd left a note to say she was all right and that she would be back later. I decided to go to Polis Bay for a swim and by chance I met her on the road. Her scooter had broken down. I gave her a lift to Exoghi because she wanted to see the house where her grandmother was born.'

'And how did she seem to you that day?'

'Fine. Embarrassed actually. I mean it was obvious that she was unhappy about something, but she certainly wasn't suicidal.'

'And after that you saw her again the following day I believe? You took her sailing on your father's boat?'

'Yes.'

'Then at the weekend you both visited the house of Alkimos Kounidis in Kioni, am I correct?'

'Yes.'

'You came to know each other quite well.'

'Quite well.'

'What was the nature of your relationship with Alex, exactly, Mr French?'

'We were friends.'

'That is all? I was led to believe that your relationship was perhaps more intimate than that.'

By whom I wondered? 'You want to know if we slept together, is that it?'

'Did you?'

'Yes.'

'You were aware that Alex was involved in a relationship with Dimitri Ramanda?'

'Yes, I know all about that. But it was over when I met her. That was why she took the sleeping pills the night I met her.'

'She told you that?'

I tried to remember if that was what Alex had actually said. 'If not, she implied it.'

'On Sunday, when you returned from spending the weekend with Alkimos Kounidis, you left Alex at the house where she had rented a room?'

'Yes.'

'And in the morning you returned, I believe. The woman who owns the house remembers you very well.'

'Yes.'

'But Alex was not there?'

'As you say, she was not there.'

'Did you see her that day, Mr French?'

I hesitated, wondering whether he knew that I had met her in the street. I guessed that he did and I could only imagine that Alex must have told Dimitri what had happened. 'Yes, I ran into her as I was leaving, actually,' I admitted.

'Did you speak to her?'

'Why don't we just get to the point?' I said impatiently.

'Very well. Did Alex tell you that she had spent the night at the house of Dimitri Ramanda?'

'Yes.'

'That must have come as a surprise to you.'

'Must it?'

'Something of a shock, in fact. You had spent the weekend together. Perhaps you had developed certain feelings. Tell me how you felt when you discovered that she had spent the night with Dimitri.'

I tried to keep my expression neutral. 'As you guessed, I was surprised.'

He raised his eyebrows. 'Unpleasantly so, I imagine.'

I made no response.

'That night you went to Dimitri's house, I understand.'

'Yes, and I'm sure you know what happened.'

'But I would like to hear it from you. Why did you go there?'

'I wanted to talk to Alex. She and Dimitri were on the terrace. I overheard them talking and I got the impression that things weren't entirely settled between them.'

'Settled?'

'I don't think Alex knew what she wanted.'

'I see. And then what happened?'

'She saw me. I said I wanted to talk to her and she came down to the street.'

'Alone?'

'Dimitri followed her. There was a scuffle. A fight I suppose, between Dimitri and me.'

'And then?'

'And then nothing. Alex had gone. I went back to Irene's house and went to bed.'

'You did not see Alex again that night?'

'No. Not until yesterday. I'd been to book a flight home. I drove to where she was staying and saw her leave on a scooter.'

'Ah yes. The ticket you bought yesterday morning. You were planning to leave Ithaca, were you not, Mr French?'

'Yes.'

'You had decided that there was no future for you with Alex perhaps.'

'Is that a question?'

He made a gesture, as if to suggest that what I said didn't matter. 'But when you saw her, what did you do?'

'I followed her.'

'To Exoghi?'

'Yes, and when I got there I couldn't find her. Look, I know where all this is going. You think I saw her on the cliff and we had some kind of argument, is that it?'

'Is that what happened?'

'No. I told you, I never spoke to her.'

'But you were angry. Of course this is

291

understandable. Alex led you to believe that her relationship with Dimitri was over, and then you discover that she spent the night with him after being with you only a few hours before. Any man would be angry. It is only natural.'

I would have laughed at his patently obvious ploy of empathy if I hadn't known that his efforts to trap me into implicating myself were completely in earnest.

'Listen,' I said. 'It wasn't me on that cliff with Alex. Maybe the boy made a mistake.'

'You believe that perhaps she went there with the intention of harming herself?' he asked sceptically.

'I don't know what I believe. The last time I saw her she was upset. It's possible.'

Theonas stared at me. 'It is a pity that you are the only person who was aware that Alex had attempted to harm herself before. I take it you did not mention this to anyone?'

'No,' I said wearily.

'Then in fact I have only your word that this incident took place at all.'

I got up and went to stand by the window with my back to him. 'I think I should wait for the lawyer to arrive before I say anything else.'

For some time I could feel him observing me, and then at last I heard the scrape of a chair followed by the sound of the door, and I was left in the company of a young female officer. She stood by the door, and when I smiled at her she merely stared back expressionlessly. I eyed the large automatic pistol holstered on her hip and settled back to think.

18

The uncommunicative female officer who'd been left to guard me was later replaced by one of her male colleagues, a swarthy mono-browed individual who sat by the door with his legs stretched out in front and passed the time idly picking his teeth and looking bored. Occasionally I wandered too close to him as I paced the room, and when I did he waved me away with one hand while the other rested menacingly close to his gun.

For the most part, however, I spent the time standing at the window with my back to the room. I contemplated the events of the past week, during which my life had been turned upside down and shaken like an old drawer. Gradually my mind began to work again and, as I thawed from the sense of shock into which I had sunk, I began to wonder about the man who was supposedly seen arguing with Alex. For the first time it occurred to me that she might not have deliberately jumped from the cliff. It was then that I remembered the car which had almost run me off the road on the way to Exoghi.

I didn't hear the door open, nor anybody enter the room, but a voice from behind broke into my troubled thoughts.

'Good afternoon, Mr French.'

I turned to find a man perhaps in his forties

regarding me with a pleasant smile. With one hand he clutched a battered leather briefcase, while the other was extended towards me. 'My name is Williams. Shall we sit down? I'm afraid the heat still rather gets to me you know. Can't get used to it.'

We shook hands and then he produced a handkerchief and mopped his flushed brow. His Home Counties accent was incongruous in our current surroundings. He was wearing a crumpled pale linen suit and beneath it a white shirt which hung limply on his fleshy frame, striped by a pair of bright red braces which ballooned outwards to accommodate his ample stomach.

'Now, first things first,' he said briskly as he dug in a pocket of his jacket. 'Yes, here we are. Let me give you my card.'

The card introduced him as Peter Williams from the law firm *Zikas and Williams*. There was an address in Argostoli. He had thinning sandy-coloured hair and glasses from behind which he examined me with a sharply observant gaze that was at odds with his slightly down-at-heel appearance.

'Irene telephoned as you know. I came as soon as I could. I expect she mentioned that our firm handled your father's affairs. By the way, may I offer my condolences? Terrible thing. Always thought he was a thoroughly decent chap, your father.'

'Thank you.'

'Actually, I was a student at Oxford when he was teaching there. Never met of course.

Different fields.' He smiled benignly, and folded his hands on the table. 'You're in business yourself I believe?'

'Yes. I run a property company in London.'

'Not an academic man then, eh? Don't blame you. That's the thing isn't it, these days? Bricks and mortar. I imagine you do very well.'

As he spoke, Williams rummaged in his briefcase and found a pad. The first few pages were covered with notes written in a small, untidy hand. He flicked over to a blank page and then unscrewed the cap from a silver fountain pen and held it poised. 'Now, shall we get down to business? I know all about your young lady-friend. Alex isn't it? Naturally I've spoken to Captain Theonas. Between him and Irene I think I've got the gist of things.'

'Theonas seems to think that I killed her.'

'Yes, well, he's not exactly saying as much actually. Not in so many words. He leans more towards the theory of a lovers' tiff I think. Perhaps things got out of hand. A tussle perhaps. But let's not get ahead of ourselves. I understand that you witnessed an incident involving Alex on the night when you first met? She threw herself into the harbour I believe.'

'I wouldn't say she threw herself.'

'But you did rescue her?'

'I think 'rescue' is a bit dramatic. I pulled her out of the water and got her back to where she was staying. Not that it matters. Theonas doesn't believe it even happened and I can't prove that it did.'

'Yes, actually while we're on that subject, it's

probably best if you don't have any more little chats with the good captain unless I'm present. Can't be too careful, you know. Words get twisted and so on.' Williams consulted his pad. 'However, it seems that there is some corroboratory evidence to support your account. A woman who lives in a cottage on the waterfront said that a bedspread she left out to dry unaccountably became damp with seawater. Also she found some money which was left by her doorstep. It would be helpful if we could also find the pills you mentioned, but apparently there's no trace of them in Alex's room.'

'She told me she got rid of them,' I said, surprised that Theonas had even bothered to check my story.

'That's a pity. But anyway, the bedspread helps to establish the possibility that Alex was prone to act rashly when in an emotional state. Who is to say that she did not acquire some more sleeping pills? She had reason to be upset yesterday, I gather?'

I shook my head. 'I don't believe she was ever suicidal.'

Williams was surprised. 'Really?'

'I've been thinking about it. I don't think she drove up to Exoghi to throw herself from the cliff. Theonas said a boy saw her with another man.'

'Yes. Naturally I enquired as to whether it had been established where this fellow Dimitri was at the time. It seems, however, that he was in Vathy for the entire day. There are witnesses.'

'Then it must have been somebody else. On

my way up there I passed a car on the way down. The driver was going too fast. It almost ran me off the road.'

Williams blinked. 'Did you mention this to our friend Captain Theonas?'

'I forgot all about it. With everything else that's been happening it slipped my mind. But there was something else. I didn't get a good look at the car, but I know it was dark coloured. It might have been blue. Possibly a Fiat.'

'I see.' Williams wore a slightly perplexed smile. With the light shining off his glasses he gave the impression of being mild-mannered, even vaguely ineffectual. It was, however, an illusion. His eyes were sharp, missing nothing. 'Am I right in assuming that this particular vehicle holds some significance?'

'A car like that followed Alex and me from Kioni on Sunday. We'd been spending the weekend at the house of a friend of my father.'

'It followed you? To what end?'

'I have no idea. I kept slowing to let it by, but it hung back every time. We took the mountain road to see if it came after us and it did. I tried to get a look at the driver when we reached Anoghi, but when he realised we'd stopped, he sped off.'

'Did you happen to report this incident?'

I shook my head. 'There didn't seem to be anything to report really.'

'But now you think that this car was the same one which passed you on the way to Exoghi?'

'I couldn't swear to it, but I think it might have been. I saw it another time too.'

Williams raised his eyebrows enquiringly.

'It was two nights ago. A man approached me. He wanted to talk to me about my father, but I brushed him off. I was a bit drunk. But there was a blue Fiat parked across the road.'

'And you think this might be the man who was seen with Alex in Exoghi?'

'Maybe. If she was in the car that I passed on the way up the hill it would explain why her body hasn't been found.'

I got the feeling Williams suspected it was wishful thinking on my part, though for a few moments he was thoughtful.

'When this car followed you from Kioni on Sunday, did Alex appear to recognise it?' he asked.

I recalled my initial suspicion that it might have been Dimitri. 'I can't say,' I said in the end. 'She didn't say so.'

Williams frowned. He stood up and took off his jacket. 'Let's take a break shall we? I'll ask for some drinks.' He went to the door and spoke in Greek to somebody outside. A few minutes later a large bottle of cold water and some glasses appeared. Williams produced a pack of cigarettes from his briefcase and, shaking one out, offered the pack to me.

'I gave it up a few years ago.'

'Very wise,' he said, lighting up a Silk Cut. 'Tried to do the same a few times myself actually, but it's never worked I'm afraid. I'm a weak man when you get to the bottom of it.' He patted his stomach. 'Always been too fond of the better things in life. Good food, fine malt whisky, and cigarettes, English of course, none of that bloody awful Greek stuff. I limit myself to six a day if I can. Not that I'm always successful,' he added wistfully.

'I suppose there could be worse vices.'

'Oh absolutely. Always had an eye for the ladies I'm afraid. Got me into all sorts of trouble.'

'You're not married?'

'Never have been. Can't say I'm much of a catch, I have to admit. Still, I've had my share of success with the fairer sex, if I do say so myself. To be honest marriage has never really appealed to me. I suppose I'm unconventional, at least compared to some of the people I was at Oxford with. I expect they're all doing rather nicely. House and family in a respectable part of town, weekends at the golf club, meetings with fellow Masons and all that. Can't say it ever appealed much to me, which is why I ended up here.' He smiled in a vaguely rueful way and stubbed out his cigarette.

'So, what happens now?' I asked.

'We get you out of here, my dear chap.' He gestured towards his notes. 'At the moment the police really have no reason to hold you. There's no actual proof that anything untoward has happened to Alex. If anything, the evidence rather leans towards the possibility that she may have done herself harm.'

'Except for this mystery man.'

'Yes, actually I was about to get to that. There is just one small matter to take care of. A formality really.'

'What kind of formality?' I questioned, suspicious of some evasive note I detected.

Just then there was a knock at the door, and a police officer put his head around the door and said something in Greek before ducking out again.

'Right then,' Williams said as he struggled to his feet. 'It appears they're ready for us.'

'Ready for what? And who are 'they'?'

'It's really nothing to worry about,' he assured me as I was ushered towards the door. 'You remember the shepherd boy who saw Alex arguing with a man on the cliff? Captain Theonas has had him brought here to see if he recognises you.'

'An identity parade?'

'Yes, I suppose you could call it that. Naturally, once the boy confirms that you weren't the man he saw, Theonas will have to let you go. As I said, it's really just a formality.'

'You knew about this when you arrived didn't you?' I guessed.

'Of course.'

'Why didn't you tell me earlier?'

'Ah. Didn't I mention it? I probably didn't want to worry you. Doesn't pay to dwell on these things for too long beforehand I find.'

Meaning, I presumed, that the less time there was for the guilty to sweat it, the less obvious their guilt would be. I wasn't exactly confident as I followed him along a short corridor. I wondered what would happen if the boy made a mistake, or if Theonas tipped him off either deliberately or inadvertently? I didn't know if such things happened in Greece, but suddenly I felt a long way from home.

'I suppose I don't have a choice in this, do I?' I asked when we reached a closed door.

'I'm afraid not,' Williams said, cheerfully unperturbed. He knocked on the door and stood aside as it opened. 'But there's nothing at all to worry about. Believe me.'

★　★　★

A few minutes later I was standing in a line with a mix of locals and other men who were probably tourists picked off the street, since they were obviously not Greek. I was heartened that at least I didn't stand out like the proverbial sore thumb. Theonas entered with his hand resting paternalistically on the shoulder of a boy of around twelve years of age. He bent down and spoke quietly to him, and the boy nodded his understanding. He seemed very young, with wide, impressionable eyes.

As he made his way along the line with Theonas following a step or two behind, the boy paused briefly in front of each man in turn, gazing at them intently before moving on. As he drew closer to me, my heart thumped harder and my palms became slippery with sweat. Though I tried not to draw attention to myself, I recalled Williams' advice not to worry, but rather than find it reassuring I felt as if guilt was stamped onto my face like a brand.

When the boy finally reached me I stared at

the wall behind him and tried to recite a nursery rhyme in my mind, though I couldn't remember anything past the first line. 'Humpty Dumpty sat on a wall . . . ' I kept repeating it over and over in my head, but my brain had turned to mush and the second line wouldn't come. I willed the boy to move on, aware that he had paused for longer than he had with the others. Every moment seemed to be drawn out excruciatingly. I was aware of Theonas's silent, watchful scrutiny. In the end I simply couldn't stand it any longer and I looked down at the boy and smiled, though unfortunately I felt as if I'd managed to twist my features into something resembling a savage grimace instead.

The boy turned and said something to Theonas and a quick exchange in Greek followed. Theonas stared at me, his expression unreadable, and then with a gesture indicated the boy should move on.

★ ★ ★

I was taken back to the interview room and for ten minutes was left alone while I contemplated my imminent incarceration. I was certain the boy had identified me. Though it had to be some kind of mistake, I knew convincing Theonas and even Williams would be almost impossible. I was so sure I was in deep trouble that when Williams finally appeared I couldn't understand why he was smiling.

'Good news,' he announced. 'You're free to leave.'

302

'Free?'

'Yes. I told you there was nothing to worry about. Have you got everything?'

'Yes. I think so.' With dizzying, uncomprehending relief I followed him out to the reception area where Theonas waited for us.

'I took the liberty of asking Irene to fetch your passport earlier,' Williams said, and passed it to Theonas.

'Wait a minute,' I protested. 'I thought you said I was in the clear.'

'Oh you are,' Williams assured me. 'Captain Theonas has assured me that as soon as he has completed the necessary formalities he will return your passport to you. Am I correct, Captain?'

Theonas acknowledged that he was with a barely discernible nod. 'Of course.'

'Excellent.' Williams shook Theonas's hand and led me to the door. 'Best if you don't say anything until we're outside I think,' he murmured quietly. I complied until we were in the street.

'What happened back there?' I demanded. 'What did the boy say?'

'Actually, he confirmed your story. He said that he did see you yesterday, but you were not the man on the cliff with Alex. He was adamant that the man had fair hair and he was taller.' Williams looked at me quizzically. 'Ring any bells?'

'Half the tourists on the island,' I said. 'Although the man I saw the other night fits that description. And as I said before, there was a blue Fiat parked in the street.'

'Can you remember anything else about him?'

'I thought he sounded German or Dutch maybe. And he asked if I knew somebody called Eric Schmidt.'

'Which is a German name, I believe. Do you know who he is?'

'I've never heard of him.' I asked Williams if he'd told Theonas about the Fiat. 'If they could find that car, maybe they'll find Alex.'

'I'm afraid the good captain was somewhat sceptical about that. He doesn't seem to like you very much, you know. Is there any particular reason for that?'

'It's complicated. He and Irene were seeing each other before my father died. I suggested that might have coloured his judgement concerning my father's death.'

'Oh? But I understood that your father died of a heart attack.'

'He drowned actually. Possibly as the result of a heart attack.'

We had reached the square. Williams looked at his watch and searched for a taxi. 'There's a ferry from Piso Aetos in half an hour. If I hurry, I can catch it. If there is any further development, Captain Theonas will inform me.'

A taxi pulled over and we shook hands before he got in. As I closed the door he wound down the window. 'This man that you met, you say he wanted to talk about your father. Was there any connection between your father and Alex?'

I was about to say no, but I remembered that there was, albeit a tenuous one. 'Have you ever heard of a ship called the *Antounnetta*?' I asked.

'Can't say that I have. Is it important?'

'It might be,' I answered.

19

The bars and cafés in the square were preparing for the evening trade. A few tourists sat drinking cold beers in the late-afternoon sun as boats sailed into the harbour in search of a mooring for the night. A sleek fifty-footer slid past the headland, the sun reflecting off her white hull. As I watched her, something tripped like a tumbler in my mind, but it was as if the parts of a lock were annoyingly not quite in synch. A half-formed association refused to yield its source. The yacht turned into what breeze there was a hundred yards from shore, and I heard the anchor chain rattle from her bow. She reminded me of something, I was sure of that, and then I turned away, thinking it would come to me.

Outside the office of *Classic Tours*, I glanced through the window at the girl behind the counter inside. Beyond her, an office door was partly ajar and I saw a movement from within. At the *kefenio* across the street I ordered a coffee and sat down to wait. Dimitri emerged about fifteen minutes later. When he reached the corner, I left some money on the table and got up to follow.

We headed away from the town, climbing the hillside along twisting streets connected by flights of steps. I hung back far enough to make sure he didn't realise I was there, but close enough that I could keep him in sight. Though the sun was slipping towards the top of the hills it was still warm, the accumulated heat of the day lying trapped in narrow lanes. The pungent smell of rosemary and sage permeated the air.

At the top of some steps I emerged onto the quiet, deserted street high above the harbour where Dimitri lived. The sun was sinking over the strait between Ithaca and Kephalonia and the sky was beginning to darken. In the soft dusk half-light I paused outside his house and knocked at the door. I heard the sound of footsteps and then Dimitri appeared. He looked ravaged by both lack of sleep and grief, but when he saw me his bewilderment turned quickly to anger.

'What the hell are you doing here?'

'I need to talk to you.'

'I have nothing to say to you! Get away from here!' He began to close the door in my face until I put a hand out to stop him.

'Have you spoken to Theonas?' I hadn't been sure what to expect when I arrived. When I had seen him that morning at Polis Bay, he had clearly blamed me for Alex's disappearance, a belief which Theonas had probably done little to discourage. If he could have got his hands on me then, he would have killed me. I'd been half-prepared to encounter the same reaction now, but though he was only holding himself together by an effort of will, I didn't see any murderous intent in his eyes. 'What did he tell you?'

'I told you to get away from here! Go before I do something I will regret.'

I kept my hand on the door. 'I can't leave. I need your help to find Alex.'

His eyes widened in surprise and for a moment I thought I saw a flare of hope, but it died as quickly as it had appeared. 'She is dead,' he said heavily. His anger turned to resignation. He released the door and began to turn away as if he couldn't summon the will to fight me any longer. 'Leave me in peace.'

'Is that what Theonas told you?' I said to his retreating back. When he didn't respond, I followed him along a narrow passage that led to a flight of stairs. 'If she's dead, where's her body?'

He paused and turned back to me and, though I could see that the question bothered him, he made a vague gesture. 'There are strong currents in the bay and there are ruins on the sea bed. Perhaps she was trapped. Captain Theonas is sending divers to search tomorrow.'

'They won't find anything,' I said.

Dimitri's eyes were dull and he hadn't shaved that morning. His clothes were creased and there was a stain on his shirt that made me think he hadn't changed since the previous evening, when Theonas would have first told him that Alex was missing. A flicker of uncertainty crossed his face. 'What do you mean?'

'I mean she isn't there.'

He shook his head. 'Captain Theonas told me what happened the night that you met her. I did not know she would do something like that. It was my fault.' He started to say something else, but broke off, his voice choked with emotion.

'If Theonas told you she killed herself, he's wrong. And if it's any consolation I don't think she really meant to harm herself the night I pulled her out of the harbour.'

Dimitri stared at me, suspicion and hope competing in his eyes. 'You'd better come up.'

I followed him the rest of the way up the stairs. At the top, a door led to a small living room. At one end was a kitchen and at the other, doors opened onto the terrace. The room was neatly if simply furnished. It had probably been built as a workman's cottage originally, though if Ithaca were more fashionable the view across Vathy and the harbour would have made it worth a small fortune. There was a glass and an open bottle of whisky on a wooden table. Dimitri picked up the glass and emptied it with a single swallow, wincing slightly.

'How do you know Theonas is wrong?' he said.

'The night I met her she'd taken some pills to help her sleep. And she was drinking. I don't think she really knew what she was doing.'

As Dimitri refilled his glass, I caught a glimpse of myself in a mirror on the wall behind him and, to my slight surprise, I saw that I didn't look much better than he did. He saw me watching him and gestured to a cupboard.

'Help yourself.' As I fetched a glass, he thought about what I'd said. 'You think she is alive?'

'Yes, I do.'

'Then where is she?'

'Did Theonas tell you there was someone else

up there yesterday? A village boy said he saw Alex with a man.'

'He said the boy must have been mistaken.'

I was incredulous. 'He didn't make a mistake, he just said it wasn't me. The man he saw was tall and had fair hair. When I was driving up to Exoghi yesterday, a car passed me going down the other way. I'm sure I've seen it before. I think it was a blue Fiat. The other night I spoke to a man who fits the description of the man the boy saw. There was a blue Fiat parked across the road then too. And the day Alex and I drove back from Kioni, we were followed by a car like that.'

The mention of Kioni was an uncomfortable reminder of the night I had spent with Alex. A muscle trembled beneath the skin of Dimitri's jaw.

'The man I spoke to claimed to know my father. It's possible they were involved in some kind of illegal smuggling. It's also possible that my dad's death wasn't an accident, and if I'm right about that it doesn't reflect well on Theonas. Did you know he and Irene were seeing each other?'

Dimitri nodded. 'Vathy is a very small place.'

'My father told Irene somebody tried to kill him. She told Theonas, but he didn't take it seriously.' I explained about the collector who had approached my father the previous year, and about his behaviour when he came out of hospital. 'Irene suspected that he'd been approached again. On the night he collapsed he'd been talking about the *Panaghia*. You know what that is?'

310

'Of course.'

'Then you know it's supposed to be on the wreck of a German ship called the *Antounnetta*. My dad claimed he'd found the statue, and if that's true he must have found the wreck. Last week I caught somebody searching his boat, probably the same person who also searched the museum. I think he was looking for a journal my dad wrote.'

'But what does any of this have to do with Alex?'

'I'm not sure, but her grandmother was in love with a German soldier. He was on the *Antounnetta* when it left Ithaca. The man I spoke to the other night had a European accent. I thought at the time it was Dutch, but now I think it was German. He asked me if I knew somebody called Eric Schmidt. A German name. It could all be coincidence, but I don't think it is. If he was the man on the cliff, then I think we have to find him. Something is going on here and I think the *Antounnetta* is the link.'

Dimitri raised his glass, then looked at the whisky and set it down again untouched. 'How do we find this man?'

'We find out how he knew my father. That's where you come in. I want to talk to a man called Spiro Petalas, but I might need an interpreter. Do you know him?'

Dimitri nodded, his grief replaced with renewed hope. 'Of course. Everybody knows Spiro.' He glanced at his watch. 'If we go now we can find him before he gets too drunk.'

★ ★ ★

We found Spiro Petalas in a taverna a short distance from the waterfront, away from the bars and restaurants catering to the tourist trade. He was sitting alone at a table in a corner, half an eye on the television screen behind the bar, and the other sullenly regarding an almost empty beer glass. He looked up, brief recognition flickering in his eyes when he saw Dimitri. He glanced curiously at me, then ground out the butt of his cigarette in a brimming ashtray.

'Yassas, Spiro,' Dimitri said cheerfully. He said something else and gestured towards the beer glass on the table, and when Spiro grunted a reply Dimitri called out to the barman.

Three beers were delivered to the table. Spiro sucked at his greedily while engaging in a brief exchange with Dimitri.

'I have told him who you are,' Dimitri said. 'Spiro and your father did not always see eye to eye.'

I had already gathered as much from the surly look Spiro directed at me when my name was mentioned. 'Ask him if he remembers the night my father collapsed. Apparently they had some kind of argument.'

The question was relayed and Spiro responded grudgingly. 'He says the police have already asked him about that. He doesn't know anything about what happened to your father after he left the bar. He says he stayed there. We can ask anyone.'

'I know that. Tell him that's not why we're

here. Tell him we want to know what he and my dad were arguing about.'

I was hoping that Spiro might recall some detail which Theonas had neglected to mention, or of which he hadn't realised the significance. However, as Dimitri questioned Spiro, I began to doubt that he could be of much help. He answered reluctantly. His entire demeanour was that of a man hard done by the world, the kind who thinks everyone is against him. When his glass was empty he put it down with a heavy and pointed thud, and when it was filled he lit another cigarette and scowled, resenting having to pay for his drink by answering Dimitri's questions.

After ten minutes or so he'd added nothing to what I already knew and I was ready to leave. 'Come on, I've had enough of this.' I started to get up. Spiro glanced at me and his face twisted into a sneer. He muttered something under his breath. 'What did he say?'

'He wants to know if you are planning to make everybody rich like your father.'

'What is he talking about?'

Another exchange followed and then Dimitri said, 'Apparently when your father was talking about the *Panaghia* he claimed that he would make Ithaca rich. Tourists from around the world would come to see what he had found.'

'But I thought it was only a religious icon.'

'It is,' Dimitri said. 'It is important only to the people of Ithaca.' He turned to Spiro and questioned him again. 'He says he told your father he was a fool.' He shrugged apologetically,

313

but I didn't care what Spiro thought. Whatever else my father had been I knew he wasn't a fool. I sat down again and asked Dimitri to get Spiro another drink.

'Ask him what else my dad said.'

Dimitri and Spiro went through another question and answer routine and, though I didn't understand a word of it, I got the feeling that progress was being made. Spiro appeared to be warming to his subject, becoming noticeably more loquacious, though I didn't know if it was a ploy to allow him to spend more of my money at the bar, or if the alcohol was loosening his tongue. Eventually, Dimitri interpreted what had been said.

'Your father hinted that he had found something else besides the *Panaghia*.'

'Does he know what?'

'Your father would not say. Spiro didn't mention it before because he thought your father had made it up. When Spiro challenged him to prove his claims your father left.'

I sat back in my chair. Up until then my theories and suspicions had been no more than that, but now Spiro had given them substance.

'There is something else,' Dimitri said, interrupting my thoughts.

'What?'

'Spiro is a fisherman, although not a very good one. I asked him if he had seen your father's boat before the night they argued. I thought if your father really had found the wreck of the *Antounnetta*, Spiro might know where he had been looking.'

'And?'

'He said that he hadn't seen the boat, but he did see your father at the marina one day with Gregory and another man.'

'Gregory?' For a moment I couldn't place the name, and then I remembered. 'You mean the man who worked for my father. I thought Irene told me he had left Ithaca?'

'Yes. He went to live with his sister on Kalamos. But this was before then. According to Spiro, perhaps a week or two before your father went into hospital.'

'What about the other man, who was he?'

'He does not know. He had not seen him before. But it was not the man you spoke to. This man was old. He had white hair. Perhaps seventy or eighty.'

'Can he remember anything else about him?'

Spiro grunted a reply when Dimitri questioned him again. 'He said he was like you. His skin was pale.'

'Then he probably wasn't Greek?'

'No. He spoke with a foreign accent.'

I felt a tingling of excitement. I knew where I had heard a description that fitted the one Spiro had just given. The clipping of the murdered tourist in my father's drawer. Theonas had described him as being an old man, and the taxi driver had said he was foreign. I told Dimitri what I was thinking.

'It should be easy enough to find out,' he said. 'The police will have a photograph.'

He went to the bar to use the phone and when he returned he said that Theonas was sending a man to fetch us. Within ten minutes a uniformed police officer had arrived, and, though Spiro was disgruntled at being asked to go with us, I gave him twenty euros and asked Dimitri to tell him there was another twenty in it for him afterwards. When he heard that, Spiro pocketed the money and drained his glass.

★　★　★

Theonas was waiting for us when we arrived at the police station. He was out of uniform and didn't look too pleased about having his free time disturbed. He gave me a cold look and glared at Spiro as if to warn him that he had better not be wasting his time, and then he led us into his office.

Wordlessly he opened a folder which contained some glossy photographs and pushed them across the desk. Spiro glanced at them quickly.

'Ne,' he said with a shrug which, despite how it sounded in Greek, I knew meant yes.

Theonas frowned and then curtly issued some instruction. Spiro grudgingly took another, closer look. When he again confirmed it was the man he'd seen with my father, Theonas questioned him at length though I gathered from Spiro's shrugs and monosyllabic replies that he wasn't being of much help.

'It is the same man,' Dimitri told me when Theonas was finished. 'But he could not tell us anything else about him.'

I took a long look at the photograph of the

corpse. His face looked sunken, and his thin white hair was badly cut. Otherwise he was simply an old man of skinny build.

'How was he dressed?' I asked.

Theonas regarded me for a measured beat and then glanced down at a sheet of paper. 'His clothes were quite new. A short-sleeve shirt and trousers. The kind of clothes that can be bought at almost any shop on the islands.'

'Not expensive then?'

'No.'

I looked again at the body. Though it may have been a natural effect of his age and metabolism, the man didn't appear to be well fed. Theonas must have guessed what I was thinking. 'Do you know anything about him at all?'

'From his hands the examiner determined that he had been used to manual work when he was younger.'

'So it's likely that he wasn't affluent?'

'That is the conclusion that I reached.' Theonas didn't look pleased that I had uncovered something that he had missed. 'It would seem that your father knew this man,' he announced, to which I made no comment. 'Do you have any idea who he was?'

'None.'

He looked from me to Dimitri and back again thoughtfully. He was clearly puzzled to find us together. 'How is it that you came to be speaking to Spiro?'

'Spiro told us that the night he and my father argued my father claimed that he'd found something which would make Ithaca prosperous.

317

I think whatever he was talking about was on the *Antounnetta*. Perhaps it still is. The man Alex was seen with in Exoghi knew my father. The same man asked me about somebody called Eric Schmidt.'

'Assuming this person exists, you think it was the same man that you spoke to, Mr French.'

'Yes, I do.'

Theonas stared at me.

I gestured to the folder on the desk. 'If I were you I'd check with Interpol and find out if somebody called Eric Schmidt who answers to this description has gone missing.'

Ignoring my suggestion he said, 'You think that Alex knows this man?'

'Not necessarily. The car I saw was in a hurry and the boy said the man and Alex were arguing. From the cliff you can see the road which runs by the bay. Maybe he saw the Jeep.'

'And wished to leave before you arrived? You are suggesting that Alex did not go with him of her own free will?'

'It seems likely.'

'But have you considered the possibility that it was Alex who wished to leave when she saw your Jeep?'

'What do you mean?'

'You had argued with her the night before had you not? In fact she had witnessed the two of you become involved in a physical fight. It is perhaps understandable that she did not wish to see you.'

I had to admit it was possible. 'But if that's true, why hasn't anybody seen her since? I assume her things are still at the place where she has been staying?'

Theonas inclined his head, reluctantly acknowledging the point.

'And why didn't she go back for her scooter?' I added. 'It doesn't make sense. She must know about the search. The whole island knows.'

We had reached an impasse. 'Naturally, I will investigate this matter further,' Theonas said with a note of finality. 'In the meantime, if you discover anything more please be so good as to inform me.' He closed the folder on his desk and opened his office door.

The interview was over, it seemed.

★　★　★

As Dimitri drove me back to the house I found myself wondering about him. His face was thrown into angular shadows by the dim glow from the instruments in the old Peugeot he drove, accentuating the darkness of his hair and eyes. In an objective way I could see why Alex had fallen for him. He had the dark, good looks and brooding sensitivity that women found so appealing. He glanced at me and caught me studying him.

'What are you looking at?'

I looked ahead through the windscreen to the lights on the road. 'Nothing. I was thinking that's all.' After a moment I said, 'Alex told me you met in London?'

I could feel him looking at me.

'Yes. At the Zannas's restaurant.'

'You knew her family before you went there?'

'Not really. But my mother is a friend of Kostas's daughter-in-law.'

'Did you know who Alex was when you met her?'

'Of course.'

'The family didn't mind you seeing her?'

'Why are you asking all these questions?'

'I'm curious.'

'Kostas didn't like it. But I didn't care what Julia Zannas had done.'

'You knew though.'

'Only a very little. Not the details. It was a long time ago. I didn't see that it had anything to do with Alex.' He was silent for a while and then he said, 'We knew each other for nearly a year, you know. When I came back to Ithaca to start my business we agreed that she would join me in the summer.'

'But you changed your mind?'

'You make it sound as if I do not really care about her! You are wrong!'

'So why did you change your mind?'

'Why do you think it is any of your business?' he demanded angrily, but then almost immediately he began explaining, as if he had to justify himself. 'Before she came, I was not so sure if we were doing the right thing any more. When Alex arrived, I told her that I thought it was too soon for us to take such a big decision. I said that I thought she should stay for a little while and then go back to England. After the season ended I would go to see her. I only wanted for us not to rush things.'

Something about Dimitri's explanation didn't gel. 'So when you saw her again after she got back from Kioni you changed your mind again, is that it? You wanted her to stay after all?'

'You think that I only said that because she told me about you, but you are wrong!'

'Is that why she went to your house that night, to tell you about me?'

'You would like to think so, wouldn't you? But that is not why she came. I love Alex. She knows that. You have only known her for a few days, but she and I have been together for much longer than that. You cannot just forget about the feelings you have for somebody you love.'

'So you're telling me she went to your house because she loves you.'

'We talked. She did not leave until the morning. When you saw her.'

I knew what he was doing. He wanted me to think she had slept with him that night. It was the conclusion I had jumped to when I had met her. 'It's funny,' I said. 'When I saw the two of you on your terrace the other night, I got the impression you were trying to persuade her to stay. I can't help wondering why she was leaving if she's in love with you.'

He didn't say anything.

A few minutes later Dimitri slowed as he made the turn off the road towards the house. We bumped up the track in silence and when he pulled over he left the engine running, the headlights piercing the olive grove. I got out and closed the door. I heard the car turn around, but as I climbed the steps to the terrace I didn't look back.

*　*　*

Theonas had already spoken to Irene so she knew everything that had happened. I wasn't surprised. I thought he wanted to get his version in before I told her what I thought of him. She was subdued. She told me Theonas had reopened the investigation into my father's death.

'I have been sitting here thinking about him,' she said. She was looking at a picture of her with my dad that had been taken years ago. They were on the *Swallow*. They looked happy together. 'I cannot believe he was doing anything wrong.'

I didn't know what to tell her. She went to bed shortly afterwards. 'You should go to bed too, Robert,' she said. 'You look exhausted.'

I felt it too, but on the way to my room I went to my dad's study and sat down at the desk. I opened the drawer where I'd found the news clippings and the Dracoulis book and took out the iron cross. As I turned it over between my fingers I wondered where it had come from. The *Antounnetta* perhaps? It was rusty, but it seemed to me that after sixty years beneath the sea there would be nothing left of it. I put it down and picked up the news clipping which described the opening of the Dracoulis exhibit. In the picture my dad had been caught chatting with another man, both of them holding champagne glasses. Behind them was a third man, and as I looked at him my senses quickened. I peered closer. The image was a little grainy and faded, but there was no doubt in my mind that it was the same man whose picture I'd seen earlier. Only then he'd been dead.

20

In the morning I left a message for Dimitri to say that I was going to the museum in Argostoli on Kephalonia and that I would see him when I returned. Irene called the director, a man who had known my father quite well, and asked if he would see me, a request he was more than happy to agree to.

I caught the early ferry from Piso Aetos. Most of the passengers were locals commuting to jobs on Kephalonia, apart from a middle-aged couple who were obviously tourists. The man nodded politely at me as I boarded. As Ithaca receded he smiled uncertainly then came over and asked if I spoke English. When he realised we were fellow countrymen his smile broadened and he asked if I would mind taking a picture of him and his wife.

They stood by the rail and I focused on them through the viewfinder, with Ithaca's dramatic landscape in the background. I imagined them showing their friends their holiday snaps when they returned home. The blue sea and sky and Ithaca's rocky coast in the background, the hills surprisingly green. It was beguilingly peaceful and idyllic, conjuring images of tranquil coves, azure bays and pretty villages. All of it accurate enough, and yet in the *Odyssey*, when Odysseus returned from his adventures to find that suitors had taken residence in his palace seeking the hand of his wife, Penelope, he had killed them all. The entire history of the island was steeped in bloody violence. Through the centuries, pirates had plagued the coast and the Turks, Venetians, French, and British had all claimed the territory as their own long before the Germans had arrived during the Second World War. Though perhaps the legacy of the German departure had still not played out.

'You just press the button on top.'

Belatedly I realised that the English couple were waiting patiently, staring with fixed, vaguely puzzled smiles. 'Sorry.' I clicked the shutter and handed the camera back.

'Looks like another nice day,' the man said.

'Yes,' I agreed. 'It does.'

When the ferry arrived at Efimia, I took a taxi across the island to Argostoli. The museum was housed in a building on the hillside above the harbour. I asked for Michael Dova and was shown to an office in the administrative wing where Dova rose from his desk to greet me warmly. He was a neat, thin man, his manner friendly.

'*Kalimera*, Mr French, I am very pleased to meet you. Can I offer you something to drink? Some coffee perhaps.'

'Thanks, coffee would be great.'

He put a pot on a small stove in the corner of the room. His office was spacious though it still managed to look cluttered. Every available surface was either crammed with books and papers or else littered with carvings and clay figures. Boxes were stacked on the floor, some with the tops open, spilling paper straw onto the carpet.

'Forgive me,' Dova said as he moved some papers from a chair. 'As you can see we are short of space.' He viewed the surrounding chaos with mild despair, then shrugged, dismissing that which he could do nothing about. 'I was very glad when Irene telephoned to say that you were coming. By the way, please accept my condolences. I was saddened to hear of your father's death. I had the greatest respect for him.'

'Thank you. Did you know him well, Mr Dova?'

'Yes quite well, I think. We were colleagues of course. However I think it would be true to say that we were also friends. Naturally we shared many common interests. In fact we worked together on various excavations.'

'On Ithaca?'

'Yes. Also here on Kephalonia and some of the other islands. But mostly on Ithaca. As I am sure you are aware, your father's great hope was to discover the site of Aphrodite's Temple. Though I believe he mentioned that you do not share his passion for archaeology.'

'That's true. But actually I want to ask you about the temple. I found a news clipping in my father's study.' I took it out and showed it to him. 'This picture was taken at the opening of an exhibit earlier this year I understand.'

'Ah yes. The Dracoulis exhibit. The artefacts you see here came from the site of the temple. You are aware of the story?'

'I know they've been lost since the war.'

'Yes that is correct. In fact until they came to light in a Swiss collection last year there was actually no proof that they even existed.'

I told Dova I'd read the book I'd found in my father's study, so I knew about the letter Dracoulis had written to his sister. The man my father was talking to in the newspaper picture I now saw was Dova himself, but I asked him about the other man in the background, who I now knew had been murdered. 'Do you know who this is?'

Dova peered carefully and then found a magnifying glass. 'Ah, yes. I remember him. A colleague of your father's from Germany I believe.'

'My father knew him?'

'Yes, of course. He asked me if he could bring a guest to the opening. It was by invitation you understand. Not a public occasion. Naturally I agreed.'

'So they came together from Ithaca?'

'Actually no. I invited your father to the opening some months earlier. I hoped that the occasion might lift his spirits. You are aware that your father had been rather depressed?'

'Yes.'

'It was a great shame. Your father was a dedicated man, Mr French, but I think that even he was worn down by the years of searching and disappointment. I was quite worried about him. I asked him to come and stay at my house for a few days before the opening. He did not seem his old self.'

I thought I detected a tactful euphemism in

Dova's choice of description. 'You mean he was drinking?'

'He was rather unhappy I think.' He paused. 'I was aware that Irene and your father were no longer living together. And he was not working. I believe that he felt his life no longer had any purpose. But, I am happy to say that his visit here appeared to restore his spirits, as I had hoped that it would. In fact I believe that meeting this colleague of his from Germany had a very beneficial effect.'

'They met here?'

'In Argostoli yes. Quite by chance I understand.'

'This man, do you remember his name?'

Dova frowned and went to a drawer in his desk. 'I wrote it down, and the address where he was staying because I promised that I would send him some information. Let me see, now where did I put it. Ah yes.' He produced a diary and leafed through the pages until he found what he was looking for. 'There, Kohl. Johann Kohl. The Hotel Ionnis.'

I was disappointed. I stared at the name.

'Is there anything wrong?' Dova asked, looking concerned.

I shook my head. 'Sorry. It's just that I thought he was somebody else. I don't suppose you've heard the name Eric Schmidt by any chance?'

'I'm afraid not.' Dova went to check on the coffee and I took the opportunity to write down the name of the hotel.

'You say my father's spirits improved after he

met this man Kohl,' I said when Dova returned with our coffee. It was strong and steaming hot.

'Yes, the transformation was quite remarkable. I put it down in part to his seeing the Dracoulis artefacts first-hand of course. It is a rather unique collection and it proves beyond doubt that the temple does actually exist. But also meeting this old colleague seemed to cheer your father up.'

'Do you know much about him?'

'Actually very little. Your father was very vague about how they knew one another. I formed the impression that it was from a dig that they worked on together some years ago.' Dova frowned thoughtfully. 'At the time I was somewhat busy with the opening you understand, so I did not have much opportunity to speak to Mr Kohl.'

'But?' I asked, sensing that there was something else.

'I may be wrong, but he did not seem like somebody that I would expect your father to know professionally.'

'What do you mean?'

'The few times I spoke to him, I felt actually that archaeology was not his field. He did not even strike me as being an academic type. Once or twice, when I mentioned some recent find which had been reported internationally, I suspected that he did not know what I was talking about.' Dova shrugged apologetically. 'Of course, it may merely have been his manner.'

'Could he have been an antiquities dealer?' I suggested.

Dova was surprised at the idea. 'I suppose it is possible. But most of the dealers I have met are very knowledgeable.'

'And this man wasn't?'

'He struck me as rather uneducated. But I may be entirely mistaken,' Dova added hurriedly. 'As I mentioned, I was very distracted at the time, and your father certainly spent a great deal of time with this man. I am sure they must have shared a great many interests.'

I wondered what those interests were exactly. 'Do you have any idea what they discussed?'

'From what I observed, they were primarily interested in the Dracoulis exhibit.' Dova gestured to a photograph on the wall. It was very old, in sepia tones, and was of a building which I didn't recognise. 'That is the original museum here in Argostoli, where Dracoulis was the curator until he died during the war. It was completely destroyed during the earthquake which devastated these islands in 1953.' He stood up from behind his desk. 'Perhaps you would like to view the exhibit for yourself? I would be happy to show you.'

I was certainly curious, and so we left his office and followed a corridor which led to the public areas of the museum. The building had been designed as a series of connecting rooms over two floors, separated into two wings with a central display hall in each. The ceilings were high, to give a feeling of light and space, and the exhibits were displayed around the walls, larger pieces mounted on plinths. As Dova led the way, he explained how the artefacts had ended up in Switzerland.

'During the war the original museum was systematically looted by the Germans. It is a well-documented event. The Germans were very thorough in that regard, even when they were stealing,' he noted wryly. 'Everything was recorded and crated and then flown off the island by transport plane destined for Berlin. Most of the records were subsequently lost during the Allied bombing and advance into the city, but there is still a manifest of the shipment of three hundred and forty-two crates. Much of what was stolen has never been returned. Of course some of it was destroyed in the bombing, but no doubt much of it was later sold by those high up in German command, to finance their escape at the end of the war.'

'And that's what happened with the artefacts Dracoulis found?'

'That is the assumption, yes. The German commander on the island who oversaw the operation was a man called Manfred Bergen.'

I mentioned that I'd seen a picture of Bergen in the book in my father's study.

'A very unpleasant man I should think,' Dova observed. 'Though actually he was known to be an amateur archaeologist.'

I hadn't been aware of that, but it was interesting to note. It seemed to lend strength to the idea that there might be something on the *Antounnetta* of value. We passed through a hall where Dova pointed out Hellenistic ceramics and votive reliefs alongside classical statues and bronze tripods which dated from the ninth

331

century BC. There were rows of cases of beautifully decorated *arybolloi* and drinking vessels of the kind I'd seen in my father's collection.

In the central hall of the west wing, a large glass case occupied a space in the centre of the room.

'These are the Dracoulis artefacts,' Dova announced.

There were perhaps two hundred different pieces, many made of clay decorated with the black figured technique. As well as the sort of goblets, jugs and amphorae I'd become used to seeing, there were several small statues and some fragments of clay masks. On a mounting in front of the display, explanatory notes described who Dracoulis had been and the history of the exhibits.

'The finds date from different periods,' Dova explained. 'Some date from the early Mycenaean, others from the Late Classical or Roman periods. From this we are able to determine that the site they came from was used as a place of worship over many thousands of years.'

There was a picture of a statue of Aphrodite which was housed in a museum in Athens, and a brief passage about her origins. She was the goddess of love, beauty and fertility. She was portrayed as a sexual creature, a goddess of earthly rather than heavenly love. Almost naked, there was something wanton and lascivious about her pose.

Dova indicated a small leather-bound book displayed open, showing slightly yellowed pages filled with neat black handwriting. Some of the pages were torn, and parts were missing. 'This is Dracoulis's diary. It was discovered with the collection. He used it to catalogue his finds and describe the remains of a structure which he concluded must be the original site of the temple.' Dova smiled wistfully. 'As you see it is incomplete, however much of it is still legible.'

As we returned through the museum I asked Dova if he had heard of the *Panaghia*.

'Yes, of course. Your father mentioned it many times. It was one of the relics stolen from the monastery at Kathara during the war.'

'Then you know that it was on a German ship called the *Antounnetta* which was attacked by the Resistance as it left Ithaca?'

'Yes.'

'Before he died, my father claimed he'd found the statue. He also hinted that he'd found something else. Did he happen to mention anything about this to you?'

Dova was mystified. 'No, I am afraid not.'

We reached the entrance and I shook Dova's hand and thanked him for his time. He told me not to hesitate to contact him if there was any way that he could be of further help. I thanked him again and went outside to find a taxi to take me to the Hotel Ionnis.

★ ★ ★

The Hotel Ionnis turned out not to be the kind of international standard hotel where a dealer of antiquities might be expected to stay. Instead, it

333

was a small low-budget hotel one street back from the working end of the wharf where the fishing boats unloaded their catches every day. The painted exterior was cracked and peeling, the steps to the door worn by the endless comings and goings of backpackers and other visitors on limited means. Outside, the smell of fish and diesel fumes hung in the air, inside, stale cigarette smoke competed with unappealing cooking aromas emanating from the kitchen.

A youth eyed me incuriously as I approached a small window set into a reception office.

'Do you speak English?' I asked hopefully.

He nodded. 'You want a room? I have very nice room on third floor. It has view of harbour. Very reasonable.'

'No, thanks. I'm looking for somebody who was staying here. His name was Johann Kohl.'

The name didn't register. Having established that I wasn't a prospective customer, the youth made an exaggerated show of indifference. 'There is nobody here called Kohl.'

I dug for my wallet and put fifty euros down on the counter. 'He's an old man. He was here some time in April.' I showed the youth the picture in the paper, but he barely glanced at it, his attention wholly taken up with my money. Reaching underneath the counter he produced a register and, after turning a couple of pages, he spun the book around for me to look at.

'Kohl. April the fifteenth. He was here four days.'

I let him have the money. Kohl had arrived a couple of days before the opening of the exhibit, and I assumed he had left to return to Ithaca with my father. The address given in the register was Hamburg, though there was no street name or number. I thanked the youth and turned to leave, but before I'd reached the door he called to me.

'If you want you can take his things.'

'What things?' I went back again and the youth gestured to a cupboard.

'Sometimes people leave things. They forget.' He opened the door to reveal a space stuffed with cardboard boxes containing bits of clothing and old books. After a bit of searching he came out with a battered holdall which he hoisted onto the counter.

'He left this?' It appeared to be full. I reached for the zip, but the youth held onto it.

'You are relative?'

'No.'

'We only give things to relative.'

I doubted that. I reached for my wallet and gave him another forty euros. 'He was my brother,' I said sardonically, at which the youth merely took the money and pushed the bag towards me. When I opened it I found it was full of clothes and a pair of shoes. There was also a toilet bag containing a toothbrush, shaving gear and a bottle of some kind of pills.

'How long do you keep things?' I asked.

'One month. Maybe two. Then we give away. There is too much.' He gestured towards the evidence of the stuffed cupboard.

'But this was left in April,' I said. 'Nearly three months ago.'

The youth took a look at the bag and pointed to some figures written on the side with a marker pen. 'June,' he said.

Around the same time that Kohl's body was discovered I realised, and also when my father had insisted on leaving the hospital. 'Let me see the register.' I grabbed it before the youth thought to demand more money from me, and flipped over the pages until I found what I was looking for. Kohl had come back to the hotel in May. He had registered the day after my father had his heart attack, but had never checked out. I knew why. Because a couple of weeks later he'd gone to Ithaca and taken a taxi from Piso Aetos to the monastery at Kathara where somebody had shoved a knife into him. But why had he come back to the hotel after my father's heart attack? And why had he gone to Ithaca again the day he was killed?

I took Kohl's bag with me when I left and found a bar near the wharf where I sat down and went through it. At the bottom, underneath his clothes, all of which were worn and of poor quality, I found a plastic zip-up case of the kind that school children use for keeping notebooks and pencils. Inside was a black-and-white photograph of a group of men wearing the uniform of German soldiers from the Second World War. They were posed for the photographer, smiling at the camera. In the background I could make out some buildings that had a Mediterranean appearance and the shadows on the ground suggested the picture had been taken somewhere sunny. Several things struck me about the soldiers. One or two were obviously middle-aged, in their fifties or so, but most were by contrast extremely young. A circle had been drawn around the face of one on the front row who was little more than a boy. His uniform looked too big for him. At the end of the row stood another man perhaps in his twenties. He was handsome, with very fair hair and he wore the uniform of an officer. On the breast of his tunic he wore an iron cross like the one I'd found in my father's study.

I turned the picture over. A date was written on the back. June 1943. The year before the Germans evacuated Ithaca. There was no indication where the picture had been taken, but I was sure that it was in Vathy. I looked again at the circled figure but, other than his youth, nothing else stood out about him.

When I replaced the picture in the case I found something else. It was a folded page from a German newspaper. It didn't matter that I couldn't understand the text. It was dated September the year before and the artefacts in the photograph matched the display I had just seen at the museum. To remove any doubt that this was an article concerning the discovery of the Dracoulis artefacts, there was a picture of a statue of Aphrodite.

I paid for my coffee and asked the waiter if there was an internet café somewhere nearby. He directed me to a *kefenio* further along the wharf which had two computers at a table in a back corner that could be hired by the minute. After I'd logged on, I typed the name

'*Antounnetta*' into the search query box, but none of the responses related to a German ship from the war. I tried several other queries using keywords such as 'Ithaca' and 'the German occupation' and, though I began turning up plenty of sites, none of them told me what I wanted to know. It wasn't until I eventually tapped into a database on the German army during the Second World War almost an hour later, and then entered the name *Hauptmann* Stefan Hassel, that I struck gold. There I found the names of all the men who had been under Hassel's last command. Beside each was a symbol denoting that they had been killed in action. There was no Johann Kohl, but among them I found the name Eric Schmidt.

21

As I sat on the ferry going back to Ithaca I watched a yacht as it turned into the wind, her mainsail flapping before somebody began hauling it down. I experienced the same nagging sensation which I'd felt the day before when I'd watched another yacht motor into the harbour at Vathy. This time, however I knew why.

I had phoned Dimitri before I left Argostoli and he was waiting for me when I arrived at Piso Aetos. There was a moment of awkwardness when we met. Neither of us was entirely comfortable about our alliance, but we needed each other. I put aside my personal feelings and told him about my conversation with Michael Dova, and my subsequent discoveries after visiting the Hotel Ionnis. Then I showed him the photograph I'd found in Johann Kohl's possessions.

'Eric Schmidt was one of the men stationed here during the war.' I pointed to the young man whose face was circled in the photograph. He was very young, little more than a youth. 'My guess is that's him. All of these men were killed in action some time during the attack on the *Antounnetta* or afterwards.' I recalled what I'd read in the book about Dracoulis in my father's study. 'There were a few survivors. They were picked up by another German ship, but it was attacked and sank before it reached the mainland.'

Dimitri handed the photograph back. 'I do not understand. Why did the man you met ask if you knew Eric Schmidt if he has been dead for sixty years? And who was Johann Kohl?'

I didn't have the answers, but once again the link was the events which had occurred during the war on Ithaca. Before I'd left Argostoli earlier I had wandered among the bars and cafés where the foreign tourists could be found until I'd heard the accent I was looking for. It didn't take long. A party of Germans were sitting down to lunch and when I approached them and asked if anybody spoke English, a mild-looking man in his forties had introduced himself. We shook hands and I told him I needed something translated. When I showed him the newspaper article he skimmed it and confirmed that it reported the discovery of the Dracoulis artefacts in Switzerland. He was good enough to translate the entire text for me, and though there was more detail about the history of the private collection where the artefacts were found, there was nothing that answered any of my questions.

'It's reasonable to assume that this article was what brought Kohl to Kephalonia, where he met my father,' I said to Dimitri. 'But I doubt that they knew each other before that. From what Dova told me it seems certain he wasn't an archaeologist, and unless he was particularly unsuccessful, he probably wasn't a collector or a dealer either.'

I studied the photograph again, willing it to

divulge its meaning. I was drawn to the figure of Hassel standing to one side, smiling faintly and squinting a little. I wondered again about the iron cross on his tunic, thinking of the one in my father's study. But in the end whatever answers were there, I saw only more questions. I put the picture aside and asked Dimitri to drive us to Polis Bay. At least there, I believed we would find one answer.

On the way, Dimitri told me that he had spoken to Theonas earlier. The police had checked all of the hotels and guesthouses on the island, but there were no reports of anybody answering the description of the man who was seen with Alex on the cliff, and no blue Fiat had been rented from the car-hire agencies. Nor had Interpol turned up any leads on Eric Schmidt, though that was hardly surprising given that I now knew he'd been dead since 1944.

When we reached Stavros, Polis Bay far below was still and clear, shades of blue becoming progressively darker as the water became deeper. Several yachts drifted at anchor, their sails neatly furled. We drove down to the beach and parked in the shade beneath the olive trees. Cicadas whirred and rattled in the trees and the water lapped gently against the shore. A light breeze carried the scent of wild sage mixed with pine from the hills. A dozen brightly-painted fishing boats were tied up at the wharf, their nets hung over the wall to dry beside the bar, and a sign outside the building next door advertised marine supplies in English and several other languages.

I told Dimitri what I'd remembered while I

was on the ferry. 'The day I followed Alex to Exoghi I saw a yacht anchored here in the bay. I watched a tender go out to it before it sailed out past the headland.' It hadn't meant anything at the time, but now I suspected that Alex was on board. 'It would explain how she managed to vanish into thin air.'

Dimitri gestured to the building at the end of the wharf. 'Perhaps you are right.' The front of a car was visible, parked along the side. It was a blue Fiat, several years old and slightly battered, but undoubtedly the one I had seen.

'Who does it belong to?' I asked.

'The man who owns this place.'

The inside of the marine supply store was cluttered with boating paraphernalia. There were shelves full of boxes of stainless steel bolts and screws, and all kinds of winches and cleats and pulleys. The kind of things that break unexpectedly and need replacing. Coils of rope and chain hung from the rafters, and fenders of all sizes lined the walls. It was an Aladdin's cave for sailors, the kind of place you could poke about in for hours and discover things you never knew you needed.

The owner was swarthy and middle-aged. His belly ballooned over the belt of his trousers. He scratched at his unshaven chin absently while Dimitri spoke to him. Though he spoke passable English, they conversed in Greek which Dimitri translated for my benefit.

'The Fiat belongs to Nikos, but he rents it to people from the boats so they can go to Stavros for supplies or to visit tourist sites.'

342

'Did he rent it out on Tuesday?'

'He thinks there was a boat in that day, but we will see. He keeps a record.'

Nikos vanished into a back room and when he returned he was carrying a book with a stained red cover. He opened it to a page of entries written in Greek. Dimitri pointed to one of the most recent and slid his finger along to the last box in the entry. 'Look at the name.'

It was a signature. I stared at it with slight shock.

K. Hassel

'Hassel?'

The same name appeared several other times. He had hired the car on Sunday, the day he'd followed Alex and I from Kioni, and also the day I'd disturbed an intruder on the *Swallow*.

'Did Nikos see a driver's licence or something?' I asked, wondering if there was something that would give us an address for him in Germany. Dimitri relayed the question, but I could tell from the man's indifferent shrug that he didn't bother with such formalities.

'He says it is a casual arrangement. For cash. I also asked if he knew the name of the boat, but he says he did not notice.'

There were hundreds, even thousands of yachts cruising the islands at that time of year. Without a name, even the combined resources of the police departments both on Ithaca and on Kephalonia had no chance of finding the one that I had seen.

When we went outside, we lingered in the shade of the olive trees. Until then I'd believed that Alex was taken from Exoghi by force. The fact that the boy who saw her arguing with someone who we now knew was Hassel supported that idea, as did her disappearance. But now I wasn't so sure. I remembered what Theonas had said. Perhaps I was the reason Alex had vanished so abruptly. I took out the photograph I had found in Kohl's possessions again and looked closely at the image of *Hauptmann* Hassel.

'There's a certain similarity between him and the man I spoke to. Fair hair. Both tall.' I couldn't be certain, but the name couldn't be simply coincidence.

'How old was he?' Dimitri asked.

'About my age. Mid-thirties, give or take a year or two.'

'That would make him Hassel's grandson.'

'Yes,' I agreed. 'But not only that. It means he and Alex are related.'

★ ★ ★

After we left the bay we drove to Stavros again where a truck had broken down in the square. A group of men were arguing about what they should do about it. A wheel had sheared off the axle and part of the truck's load of rubble had tipped out, blocking the road to the coast. Rather than wait, we decided to take the mountain route back to Vathy.

Dimitri drove silently, no doubt thinking as I was about what we'd found. I asked him if he thought Alex could have gone with Hassel of her own choice on the day she had vanished, but he shook his head emphatically.

'What about the boy who saw them arguing?'

'He thought they were arguing,' I pointed out. 'But maybe he misinterpreted what he saw. Alex had just been confronted by somebody claiming to be her cousin.'

Dimitri wasn't convinced. 'Why has she not been back for her belongings? And how could she not know about the concerns for her safety?'

Both were valid points, I admitted. And I didn't have an answer for either of them.

The road climbed steeply in a series of sharp curves, often so narrow that there was barely enough room for two vehicles to pass, though we didn't encounter any other traffic. The landscape became increasingly barren as olive groves and cypress trees gave way to thick, almost impenetrable wild oak and laurel. Bare rock escarpments loomed over the road.

The village of Anoghi near the top was almost deserted, though an old man sat outside the *kefenio* opposite the church. He stared as we passed. Two old women in the street wearing heavy black dresses and stockings stopped to watch us with the frank gaze common to Greek villagers. A couple of miles beyond the village, a turning led to the Kathara monastery perched on the very summit of the mountain where, according to Theonas, Kohl had been murdered. On impulse I asked Dimitri to go there.

At the top of the road we parked outside the monastery walls. A pair of heavy iron gates stood open revealing a courtyard within where a single old Citroën was parked.

'Does anybody live here?' I asked, wondering why anyone would choose such an austere and remote place to build a monastery.

'The car belongs to the priest. There are no monks here any more, but the priest comes from Vathy for a few hours every day.'

By then it was late afternoon, but it was still hot. I knew from looking at maps that we were about eight hundred yards above sea level. Practically the entire north of the island and much of the south could be seen from where we stood. To the west, Kephalonia looked almost close enough to touch, while the islands and mainland to the north-east were visible as hazy blue-grey shapes on the horizon. The road beneath us vanished and reappeared as it twisted down the mountain side all the way to the coast road far below.

Theonas had said that the only vehicle known to have gone to the monastery on the day Kohl was killed, other than the taxi which had picked him up from the ferry, was a tourist bus from Vathy. I saw now how he could know that with such certainty. There was practically no traffic on the mountain. It was difficult to see how another vehicle could have driven up there and gone unnoticed. But what had Kohl been doing there? Was it significant that this was the place where *Hauptmann* Hassel's convoy had paused on the way to Frikes in order to loot the monastery?

There was a movement from inside the monastery gates. The door to the church was open and I glimpsed a figure.

'The priest,' Dimitri said.

We followed him inside. The church was decorated in the Orthodox style, though this one was faded and less gaudy than the one in Stavros where I'd been with Irene. The most striking features were the richly illustrated icons on the wooden panels around the walls. Images of Christ and the disciples gazed down on us as we walked down the aisle. In an alcove behind a high throne-like chair stood a life-sized statue of Mary. Her hands were clasped in front, her face tilted slightly downward, her features as always serene and beautiful, yet imbued with sorrow. She was painted in pale flesh tones, and her dress was robin's egg blue beneath a white headdress and shawl. I turned questioningly to Dimitri and he confirmed what I'd guessed.

'The *Panaghia*.'

There was a sound from close by and a figure emerged from a small door set back in an alcove. He was tall with dark eyes, dressed in the black regalia of an Orthodox priest. The only adornment on an otherwise austere and somehow forbidding costume was a large, heavy-looking crucifix.

'Unfortunately this one is only a plaster copy of the original.' He came towards us, the warmth of his smile a marked contrast to the manner of the priest I'd spoken to in Exoghi the day Alex had disappeared. '*Kalispera*,' he said to us both. He and Dimitri appeared to know one another, and a brief exchange followed in Greek during which I heard my name mentioned.

'French? Ah yes. I knew your father,' the priest

347

said. 'The archaeologist. He came here many times.' He gestured to the statue. 'Perhaps you are aware that the original was stolen during the war?'

'Yes, but I'm curious to know why. I understood it wasn't valuable.'

'That is true. But the Germans took many things from the monastery in the mistaken belief that there might be something of value among them. The original statue was carved from marble. It was believed to have come from a town on the mainland, and when this monastery was built in 1745 it was given as a gift. But there are many such statues in Greece. The *Panaghia* is a symbol to the people of Ithaca. In the past soldiers claimed sanctuary here from the armies of the Turks. It was believed that no harm could come to those who prayed to her.' The priest smiled sadly. 'This copy was made after the war, but it is not the same.'

'Did you know that before he died, my father talked about returning the original?' I asked.

'Yes, of course.'

'You said he came here sometimes. When was the last time you saw him?'

'It was not long before his heart attack. A week or two. I remember because he asked to see our small collection. It is a kind of museum containing items relating to the history of the monastery, though of course there was not much left after the Germans came. Only a few things that the monks managed to hide when they saw the convoy coming. Perhaps you would like to see it yourself?'

'Thank you, I would, if it's no trouble.'

'Please.' The priest gestured towards the door he had emerged from, and led the way along a narrow passage which connected the church with the main building. We passed several other passageways which the priest explained led to secret rooms and tunnels beneath the monastery. 'In the old days they were used to hide from invaders. They are all locked now.'

The room which housed the museum was in the main building. It contained a few religious artefacts, but the collection was made up primarily of books and various letters and papers, some of them centuries old, which gave an indication of what life had been like for the monks who had once lived there. There was one document which was a diary of sorts, kept by a man who had sought sanctuary from Turkish invaders and had remained hidden in the subterranean rooms and tunnels for more than two years, until he had eventually decided to become a monk himself.

One item in particular caught my attention. It was a document written on several pages torn from a notepad and was clearly relatively recent, though what caught my eye was a familiar-looking stamp at the top incorporating the image of an eagle and underneath a phrase written in German.

'What's this?' I asked.

'It is what your father wished to see when he last came here,' the priest replied. Nearby was a framed picture of a statue similar to the one in the church. He showed me a notation written in

German which was part of a long handwritten list. The ink had faded, though the text was still decipherable. 'It says, 'a statue in marble of the Virgin Mary'.'

'The *Panaghia*?'

'Yes.' The priest explained that the Germans had recorded every item that they had removed. He turned over the page, and at the bottom was a dated signature and another stamp. The signature belonged to *Hauptmann* Hassel.

I wondered what had interested my father about this list. The priest didn't know. 'Surely he must have seen it before,' I said.

'Yes, of course,' the priest agreed with a mild shrug. Though he didn't read or speak German, he knew every item. He recited the entire document for us, but as far as we could tell it was simply an exhaustive record of every chalice, icon and crucifix which had been stolen, though none of it was of any great value.

When we left to go outside again I asked the priest about the man who had been murdered at the monastery.

'Ah, yes, a terrible thing,' he said.

'Were you here that day?'

'Actually yes, though, as I told Captain Theonas, I do not remember the man at all. There was a tourist bus here. I escorted the people around the buildings and explained a little of the history of the monastery to them. It is an arrangement I have with the tour company. In return for my commentary, the tourists may make a donation to the church. But I am sure the man who was killed was not among them. Of course it is possible that I may have simply not noticed him.'

'Where exactly was his body found?'

'Outside. A little way down the hillside.'

We emerged into the courtyard again and I thanked the priest for his help. As we returned to the car I said to Dimitri, 'Kohl must have come here for a reason.'

'Perhaps to meet somebody.'

'Hassel?'

'Perhaps Kohl had your father's journal.'

I thought about that. Even if it were true, he couldn't have brought it with him because Hassel had still been looking for it a few days ago. Unless it wasn't Hassel who he had come there to meet. Or perhaps the journal wasn't why he was there at all.

★ ★ ★

When we arrived back at Irene's house a Mercedes was parked outside and the man who drove for Alkimos Kounidis was leaning against the side smoking a cigarette. He nodded to me and greeted Dimitri by name. We found Kounidis and Irene sitting on the terrace.

'*Kalispera*, Robert,' Kounidis said, getting to his feet. '*Kalispera*, Dimitri.' He shook both of our hands in turn. Dimitri said hello to Irene. I noticed the quick look of surprise she and Kounidis exchanged at seeing us together, though neither of them said anything.

'You have just missed Miros,' Irene said to me. 'He left only a few minutes ago.'

351

'Has there been any news?'

'No, I am sorry. He wished to return this.' She handed me my passport.

'I'm free to leave?'

'Yes.'

'So what is he doing to find Alex?'

'A description of the man she was seen with has been sent to Kephalonia. The police will contact the hotels there.'

'It won't do them any good,' I said, and I explained everything that had happened that day. I showed them the photograph which I'd found at the Hotel Ionnis. When Kounidis saw it he became silent, his expression clouded with the memories it evoked.

'I think the circled one is Eric Schmidt, but I don't know who Kohl was or why he had this picture.'

Kounidis handed it back. 'The man who was seen with Alex . . . '

' . . . Is Hassel's grandson. At least that's our guess.'

'But why is he here? What is this all about?' Irene questioned.

'The *Antounnetta*.' Of that much I was convinced. 'If we can find the wreck, I think we'll find Hassel. And Alex too.'

'But how are we going to do that?' Dimitri asked. 'Your father spent more than twenty years looking for the *Antounnetta* before he found it.'

'If he really did,' Kounidis reminded us. 'Without his journal there is no proof of that. I understand you have not found it?'

I shook my head. 'It's not in the house and it's

352

not at the museum or on the boat.' I turned to Dimitri. 'But maybe there's another way we can find the wreck. Remember what Spiro Petalas said? He saw Kohl at the marina, but he said Gregory was there too.'

'But Gregory went to live with his sister on Kalamos,' Irene cut in.

'Yes, but when was that? If Spiro was right, it must have been after Kohl came back with my father from Kephalonia.'

Irene considered this for a few moments and then agreed that she thought it was shortly before my father's heart attack. No more than a few weeks.

'Then it must be worth talking to him. If Dad found the *Antounnetta* maybe Gregory knows where it is,' I said.

Kounidis looked thoughtful. 'It occurs to me, Robert, that if you are right then there is also another avenue we could try. Your father and Gregory were old. They could not dive the way they used to. In recent years your father would hire somebody to help them.'

I remembered reading something to that effect in my dad's old journals.

'Alkimos is right,' Irene said. 'Johnny would put a card up in the dive shop in Kioni.'

'I know the man who runs this place,' Kounidis said. 'Perhaps he may remember if your father hired anybody this year. I will go and see him.' He looked at his watch. 'But it is late, I will have to wait until morning.'

'In the meantime, I'd like to talk to Gregory,' I

said. 'Where is this place Kalamos where he lives?'

'It is an island north of here,' Dimitri said. 'Near the mainland.'

I turned to Irene. 'Can we take the *Swallow*?'

'Of course.'

'Then I'll meet you at the marina first thing in the morning,' I said to Dimitri.

★　★　★

I went to bed early feeling drained, but so much was swimming in my head that I couldn't sleep. It must have been an hour after I heard Irene go to bed when I heard the phone. I got up to answer it. As I passed Irene's door I stopped to listen, but there was no sound from inside. It was dark downstairs and as I groped to find the phone I wondered who would allow it to ring for so long at such a late hour.

'Hello?' I said when I picked up the receiver.

'Mr French?'

I came awake immediately, recognising the accent at once. 'Yes.'

There was a muffled sound as the phone was passed to somebody else. 'Robert?'

My heart jumped. 'Alex? Alex is that you?'

'Yes, it's me.'

A flood of questions rose up in my mind in a tangled, jostling mass. 'Where are you? What the hell is going on?' I felt a stab of anger and my voice rose. 'Do you realise I've been suspected of killing you?'

'Mr French.'

354

It was Hassel's voice again, curtly cutting me off in mid flow. 'Please come to the marina where your father's boat is. Do not tell anybody where you are going and come alone.'

'Put Alex back on damn it!' I demanded.

'Thirty minutes, Mr French.'

Before I could say anything else there was a click and the line went dead. I stared at the phone and then hung up. My heart was pounding. The rush of anger I'd felt ebbed as I started to think rationally. On reflection I thought Alex had sounded tense and uncertain. With the few words she had spoken she had done no more than confirm her presence before the phone had what? Been taken from her? And Hassel's instruction to meet him had been exactly that; an instruction rather than a request.

I thought about calling somebody. Dimitri perhaps. I even thought briefly of Theonas, but Hassel's warning to come alone and tell nobody rang in my mind. Time was already ticking away fast which I thought was probably intentional. I had been given a tight deadline so that I didn't have time to consider my options. I went back upstairs and dressed hurriedly and five minutes later I was driving down to the coast road.

There were no streetlights beyond the town. The road plunged into darkness where it passed beneath a tall avenue of gum trees which obscured the moonlight. Beyond them the harbour was cast in a ghostly grey wash. When I arrived, I parked a hundred yards from the marina and went the rest of the way on foot. Cicadas chattered from the hillside, a sound which, after a while, became almost invisible, like atmospheric static. The shifting water slapped against the hulls of the moored boats. I identified other night sounds; the rattle of rigging in the masts; the creaking of timbers and ropes straining against cleats. When I reached the buildings by the road I paused in a deep wedge of black shadow. I listened for something out of place; a stealthy footfall or a rustle of clothing, and I watched for a movement or the glow of a cigarette tip. But there was nothing there.

The *Swallow* lay twenty yards ahead of me. I moved through the pitch-black alleyway between two buildings, feeling my way blindly. As I stepped into the open, cloud gathered above the harbour smothering the moon. On a boat somewhere nearby a wind chime made a mournful lament. The moon appeared again, hazy behind thin drifting cloud. I thought I saw a movement from the deck of a nearby launch, but it was only a flag fluttering in the breeze.

Just then I heard the sound of a car approaching from the direction of the town, though no headlights were visible. I froze and listened as it drew nearer. Abruptly it stopped somewhere back along the road. My sense of disquiet grew and then I became aware of a faint buzz. As it became louder I realised that it was an outboard motor running at low revs. A boat was approaching from out on the water. Suddenly the motor was cut and that sound died too.

My senses jangled. It occurred to me that I'd been set up and that I was trapped between unseen figures on both my seaward and landward sides. I heard a bump as something nudged the wharf and then a sound like somebody jumping ashore. I turned and ran back towards the cover of the buildings. Moonlight cast the marina in patches of grey light and dark jutting shadows and, as I darted across open space, I felt exposed. The alley between the sheds beckoned, a deep tunnel which swallowed light like a black hole. From its safety I paused to listen as footsteps moved towards me from the wharf. Behind me, towards the road, there was only darkness, but I sensed that somebody was waiting there. I heard a scraping noise and was startled by how close it was. No more than ten feet away. Somebody was edging along the front of the shed. I turned and made for the road, but as the end of the building loomed close I snagged my foot and pitched forward, instinctively throwing out my hands to break my fall. I hit the nearest wall with a loud thud and for a moment I held my breath.

From behind I heard footsteps moving quickly. Too many to be one person. Perhaps two. Abandoning any attempt at stealth I staggered to my feet and lunged for the corner. I tensed, half expecting somebody to jump out, but nothing happened and then I was in the road.

A car engine started somewhere close by and in the same instant I was pinned by the sudden glare of lights. There was a shout from behind and, as I raised my arm, momentarily dazzled, everything happened at once. I saw two people.

An impression of movement and then for just an instant I saw Alex's face clearly. Her expression was fraught, desperate, but something else struck me, though it was too fleeting for me to pin down. An engine accelerated hard and I wheeled around as rubber squealed against the Tarmac. Lights bore down on me, moving very fast. Something slammed into me from behind and pitched me face-down. Acting more by instinct than anything else I rolled to avoid the car rushing towards me and, as I did, I glimpsed a figure on all fours lunging after me. It was Hassel. His face was caught in the lights for a split second before I kicked out and scrambled to the edge of the road.

As I dived to get out of the way, the car passed close enough to clip me, the force spinning me into the air. I landed heavily and a sharp pain exploded along my left side, but I ignored it and scrambled to my feet again. Behind me the car screeched to a stop and the engine howled as it reversed at speed. The cloud slid over the moon again and in the cover of darkness I changed direction and stumbled up the hillside. The lower branches of a tree raked my face, but I barely felt it. I heard what sounded like a series of popping sounds, and when something hit a tree close by I realised with a shock that somebody was shooting at me. I crouched low and changed direction again without breaking stride and after that, though I heard a few more shots, they went well wide of me.

I had been running for no more than thirty seconds, though it felt longer, when I heard a sound which stopped me dead. It was a woman's scream, cut off abruptly. I hesitated, panting heavily. There was no mistaking what I'd heard. It was Alex and something had happened to her. Without thinking, I turned and started back down the hill, but almost immediately I fell. I rolled head over heels and half rose to my feet again before I slammed into a tree and crumpled to the ground. Stunned, I lay on the ground gasping for breath, my chest on fire, my heart pumping too fast.

Eventually, after perhaps half a minute, my senses cleared and I got to my knees. Through eyes blurred with sweat I saw the harbour below. The lights of the town glittered prettily a couple of miles away. Headlights lit the road in the distance moving steadily towards the town, and beyond the wharf where the *Swallow* was moored I thought I saw the faint white smear of a wake on the harbour.

I made my way down to the marina again, but I already knew what I'd find. It was deserted.

22

Irene dabbed at the cuts and scrapes on my face with cotton wool soaked in some foul-smelling antiseptic lotion. She didn't speak and she wasn't too gentle with her ministrations. Her mouth was pressed into a tight line of stern disapproval. She dabbed forcefully at a cut over my eye and put the blood-stained wad of cotton wool in a dish on the table.

When she was finished, she regarded her handiwork with arms tightly folded across her chest. 'There, that is the best that I can do.'

'Thanks.' I picked up a small mirror and examined myself. I looked a lot better than I had when I'd woken up earlier, my face covered with encrusted blood. I was pale and hollow-eyed, but though slightly battered, the cuts and bruises were superficial.

'This is ridiculous,' Irene said suddenly. 'I am going to phone Miros.'

She turned on her heel, but I leapt to my feet and caught her before she reached the phone. 'Irene, wait. We've been over this. I'm fine. These are nothing more than scratches.'

'Robert, you could have been killed.'

'But I wasn't,' I pointed out. In fact my injuries were the result of my scramble up the hillside in the dark, though I was far more shaken up than I was letting on. It hadn't really hit me until later that I had actually been shot at.

I kept flashing back to the split second when the car had started as I stumbled onto the road and I'd turned to see Alex frozen in the headlights. If I closed my eyes I could picture her with absolute clarity. She was tense, wary, but something else had made a fleeting impression on me. It wasn't what I saw, so much as what I didn't see. She should have been frightened, even terrified by what she'd been through. Fear is a powerful emotion and it is expressed powerfully. There was a boy I went to school with who suffered from night terrors. He would wake in the dormitory from some terrible nightmare and sit up in bed with his eyes bugging, his face frozen in a terrible rictus of horror. Some reflection of that kind of fear should have been apparent in Alex's expression, but it wasn't. But there was the scream I'd heard too. I remembered the way it had ended so abruptly.

'If you tell Theonas about this I'll spend the rest of the day answering his questions,' I said to Irene. 'There isn't time for that.'

She wavered for a few moments, but then her resistance crumbled. It was beginning to get light and I rose stiffly from the chair and put on a shirt.

'You are still going to Kalamos?' Irene asked. 'Yes.'

She sighed. 'I will make some coffee.'

★   ★   ★

Dimitri was already on board the *Swallow* when I got there. 'What happened to you?' he asked as

361

soon as he saw me. When I told him, he responded angrily. 'You should not have gone without me.'

'There was no time. He would have known anyway. I must have been followed.'

'But you saw Alex? How did she seem?'

I hesitated, unsure how to answer, but I told him everything that had happened, including that I'd heard her scream.

'She must have tried to get away,' Dimitri said.

'Perhaps,' I agreed, but he picked up on my uncertainty.

'What is it? This proves that Hassel must have forced her to go with him from Exoghi.'

'But why? And why did he want me to meet him last night?'

'Because he does not want you to find the *Antounnetta*.'

I wasn't so sure that was the answer. 'Something about this doesn't seem right to me.'

'What are you saying? That Alex is involved? You said yourself that you heard her scream. This man tried to shoot you.'

He was right, but I was plagued by a sliver of doubt. I remembered Hassel jumping me as I was caught in the headlights of the car. I'd assumed I'd been led into a trap. But maybe I was wrong. Someone had shot at me, but perhaps it wasn't Hassel. The night I'd met him when I was drunk he had asked if I knew Eric Schmidt. Why would he ask if I knew a youth who'd died in a long ago war? Unless, just as there was more than one Hassel, there was more than one Schmidt. Were the descendants of the people who had been here during the war finishing something that had begun then? If so, what was Schmidt's part in it all? Come to that what was mine?

I looked up at the hills surrounding the harbour and it struck me that nothing had changed there for thousands of years except the human inhabitants, who crawled like ants over the land. Their affairs had always been riven by intrigue and betrayal, fuelled by the emotions of love, hate and greed which had competed restlessly through the ages. And since the times of Odysseus they had brought death in their wake.

We threw off the lines and took the *Swallow* out of her berth, and when we were beyond the harbour entrance I went below. Years earlier when I was a boy, my father had caught a six-foot shark when we were fishing. When he'd brought it alongside the boat it was clear that it had become hopelessly fouled in the line and cutting it free would have simply condemned it to a slow death, so he'd shot it with a rifle which he kept on board. I remembered the gun was kept in a locker beside the galley. It was still there, along with a box of ammunition. It was old, with a worn wooden stock and a single bolt action, but the mechanism worked smoothly and the barrel and metal parts glistened with a thin sheen of cleaning oil.

I went on deck and showed it to Dimitri. 'I don't know much about guns. But it might be a good idea if we learned to use it.'

He took it from me and sighted along the

barrel, then worked the action with a practised ease which demonstrated that he had less to learn than I did.

The journey to Kalamos took most of the day. The *Swallow* wasn't built for speed and during the morning there was no wind. When we were well underway, Dimitri found some plastic bottles in the galley and strung them together on a line. He threw them over the stern and let them drift a hundred feet behind us, then showed me how to load and fire the rifle. For the next hour or so we took turns shooting at them. The recoil initially sent all my shots high, but eventually I got the hang of it. We pulled each bottle in as it began to sink, and the last one had two holes in it for only four of my shots. I was quite pleased, but Dimitri was less enthusiastic.

'It doesn't matter,' he commented. 'If we have to use it, the range will be much closer.'

I thought about this later. I wondered if I could point a gun at a living human being and pull the trigger. Whatever my own reservations, Dimitri didn't appear to share them. He went about the boat wearing a look of resigned determination.

By midday, the sun was beating fiercely onto the deck. We passed a number of yachts, all of them making way under engine power. A little later, a slight breeze came up from the west so, while I took the helm, Dimitri went out on deck to raise the sails. He worked quickly and expertly, winching sheets to trim for maximum advantage of the wind.

'You know your way around boats,' I

commented when he came back.

'When I was a boy I used to go fishing with my father.'

'He's a fisherman?'

'On the islands many families own fishing boats. Once it was necessary to feed themselves, but for most these days it is only a pastime. My father was a teacher. He is retired now.'

'So how did you get into the travel business?'

He shrugged and lit a cigarette. 'There are not so many opportunities for work on Ithaca. Many people leave to live somewhere else, but Ithaca is my home. For a long time I ran a small *kefenio*, but I did not want to do that for my entire life, so I decided to bring people here who are interested in the history of the island.'

'That's how you ended up in London?'

'I needed to make contacts and to learn how to sell my ideas to the travel companies. I also needed to make some money to get started.'

I remembered that Dimitri had told me it didn't matter to him that the Zannas family weren't exactly enthusiastic about his relationship with Alex after they met. But that was in London, a long way from here. I told him that Kounidis had warned me that plenty of people on Ithaca would dislike Alex if they knew who she was.

'It seems unfair to blame her for what happened.'

Dimitri gave a wry smile. 'You are not Greek. You cannot understand how people here think.'

'So explain it to me.'

'The people of Ithaca did not resent Julia

Zannas. They hated her. Such strong emotions spill over onto the innocent.'

'Even after all this time?'

'Families are close here. They remember.'

I thought about the resemblance between Alex and her grandmother, and the way the old man in Exoghi had reacted the day we went there. 'Even though her name isn't Zannas, I suppose it wouldn't take long for people to make the connection.'

'Perhaps,' Dimitri agreed. He turned away and busied himself coiling a line over a winch. He was avoiding looking at me and I thought I knew why.

'I expect it could make things awkward,' I suggested.

He put the line down and turned to look at me. 'Awkward for who?'

'Somebody who might be tainted by association if you like. Maybe someone who needed local support, for a new business perhaps.'

'What the hell are you trying to say?' Dimitri demanded.

'I'm saying that's why you wanted her to go back to England isn't it? You were afraid of how people would react.'

'That is a lie!'

'Is it? I don't think so. That's why you wanted her back when she told you about me. It must have really got to you. It's ironic isn't it? You really do care for her.'

He didn't try to deny that I was right any more. 'I love her. I only wanted some time. By next year my business would be a success and it wouldn't matter so much.'

'Why didn't you tell her the truth?'

He looked away, ashamed of his actions but also angry that I knew. He didn't have to answer. I knew why he hadn't told her.

'I'm not going to tell her, if that's what you're worried about,' I said. 'I'm just making an observation.'

He regarded me with hostile scepticism. 'I think it would be a good idea if you kept your observations to yourself.'

★ ★ ★

Kalamos town was on the eastern coast of the island. We arrived early in the evening and entered a small harbour where a few yachts were tied up alongside the fishing boats. A couple of tavernas and restaurants on the waterfront catered to the passing boat trade, but the island itself was small and only lightly inhabited. After we had tied up at a berth, Dimitri went ashore to see if he could find out where Gregory lived. He returned an hour later with news that the old man lived with his sister a few miles away along the coast, but that he came into town every night to drink at one of the tavernas.

I waited until the light was fading and people were beginning to gather at the tables along the waterfront before I went to find him. Since Gregory spoke English and, according to Dimitri, he was taciturn at the best of times I went alone. I was glad of the chance to escape Dimitri for a while anyway. We had spent most of the afternoon avoiding one another.

I found the taverna where Gregory drank easily enough and as I approached, I saw an old man at a table outside gazing vacantly across the harbour, an empty glass in front of him. There was something vaguely familiar about him though I hadn't seen Gregory for years. He looked to be in his seventies. Tufts of grey hair stuck out from his head as if somebody had trimmed it with a pair of garden shears.

'Gregory?' I said.

When he looked up I saw that one of his eyes was heavily bloodshot, the pupil milky-coloured. 'Who are you?' he demanded suspiciously in a voice roughened by years of smoking.

'I'm Robert French. You used to work for my father.'

His eyes widened in vague confusion. 'Your father?'

'Johnny French.'

Comprehension leaked slowly into Gregory's expression. 'Ah yes. Johnny. I worked for him for many years.' His mood abruptly soured. 'Until he sent me here.' He muttered something in Greek and picked up his glass, but when he remembered it was empty he slammed it down again irritably.

'What do you want with me? Did your father send you?' He looked around, craning his neck belligerently as if he expected to see him at any moment. 'I expect he has told you to ask me to come back, has he? I knew he could not manage alone.'

'My father didn't send me.' It hadn't occurred

368

to me that Gregory wouldn't know that he was dead. 'Look, can I get you a drink?' I signalled to a waiter and ordered a beer for myself and another of whatever Gregory was drinking, which seemed to go a long way towards making him more amenable.

As I drew up a chair he peered more closely at me and then wagged a finger. 'Now I remember you. You came with your father on the boat when you were a boy.'

'That's right.'

'I remember,' he said again. He lit a cigarette, striking a match with short thick fingers. The waiter brought our drinks to the table, pouring ouzo for Gregory from a bottle that I asked him to leave. Gregory downed the glass in a single gulp. 'I drink more than I should.'

'There's something I should tell you,' I said as he reached for the bottle. 'My father died.'

The old man froze with his glass half-way to his mouth. 'He's dead?'

'Yes. A heart attack,' I added, not wanting to complicate things.

The news seemed to deflate the old man. His hand holding the glass dropped to the table again and he gazed beyond me. 'Ah, I am sorry,' he said heavily after a while. He shook his head regretfully and murmured some salute before raising his glass and draining it.

'I'm trying to find out what he was doing before he died,' I said.

Gregory appeared not to have heard me. 'How did you get here?'

'On the *Swallow*.'

'Your father's boat?' He looked towards the harbour, but the boat couldn't be seen from where we were sitting. 'She is a good boat. Where are you taking her?'

'I'm not taking her anywhere. I came here to talk to you.'

He filled his glass again with trembling fingers. 'All this way. To talk to me? What for?'

'About what my father was doing before he died.'

The old man shook his head. 'He should not have sent me away. He said I was too old, but I am still here.'

'He sent you away?'

'Yes. Why else would I be here? He said I should help my sister. She is old. She wanted me to come after that husband of hers died. Your father said it was time for me to retire. He gave me some money. He was generous, but I told him I did not want to retire. To be honest with you I did not want to live with my sister. She complains that I drink too much.'

He eyed the bottle and, losing some brief internal battle, he filled his glass again. 'What does it matter what I drink at my age? I told your father he was the one who should stop working. I said I would live ten years after he was dead. And you see, I was right.'

A look of sly triumph crept into his eyes, but then it faded and was replaced with sadness. He raised his glass to me. 'Your father was a good man. May he rest in peace.' He tossed off his drink, but as he reached for the bottle again I stopped him, afraid that he would be too drunk to talk to me soon.

'In a minute. First let me ask you a few things. When was it that you came here, can you remember?'

'Of course I remember,' he exclaimed with obvious affront. 'I am old but I am not stupid!'

'Sorry. Of course not. So when was it?'

'In May. The beginning of the month.'

'So that was after my father came back from Kephalonia. You remember he went there in April?'

'Yes. Yes. I remember.' He licked his lips, his eyes greedily fixed on the bottle in my hand.

'When he came back, did he come alone?'

'Alone?'

'Somebody saw you and my father on the *Swallow*. There was another man with you.'

'Ah, yes. I remember now. He was a man like your father. An archaeologist. We took him out on the boat. For a cruise, you know, so that he could see the island. He was on holiday.'

'What was his name, can you remember?'

'He was foreign. He said I should call him Johann. I don't remember anything else.'

'But you remember taking him out on the boat. How many times did you take him?'

'Only one time,' Gregory said, scowling. 'Then your father gave me money and said I should retire. It was the same night. I told him I did not want to come to live with my sister. He should not have made me come.'

I wondered why my dad had done that to Gregory after he had worked for him for all those years. And why so suddenly? 'When he came back from Kephalonia, how did he seem to you?'

'What do you mean?'

'I mean, did he behave differently?'

Gregory shrugged. 'He did not talk to me much. He talked to this other man. They talked about their work.'

'Their work? Did you hear them? Did they mention the *Antounnetta*?'

The old man's eyes slid back to the bottle. 'Perhaps I could remember more if I had something to take away my thirst.'

I poured him another ouzo, a smaller one this time and watched while he drank it down. 'So did they talk about the *Antounnetta*?'

'Maybe. They might have mentioned it.'

'When? When you were on the boat?'

'Yes. On the boat I think.'

'Where did you go to that day?'

'To a bay in the south. Pigania. You know this place?' I shook my head. 'There is nothing there. You can only get to it by boat. It is very deep.'

I was surprised at this. The search pattern on the charts I'd seen on the boat covered an area toward the mainland, beginning at a point at least a mile off the coast of Ithaca. 'What did you do there? Did you dive?'

Gregory looked surprised at the suggestion. 'Why would we dive there? Besides, we are too old. When your father wanted somebody to dive, he hired young people. Students. Foreigners. We did nothing.'

'Nothing at all? You mean you went to this place and then you just turned around and went

372

back to Vathy again?'

'Your father and his friend went ashore for a while. They wanted to go for a walk. I stayed on the boat. It was hot. Too hot for walking.'

'How long were they gone?'

'I do not remember clearly. I had a drink or two while I waited. The sun made me thirsty. An hour or two perhaps.' He waved a hand in a vague gesture.

'Did they say anything about where they went or what they were doing?'

'No, I told you. They wanted to walk. This friend of your father's, he liked to walk he said. Where he came from he walked every day.'

'And you didn't hear them talking about anything else?'

'No. I heard nothing.' Gregory's face sagged and he shook his head. 'Your father, he was a good man. A good friend. I am sorry that he is dead.'

His voice was becoming slurred, and his eyes were glazing over. I asked a few more questions, but it was clear that I wouldn't get anything else out of him. Before I left I went to see the owner of the taverna to give him some money to make sure that Gregory got home safely. When I went back to say good-night, Gregory didn't appear to hear me. He was more than half drunk, lost in some silent memory.

★   ★   ★

We left Kalamos that night, planning to sail back to Ithaca by morning. We agreed to take turns to keep watch. I volunteered to stay up first and while Dimitri went down below to snatch a few hours' sleep, I plotted a course and set the auto-helm. There was virtually no wind, so we planned to make the journey under engine power. All I had to do was keep watch for other vessels and stay awake.

The night was clear and once we were out of the harbour I brought my father's charts up to the wheelhouse. The pattern of crosses annotated with the dates of dives going back years clearly followed the likely course the *Antounnetta* would have taken towards Patras on the mainland to the south-east. But when I looked for the bay where Gregory said he and my father had taken Kohl, I found it at the bottom south-western tip of Ithaca, practically in the opposite direction. They must have gone there for a reason, though I had no idea what it had to do with the *Antounnetta*.

Later, I sat on deck with a cup of coffee and stared at the sky. The stars were mesmerising, vividly clear in the absence of any light from the land. I felt adrift in the universe, following a course among the planets instead of between two islands in the Ionian Sea. The moon rose above the horizon, a massive, hauntingly beautiful sphere which cast an eerie light over the swell.

The steady thump of the diesel and the constant suck of water gradually lulled my senses. A series of sleepless nights and the battering inflicted on my body had taken their toll. My heartbeat became attuned to the rhythm of the boat and the rocking of the sea. My eyelids fluttered closed and, without realising it, I fell asleep.

I woke abruptly, disoriented and uncertain where I was. Realisation hit me in a flood and, panicked, I scrambled to my feet instinctively sensing danger. I didn't know how long I'd been asleep. I half expected to see either a tanker bearing down on us or else the looming, rocky coast of Ithaca against which we were about to be smashed.

'It is all right,' a voice from the darkness said.

I spun around and heaved a breath of relief. There was no tanker or anything else, only the sea and the stars and Dimitri. I checked my watch guiltily.

'I must have nodded off. It couldn't have been for more than a few minutes.'

It must have been more like an hour. Belatedly I noticed the rifle which Dimitri was holding. The moonlight gave the metal a chilling grey sheen.

'I woke up and couldn't see you. I was worried,' he said.

It was a plausible enough explanation, but something gave me the impression that he'd been there for a while, watching me sleep. A shiver ran up my back. For a few moments we regarded each other silently, then he turned and went back to the wheelhouse.

'Your turn to get some rest,' he said.

But after that I couldn't sleep.

The wind came up later so we raised the sails and made better time. By four in the morning we could see the outline of Ithaca rising from the grey sea.

23

As Ithaca drew closer, first light streaked the horizon. The radio in the wheelhouse crackled into life. It was set to a local ship-to-shore channel and left permanently on at low volume, so I was used to hearing intermittent traffic, but this time I was sure I heard the *Swallow* mentioned. I turned up the volume and waited, and a few moments later I heard it again. Dimitri had heard it too and he came in from the deck and picked up the microphone to respond. There was a brief conversation.

'It was the harbourmaster at Kioni. Alkimos Kounidis asked him to pass on a message to us to ask us to go to his house when we return.'

'Did he say why?'

'Only that it was important. We can anchor in the cove below his house.'

I left Dimitri to set the course and went out onto the deck. Since I'd woken earlier to find him standing over me holding the rifle, a state of unease had existed between us. I couldn't really believe that he had been contemplating anything murderous, but at the same time I didn't entirely trust him. Since I had suggested that the real reason he had wanted to cool his relationship with Alex was because he was afraid she would jeopardise the success of his business, I couldn't help wondering how far he would go to make sure she never knew about it.

Within half an hour we had dropped anchor and were rowing ashore. When we climbed up to the house, Kounidis was waiting for us though it was still barely light. He told us the harbourmaster had phoned to tell him that we were on our way, adding that he was always awake early. 'At my age to find it difficult to sleep should be regarded as a blessing,' he observed wryly. 'Soon there will be an eternity of sleep.'

Eleni was already preparing coffee and something to eat. Before we could discover what it was he wanted to tell us, Kounidis asked if we had found Gregory. I told him about our conversation and spread the charts I'd brought from the boat out on the table. Kounidis was as puzzled as we were to learn that my father and Kohl had gone to Pigania Bay, but he said that he had learned something that added weight to what Gregory had told me.

'Yesterday I contacted the owner of the dive shop in Kioni. It seems that in May your father hired a young American to work for him.'

'After he came back from Kephalonia?'

'Yes.'

And after Gregory had been banished out of the way to Kalamos, I guessed.

'The American spoke about another man on the boat, though he was quiet and kept out of the way. Apparently he stayed below for most of the time, except when they were diving.'

'Because he didn't want to be seen?'

'Possibly,' Kounidis agreed.

'I don't suppose this American is still around?'

'Unfortunately no. After your father's heart

attack the young man left to find another job. He said he was going to try Crete or perhaps Rhodes. But he did say that the place he had been diving was a bay to the south.'

'Pigania?'

'Perhaps.'

'Did he say what they were looking for?'

'Only that it was something of archaeological interest. I imagine that he was paid to be discreet. Possibly your father did not reveal the truth to him anyway.'

'I'm beginning to wonder what the truth is,' I said as I looked at the chart on the table. 'Maybe they weren't looking for the *Antounnetta* after all.' The pattern of crosses and dates which marked the progress of my father's search over the years was nowhere near Pigania Bay. Everything that was known about the last hours of the ship suggested that it had set a course eastwards towards the mainland after it left Frikes. I pointed to the large cross on the chart toward the mainland coast which I had first noticed the day I'd taken Alex out on my father's boat.

'Do you know what this is?' I asked Kounidis.

'It is the place where the survivors from the *Antounnetta* were picked up by another ship.'

It was this reference point along with calculations estimating speed, tidal charts and weather records that had given my father a broad search area, taking into account also where Kounidis had eventually come ashore on the southern tip of Kephalonia. I turned my attention to Pigania Bay. It was the largest bay

378

on the southern coast, though Kounidis said it was rocky and inhospitable. There were no beaches marked on the chart, and that entire part of the island was mountainous and completely uninhabited.

'Whatever they were looking for, it must be here,' I said. I started to get up, ready to leave, but Kounidis stopped me.

'Wait. There is something else I must tell you. The reason I asked the harbourmaster to contact you is that I have received some other news.' He paused. 'It is about Alex.'

Some inner part of me lurched at his hesitant manner and I envisaged the worst; Alex washed up dead somewhere. In my mind's eye I saw her pale face bleached by the seawater, her hair entwined with seaweed. I glanced at Dimitri. He gripped the table edge tensely.

'Please,' Kounidis said anxiously, raising both hands in reassurance. 'I did not wish to alarm either of you. She is not hurt. Yesterday afternoon Alex went to the house where she had been staying, to collect her things. She told the woman who owns it that she was returning to England.'

I was stunned. 'There must be some mistake.'

'I am afraid not. The woman was quite certain. Alex left a note for the police.' Kounidis took a folded sheet of paper from his pocket and placed it on the table. 'Miros Theonas allowed me to take a copy so that I could show you both.'

I read what she'd written with a sense of growing confusion. The note was short. She apologised for any trouble that she had caused the police, explaining that she had left Exoghi so suddenly to avoid another confrontation with me. She wrote that she had met somebody who invited her to his yacht and they had not been aware of the clamour surrounding her disappearance until they returned from Zakynthos, an island to the south, where they had been for the past few days.

'This is ridiculous,' I said after I had quickly read it through once. I turned to Dimitri. 'Is this her writing? Do you recognise the signature?'

He nodded heavily.

'It must be a forgery,' I insisted. 'Surely Theonas spoke to her. He didn't just let her go.'

'After she collected her things, Alex caught a ferry to Sami,' Kounidis said. 'The travel company confirmed that she had bought a ticket, and also a ticket for a flight to London from Argostoli. Theonas phoned the airline and they confirmed that she had checked in. Under the circumstances he has officially called off his investigation.'

'And I suppose the fact that somebody tried to kill me the other night was my imagination,' I said cynically.

'When Irene told me what happened I of course mentioned it to Miros Theonas. He wondered why you had not reported such a serious matter to the authorities.'

'Because I didn't have time to spend the entire day answering his questions,' I protested.

'Which I again explained to Theonas on your behalf,' Kounidis said. 'He made the comment that perhaps it was understandable that you did not wish to waste time as no doubt you were eager to prove your conviction that your father had indeed made a discovery of some value.'

'Theonas thinks I'm looking to cash in, is that it?'

'He believes you are convinced that your father planned to smuggle something he had found out of Greece.'

'And now I'm looking to take up where he left off? And what about Kohl?'

'A coincidence. Theonas is of the opinion that his original theory is correct, that the murder was the result of a bungled robbery. He points to the fact that the only other people at the monastery that day were the tourists on the bus. Also the body has now been tentatively identified as that of Johann Kohl, a retired builder from Hamburg. A man with no connection with the dealing of antiquities, and with no criminal record.'

I shook my head in disbelief. 'He was in the photograph with my father at the museum, for Christ's sake! I suppose Theonas thinks my father's death was another coincidence? No doubt an unfortunate accident.'

'He insists there is no evidence to the contrary.'

Suddenly I saw Alex's appearance, her note and convenient departure for what it really was; a means to fool the police. And in this case, Theonas was all too ready to accept it at face value. But there were too many questions, too many inconsistencies.

'Alex hasn't left,' I said. 'I'm sure of it.'

'I believe that you may be right,' Kounidis agreed and smiled at my surprise. 'Unlike Theonas, I share your concerns, Robert, and so I spoke to somebody that I know who works for the airline. It seems that, upon examination, the passenger numbers for the flight Alex bought a ticket for do not tally with the number of people who actually checked in.'

'Let me guess,' I said. 'The numbers were out by one.'

★　★　★

Kounidis's news had unsettled me. I no longer presumed to know what was going on. After we had eaten the breakfast Eleni had made for us, Dimitri and I prepared to leave for Pigania Bay. Dimitri was certain that Hassel had somehow forced Alex to go through the charade of pretending to leave, but I couldn't see how he had managed it. Kounidis told us that when she had collected her things from the house where she had been staying she was alone. Even if Hassel had threatened her, surely she could have taken her chance to escape or at least tip the police off. But then I thought of the scream I'd heard at the marina. I had no doubt that it had been Alex.

The coast around the south of the island was quite different from the north. The sea surged against barren rocks and, though there were numerous inlets and coves, most of them were fringed with vertical cliffs topped with dense, impenetrable vegetation.

382

A wall of rock surrounded Pigania Bay and the water was still and deep green, more like a fjord than a bay. The headland on the western side jutted out to sea and formed a prominent point. Along its shoreline there was a platform of smooth, flat rock where a small boat could easily land. It was the only place where my father and Kohl could have gone ashore.

Dimitri steered the *Swallow* in close until we were less than fifty yards away then hit a switch to drop the anchor over the side. Half a minute later we were motionless, the winch and engine turned off. Around us the water shifted in a single molten mass. We took the dinghy ashore, where I clambered up onto the rocks and secured a line. A trickle of fresh water dripped down a narrow ravine in the cliff above, where a rough goat track vanished into the tangled undergrowth. When we followed it, we found ourselves climbing alongside the ravine. In places the ground was dry and covered with loose rock which made it difficult to get a foothold, but higher up the slope levelled out. A few pine trees had gained a hold marking the edge of a wood where we walked through a world in permanent twilight. Even so, by the time we emerged onto the flat open ground of the headland high above the bay, we were both soaked in sweat. Far below us we could see the *Swallow* as she lay serenely at anchor in the bay.

Straggly clumps of grass scorched brown by the sun grew in the thin soil near the cliff edge. To the south, the sky and sea merged in a smoky haze on the horizon, and to the west, Kephalonia rose from the strait.

At first sight there was nothing to indicate if this was where my father and Kohl had come, but then, near a lightning-struck burned out stump at the edge of the trees, we came across a circular depression in the ground. It was perhaps ten feet across and three or four deep. At the bottom, the ground cover had been cleared exposing loose earth. Though fresh growth was already regaining a foothold, it was clear that somebody had dug there recently. As I stood on the lip of the hollow, what I had at first thought to be a natural feature took on a different interpretation. There was a low hump of similar proportions to one side. At first the growth of many years had tricked my eye, but now I could see that the hollow was in fact man-made, the earth which had been removed from it forming the hump. It had been dug a long time ago, probably decades earlier, though the evidence of fresh earth at the bottom was much more recent. I guessed that it had to have been disturbed by my father.

I hunted around for a stick, and then went down and used it to scoop out the loose earth. It was easy work but dirty and hot and another pair of hands would have made it easier still, but when I looked for Dimitri he had vanished.

'Thanks for your help,' I muttered to myself.

Even without him, within half an hour I had removed the loose earth to reveal the shape of a hole a few feet deep and about six feet long. But whatever had been buried there was long gone. As I regarded the result of my efforts, wiping the sweat and dirt from my face and trying to make sense of it, Dimitri reappeared.

'Did you find anything?' he asked.

I ignored him. Something caught my eye in the dirt. It was small and round, too regular in shape to be natural, and I bent down to pick it up. It was made of some kind of metal, though it was pitted and rusted. I turned it over in my fingers and tossed it up to Dimitri.

'What do you make of that?'

He examined it, then said, 'Come with me. I want to show you something.'

It was only then that I noticed that he was as sweaty and dirty as I was. Intrigued, I followed him toward the point of the headland. As we got closer I saw a pile of earth heaped next to a single tree, its trunk bent almost at right angles away from the winds to which it was constantly exposed. The hole Dimitri had uncovered was about a third of the size of the one I'd just dug out. A pile of stones lay close by. Beside them he'd laid out the bones he'd found. There were two almost complete skeletons.

'How did you know they were here?' I asked.

He gestured to something he'd propped by the tree. It was a rudimentary cross, formed by two lengths of pine lashed together. He lit a cigarette and squatted by one of the skeletons. He picked up the skull to show to me. There was a small round hole at the back, and a much larger one at the front which had obliterated much of the forehead. He put his finger in the one at the back.

'What does this look like to you?'

'A bullet hole?'

He nodded. 'This is where it entered.' Then he indicated the jagged mess at the front. 'This is the exit.' He showed me the second skull, which was unmarked, and then he gestured to the rest of the remains. 'I looked for some other injury, but I could not find anything.'

Two people. One shot at close range in the back of the head, execution style. The other possibly also shot, but the bullet having hit only soft tissue.

'The earth was loose,' Dimitri said. 'But the bones are old.' He showed me a small pile of objects, some similar to the round piece of metal I had found. These too were rusted and pitted. 'They are buttons,' he said and showed me a rusted hollow square of metal which I recognised as a buckle. 'They are from a uniform I think.'

'Soldiers?'

I looked back to the treeline, trying to figure it out. 'Somebody dug these up from the bottom of the hollow over there. Presumably my father and Kohl. And then they reburied them here. Why?'

With a sweep of his arm Dimitri indicated the view across the sea. 'It is a nice place to be buried.'

He was right, of course. But why go to so much trouble? There was a certain ritual aspect to it, though my father had not been a religious man. What was more puzzling was that the hollow they had come from had obviously been dug many years before and left for nature to reclaim. Why would anyone dig a large hole only to bury two bodies at the bottom and leave the rest uncovered?

Like everything else, it made no sense.

* * *

That evening we returned to Kounidis's house as he had suggested earlier, and after dinner I saw the glow of a cigarette tip outside near the cliff. Somebody else who couldn't sleep. The faint sound of music drifted on the air. I recognised it as the same haunting rhythm I'd heard when I was there with Alex. Because I couldn't sleep and because I was curious, I left my room and went downstairs to the terrace. Dimitri emerged from the darkness at the same time and together we listened. The music appeared to come from the far end of the terrace where a sliver of dim light escaped the shuttered windows of a room.

'Do you know what it is?' I asked.

'A traditional song,' he said. 'It is about a young shepherd who falls in love with a beautiful girl. A stranger arrives in the village and he steals the girl away. The shepherd is heartbroken.'

I wasn't sure if he was serious. His face was shadowed, making it difficult to read his expression. Was I imagining it, or was he alluding to Alex? Was I the stranger?

'What happens?' I said.

'There is a fight between the stranger and the shepherd. One of them is killed.'

I was almost afraid to ask. 'Which one?'

He stared at me for a moment then shrugged,

the tiniest movement of his shoulders. 'I don't remember.'

As if on cue the music abruptly ended. Without another word he passed me by and went into the house.

★　★　★

In the morning at first light I turned the wheel towards the open sea and we motored out of the cove. We made the short journey to Kioni where there was a place to rent diving tanks, and then headed south. By the time we reached Pigania it was only mid-morning but it was already hot, though much of the bay itself was shaded from the morning sun by the steep hills surrounding it. The water was dark and green, unruffled by even a tremor of breeze.

We dropped anchor and dragged the scuba gear up from below. I had taken a five-day course once years ago during a holiday in Malta, but hadn't done any diving since then. I'd been keen on the idea, but I soon found I hadn't liked the reality much. Once the initial novelty of swimming among multi-coloured fish had worn off, I'd spent most of the time worrying about sharks and constantly checking my oxygen gauge.

Nevertheless, I volunteered to go down first and Dimitri reminded me how to check the gauges and make sure air was flowing through the mouthpiece. When everything seemed to be working, I started pulling on a wet suit.

The charts showed that the depth in the bay

was fairly uniform at between fifty and sixty feet until the beginning of a trench about a quarter of a mile out. We planned to search the seabed methodically out to the trench, working on the assumption that whatever my father and Kohl had found was still down there. If we were right, it wouldn't be long before Hassel showed up.

When I was ready for my first dive, Dimitri handed me a line and told me to tie it on my buoyancy vest. 'If you get into trouble, tug it twice like this.' He demonstrated, giving two sharp but long pulls which gave a clear signal. 'Then I will pull you up.'

'And if you see anything up here do the same,' I said.

My safety was in his hands. I was uncomfortably aware that if anything went wrong I had to rely on Dimitri for help, and I tried not to think about our conversation the night before. If he knew what I was thinking he gave no sign of it, however.

'If you find anything, tie the line on to mark it,' he said.

Finally I climbed down into the water and rinsed out my mask. Dimitri watched from the boat as I put the mouthpiece in and began to breathe air from my tank. I gave him the thumbs up sign then I opened the valve to let some air out of my vest and quickly sank beneath the surface.

For a few minutes I trod water several feet down, getting used to the sound of my own breathing and the feel of the rubber in my mouth. In Malta I'd had an illogical desire to rip it out. The water was clear and sunlit near the surface, but when I looked down it was dark and I couldn't see much. I wondered what might be lurking down there. My heart was beating too fast and I was breathing too quickly. I told myself to calm down and take slower breaths.

At a depth of ten or twelve yards I paused to look back toward the *Swallow*. The line tied to my vest trailed reassuringly like an umbilical cord back to the comforting presence of her hull. Below me the rocky terrain was cut through with valleys and ravines where the darkness was only pierced by the beam of my torch. I continued down perhaps another seven yards or so. Schools of fish cruised around me, some as small as my thumb, others that must have weighed ten pounds or more. Plant life floated exotically in the current, the colours mostly browns and greens and yellows.

Other than the sound of my breathing it was a silent world. I was out of my element. I kept panic at bay only by a conscious act of will. Every time I saw a movement in the periphery of my vision my heart rate quickened. I peered around anxiously, shining my torch beam back and forth, forever expecting something from *Jaws* to materialise out of the gloom.

When I checked my watch, only ten minutes had passed, though it felt like half an hour. I began swimming slowly eastwards across the bay searching for anything out of place.

Having something to concentrate on helped take my mind off imagined dangers, and after a while I even stopped looking over my shoulder every fifteen seconds. Take it easy, I repeated endlessly. Stay calm. Breathe.

When another ten minutes had passed I looked back and was alarmed to find that I couldn't see the *Swallow*. Panic fluttered in my chest. I breathed in gulps. My heart rate soared, gobbling oxygen. I was suddenly disoriented. I thought the current had swept me away from the bay. A grey shape flitted past at the very edge of the light and I thought I glimpsed a fin. I struck out for the surface, suddenly consumed with the notion that I was running out of air. I gulped and then gulped again and a part of me knew that I was losing control. A tiny voice in my brain struggled to be heard. Stay calm, it said. Just relax.

Somehow, with a great effort of will, I managed it. There were no sharks, I wasn't lost and I hadn't run out of air. I took deep breaths.

I remembered that I should wait a few minutes before I went the rest of the way up to avoid nitrogen sickness. I floated twenty feet down, thinking calming thoughts. When at last my time was up I filled my vest and kicked for the surface. I emerged into the welcome warmth of the sun, took off my mask and removed the mouthpiece, flexing my aching jaw. I had never felt so relieved in all my life.

The *Swallow* was a hundred yards away. As I struck out towards her, Dimitri began hauling in the line and when I reached the stern he helped me aboard. As I sat on the deck and took off my gear I told him that I hadn't found anything, hoping that he couldn't tell how close to losing it I'd been.

He checked my tank to see how much air was left and, though he didn't comment, I knew I'd used it up too fast and told myself I'd do better the next time. 'Anything up here?' I asked.

'A few yachts passed by, but they were a long way off.'

We swapped roles. This time Dimitri put on the wet suit and strapped on a tank. I handed him the weight belt and the line.

'Same arrangement, OK?'

He nodded and gave me the binoculars, then quickly checked over the equipment with practised ease. When he was ready, he glanced at his watch then climbed down into the water and quickly vanished.

That day we each did two more dives, moving further out in the bay each time as we systematically covered more ground. By the end of the afternoon we had to return to Kioni to swap our empty tanks, and I phoned Kounidis to tell him we were spending the night on board the boat.

We motored back to Pigania and anchored for the night, then ate a meal of pasta and sausage washed down with beer. We agreed to take four-hour watches, and when we tossed for the first shift I lost, so Dimitri went below to rest while I stayed above and drank coffee to stay awake. I kept the rifle by my side and a torch handy, and every fifteen minutes I walked the deck, listening for the sound of a stealthily approaching boat.

Sooner or later I knew somebody would come.

24

We spent two days searching the bay, gradually moving further out until we were almost beyond the headland. Dimitri and I existed in a state of undeclared truce, though I wondered how long it would last. We avoided any mention of Alex. In fact we avoided talking about anything at all, instead absorbing ourselves in preparations for our repeated dives, and in between times returning each day to Kioni to refill our tanks. Given that at night we took alternate watches, the only occasions when we were briefly together with time on our hands was when we ate. Even then we made sure our breaks were kept to a minimum.

On our third night on the boat I had fallen asleep, the still, quiet hour before the end of my watch getting the better of me. Lulled by the gentle motion of the waves my eyelids flickered and closed. In the moment before consciousness departed I told myself it would just be for a few moments. But during that time somebody had crept aboard the *Swallow*.

I'd been having a dream. In it I had watched my father walk along the wharf towards the boat. It was early, the darkness melting to grey. I saw a figure emerge silently from the shadows and move towards him. I knew what was going to happen and though I wanted to call out a warning, I couldn't move, I couldn't speak. I could only watch with mounting helplessness as the figure moved closer. My father was oblivious to the danger. The figure raised his arm, something heavy in his hand, and then he brought it down in a sudden blur of motion. At the very last moment, my father sensed something and began to turn, but he was too slow. His eyes locked on mine, registering surprise and then accusation in a silently begged question. Why didn't you warn me? I heard the crack of something hard against his skull and he crumpled and fell. There was a splash and then he was gone.

A hand gripped my arm and I opened my eyes in panic as the images of my dream fragmented. I registered the barrel of a gun and flinched. It was Dimitri.

'Your watch,' he said.

Groggily I sat up. The air in the confines of the cabin was sticky and hot and I was soaked in sweat.

'You were dreaming.'

I came awake, realising that in fact I had not fallen asleep on my watch. I had stayed awake until I'd woken Dimitri at two in the morning before stumbling to bed myself. 'What time is it?'

'Six. I am going to get a couple of hours rest.'

'Right. Everything OK?'

He nodded. 'It is quiet.'

I went up on deck feeling thick-headed from the heat and not enough sleep. Light crept into the sky as the sun came up. The water mirrored the green hills, as still as glass. I drank a hot cup of coffee then stripped off and dived over the side. The water was cool enough to take my breath away, but instantly it cleared my head. I struck out and swam fifty yards from the boat then turned and came back, digging my arms in deep, breathing on every third stroke, concentrating on kicking hard and fast. I emerged panting, and dripping water onto the deck.

By the time I roused Dimitri, the heat of the day was building. We drank coffee and ate a light breakfast before getting ready to repeat the procedure we'd followed on each preceding day. We were beyond the bay itself by lunch time. I studied the chart and realised that within another day we would reach the trench where it was too deep for us to dive. So far we had found nothing, and nobody had found us. Though occasionally boats passed by, they were usually a long way out and nothing came within a mile of us.

The yacht appeared while Dimitri was doing his last dive of the day, though even with binoculars I couldn't make out the name. The sail had no charter company logo, which meant that it was privately owned. I compared it with the one I'd seen at Polis Bay the day Alex vanished, but although they seemed to be about the same size, I couldn't tell if it was the same boat. It was sleek and white and looked like almost every other yacht cruising the islands. It was sailing east-west, making slow progress. As I watched, she came around into the wind and the sail flapped and came down.

The line I was playing out through my free hand stopped moving, distracting my attention. I put the binoculars down. Dimitri had been gone for twenty minutes. The line started moving again. I picked the glasses up again and took another look at the yacht, but couldn't see anything.

When Dimitri surfaced I helped him back onto the boat and coiled the line. As I stripped off my T-shirt and started pulling on the wet suit I pointed out the yacht.

'It arrived about twenty minutes ago.'

'Did you see anybody on board?'

'It's too far away to make out any detail.'

'Do you still want to dive?'

I thought about it. If we were being watched we needed to make it look as if nothing was amiss. 'If anything happens you can get me up,' I decided.

When I was ready, I climbed down into the water and when I was six feet beneath the surface I paused to look back. Dimitri stood by the rail, his outline distorted by the reflection of sunlight on the water. He raised a hand and then I turned and swam down.

The water was cool. The rocks formed towers and plateaux cut through with deep fissures and ravines. At times I swam around structures no more than thirty feet from the surface, at others I descended into the half light, fifty and sixty feet down, always checking to make sure that the line wasn't getting snagged. Time passed. A lone fish flitted by hunting smaller prey. A stingray floated ghost-like beneath me and schools of smaller fish darted this way and that in some curious concert of movement. The unhurried rhythm of my

397

breathing relaxed me. I had become used to diving now, was even starting to enjoy the strange quiet and weightlessness. I paused to check the line and my gauge.

Sunlight diffused through the depths, broken by the rocks which cast shadows on the sea-bed. I was deeper than I should have been. About seventy feet down. I'd have to stop for a little while longer on the way up. I began rising slowly, watching tendrils of seaweed undulating in the current. Rocks formed strange shapes. Another ray passed by, effortlessly gliding and changing direction in a sweeping turn. Not far away I glimpsed a black chasm, the beginning of the trench. I hadn't realised I had come that far. It looked cold and empty. On the edge was a rock formation with an oddly regular shape. It reminded me of something.

I remembered my depth and glanced toward the surface. It was time to stop. I searched for the rock again while I waited, but now I couldn't see it. It had become lost among the formless shapes below me, but then I found it again. What did it remind me of? A square structure, a dark long shape . . . My heart started thumping.

Gradually the shape emerged and took form. Damaged and broken, her lines disguised by the rocks she had come to rest among was the wreck of a ship. Her superstructure had been colonised by the sea, barnacles and seaweed slowly transforming her into a reef. I could make out her bow and a dark hole in the midsection of her hull. If I looked away even for a moment, she vanished, only reappearing again little by little in the gloom as I distinguished her from the sea-bed.

Then I was almost out of air and there was no time left. I kicked for the surface and when I came up Dimitri began hauling me in.

As I took my gear off I told him what I'd seen, excitement making me speak in a rush. 'It must be the *Antounnetta*.'

It was no wonder that my father had never found her before. He had been looking in entirely the wrong place until he met Johann Kohl. We were no more than a few hundred yards from the mouth of the bay, but I could see how Kounidis might not have realised he was so close to the island when the *Antounnetta* had gone down all those years ago. The weather had been bad and there would have been no lights from that part of the island. When he went into the sea, the currents had swept him around the headland into the strait and eventually to the southern tip of Kephalonia.

It was only then that I remembered the yacht I'd seen earlier, but when I looked, it was gone.

'It left a few minutes after you went down,' Dimitri said.

★ ★ ★

By the time we reached Kioni, the light was going. Dimitri took the dinghy and sped across the harbour to fill our tanks. While he was gone, I phoned Kounidis and told him what we'd found.

'We also saw a yacht today. It left after a while,

399

but I've got a feeling it'll be back.'

Kounidis was still stunned by the news that the *Antounnetta* had been there all that time. When he spoke, the strain was evident in his voice. 'I think that now we should inform Miros Theonas,' he said quietly. 'This proves that you were right, Robert. He will have to listen.'

'And then what? If Hassel sees the bay swarming with police he might vanish again. No, let's play it out. Let Hassel come to us.'

'That may be dangerous.'

I knew that he was right, but I had thought this through and Dimitri and I had talked it over. 'There are two of us and we've got a rifle. Give us until lunch time tomorrow. If you haven't heard from us by then, you call Theonas. We'll leave a message with the harbourmaster.'

Though he was reluctant, Kounidis agreed in the end. By the time I got back to the boat, Dimitri had returned and I helped him aboard with the tanks. A few minutes later we slipped our lines and were heading back to Pigania. It was dark by the time we arrived. The moon had risen, painting the water in grey and silver while around us the hills were black against the sky.

Dimitri volunteered to take the first watch. I left him smoking a cigarette on deck and went below to my cabin. There was little chance of sleeping however, and after a while I gave up trying. Instead I lay on my back staring into the darkness, my mind a whirlwind of thoughts and images. I got up and went through my bag to find the photograph which I had found among Kohl's things at the Hotel Ionnis. I stared at the slightly blurred faces, trying to discern details of their features as if somehow that would allow me an insight as to who they had been. Sons and fathers, somebody's brother, somebody's loved one. They were all long dead. I wondered if their relatives still thought of them. They looked so young. Take away the uniforms and they might have been on a school outing, the few older ones perhaps teachers.

I turned my attention to Hassel, standing to one side and slightly apart, and I thought about the story Irene had told us of how he and Julia had fallen in love. I went to fetch a magnifying glass which I had seen on the chart table in the main cabin, and when I looked through it the faces of the soldiers swam into startling clarity. Irene had said that Hassel was in his late-twenties, but he appeared younger. He was smiling slightly in the picture, though there was a faint but unmistakable stamp of melancholy in his expression. Amongst the others there was a visible camaraderie in their shared grins, their shoulders touching, but Hassel seemed separate from them. Perhaps when the picture was taken he had already met Julia and he was thinking of her. I noticed the iron cross on his uniform, and once again recalled the one I'd found in my father's study. In a flash of realisation I understood something which I should have seen before and my blood quickened.

When Dimitri came for me I was still awake and deep in thought. He seemed subdued as if he too had spent the last few hours plagued by doubts and questions. When he saw the photograph on my bunk he looked at me questioningly, but I hadn't yet made sense of what I suspected so I didn't say anything. He handed me the rifle and went to his cabin, while I got up and made myself a pot of strong coffee. I sat on deck in the hope of feeling a cooling breeze but the air was utterly still. Ironically, now that I was up the minutes seemed to drag with infinite slowness and despite the coffee I was tired. I knew that if I lay down for just a minute I would fall into a deep sleep.

After twenty minutes I took the empty coffee pot down below. I could hear faint snoring from the direction of Dimitri's cabin. Fatigue had eventually got the better of him and I envied him for having taken the first watch. Back on deck, the bay was calm. By the light of the moon I could see the shore fifty yards away where the track led up the ravine to the headland. I knew I would never remain awake if I stayed on the boat, and five minutes later I was rowing the dinghy ashore.

It took only a couple of minutes before I heard the scrape of rocks and I hauled the dinghy safely out. Making my way up the track was difficult in the darkness of the ravine where the moonlight barely penetrated, and I had to feel my way along. Eventually the going became easier and I reached the top and walked among the ghostly grey pines towards the headland. When I emerged from the trees it was empty and still. I looked down on the dark outline of the *Swallow* against the moonlit bay.

From somewhere close by I heard the skitter

of a stone, but when I turned there was nothing to be seen other than the single bent tree where Dimitri had uncovered the grave. My pulse raced and my heart thudded in my chest. I sensed that I wasn't alone. I felt unseen eyes watching me. A movement caught my eye and then a figure moved away from the shadow of the tree.

'Mr French,' a voice said.

I recognised it immediately. He came closer so that I could see him clearly. He held both hands out slightly from his body, showing me his open palms so that I would know he wasn't armed.

'*Herr* Hassel,' I said. He looked a little surprised that I knew who he was, but he inclined his head in acknowledgement. I gestured toward the grave where Dimitri and I had reburied the bones he'd found. 'Is that your grandfather?'

He looked over his shoulder. 'I believe so, yes. How did you know?'

'I found a medal which I think my father dug up here. I think it belonged to your grandfather.'

'Yes, you are right. He was awarded it during fighting in North Africa where he was badly wounded. It was before he was sent to Greece of course.'

'You knew he was buried here?'

'Yes.'

'My father told you?'

'I never spoke to your father. But he wrote me a letter.'

I thought about that, and then I said, 'What exactly is this all about? And where is Alex?'

I looked around, thinking she might appear at

any moment, but then I was struck by how tense Hassel was. His eyes held a gleam of anxiety which was dulled only by exhaustion.

'We must talk,' he replied. 'I am very worried about her.'

★ ★ ★

Hassel had anchored his yacht on the far side of the headland and had moored a dinghy just off the nearest beach. We left it there and he came with me when I rowed back out to the *Swallow*. When Dimitri saw that I wasn't alone he pointed the rifle at us until I called out to assure him that everything was all right. Nevertheless he kept the gun trained on us until we were aboard. I introduced Kurt Hassel, as I had discovered his full name was, and then I suggested we go below.

'I think we all need a drink.'

I found my dad's Scotch and poured three glasses. I had so many questions I didn't know where to start, but Hassel had questions too. He wanted to know where I had found my father's journal.

'Is that what you were looking for when I disturbed you at the harbour?' I asked.

'Yes,' he admitted. 'Though I did not know who you were then.'

'But you said my father wrote to you, so you must have known about this place,' I reasoned. 'Why did you need the journal?'

'Your father did not tell me about Pigania. I only knew to come here because I followed you from Kioni this morning. I plotted you on radar.

May I ask where you found your father's journal?'

'I didn't. We discovered that my father brought a man called Johann Kohl here.' I saw the name register. 'You knew him?'

'Yes. Earlier this year he arrived at my house unannounced one evening. He claimed to have served with my grandfather during the war here on Ithaca. At first I did not believe him because all of the men under my grandfather's command were listed as having been killed. Kohl claimed that he had in fact survived the attack on the ship which had picked up the survivors from the *Antounnetta*. When he reached the mainland shore he decided to desert. As proof of this he showed me a photograph which had been taken during the occupation. He claimed that he was one of the men in the picture.'

'Wait a minute,' I said, and I got up and fetched the picture I'd found among Kohl's possessions. 'Is this it?'

Hassel nodded. 'Yes. Where did you get it?'

'From a hotel in Argostoli. But there was nobody called Kohl stationed here during the war. Though there was a soldier called Eric Schmidt. You asked me if I knew anybody by that name the night we met.' I paused, guessing the truth. 'Kohl and Schmidt were the same person?'

'Yes. Though his documents showed that his name was Johann Kohl, he claimed to have assumed the identity from a dead soldier at the end of the war.'

At first Kurt hadn't been entirely convinced by Kohl's story but the more they talked the more inclined he was to believe him. Kohl had detailed knowledge about Kurt's grandfather and the occupation of Ithaca. In the end Kurt gave him some money.

'Why did he want money?' I asked.

'To come to Greece. He told me that the official version of my grandfather's death was not what had really happened, and that if he could come here he would be able to prove it to me.'

'The official version being what?'

'That he was killed during the attack on the *Antounnetta*.'

'But even if what he said was true, why should it matter after all this time?'

'It did not,' Kurt said. 'At least not until I came here and discovered that my grandfather is remembered as a Nazi.'

'But you didn't know that when Kohl approached you.'

'No. I gave him money because I felt sorry for him. He was old. I believed that he had led a hard life and I thought that it may have been true that he served with my grandfather. He spoke of him with great respect. Also my family is quite wealthy and the money I gave him was really very little. A few thousand euros, that is all.'

'This was last year, you said. When exactly?'

'In September.'

'He never mentioned anything about the Dracoulis artefacts?'

'No.' Kurt looked blank. 'What are they?'

I was surprised that he didn't know. I showed him the German newspaper cutting I'd found among Kohl's things. 'I think Kohl must have seen this last year. This was the real reason he came to you for money. The artefacts were originally discovered by a man called Dracoulis, but they were stolen from Kephalonia during the war. I think Kohl read about their return and that's when he decided to come here himself.'

'But why?'

'I'm not sure. Did you hear from Kohl again after you gave him the money?'

'No.' Kurt told us that Kohl had promised to stay in touch, but he wasn't surprised when he didn't hear from him again. He might have thought no more about it if he hadn't received a letter a few months later from a man he had never met who lived on Ithaca.

'My father?'

'Yes. He said that he had met Kohl, but that Kohl had been murdered. He told me that his death was connected to events which had taken place during the war and that there were things which I should be aware of regarding my grandfather. He hinted that I may have relatives I did not know of.'

'He knew about Alex?' I interrupted.

'Not directly I think, but he would have known that Julia was pregnant when she left the island.'

I realised that was true. 'What else did he say?'

'He asked me to come here, but he warned me that when I arrived I should take care not to let anyone know my identity or what the purpose of my visit was. He said that in the event that anything should happen to him he had written all I needed to know in a journal which I would find on his boat. Which of course is where you and I first encountered one another. But as I said, I did not know who you were at that time.'

'But you did when we met outside a bar in Vathy.'

'Yes, though I had very little idea of what was going on. That is why I wished to talk to you, but I was not sure how much to say. Your father's death was recorded as an accident. And when we spoke . . . '

'I wasn't exactly communicative. It was bad timing.'

'This I understand now.'

'From Alex?'

'Yes. By then I knew who she was. Since I could not speak to you I left a note for her asking her to meet me in Exoghi. Of course it came as a great shock to her to realise that we were related. While we were talking we saw your Jeep driving past the bay. I think everything had become too much for Alex at that point. She said that she could not see you.'

'So you took her to your yacht?'

'Yes.'

They had sailed to Zakynthos, just as Alex's note to Theonas had claimed, and it was true that they hadn't realised that she was considered as a missing person or that I was suspected of having pushed her from the cliff. However, once Alex knew about the letter my father had sent to Kurt, she realised that they had to tell me and that's when they had returned to Ithaca and phoned me.

'We did not want anyone to know,' Hassel explained. 'We did not know who to trust. But somebody followed you to the marina.'

'The driver of the car.'

'Yes. He tried to kill us both.'

I knew who it must have been. Earlier, when I had been studying the photograph of *Hauptmann* Hassel and his men, I'd realised that if the iron cross in my father's drawer came from the grave on the headland then it was likely that one set of the remains probably belonged to *Hauptmann* Hassel. That could only mean that Kounidis's account of Hassel's death was a lie. 'It was Kounidis in the car,' I guessed.

'Or the man who works for him,' Kurt agreed, though he explained that at the time he was not aware of this. He suspected Kounidis's involvement only because there was a strong suggestion that the account of his grandfather's death was untrue.

That night at the marina Kurt had escaped unharmed as had I, but Alex was not so lucky. I remembered the scream I had heard and now I understood.

'So Kounidis has got her?'

'Yes. I could not go to the police because I could prove nothing and I was afraid for her safety. And so I decided to look for you. When I saw this boat in the harbour at Kioni I followed you here.'

Dimitri, who had all this time listened without comment, now spoke. 'But the note Alex wrote when she went to fetch her things. You are saying Kounidis forced her? Why did she not say something to the owner of the house, or send a message to Theonas?'

Kurt didn't know about the note, but it wasn't hard to guess the answer.

'Kounidis probably told her that if she did she wouldn't see either of us again,' I said. He had been clever. Even to the point that it was he who had told me she never made the flight she was supposed to have taken back to England.

'But why?' Dimitri questioned.

'Because it was Theonas he wanted to put off, not us. He wanted us to keep looking. That way he knew we'd come here. All along he's been manipulating us. He even told us about the American my father hired to dive for him, just so there would be no doubt we were looking in the right place.'

'Because he wanted us to find the *Antounnetta*?' Dimitri asked.

I shook my head. 'He's always known she was here. There was something else he wanted.'

'What?' Kurt asked.

'You,' I said.

Kounidis had used us to draw Kurt out. And he had succeeded.

25

The sun was beginning to rise. To the east, the horizon was changing colour as the night slowly dissolved. I had gone up on deck for some air. There was no movement, everything utterly still. I heard a sound and when I turned, Kurt was standing by the wheelhouse.

'May I join you?' he asked.

I made a gesture of assent and together we watched as fire streaked the sky.

'It was very strange for me to meet Alex,' Kurt said. 'To know that we are related. I have a sister and several cousins on my mother's side, but my father was an only child. At least I always thought so. He was born while my grandfather was in North Africa. Of course he was only a baby when my grandfather came home, before he was sent here. He does not remember him.'

'Did your grandmother know about Julia?'

'No. My grandmother remarried after the war. But she never had any more children. Her second husband died before I was born. I think he was a good man, a good husband for her and a father to her son. But I do not think she ever loved him the way she loved my grandfather. She used to talk about him when I was young.'

'Is she still alive?'

'Yes. And my father also. I do not know how he will react when he discovers that he has a half-sister living in England.'

'You'll tell them?'

Kurt looked surprised. 'Of course. Why would I keep such a thing from them?'

'Maybe it's better not to know some things,' I suggested. 'You say your grandmother loved your grandfather, but she didn't know about Julia.'

'Yes,' he mused, 'I have thought about that. However my grandmother has always been a very practical woman. And an understanding one. I know that when my grandfather came back from Africa he was a changed man. He was very young. No doubt he had seen many terrible things. I think that she will understand how he might have fallen in love here.' Kurt swept his arm in a gesture to encompass our surroundings. 'It is very beautiful. The war must have seemed a long way away, and I think he had had enough of war. I think he may have needed to believe in people again.'

'You know what Julia told her daughter about your grandfather?' I asked.

'That she was raped by him? Yes, Alex told me.'

'She doesn't believe it was true. Do you?'

'No. As I mentioned, my grandmother talked about him often. I believe he was a good man, a gentle man. Perhaps Julia did not want her daughter to find my family. It is understandable. She could not have known how we would react. She invented a story that made certain the past remained where she thought it belonged.'

I thought he was probably right. The account that Kounidis had given of the end of the occupation was undoubtedly untrue. He was the

412

only living witness to the cruel acts he'd ascribed to Hassel. 'I wonder what really happened here,' I said. I thought about the hollow on the headland where my father and Kohl had uncovered the bones of two men, one of whom we knew was *Hauptmann* Hassel. But who had killed them? And why had their remains been buried at the bottom of what must have then been an empty hole?

'The truth must be in your father's journal,' Kurt said. 'Do you have any idea where it could be?'

'I think Kounidis must have it. I think my father went to fetch it from the boat on the morning he vanished.'

'You believe Kounidis murdered him?'

I nodded.

'Because of what is down there?' Kurt gestured to the water.

'In a sense. It's ironic, but I thought this was about money. I thought you, my father, Kohl, you all wanted whatever is down there for the same reason. But now it looks as if I couldn't have been more wrong. You want to know the truth about your grandfather. So does Alex. And Kounidis certainly doesn't need money. In fact I don't think he wanted the *Antounnetta* found at all. That's what this is all about for him. He doesn't want the truth to be known.'

'And your father?' Kurt asked. 'What do you think he wanted?'

'What he always wanted. To be remembered for something. Perhaps Kohl was the only one in it for the money. If my dad had planned to smuggle whatever it is down there out of the country, he never would have talked about any of it in the first place. And he wouldn't have written to you.'

It was getting light. Kurt saw me searching the horizon and guessed what I was looking for. 'Do you think Kounidis will come?'

I told him we saw a yacht yesterday. It turned out the yacht was actually Kurt's. He'd told us earlier that it was moored in the next bay around the headland. 'Kounidis knew you'd turn up sooner or later and he knows we won't go to the police while he's got Alex.'

I didn't think there was much we could do except wait.

*   *   *

An hour later I had decided that I was wrong to think there was nothing we could do. There was one thing.

The sun was up and the heat already building as I strapped on my tank. Another tank which I was going to take with me as a spare lay by the stern rail. When I climbed down to the water, Dimitri let out some of the line attached to my vest. I took a final look around. There was still no sign of Kounidis.

'Be careful,' Kurt said to me.

I nodded and then I moved away from the boat. When I was twenty feet away, I released some air from my vest and sank beneath the surface. As I swam down I felt the change in pressure and the temperature became cooler. I could see the dark chasm of the trench and the rock formation below me and, when I turned on the torch, the wreck began to emerge from her surroundings. The *Antounnetta* was lying on her starboard side, her bow partly out over the edge of the trench. I ran the beam back along the length of her hull, lingering over the damage to the forward gun and the bridge. Twisted metal plates had peeled back like the skin of an orange. The parts of her hull which weren't encrusted with shellfish or cloaked in seaweed were completely rusted. Fish swam in and out of empty windows and doors.

I tied the line off on a rail near an open door amidships, and left my spare tank there while I swam inside. It was almost completely black except for the beam from my torch. I tried not to think about the tons of metal encasing me as I moved deeper into the wreck. At the bottom of a metal stairway I found a partly open door, but when I tried to push it wider it was firmly stuck. Using the torch I peered through the gap to the passage beyond where I saw the bulkhead had buckled, either from an explosion somewhere in the bowels of the boat or perhaps from the heat of a fire.

I turned and went back to look for another route in. When I emerged onto the outer deck I retrieved the spare tank and swam over the top of the wreck until I found an open door on the other side where I left the tank. Inside, I found a ladder which led down to the deck below and another closed door. The mechanism was rusted solid and it wouldn't open at all, but further down I found another door, and this one was open. It led into a passage which took me into the belly of the boat. The darkness was total and the silence claustrophobic. Without the torch I would have been totally blind. I tried not to think about the trench. Now and then the sound of grinding metal against rock reverberated through the wreck as if she were shifting inch by inch. I imagined her teetering at the edge of the abyss, then slowly falling into the freezing black depths with me trapped inside, the pressure steadily increasing as she fell, until it crushed my lungs.

As I searched the *Antounnetta*, sometimes I found a passage was blocked and I had to go back and try another route. My tank clanked eerily against the bulkhead. An eel darted from the light, startling me so that my heart thudded like a piston. I found the galley, where pots and pans still hung in their racks above the stoves, and nearby was a room which might have been the mess. I checked my gauge and saw that I would soon need to go back and swap tanks, but first I swam down a stairway which took me down another level to the engine rooms.

Twisted wreckage littered the space, the internal bulkheads buckled and smashed. A gaping hole in the hull revealed what had finally sunk the *Antounnetta*, though for me it was a convenient exit and I swam through it and up the side of the ship to the open deck where I'd left my tank. I unbuckled the one on my back and swapped them over. When I turned on the air a stream of bubbles rose from the mouthpiece. I put it in my mouth and blew out sharply before I started breathing again.

When I got back down to the engine room I found another passage which led past cramped cabins with rows of bunks. A locker door hung open and, though most of the contents had long since rotted away, a pair of spectacles remained on a shelf. At the end, I found myself in what appeared to be a storage hold. Broken debris littered the floor. Something was wrapped in what was left of a tarpaulin. I shone the torch over it, and when I tugged at a section of rotted material a pile of rusted metal fell out and drifted to the floor. A cross. A candle holder. Traces of gold paint glinted in the beam of my torch. The remains of a framed picture lay against the bulkhead, the canvas itself gone save for a few tattered threads. Everywhere I looked I saw the remains of what I assumed was what had been looted from the monastery at Kathara.

I had disturbed clouds of silt and rotting matter, which swirled in the current making it harder to see. I glimpsed something pale and went closer. A face stared up at me. For an instant my heart leapt, but it was only a statue. It was life-sized, the paint largely gone, but clearly the original *Panaghia*. Her features were beautifully fashioned. Even in this dark and gloomy cavern, her expression was achingly serene. For several long moments I stared at her image, knowing that my father never had. This was the symbol of faith which he had wanted to return to the people of Ithaca to repay the kindness they had shown him. But there was

417

something else he had expected to find on the *Antounnetta*. He had spoken of the attention of the world, of something which would make Ithaca prosper. But though I looked all around, peering through the murky debris, I couldn't see anything.

Time was getting short. I searched amongst the rotting junk on the floor. My hands stirred up more silt and I came up with a rusted crucifix, a small bowl. I swept back and forth, but all I found was more religious paraphernalia. Then I grasped something which resisted when I tugged. I pulled again and it came away in disintegrating clouds of murk. I felt again and burrowed underneath what I thought must be some kind of material and found something hard and smooth with rounded contours. It was wrapped in canvas and blankets which yielded like wet tissue paper as I uncovered a long, pale shape lying prone. When I shone the torch along its length I saw that it was another statue. It was classical in style. A female form, naked except for a garment draped low around the hips. In contrast to the chaste, slightly sorrowful representation of the *Panaghia*, the smile and pose the sculptor of this statue had fashioned was suggestive, even playful. As I shone the light directly at her lifelike face I was struck by the notion that she stared back at me, amused, and I knew where I had seen this face before. Then silt drifted like soot and the image was clouded. I checked my watch and saw that I was out of time.

On land I would never have been able to lift the statue alone, but underwater I managed to manoeuvre it back to the engine room where I left it while I swam back up the side of the wreck for the line. When I returned and had it secured, I began my ascent. I had been down a long time, at a depth of sixty to seventy feet, so I had to make several stops to allow the nitrogen to leak out of my blood. I kept checking my gauge, hoping I had enough air, trying to relax while I counted off the minutes. I could see the hull of the *Swallow* above and to my left where the water was bright with sunlight.

Finally, I checked my gauge again and, though I was cutting it fine, I was out of air and I had no choice. I kicked for the surface.

⋆　⋆　⋆

I knew immediately that something was wrong. The *Swallow* appeared to be deserted. I looked around, but there was no other boat in sight. I called out, thinking maybe Hassel and Dimitri were in the wheelhouse, but there was no response.

I began to swim to the stern. The closer I got the more certain I was that something had happened. When I reached the boat I hauled myself onto the platform at the back. The silence was total. The hairs on the back of my neck prickled. Unbuckling my tank, I stood up cautiously. The deck was empty. There was no evidence of mayhem or violence. There was no evidence of anything at all. Increasingly puzzled, I climbed up and looked around. There was no sign of life anywhere. The boat was deserted and the bay was still and empty.

A few minutes later I had been through the *Swallow* from bow to stern. Dimitri's things were still in his cabin. Three glasses smelling of whisky stood on the bench in the galley, but there was definitely nobody on board. I wondered briefly if Dimitri and Hassel had taken the dinghy to fetch Hassel's yacht, but even before I found the dinghy still tied alongside, I knew they wouldn't both have gone. The only possible explanation was that Kounidis had come, though I couldn't understand why he had left without waiting for me.

When I went to the wheelhouse I found something puzzling. The wires which fed into the back of the radio had been cut, rendering it useless. The key to start the engine remained in position however, and I wondered why Kounidis had made sure I couldn't use the radio and yet had left me the means to drive the boat. It occurred to me that the engine had been disabled, though again I wondered why, unless Kounidis was planning to return. I looked up quickly, half-expecting to see another boat bearing down on me, but there was nothing there save for some distant sails on the horizon.

I turned the key and to my surprise the engine turned over, but as it caught I heard something from below, like a dull thud. Almost simultaneously the smell of smoke and a blast of hot air came up from the cabin and, in an instant, I knew what had happened. Acting purely on instinct I bolted for the door. Even before I reached it I leapt for the side. At first I felt rather

420

than heard the explosion. It was as if something had caught hold of my body as I left the deck and violently tossed me into the air.

I was aware of spinning in an impossibly high arc, my arms and legs cartwheeling. The sound of the blast and the heat enveloped me, and then I was falling to the water below. I hit the surface and sank, and as I went down I struggled to stay conscious. Looking up I saw fire, and debris rained down. Pieces of hissing wreckage shot like bullets through the water around me. Several chunks of metal hit me, though by that time their force had been dissipated and I felt little more than a sharp nudge.

Gradually, the firestorm became a shower and then a trickle. With my lungs bursting, I struck out for the surface and when I broke through, I gulped in the acrid air.

The *Swallow* was already sinking, her hull and decks ablaze as a thick pall of black smoke stained the sky. Had I reacted half a second later and not already leapt for the side, I knew I would have been directly above the centre of the explosion. As it was, the force of the blast had added impetus to the trajectory I had already begun and, by a virtual miracle, it had propelled me away from the boat. I trod water, numbed by the shock of what had happened. The boat burned fiercely and then, in a frighteningly short space of time, began to go down at the stern. Her bow rose and within seconds she had vanished, and all that remained was a slick of oil to match the smoke which was already beginning to disperse above.

26

After the *Swallow* had sunk, I swam towards the headland at the entrance to the bay. I guessed that the explosion had been meant to kill me and neatly account for Dimitri's disappearance. As far as anybody was aware, Alex had already left the island, and nobody even knew about Kurt Hassel. At some point in the future his family in Germany, and also Alex's family, would report them missing and an investigation would ensue, but by then Kounidis would have made sure that they would never be found. I doubted that their disappearance would ever be connected to him, and whatever fate he had planned for them I knew time was short.

By the time I reached the shore and hauled myself onto the rocks, I was beginning to appreciate my immediate problem. I was miles from the closest habitation. To walk would have taken days, but without a boat I had no other choice. The bay was still and empty. All that remained of the *Swallow* was an oil slick which would eventually wash up on the rocks. Even the smoke from the blast had vanished except for a thin murky haze which was drifting eastward. I scanned the horizon, wondering if anybody would come to investigate. There were some yachts a long way out, but after I had watched them for a few minutes, I was fairly sure none of them was headed this way. It appeared that I couldn't count on being picked up by any of them, but they did give me an idea.

The previous night, Kurt had anchored his yacht in the next bay around the headland. I knew Kounidis wouldn't have overlooked it. No doubt it was already lying on the bottom of the sea in deep water, but I wondered if he had noticed that the dinghy was gone. There was a chance it might still be where Kurt had left it.

I made my way around to the next cove by scrambling over the rocks and occasionally swimming when the cliff face plunged directly into the sea. As I'd expected there was no yacht, but I eventually found an inflatable dinghy beached out of sight where the trees came almost to the water. There was a pair of oars in the bottom, but there was also a twenty-five horsepower motor attached to the back and when I checked the fuel tank I found it was almost full.

Within minutes I had it running and was heading out of the cove. About an hour had passed since the explosion, but it was still early. It would take an hour or so to reach Vathy, though I reasoned that by the time I found Theonas and managed to convince him that I wasn't mad it would be another thirty or forty minutes on top before we reached Kioni. By then it might be too late. In fact, for all I knew I was already too late. I thought it would be much quicker if I went directly to the cove below Kounidis's house, though there was no guarantee I would find anybody there and I wasn't sure what I could do if there was.

I was still debating the options when fifty minutes later I reached the southern point which marked the entrance to Molos Bay. My sense of urgency had grown. I knew that if I made the wrong decision it could cost three people their lives. If I kept going, the northern point of Molos was no more than ten minutes away and Kounidis's house only another five minutes beyond there. At the last moment I steered a course straight ahead, praying that I wasn't making a huge mistake.

★ ★ ★

When I reached the cove it was empty. I stayed close to the cliff edge and idled the dinghy into shore so that the sound of the motor wouldn't alert anyone at the house. As soon as I felt the bottom scrape the beach I jumped ashore and ran for the steps. I had no plan except the vague idea that if I confronted Kounidis and told him that I had sent a message to Theonas via a passing fishing boat, he would realise that it was over and give in without getting any more blood on his hands. But as soon as I reached the top of the steps I saw with a crushing sense of despair that the house appeared to be deserted.

I crouched out of sight for a few seconds to make sure. There was no sign of movement and the shutters over the windows were all fastened. I crossed the lawn and tried a door, but it was locked. I looked around for something to use to break in, knowing that all I could do now was phone the police for help. There was no time for subtlety, and I grabbed a chair from the terrace and swung it towards the shutters over a nearby window. It connected with a resounding crash and splinter of wood. The impact jarred my hands, but I barely noticed the brief flash of pain which shot up my arms. Instead, I grabbed the mangled shutters and wrenched them free. The glass beyond was cracked and, without pausing, I seized a broken piece of wood to smash it from the frame and then I climbed inside.

At first I saw just an ordinary room, though it was much more simply furnished than the rest of the house. Splintered glass crunched beneath my feet. A wooden cabinet against the wall contained a few framed photographs and an armchair faced the window, beside it a small table on top of which stood an old-fashioned record player. It was only then that I realised this was the locked room I'd come across during the weekend I'd been to the house with Alex. I looked for a phone, but there wasn't one so I went to the door and made my way towards the front of the house. I found one in the entrance hall, but when I picked up the receiver, the line was dead.

For a moment I didn't know what to do and then, as I put the receiver down, I heard a sound from somewhere in the house. I listened for it again. I thought I must have imagined it until a door a few feet away, which I knew led to the kitchen, began to open and Kounidis's driver emerged. He was holding a pistol and was heading for the passage across the hall from which I had emerged less than a minute earlier.

As he took a step forward, he glimpsed me in his peripheral vision and, startled, he began to turn, but my reaction was faster. I still held the length of wood which I'd used to smash the window, and I swung it at his head. I saw the barrel of the pistol rise in competition with the arc of my arm and then the jagged edge of the wood connected with the bridge of his nose and bounced off again with a sharp crack. Blood and cartilage bloomed in a fine mist and splattered against my wetsuit and, without a sound, he crumpled. His skull hit the floor with a sickening thud.

It had happened so fast there was no time to think about what I was doing. I had acted instinctively, but now I stared in fascinated horror as dark red blood began to fill the cracks between the tiles, flowing like small canals which began to interconnect and spill over to merge with one another in a rapidly spreading slick. I thought he was still breathing, but when I bent down to him I wasn't sure. As I retrieved the gun and stood up again another figure appeared in the doorway from which he had emerged. It was Eleni. She froze. Her shock turned to a hostile stare as she met my eye.

'Where's Kounidis?' I demanded.

She shook her head and said something rapidly in Greek, pantomiming that she didn't understand. I thought about how long it had been since I'd left Pigania Bay.

'Where is he?' I repeated, and this time I pointed the pistol at her. Her eyes widened fractionally. A second passed and I thought she was wondering if I would really shoot her. Her gaze dropped to the prone figure whose blood was even then reaching out for her feet.

'Kathara,' she said.

For a moment I didn't understand, and then it made sense. 'The monastery?'

She nodded. I knew then why Kohl had taken a taxi there on the day he was murdered, and why nobody had seen another vehicle apart from the tourist bus. When I had been there with Dimitri the priest had even shown us the doors to the underground tunnels and chambers which Kounidis must have used to come and go unobserved. I recalled the diary written by the soldier who centuries ago had hidden for two years from the Turks. Three people locked in a chamber deep underground might never be found. Certainly not until long after Kounidis had ended his natural life. There had been something else in the monastery museum. The list which *Hauptmann* Hassel had left, and I understood why my father had wanted to see it again. It was a receipt. Not the result of a fastidious looter, but a mark of regret from a good man who had no choice but to carry out his orders.

I grabbed Eleni by the arm and roughly shoved her toward the passage. In the room I had broken into, I made her stand against the wall where I could see her while I went to the record player.

When I turned it on and moved the arm across the record, a scratchy hiss emanated from the speakers followed by the opening notes of the same haunting melody which I had heard before.

427

Once when I was there with Alex, the second time with Dimitri.

I imagined Kounidis sitting in the chair and my eye fell to the cabinet it faced where half a dozen framed pictures stood on the shelves. The quality was poor and they were in black-and-white. They were all of the same girl. They had been taken when she was very young, perhaps between the ages of fifteen and sixteen, but as I stared at these images of Julia Zannas I might have been looking at a young Alex.

Beside them was a slim volume with a leather cover. I opened it to the first page and saw my father's handwriting. I made Eleni lie face-down on the floor while I read what he had written.

27

The journal was not a record of a series of dives like the others. Instead it was the story which Eric Schmidt, alias Johann Kohl, had told my father after they had met in Argostoli. He had written it down as he remembered it. As I read his words they conjured the events played out like an old film. I could see the faces of the characters, discern what they thought and felt. I had heard enough about them that they sprang to life before my eyes, like the real people they had once been.

* * *

The day that *Hauptmann* Hassel returned to Vathy having escaped the ambush Metkas had planned, his driver roared along the waterfront at full speed. The soldiers in the back kept their weapons trained at the ready, fully expecting an attack at any moment. Between them, the owner of the taverna sat white-faced, rigid with fear. In the front sat Julia Zannas. She was pale and stared straight ahead, never looking directly at any of the people they passed who stopped to stare.

As soon as they reached the waterfront mansion which served as the German garrison headquarters, Hassel climbed from the vehicle and, with his pistol drawn, began issuing orders.

The taverna owner was taken away to be locked up, while soldiers snatched up their weapons and ran to man defensive positions. In a few short minutes, what had been a tranquil scene was transformed into a hurricane of activity. As word of what had transpired spread among the soldiers they felt a universal sense of betrayal and anger. Mixed with fear, their reaction became one of hostility. The people of the town suddenly found themselves staring down the barrels of guns. They were roughly pushed aside and told to leave the streets or be shot. An immediate curfew was put in place and within the hour the town of Vathy had fallen eerily quiet in the middle of the day. The soldiers waited nervously for the sound of gunfire, the roar of explosions.

When it was clear to *Hauptmann* Hassel that the attack he expected would not take place, he contemplated his options. As a soldier, his duty was to follow standing orders and report the conspiracy to *Standartenführer* Bergen in Kephalonia. However, he was afraid of the consequences for the island if he followed such a course. What nobody but he was aware of was that Bergen was due to arrive on the gunship *Antounnetta* to evacuate all German forces from Ithaca. Hassel had already been ordered to assemble his men at Frikes in preparation for this event. His instructions included the directive that he was to go to the monastery at Kathara *en route* and remove all icons, statues and religious paraphernalia which might be of value and transport them to Frikes.

In a room in the mansion which served as

Hassel's office, he stood at the window looking onto the yard outside. He was deeply troubled. Julia Zannas sat quietly in a chair watching him. She was beautiful, he thought. More beautiful than ever, though her eyes were filled with the pain of the slowly-dawning comprehension of what she had done. He had gone to her home that morning to say goodbye. He had wanted to tell her that he was leaving soon, but once he was there he could not bring himself to do so. Sometimes he dreamed about coming back for her when the war was over. But he already had a wife and a baby child in Germany. He felt a powerful sense of guilt for having fallen in love with Julia. He had not wished it to happen. He had always known it was folly, but he had not been able to help himself.

He went to Julia and knelt on the floor. He took her hand in his own and held it against his cheek. She regarded him uncomprehendingly, her eyes brimming with uncertainty.

'I owe you my life,' he said. He did not attempt to speak Greek, since the things he wished to say were far beyond his comprehension of the language. 'Do you know what it is you have done today?'

She did not understand, he knew that. Nevertheless, he needed to talk to her.

'What can I do?' he asked. 'If I report what has happened, *Standartenführer* Bergen will undoubtedly order reprisals.'

Hassel knew this would happen. On a neighbouring island, Bergen had ordered the captain of the *Antounnetta* to open fire on the villages. Many people had been killed and wounded.

But he could not fail to report the incident. It went against everything that he stood for as an officer of the German Army. Such a thing was unthinkable.

'And you, Julia, what am I to do with you?'

He knew that Bergen would never allow him to take her with him. But how could he leave her here after what had happened? In an agony of indecision he cursed himself for having created this situation. If he had resisted his feelings, if he had only thought of Julia and not himself, none of this would ever have happened. But though he had tried many times to forget her since the first time he had seen her face, she had captivated his dreams. He had allowed himself to believe in a fantasy; that the war had not touched Ithaca, that here things were different and the people did not think of him and his men as invaders, forcibly occupying the island. He had been wrong of course. And he had always known it.

Hassel bowed his head, resting for a moment against Julia's knees. He felt her hands lift his face. She spoke softly, though he didn't understand what she said, and then tears escaped from her eyes and slid down her cheeks. He stood up and, taking her hands, raised her with him. He kissed her cheek. She leaned against him and he held her. His senses were filled with the scent of her skin, the feel of her hair, her breath against his neck. He held her close, so close that he could feel the beat of her heart.

It was dark when he went down to the basement where the owner of the taverna had been confined. The man was huddled in a corner, and it was immediately apparent that he had been beaten, though not badly. One eye was bruised, and his cheek was grazed, perhaps where he had been thrown to the floor. He looked up fearfully.

Hassel turned to the soldier beside him. He was very young. Perhaps seventeen, not even shaving yet. 'What happened to this man?' he demanded.

The soldier stammered a reply. 'He fell, *Herr Hauptmann*. When we brought him in. It was an accident.'

'Then you will ensure that there are no further 'accidents'. Is that understood? We are soldiers of the German Army. We are not members of the SS.'

'Yes, *Herr Hauptmann*.'

He could not really blame them, Hassel thought. This man had got off lightly. He had offered wine to boys in uniform so that they would be slow to react when men came to kill them. Nevertheless, there would be no more beatings.

A second soldier stood in the passage outside. Another boy wearing an ill-fitting uniform and carrying a rifle almost as big as he was. His name was Schmidt, Hassel recalled. He had learned to speak a little Greek. Better than he had himself. It seemed he had an ear for languages. Hassel ordered him to step forward.

'Tell this man that I want to know the names

of the leaders of the group who planned to attack the garrison.' He fixed the taverna owner with a hard stare which he hoped would add weight to the words which were about to be translated. 'Tell him that if he does not give me those names then I will have no choice but to hand him over to the SS. Explain to him that he will be tortured. Make this very clear. Explain that he will give the information in the end anyway. Tell him that many people on the island will be killed as a reprisal for what has happened. Make sure that he understands this. Men, women and children.'

Hassel waited while all of this was relayed. The soldier's Greek was not perfect and it took some time, but from the increasing fear apparent in the taverna owner's eyes it was clear that he understood the gist of it.

'Now tell him this,' Hassel said. 'If he gives me the names of the leaders and tells me where to find them, I give him my word that there will be no reprisals. Only these men will be taken. Tell him that I understand that what I am asking is a difficult thing, but tell him that it is better that a few men who knew what they were doing are shot, rather than hundreds of the innocent.' Hassel paused, then added, 'He has one hour to reach a decision.'

Hassel spent the hour in his office. He explained to an uncomprehending Julia that this was the only way he could reconcile his duty with his own sense of moral conduct. If he were able to produce the ringleaders of the Resistance, perhaps Bergen would be appeased and there would be no question of reprisals. It was the best that Hassel could do.

Julia, of course, did not understand what he was saying, but as he stood by the window she came to him and leaned against him, entwining the fingers of her hand in his own.

When the hour was up, Hassel returned to the basement. The taverna owner gave him one name, but it was a name which Hassel knew would satisfy *Standartenführer* Bergen. The name was Metkas, and he was hiding in the monastery at Kathara.

Hassel ordered a squad of men to be assembled immediately. When they arrived at Kathara, soldiers were posted around the perimeter of the monastery before Hassel drove in through the main gates. Metkas was alone except for one young man who had been left to keep look-out for him, but who had fallen asleep. They were both captured without a shot being fired and taken back to Vathy where they were imprisoned with the taverna owner.

It turned out that this was a mistake. During the night, Metkas beat the man to death with his bare hands.

*   *   *

The *Antounnetta* was already anchored in the small harbour at Frikes when *Hauptmann* Hassel led the small convoy of men and vehicles into the town. He made his report to *Standartenführer* Bergen in the house which Bergen had temporarily seized while the

435

evacuation took place. When he got to the part Julia Zannas had played in preventing the guerrillas' plan from succeeding, Hassel took care to emphasise that without her help he would undoubtedly have been killed.

Bergen regarded him with cold contempt. 'Perhaps it has not occurred to you, *Hauptmann*, that without the girl's part in this it would not have been so easy to ambush you away from your men.'

'Yes, *Standartenführer*,' Hassel said obediently while he remained stiffly at attention. 'However if I may . . . '

'Silence!' Bergen rose and came around the table, his thin lips drawn tightly. 'I do not have time for your pathetic explanations. You may be sure that when we reach Patras, *Hauptmann*, you will be held accountable for your actions. Where is Metkas now?'

'Under guard in the house next door, *Standartenführer*.'

'Have him and the other one taken to the ship. And the girl? Presumably you brought her with you?'

Hassel hesitated, then answered, 'Yes, *Standartenführer*.'

'I hope you do not imagine that we will be taking her with us when we leave.'

'With your permission, *Standartenführer*, I cannot leave her here after what she has done. I respectfully request that she be taken to the mainland.'

Bergen smiled mirthlessly. 'Your request is denied. Do you think that I care what happens to

436

your peasant whore? She may consider herself lucky that I do not order her to be shot. As it is, she can take her chances with her own people. I am quite sure they will know what to do with her. Now continue with the evacuation immediately.'

Hassel knew that he had no choice. To further plead for Julia risked her being shot.

* * *

While arrangements were made to depart, *Standartenführer* Bergen made arrangements of his own. He emerged from the house and called out to a passing soldier. Schmidt nervously snapped off a raised arm salute as Bergen ordered him to fetch half a dozen men and a truck. When he returned with the men in the back, Bergen climbed into the passenger seat and told him to drive towards the village of Stavros.

As he followed the road, anxiously keeping an eye out for any sign of an ambush, Schmidt occasionally glanced at the piece of paper Bergen held in his hand. Bergen made no attempt to hide what was written on it because it was in Greek, though it was not Greek as Schmidt had seen it before. Nevertheless, he understood enough to know that it was a verse of some kind. Certain hills were mentioned, as were two seas. There was more, but he could not understand it, and he did not want to make his scrutiny obvious.

Eventually, after ordering Schmidt to take

several turns and after following a bumpy donkey track past a church on a low hill, Bergen ordered him to stop. He got out and withdrew his pistol.

'Wait here,' he commanded, and then he vanished on foot around the bend.

Schmidt and the other men waited for two hours. They were nervous and debating amongst themselves what they should do, when Bergen finally returned. He was dusty and sweating, but he looked strangely pleased with himself. Without a word, he climbed back into the truck and ordered Schmidt to turn around and drive back to Frikes.

★ ★ ★

By the time Bergen returned, the light was beginning to fade. Preparations to leave were almost complete. Hassel watched with a heavy heart. He tried to explain to Julia, but she regarded him with uncomprehending eyes and eventually she put her finger against his lips to silence him. Then she came into his arms and for a long time he held her. A few final explosions could be heard from beyond the village where the equipment which could not be taken with them was being destroyed. The flames from burning vehicles could be seen in the sky and the smell of burning fuel and rubber lay heavy in the air.

At the wharf, Schmidt was waiting with the last boat.

'Tell her this,' Hassel said. He turned to Julia

and held her face in his hands and told her that he loved her. He said that he was sorry for everything, that if he survived the war he would come back to find her. Even as he spoke the words he knew it was a lie, though it was not meant as such.

Masking his surprise, Schmidt did his best to translate. Like the rest of the men under Hassel's command, he had great respect for his commanding officer. To Schmidt and many of the other men, *Hauptmann* Hassel seemed so much older than they were. He had done his best for them, and he had done his best for the people of Ithaca.

Julia's eyes filled with tears.

'Tell her there is a fishing boat and a man who will take her to Kephalonia,' Hassel continued. He had bribed the man to do this. He was a fisherman from Frikes, a man who was more interested in the money Hassel had given him than anything some village girl he didn't even know might have done.

Schmidt repeated this too and Julia nodded her understanding.

'Make her promise she will go,' Hassel said.

Again Julia nodded.

There was nothing more he could say. He held Julia one last time before he climbed into the boat and, as it left the wharf, he stood in the bow watching her grow steadily smaller. She seemed alone and vulnerable. He felt sure that he would never see her again and the pain this caused him was like a dagger through his heart. He prayed with all of his might that no matter what happened to him she would survive. She did not deserve to pay for his mistakes.

In a few minutes the boat reached the *Antounnetta*, but, as Hassel climbed aboard, he heard the sound of a shell fired from somewhere on the cliffs above the harbour. He registered the flash and roar of flame as a blast of hot air lifted him from his feet and threw him to the deck, and he knew that they were under attack.

★ ★ ★

The *Antounnetta* limped into a dark and remote bay in the south of Ithaca. There was no moon and the wind whipped the sea into whitecaps. Off the coast, the ship had rolled and listed badly. She was already taking on water, and though the fires had all been put out, the damage was severe. More than three-quarters of the crew and men who had been aboard when the attack began were dead. Of those who were left, many were severely wounded. As well as all of this, an unexploded shell had pierced the upper deck and was lodged in a mass of twisted metal close to the engine room.

Once in the relative shelter of the bay, Bergen ordered Schmidt and a party of other men to the hold below. Among the pictures and religious paraphernalia which had been removed on Bergen's orders from the monastery at Kathara, there were several wooden crates which had been nailed shut.

'Take these onto the deck,' Bergen ordered. 'And be careful with them!'

He watched as the crates were lifted and, when a young soldier lost his grip and dropped one of them, Bergen was furious.

'Fool! I told you to be careful.'

The lid had come off and some of the contents had spilled out. Schmidt helped to put them back, placing them carefully in the straw under Bergen's supervision. He did not know where they had come from, but there were small jars and bowls made of clay decorated with tiny detailed designs. When the lid had been nailed down again, Bergen turned on the soldier who had dropped the crate.

'If you are so careless again I will have you shot. That goes for all of you.' He stared at them with a cold, fanatical intensity. 'Now move!'

While the crates were taken above, Schmidt and another man were ordered to remain behind. They watched as Bergen examined the statue of the Virgin Mary which had been brought from the monastery. His mouth curled in a disdainful sneer. 'Leave this worthless rubbish,' he said and instead directed them towards another smaller statue of an almost naked woman.

He instructed them to fetch blankets to wrap it in and, when they had done that, they secured it with a canvas cover. As Schmidt tied the cords he noticed the inscription which was carved into the base, and recognised that it was the verse he'd glimpsed written on the piece of paper which he'd seen Bergen with earlier.

When they were finished, Bergen ordered them to leave the statue and to fetch the two prisoners. The crates and the prisoners were put into a boat and Schmidt and another soldier were ordered to guard them while Bergen turned to *Hauptmann* Hassel.

'You will wait here until I return,' he instructed. 'Have your men work on whatever repairs they can effect while I am gone.'

Hauptmann Hassel began to protest. The ship was already in danger of sinking. If they were to have any chance of escaping, they must leave immediately. Bergen regarded him with cold fury.

'Must I remind you, *Hauptmann*, that the responsibility for what has happened rests with you? This island was under your command. Had you dealt with the guerrilla element properly instead of behaving as if you and your men were sent here to enjoy some kind of holiday, we would not be in this position. Trust me, if I did not need you for the moment, I would have you shot. Question my orders again and I will do so myself.'

To emphasise his threat, Bergen removed his pistol from the holster at his side. 'Do I make myself clear?'

'Yes, *Standartenführer*.'

The prisoners were forced to row the boat to the shore and, once there, they and the two soldiers unloaded the crates while Bergen looked on with his pistol drawn. He directed them to follow a goat track which led up a ravine. The path was steep and it was dark and whenever any of them stumbled, Bergen would threaten them furiously. After they had paused several times to rest, the path levelled and they emerged into woodland. Eventually Bergen stopped. He told them to put down their crates and then he ordered Schmidt and the other soldier to return to the shore and wait.

Schmidt glanced at the prisoners. The young one looked frightened and he felt a stab of sympathy for him. The older one glared at them with dark, hostile eyes. He did not think he would see either of them again.

★　★　★

On the *Antounnetta*, Hassel had organised his remaining men into repair crews, though there was little that they could do. As they worked, Hassel was plagued by a vision of the young prisoner's face as he had rowed away from the ship. His eyes had been wide with apprehension, his colour pale. Perhaps Bergen was right, Hassel thought. Perhaps all of this was his fault. But if that was so, he could at least stop one more innocent life being wasted. He told his men to wait for his return and then he took one of the remaining lifeboats and went ashore.

There was only one way up the hillside, through a narrow ravine beside a trickle of water. Before he had gone very far he met Schmidt and the other soldier coming down. He ordered them to take one of the boats and return to the ship and then he continued his climb.

Schmidt watched him vanish into the darkness and then he told the other man to go ahead without him.

'We have our orders,' the man said. 'If that bastard Bergen sees you he will shoot you.' But Schmidt would not be deterred and eventually the other man shrugged. 'It's your funeral.'

When he had gone, Schmidt followed Hassel, though he kept well back so that his presence wouldn't be detected. He was not sure why he was disobeying his orders. He wished that he was armed, but his rifle was in the boat on the shore.

When he emerged into the woods at the top of the hill, Hassel saw the glow of lanterns through the trees and approached quietly. It was almost pitch black on the headland except for the pool of yellow light where Bergen was standing guard over Metkas and the young one as they finished digging a large hole. The two prisoners were filthy and streaked with sweat. When Bergen ordered them out, they staggered with fatigue. He gestured towards the crates and they carried them over and lowered them into the hole. When they were finished, Bergen made them begin putting back the dirt they had laboriously removed.

It didn't take long. Hassel knew he had only a few more minutes. He approached from behind with his pistol drawn. 'Please put down your gun, *Standartenführer*,' he said.

Bergen whirled around, his surprise quickly turning to anger. 'I will have you shot for this,' he hissed.

Hassel managed a sardonic smile. Bergen's constant promises to have him shot had lost some of their impact. The two prisoners had stopped their work, uncertain what was going on. Hassel told Bergen again to put his pistol down.

What happened next happened very quickly. Metkas suddenly lunged toward Bergen with his shovel raised above his head. He must have believed that this was his one chance to survive and he took it almost without thought. Bergen began to raise his pistol but the shovel fell first and caught him on the shoulder and the pistol fell from his hand. Bergen shrieked with pain as Metkas dived for the gun and Hassel knew that if he reached it, Metkas would not differentiate between one German soldier and another. He hesitated for a fraction of a second before he did the only thing he could. He fired.

The bullet hit Metkas in the back. He grunted as he hit the ground and then lay still. The other prisoner had frozen in surprise but now, certain that he was about to be shot, he flung his shovel aside and made a dash through the woods. Hassel let him go, watching until he had vanished in the darkness. With his pistol still trained on Metkas he went closer. He was still breathing. He bent down on one knee and felt for the pulse in his neck but it was very weak. He looked around for Bergen's pistol, but couldn't see it. He thought perhaps it was underneath Metkas, but then he heard a movement behind him and he realised his mistake.

He felt the barrel of the gun touch his head, but he never heard the shot which sent a bullet through his brain and blew off the front of his skull.

The remainder of Schmidt's account described what had happened after he returned to the *Antounnetta*. Bergen ordered the ship to leave the bay on a course for the mainland, but she had barely gone past the headland before there was an explosion from the engine room. The *Antounnetta* had gone down quickly, but Bergen and the handful of remaining survivors had taken to the lifeboats. Bergen had ordered the men to continue on their course. The next day they were picked up by a German ship from Patras, but by then Bergen was dead. During the night when he had fallen asleep, Schmidt had strangled him with a bootlace and then dumped his body over the side.

When the ship which rescued them was attacked by Allied planes, Schmidt had found himself in the oily water swimming for his life. Amid the screams and cries of the dying he had struck out for the mainland shore where he had eventually washed up half drowned. Afterwards he had stolen some clothes and discarded his uniform. For him the war was over.

It was only much later that he discovered that he had been the sole survivor from the *Antounnetta*. He returned to Germany after the war having assumed the identity of a dead soldier, and eventually became a builder. He married a girl he met and together they had a family of three children, but when they were quite young his wife had left him. As he grew older he became bitter and disillusioned, he began drinking and fell on hard times. Sometimes he thought about what had happened during the war. He suffered from nightmares. He remembered the crates which Bergen had forced the prisoners to bury, though he was certain that the young one who had escaped would have gone back soon afterwards and recovered whatever treasure they contained.

It was only when he read by chance of the discovery of some artefacts in a collection in Switzerland that he recognised the pictures and thought of the statue he had seen on the *Antounnetta*. He guessed that the young prisoner must have sold the artefacts he had dug up after the war, which explained how they came to be in Switzerland. But the statue played on Schmidt's mind for weeks afterwards. He wondered if it could still be on the wreck of the *Antounnetta*. If the statue had been found, why was there no mention of it? In the end, he resolved to get enough money somehow to travel to Greece, and when he read that the artefacts would be returned to the museum in Argostoli he decided to go there.

It was there that he had met my father, who had realised that the verse Schmidt described must reveal the location of the temple. He already guessed from what Schmidt had told him that it was somewhere near Platrithias. There was a church on a low hill there which matched the description of the one Schmidt had seen all those years earlier, and he believed the two seas referred to the strait between Ithaca and Kephalonia and the Ionian sea that stretched to the mainland.

My father had also realised that the young prisoner who had escaped must have been Alkimos Kounidis. He had used the money he made to buy a freighter to start his shipping business.

Now I understood the hollow in the ground on the headland. Kounidis had buried Hassel and Metkas after he had recovered the crates, but had not bothered to refill the hole. He knew that nobody ever went there and even if somebody did stumble over it, by then nature would have disguised what had happened.

I closed the journal. Eleni was still lying on the floor. I ordered her up. Her eyes glowed with malice. I wondered how much of this she knew, and what made her and her husband loyal to a man like Kounidis. Perhaps they owed him a debt of loyalty. Another blood tie from the war.

There was one thing I hadn't understood about Kounidis's fictional account of the sinking of the *Antounnetta*. Why had he portrayed Hassel as being no better than the SS man Bergen, when Hassel had saved his life? But when I looked again at the pictures of Julia Zannas on the shelf, I knew the answer.

I tossed the journal on the table and brushed past Eleni without another word.

28

I found a pick-up truck outside the house which I assumed belonged to Kounidis's retainers who appeared to have been in the process of packing to leave. The keys were in it and within a few minutes I was heading north along the coast road. At Stavros I took the mountain road. As it climbed, the air became cooler. When I arrived at the monastery it was still and quiet except for the distant clank of goat bells.

I parked outside the closed gates. On the road below, a truck headed down the mountain from the village of Anoghi, the sound of the engine rising and falling as the driver negotiated the bends. The noise grew fainter as it wound back and forth towards the coast.

A chain was looped through the metal bars on the gate but there was no padlock. Though the courtyard inside was empty, the door to the church was open and I wondered if I was expected. As I pushed the gate open I could feel unseen eyes observing me. My footsteps echoed around the walls.

The light was dim inside the church. There was nobody there. The silence was oppressive. I thought of the chapel at school, remembering how even a cough seemed an insult to the solemnity which was steeped into the very stones. At the end of the aisle beneath the domed roof, the *Panaghia* looked down at me from her alcove.

A sound came from the door which led to the passage connecting the church to the main building, and Kounidis appeared. He had Alex with him, a pistol held against her back. Uncertainty and fear flashed in her eyes. There was no sign of the others, but I assumed they were already locked in a room somewhere underneath the monastery.

Kounidis regarded me quizzically, as if he was surprised that I had come, but he didn't appear concerned.

'I get the feeling you were expecting me,' I said.

He produced a mobile phone from his pocket. 'I had hoped you might change your mind. But, of course, Eleni told me you were coming.'

I didn't know what he meant by his first remark, but I could almost have laughed at the irony of his producing a cell phone, such a symbol of modernity amidst all the tangled remnants of the past. 'Did Eleni tell you about your chauffeur? I'm afraid he's going to have a bit of a headache.'

'Actually, he is dead.'

I was shocked. Not only because I had killed a man, but also because Kounidis relayed the information with apparent unconcern. He smiled at my reaction.

'Do not distress yourself, Robert. I am sure you did not mean to kill him. Any more than I intended to kill your father. You may not believe me, but his death was an accident.'

450

'He's lying, Robert,' Alex cut in. 'He murdered Eric Schmidt and he killed your father because he didn't want anyone to know the truth about where he got the money to start his business after the war.'

'It is true I did not want your father to find the *Antounnetta*,' Kounidis said. 'But I did not kill him. I tried to persuade him to leave the past where it belongs. But he would not listen. That morning we argued. He clutched at his chest. It was his heart. Before I could help him he fell into the harbour. There was nothing I could do. Whether you believe it or not, I am telling you the truth, Robert. Your father was my friend for many years.'

'What about Schmidt? Was that an accident too?' I said sceptically.

Kounidis made a dismissive gesture. 'I have no qualms about killing Schmidt. After your father's heart attack, Schmidt tried to blackmail me. He said if I gave him money he would leave and nobody would know.'

'But that wasn't true,' I pointed out. 'My father already knew.'

'Schmidt betrayed your father.' Kounidis gestured for me to move towards the window, keeping Alex between us. 'You came alone,' he said when he saw the empty road.

'How do you know I didn't call the police before I came?'

He smiled tolerantly. 'I think if that were true, Miros Theonas would be here by now, don't you? Perhaps you believed that you would single-handedly save the day using the pistol that

451

I know you have in your possession. Please give it to me.'

'I left it in the car.' I held my arms away from my body.

'Please, do not insult me,' Kounidis chided.

'See for yourself.'

He smiled at the invitation, suspecting trickery, but pushed Alex forward. 'Empty his pockets,' he told her, while pointing the pistol at us with a steady hand.

She looked at me questioningly. I told her to go ahead. She searched hesitantly as if she expected that I had some kind of plan in mind, but when she found nothing she looked bewildered.

'Again you surprise me,' Kounidis said. 'I assume that your judgement has been affected by the desire for revenge. Or is it perhaps the misplaced gallantry of youth?' He looked at Alex coldly. 'Is that it, Robert? You came to save Alex, even though she betrayed you.'

'You mean the way Julia betrayed you?' I said.

He wasn't surprised that I knew, but Alex looked at me uncomprehendingly. 'Hasn't he told you? There's a room in his house full of pictures of Julia taken when she was young. He was in love with her.'

She turned to him in disbelief. 'I don't understand.'

'At first I couldn't work out why he had made up that whole story about Hassel being a torturer and a killer,' I said, and then I addressed Kounidis directly again. 'But when I saw that room I understood. You did it for revenge. To punish Julia. You wanted to hurt her. And to make sure the people of Ithaca hated her.'

'She was lucky to survive after what she did!' Kounidis said bitterly. 'Her own father would have killed her if she had not escaped to Kephalonia.'

'What did she do except save a man into whose arms she was practically forced?'

'She was a whore for that Nazi!' The gun in his hand trembled. 'She knew that I loved her. It was only because her father would not accept me that I could not marry her. My family was poor.'

Kounidis stared at Alex with such loathing that she shrank back from him. 'You should know how I felt, Robert. I watched you and Dimitri pant after Alex like dogs after a bitch in heat. She made fools of you both. She betrayed you just as her grandmother betrayed me when she had that Nazi's bastard!'

I shook my head. 'You're wrong. Julia loved Hassel, but she never slept with him.'

'What are you talking about?' Alex asked.

I kept my gaze fixed on Kounidis. 'Think about it. She was a simple Greek girl brought up in a traditional family. She'd had loyalty to the church and her family drummed into her since before she could walk. She'd never even been alone with a man before she met Hassel. I don't believe she just cast all that aside.'

'She went with him willingly that day!' Kounidis cut in.

'Yes, because she wanted to save him. But that doesn't mean she slept with him. Julia told Alex's mother that she was raped.'

Kounidis hesitated. The beginnings of doubt, and perhaps understanding flickered in his eye, though he wasn't ready to acknowledge what I knew to be the truth. 'She lied!'

'That's what Alex thought. She believed her grandmother was trying to protect his family.' I looked at Alex. I hated the fact that she had to find out the truth this way. 'You said when she died she still loved Hassel after all these years. You didn't see how that could be if he had raped her? You were right. But it wasn't Hassel's family she was protecting. It was your mother.'

Her confusion began to clear. She looked at Kounidis with growing horror as he too began to suspect the truth which hatred had blinded him to for all these years.

'What happened?' I said to him. 'After you escaped from the headland that night you went to her didn't you? You told her Hassel was dead. The man she loved was dead.'

'Yes, I told her that,' Kounidis said, though suddenly he sounded uncertain as he struggled to hold on to the delusion he had maintained for all these years. 'I told her that I saw his brains blown out with my own eyes.'

'And I bet you enjoyed telling her about it. It was your revenge. But that wasn't enough. You couldn't stand the fact that even then it was still him that she loved. Was it you who took her to Kephalonia?' I saw that I was right. 'Despite everything, you didn't want her to be killed, did you? Instead you raped her.'

Kounidis shook his head, but his mute denial lacked conviction. He stared at Alex. The hand that held the gun dropped to his side.

'Hassel was a good man,' I went on. 'He wouldn't have slept with Julia even if she had been willing. He would have understood what it meant to her. On the way here I wondered why she didn't tell you. She didn't did she? But maybe it was because she didn't want you to have the satisfaction. Instead she endured what you did to her, and for the rest of her life she hated you. But she lived. She got away to England and she had a daughter. Your daughter.'

Kounidis sagged like a man who suddenly had to bear a tremendous weight. The pistol fell from his hand and clattered to the ground. As the terrible realisation of what he had done hit home, the flesh on his face appeared to cave in. He had grown rich, but he had never had children or found happiness. Though he'd been married once, I suspected that the only woman he had ever really loved was Julia. But bitterness had turned his love to hate. In the end it had poisoned his life far more than it had Julia's.

And all the time the child that Julia carried was his. Alex was his grandchild. He saw before him living proof of the ultimate waste of his life. His flesh and blood, who stared back at him with horror and disgust.

The final irony was too much for him. The light faded from his eyes. It was as if he died right before us. Neither of us tried to stop him as he shambled, ashen-faced from the church. At the doorway he paused, and I thought for a moment that he would look back, but then he stepped outside and was gone.

455

★ ★ ★

He was found days later on the mountainside. His body had been gnawed at by animals and the crows had taken his eyes. The empty sockets gazed unseeing towards the sky, as blind in death as he had been in life.

29

The smell of roasting corn drifted from a food stand on the wharf. There was a festive mood in the air. The cafés were busy serving coffee and sweets. People from all over the island had gathered at the square in Vathy. Many were dressed in their best church clothes, the older women in black and the young in bright-coloured skirts. The devout murmured solemn prayers and fingered icons of the Virgin, others smiled and talked happily to friends and neighbours. Men stood in groups smoking cigarettes, fingering newly-shaved jaws, their jackets already thrown over their shoulders in the heat, while children ran in between them playing noisily.

It was almost two months since Kounidis had died. I hadn't seen Alex since that day. Shortly afterwards I had returned to London to devote some time to my ailing business. The distraction had been time-consuming and welcome. I had deliberately immersed myself in work to the exclusion of all else. By the time I went home each night I was so tired I fell into bed exhausted, and if I dreamed I didn't remember what about. As the weeks went by I rearranged my business finances and sold the Fulham warehouse on at a loss. I would survive, though for a while it was touch and go.

Eventually I began to ease off. I gave myself

457

time to think about my father and the way I had lived my life. One night, quite unexpectedly I was cooking something in the microwave and I felt my eyes brim with tears. Before I could control myself I was choking back heaving sobs. I gave in. All the repressed feelings, the confusion of love and resentment, the knowledge of wasted years, I let it all go, and afterwards I felt better.

I found Alicia. She was living with a friend, and when I approached her one day as she left the flat, her eyes widened and she started in surprise. I asked her to go for a coffee with me, and though at first she refused, I persuaded her. She was quiet initially, but gradually as I told her some of what had happened on Ithaca, she began to ask questions.

She wanted to know why I had found her. I told her that I was sorry about what had happened between us. I should have tried to understand her. I had seen the world in black-and-white then, and I now knew it was wrong to think that way because people make mistakes. I told her I understood that we are all of us made of shades of grey. People can never be exactly what we want them to be.

Tears filled her eyes. She looked down at the table, and when she looked up again she tried to smile. She told me she had met somebody and that things were working out so far. She asked me about Alex. She asked if I was in love with her.

When we left the café we hugged and wished each other well. As I watched her leave, I felt a lingering ache of regret.

Now I had returned to Ithaca for the festival of the *Panaghia*. As I sat with Irene at a table outside a *kefenio* in the square, the crowd lowered their heads while the priest performed the blessing. The statue of the *Panaghia* had been placed on the back of a truck. Since being salvaged from the wreck, she had been painted and restored and though her smile remained imbued with deep sadness, somehow the colours she now wore made her seem less melancholy.

I searched the crowd, looking for Alex. Irene had told me that she too had come back to the island. She had seen her with Dimitri a few days before. When I finally spotted her, they were together. They were talking, her hand resting on his arm. I experienced a terrible emptiness when I saw them together. She looked beautiful. Her skin was tanned the colour of honey and she seemed almost to glow. She was smiling happily, but then for a moment she was distracted and her gaze swept restlessly over the crowd. When she saw me she faltered, then she turned and said something to Dimitri. His smile faded a little and he looked across at me, then she was coming towards me and I got up to meet her.

I had forgotten how startling her eyes were, and for a moment I didn't know what to say.

'My dad would have liked to see this,' I said at last, making a gesture to encompass the crowd. Alex smiled.

'Are you going to do the walk?'

The procession would follow the *Panaghia* all the way to the monastery at Kathara, which was a long, hot walk even in autumn, but I had decided that I would make the pilgrimage. 'I think I'm up to it. And you?'

She nodded. 'We could go together if you like.'

I glanced at Dimitri who was standing among a group of friends. I had learned a lot, but Rome wasn't built in a day.

Alex saw where I was looking. 'I meant just you and I.'

I was surprised. 'I assumed . . . '

She shook her head. 'He told me, you know.'

'Told you what?'

'Why he wasn't sure about us any more. Because he was worried about his business.'

'And that's why you're not together?'

'No.' She shook her head. She didn't tell me what the reason was, but my heart was thudding in my chest.

'About walking together. I'd like that.' I held out my hand, but she hesitated.

'There's something you should know. That night, when I stayed with Dimitri . . . '

'It doesn't matter.'

She shook her head again. 'No. It does matter. You can't not talk about things. I want you to know. I went to see him to tell him about you. Maybe also because I wasn't sure how I felt. When he told me he'd made a mistake, I was confused. I don't know what happened. I slept with him.' She looked at me searchingly. 'Do you understand?'

'Yes,' I said. 'I think so.'

★ ★ ★

The walk to Kathara was long and hot. At first people talked and laughed, and children ran about and played as the procession wound out of the town along the coast. When we passed the beach at Molos Bay many stopped to rest. Some had brought towels and swimming costumes. When we continued, some of the older people and younger children remained behind. Those who went on were more subdued, saving their energy for the mountain, though a genial mood of good spirits remained.

Now and then people would come alongside us and speak a few words to Irene, always smiling and nodding to Alex and me. A woman and her husband and two children resting by the roadside got to their feet as we approached and fell in with us.

'*Kalimera*,' the man said, and the woman murmured a greeting too. They spoke a little to Irene, asking polite questions. When they fell behind again they wished us all a good day.

When we finally reached the monastery, the *Panaghia* was restored to her rightful place and afterwards there was a service. When it was over, we went outside where Theonas was waiting with a car to drive us back to town. He took off his sunglasses as we approached, his expression, as ever, unreadable.

'*Kalimera*, Alex,' he said, and nodded coolly to me.

Instead of going straight to Vathy, we took a detour to the site which was being excavated near Platrithias. As we passed Polis Bay I half expected to see Kurt's yacht, though it wasn't there. He had returned to Germany but he was planning to come back when the museum which was being built was finished. It would house the artefacts which they had begun to uncover from the site of the temple.

The foundations had already been laid and a fenced enclosure kept people away from the excavation itself. There would be a plaque I was told, acknowledging my father's part in the rediscovery of the temple. The remains of both *Hauptmann* Hassel and the guerrilla Metkas had been interred in the cemetery on a nearby hill.

While Theonas and Irene waited by the car, Alex and I walked hand in hand. Our feet stirred dust from the path. The sun was still hot, but it was pleasant in the shade of the olive trees. From the temple, we could see the sea to the east and west, shimmering blue and silver. The scent of wild mint laced the air. I told her that I had been to see the statue of Aphrodite in the museum at Argostoli where it was being kept for the time being.

'I wish my father could have seen her.'

'He knew she was there. Perhaps that was enough.'

I wondered whether that was true. He'd searched half his life for the temple and, right as he was on the verge of a discovery which would rock the archaeological world, he had been denied his moment of glory.

I remembered being struck by how lifelike Aphrodite's face seemed. Her expression radiated a sense of benevolent humour and a certain sensual lasciviousness. She was beautifully carved and preserved, her naked form almost flawlessly perfect.

'I couldn't help comparing her with the *Panaghia*,' I said.

'And what did you think?' Alex asked.

'The *Panaghia* is depicted as chaste and virginal, but her expression is sorrowful, almost pitying. It's like a comment on humankind.'

'And what about Aphrodite?'

'She seems amused,' I said. 'But in a compassionate way. You get the feeling she likes what she sees, warts and all, whereas the *Panaghia* is an expression of a religious desire for mankind to be perfect. She's disappointed in us.' I took Alex's hand and we started back towards the car. 'It's about understanding that we all screw up, isn't it?'

'Yes, I think it is,' Alex said.

We stopped and turned towards one another.

'I want to say that I'll never make the same mistakes again,' I said. 'But that's probably not true, is it?'

'No,' she laughed. 'Not for any of us.'

In that moment, I thought we would be OK despite that. I put my arms around her and we kissed.

And in the back of my mind I hoped my father was watching.

Author's Note

Many of the places described in this book are real, but almost nothing else is. The original idea for the story was inspired by a holiday on the island of Ithaca taken several years ago. In the village of Frikes there is a plaque set into the cliff beside the harbour commemorating an attack on the German ship, the *Antounnetta*, during the Second World War. Although I have used that event in this story, the characters and the event itself as described in this novel are completely fictional. In fact I would like to stress that the depiction of the occupation of the island in this story is entirely of my making.

Ithaca is reputed to have been the home of Homer's hero Odysseus, but as far as I am aware, Homer does not mention a temple dedicated to Aphrodite.

Finally, the descriptions in this story of the island and its present-day character and beauty do not do the reality justice. Ithaca is truly an unspoilt gem. I would like to thank the people of Ithaca for the warm welcome I have enjoyed on both my visits there.

We do hope that you have enjoyed reading this large print book.

Did you know that all of our titles are available for purchase?

We publish a wide range of high quality large print books including:
Romances, Mysteries, Classics
General Fiction
Non Fiction and Westerns

Special interest titles available in large print are:
The Little Oxford Dictionary
Music Book
Song Book
Hymn Book
Service Book

Also available from us courtesy of Oxford University Press:
Young Readers' Dictionary
(large print edition)
Young Readers' Thesaurus
(large print edition)

For further information or a free brochure, please contact us at:
Ulverscroft Large Print Books Ltd.,
The Green, Bradgate Road, Anstey,
Leicester, LE7 7FU, England.
Tel: (00 44) 0116 236 4325
Fax: (00 44) 0116 234 0205

Other titles published by
The House of Ulverscroft:

LOST SUMMER

Stuart Harrison

A remote lake; a unique forest; a close community. How could anything terrible happen in such a place? Adam Turner is an investigative journalist plagued by the memory of a girl who vanished from the town where he grew up. When he is asked to look into a suspicious car accident in which three students were killed, he sees a chance to exorcise the demons that have haunted him since his youth. Past and present rapidly and painfully collide as Adam finds himself in conflict with the friend who once betrayed him and becomes embroiled in a classic love triangle. Amid the rugged landscape of the fells and the surrounding forests the tension escalates, breeding violence . . .

A PLACE OF SAFETY

Natasha Cooper

Barrister Trish Maguire needs all the time she can find to help her young half-brother adjust to life after the violent death of his mother. Sir Henry Buxford, an influential acquaintance, has other ideas. He asks Trish to investigate one of his private charities, a magnificent art collection that has been lost for most of the twentieth century. Trish's research takes her not only into the heart of an engrossing love story, but also the agonizing reality of life in the trenches of the First World War. She soon discovers a web of deceit that has spanned the decades since, catching all kinds of people in its filaments.

PARANOIA

Joseph Finder

Adam Cassidy is twenty-six and a low-level employee at a high-tech corporation who hates his job. When he manipulates the system to do something nice for a friend, he finds himself charged with a federal crime. Corporate Security gives him a choice: prison — or become a spy in the headquarters of their chief competitor. It's no choice at all . . . They train him for his 'mission' and feed him inside information when he lands a top job with the rival company. But then he finds that he has talents he never knew he possessed. He's rich, drives a Porsche, and lives in a fabulous apartment. And he's dating the girl of his dreams . . . All he has to do is betray everyone he cares about and everything he believes in.

R IS FOR RICOCHET

Sue Grafton

Kinsey Millhone, employed by Nord Lafferty to drive his daughter home from her incarceration at the California Institute for Women, marvels at the simplicity of the task. But Reba Lafferty emerges feisty and rebellious. As Kinsey finds herself befriending the ex-gambler, ex-alcoholic and ex-con, she discovers that Reba had taken the fall for her boss, also her lover, when he conducted a money-laundering scam. Alan Beckwith has so far escaped the clutches of the FBI; now they believe he is laundering money for a Colombian drug cartel — they just need the proof. When Reba hears shocking new information about her lover, she is suddenly eager to ruin him, and Kinsey must try to control her as she launches her dangerous revenge . . .

A PARTY IN SAN NICCOLÒ

Christobel Kent

Gina Donovan arrives in Florence on a beautiful spring morning to stay with an old friend. She is hoping for nothing more than a break from her demanding young family, but as she soon finds out, this most ancient and beautiful of cities has its dark side. Within hours of her arrival, Gina meets the elegant Frances Richardson, who invites her to her birthday party. It is the highlight of the expatriate calendar, and this year it is to be held in the gardens beneath the city's medieval wall. However, as the party draws near, a terrible discovery is made — and no one in this close-knit community of locals and exiles is free of suspicion . . .